PRAISE FOR THEY'RE NOT YOUR FRIENDS

"An entertaining and eye-opening look at the reality behind celebrity, and the darker side of the Hollywood spotlight."

—Jennifer O'Connell, author of DRESS REHEARSAL and BACHELORETTE #1

"Irene Zutell's firsthand experience as a celebrity journalist makes for a decadently satisfying first novel—her unapologetic, take-no-prisoners candor scintillates like the hottest Hollywood bombshell."

—Elise Miller, author of STAR CRAVING MAD

ALSO BY IRENE ZUTELL

I'll Never Have Sex with You Again!

They're Not Your Friends

A Novel

Irene Zutell

THREE RIVERS PRESS • NEW YORK

 Published in the United States by
Three Rivers Press, an imprint of the Crown Publishing Group,
a division of Random House, Inc., New York.
www.crownpublishing.com

Library of Congress Cataloging-in-Publication Data
Zutell, Irene.
They're not your friends : a novel / Irene Zutell.—1st ed.
1. Hollywood (Los Angeles, Calif.)—Fiction. 2. Motion-picture industry—Fiction 3. Women journalists—Fiction. 4. Celebrities—Fiction. 5. Young women—Fiction. I. Title.
PS3626.U84T47 2005
813'.6—dc22 2004026536

ISBN 1-4000-9758-4

Printed in the United States of America

DESIGN BY KAREN MINSTER

10 9 8 7 6 5 4 3 2 1

First Edition

FOR THE TWO MEN IN MY LIFE, LARRY AND DAD

IT WAS BETTER THAN SHE'D IMAGINED. THERE WAS APPLAUSE, some whistling, even a couple of standing ovations. Lottie's heart hammered at her ribs. She closed her eyes and inhaled, opened and exhaled. She pushed out an enormous fluorescent smile.

"Hello, my name is Lottie Love, and I'm . . . well, it's so hard to say this."

Lottie's eyes flitted around the room, checking for familiar faces. She spotted a soap actor and quickly averted her gaze so he wouldn't sense her recognition. She swilled some Red Bull. This wasn't what she had in mind when she dreamed about the spotlight, but, hell, at least she was onstage.

"I'm . . . I'm . . . I'm an alcoholic."

The group cheered. "All right, Lottie!" "Way to go!"

When she had rehearsed in front of the mirror, Lottie hadn't imagined the applause. She had planned to stop there. But now, she couldn't help herself.

"When I was lit-rully barely a teenager, I'd sneak into the liquor cabinet when my parents weren't around. It was fun? All my friends did it. But the difference was, I couldn't stop. I started drinking before school. Then I'd fill up my Boyz II Men thermos with Absolut and orange juice. The teachers thought I couldn't be more of a typical L.A. kid—loud and always performing. No one knew I was always drunk. It got to a point where I didn't even know how to function sober?"

Words spilled out of her. She spoke about smashing her dad's plumbing truck into the neighbor's kitchen, passing out during the SATs, vomiting on the valedictorian's mortarboard during high school graduation.

Afterward, a throng crowded her.

"What you did was courageous. I hate to sound, well, cliché, but it's the first step. And the first step is the hardest."

"Let's get a soy latte sometime."

"Did you ever think about selling your life story?"

Catherine, her sponsor, wrapped her arms around her. "You did great, Lot. I'm so proud of you."

"Thanks." From the corner of her eye, Lottie watched them file out. Then Lottie saw *him*. He stared right at her and smiled. *I understand what you're going through. I'm there for you,* the look said.

Lottie's eyes stalked him. It was ironic. She'd seen his movies, and now he was her captive audience. How to break free of Catherine? But then he was vacuumed up into the crowd. She couldn't wait for the next meeting. Maybe there was one tomorrow. The Hollywood branch of Alcoholics Anonymous was the hottest ticket in town. Chris Mercer was the hottest celebrity.

And soon he would be Lottie's latest conquest.

CHARLOTTE LOVE was born and raised in Tarzana, just another strip-mall town buried in the hills off the 101 freeway in the San Fernando Valley. It was a peripheral place, and Lottie and her family were peripheral people. They could almost see the beacons of light swirling in the lavender sky when a movie debuted at Mann's. They could nearly hear the fans' applause as celebrities strutted along the red carpet. But though Hollywood was only a few miles down the road, they were as removed from it as Aunt Bertha in Buffalo. When searchlights scanned the heavens in Tarzana, they led to another going-out-of-business sale at Ali Baba's Imported Rugs.

Charlotte, or Charlie, as her parents called her (an only child, she's convinced they wanted a boy), vowed that one day she'd be part of it. She wanted to be the one vogueing along the velvet rope. She took acting lessons. She auditioned for shampoo commercials and modeled for Loehmann's. In high school she was voted most likely to win an Emmy. But her mother begged her to choose otherwise.

"Don't be an actress, Charlie. Look what it did to your father. Hollywood will eat you alive. Get an education."

Her mother recited this, over and over, year after year, fueling Lottie's desire to act even more. "All acting ever did for us was leave us with a phony last name. *Love. Love.* God, I hate myself for allowing him to do that to us. What was wrong with Lutz? We have no identity, no past, no history whatsoever, because of Hollywood."

Lottie screamed at her mother that it was her life and she had more talent than her father ever dreamed of and that no one believed in her and they'd all be sorry when she became a big actress and emancipated herself.

They fought like this for years. One day, they stopped fighting. Her mother had a bad biopsy. So in between sobs, Lottie promised that she'd go to college and put aside her silly dreams. Right after her mother's funeral, Lottie enrolled at UCLA.

Charlie Love reinvented herself. No more tomboy name. Charlie was okay when she was a kid climbing trees. But from the moment she set foot on campus, she decided to go by Lottie. Lottie Love. She liked the singsongy sound of it. The name fit perfectly into her new plan—she majored in communications because it was the easiest way to coast while attending nightly fraternity parties and daily tanning sessions, and because if she couldn't be a star, she'd cover those who could. She told herself that one day she'd be a young and hip Mary Hart. She would live in Bel Air or the Pacific Palisades or Beverly Hills. She would never spend her life looking in from the outside. Never.

During Lottie's final semester, one of her journalism professors was so hypnotized by the way her tiny tank tops barely contained her chest that he arranged a postgraduate internship for her at *Personality* magazine. The minute Lottie walked into the Wilshire office, she felt as though she belonged there. She had grown up reading about life just over the hill in the pages of *Personality*. It had been her conduit between the life in the Valley and the only life that mattered.

Lottie was pleasantly surprised by Vince Reggio, the bureau chief. She had thought he'd be polyester garbed, fat, and bald—a guy with ink stains on a wide paisley tie. Instead, Vince was handsome and well dressed in a taupe Armani suit and Gucci loafers. His face was bronzed and his black hair was peppered with gray and gelled in place, with a curlicue casually yet purposefully fixed in the center of his forehead. He looked like a middle-aged Gerber baby.

"All my life, all I've ever wanted to do was write. I couldn't be a stronger asset to your magazine. I can write well and I'm a people person. For some reason, people like to tell me things? So I'll be able to get lots of scoops."

As she spoke, Lottie surveyed the walls of Vince's office, a floor-to-ceiling chronicle of his brushes with fame. There was Vince sipping cocktails with Al Pacino. Vince grinning ear to ear, standing next to Cindy Crawford. Vince gazing at Gwyneth Paltrow. Lottie was so impressed that she interrupted herself in the middle of her own sales pitch. "Oh my God, that's you and Tom Cruise."

"Yep. And he's laughing at a joke *I* told him." Vince leaned forward in his chair and lightly rested his chin in a fist. He cleared his throat. "Lottie, meeting celebrities is one of the perks you get working here. Don't drop the ball and you'll be hanging out with the best of them."

THAT DIDN'T HAPPEN.

Lottie spent months answering phones and updating agent and publicist contact lists for the magazine. Her coworkers threw menial work at her as if she was some kind of housekeeper. They'd go to lunch without asking her. They ignored her in meetings. Just because she had a mane of auburn hair with a great body and big boobs, everyone assumed she was stupid, probably hired because she slept with Vince Reggio—which was just ridiculous. Lottie wasn't one of those desperate wannabes who'd screw *just anyone* to get ahead. Besides, she was a serious journalist. She'd teach them not to underestimate Lottie Love.

And she did. While those dour-faced reporters left the office and went home to the kids and the latest episodes of *The West Wing, Survivor,* and *The Bachelor,* Lottie hung out anywhere a celebrity would: Dolce, Luna Park, Avalon, Belly, Velvet Margarita Cantina, Jones, Vermont, Lotus, Sky Bar, Fred Segal on Melrose, all the trendy bars at all the boutique hotels, the Coffee Bean & Tea Leaf on Sunset, Booksoup, Malibu Kitchen, Starbucks at Cross Creek.

As a teenager she had turned her bedroom into a shrine of famous faces. She augmented centerfolds ripped from *Tiger Beat* and *Personality* with posters bought with her weekly allowance. By the time she went to college, every inch of the floral wallpaper her mother had painstakingly hung was covered by a celebrity. There was Brad, Tom, Christian, Johnny, Denzel, Luke, Jason, George, Noah, Matthew, Matt, Keanu, James, Freddy, Steven, Tobey, Leo, Ricky, Hugh, Marky. She wrote letters to Joaquin Phoenix asking him to her prom. She was crushed when she didn't get a reply.

But now she saw him up close. She kept a list of her sightings: Ben and Matt; Paris and Nicky; Reese and Ryan; Justin; Tobey; Vin; Leo; Kate; Katie; Gwyn and Chris; Gwen and Gavin; Britney; Julia and Danny; Ashton; Beyoncé; J.Lo. At work, she'd brag about her encounters and recount anecdotes, such as when that hot boy-band singer left Barfly without paying the tab. Or when an actor with a nice-guy image beat up the bouncer at the Viper. Or when a famous actor/recovered drug addict bumped into her looking dazed and disheveled. Or when a devoted family man superstar hit on her. Before she knew it, Vince let her write about most of it for *Personality.*

And then they started paying her for going out at night. Getting paid to rub shoulders with the stars, at parties she once only imagined! They created a title just for her: Lottie Love, Chief Party Correspondent. After barely six months she had rocketed from anonymous intern to a name on the *Personality* masthead. It was a dream come true. Lottie had wriggled her way inside. She was reporting for the magazine she had read and devoured and recited as gospel. She vowed to remember the little girl from Tarzana, to write for her. No more watching a searchlight from across the freeway.

Lottie was in the light.

HANK LOVE, HER father, had spent years and years vying to be in that light until he finally retreated to Tarzana and opened up his own plumbing company. Hank Love Plumbing. He ran the business while occasionally auditioning for toothpaste commercials and bit parts on cop shows. He had great teeth. Lottie's mother had been attracted to his thousand-watt smile back in Duluth, where she first saw him play the Messiah in *Jesus Christ Superstar.*

When she became pregnant with Lottie, Mrs. Love made it quite clear that it was time to call it quits. Time to have a bankable profession. For Hank, that meant one thing—toilets. Lottie knew that replacing his dreams of fame and fortune for a lifetime of shit and piss was beyond depressing. And she felt he always resented her for it, but he went into the plumbing business with a vengeance. He took the inheritance his father had left him and bought a big white van, shiny new tools, and a couple of starched white jumpsuits with his italicized name embroidered inside a star on the chest pocket. Hank hired some artist friend to paint his likeness on both sides of the van. If he couldn't have billboards and marquees, he'd have the sides of a truck. HANK LOVE PLUMBING, INC. WE'LL MAKE YOUR PIPES SING. Next to his motto was the artist's rendering of Hank, jet-black hair slicked back and a mouthful of sparkling white teeth occupying more than half of his chiseled face. Instead of his long, crooked nose—the nose that ruined his career, Lottie's mom confided to her when she took Lottie to the plastic surgeon—the van nose was straight and curled up slightly at the end. Lottie thought it looked a lot like the one her mother eventually ordered for her.

HANK LOVE'S EMPIRE grew. Soon there was a fleet of vans with his mug on either side rumbling along the freeway. LUVPLMG, his license plate read. With each addition to the fleet, a U was deleted from the plate and a numeral added. At last count there was a LVPLMG-5. All the plumbers were struggling actors who'd arrive at appointments as if ready for auditions—their mouths curled in bleached grins, their jumpsuits stretched against muscular arms and legs, their taut stomachs squeezed in, their bulging chests heaved out. Still hoping for that big break, they'd leave a headshot at the home of some high-powered executive or casting director or producer who had clogged up a toilet.

Lottie had spent her childhood embarrassed by her father. "My dad says your dad's full of crap." "Your dad smells like shit." She would turn purple when one of his vans chugged up a street near school. At least once a month, vandals would spray-paint messages next to his enormous mouth with its twinkling teeth. "I eat shit." They'd color his teeth brown.

"All those friends of yours with attitude, well, your father will be the first one to tell them that their doo-doo does stink," her mother lectured. "It's an honest profession, and it's a lucrative one. You should be very proud of your father. Look at all he's done for you. He could have been a star."

Lottie tried to imagine what her life would have been like if her dad had become a star. At her elementary school there was a handful of kids with famous parents. A hush seemed to follow them wherever they went. They were treated better than the rest. Teachers smiled at them more. If they disrupted class, it was only because they were performers—just like their parents. If they failed math or science, it was only because they were so artistic.

When their famous parent showed up at school, it was like Christmas.

She remembered when an action-hero actor picked up his son from theater practice. Lottie was in the auditorium rehearsing for her role as an orphan in *Annie*. She watched as the usually sour-faced principal giggled and flirted with him. Her voice trilled. "Would you honor us with some advice for our young thespians?"

"You have to love what you do. Once you don't love it, you should stop. Because it's a lot of hard work." The principal nodded and applauded wildly as if this were the most brilliant thing she'd ever heard.

Out of the corner of her eye, Lottie saw the peroxide-white jumpsuit enter the auditorium. *Please, please let it be one of his employees,* she begged. No, it was the original. Hank Love.

The principal cleared her throat. Her voice was sharp. "Service entrance is in the back."

Lottie was not going to become her father. She wasn't going to live her life with regrets while making pipes sing.

ALTHOUGH LOTTIE HAD spent months silently studying celebrities at bars and clubs and parties, she was surprised how nervous the prospect of actually speaking with them made her. Before driving to her first assignment she spent an entire hour vomiting. To settle her nerves, she downed a few screwdrivers before leaving her Santa Monica apartment for some producer's home in Bel Air.

Lottie pretended that tossing her Cabrio keys to a valet was an everyday thing, then strutted to the Doric-columned entranceway in a low-cut black lace Bebe dress. She gave her name to a tuxedoed man at the door. Lottie Love, Chief Party Correspondent for *Personality* magazine. He smiled at her and said, "Go right in, Miss Love."

Personality expected a lot from her. When Vince assigned her to cover the party, a fund-raising event for an animal rescue shelter, he instructed her to "get the color of the party as well as quotes from as many high-profile guests as possible. Find out who designed their outfits. Describe what they're wearing, thinking, doing. Who are they hanging out with? Who do they leave with? What are the latest style trends? If you see three celebs holding faux crocodile clutches or wearing short waist-tied pleated skirts or sporting updated versions of the perm or painting their lips with gold lip gloss, your trend alarm should go off. Remember: one means nothing—unless Gwyn, Nicole, or Julia's wearing it, two is a coincidence—again, unless it's an A-lister, and three is a trend. *Personality* readers want the scoop. They want the dirt. They want to dress like celebrities. It's up to Lottie Love to step up to the plate and go to bat for them. Don't strike out."

As Vince's words echoed in her head, Lottie's stomach somersaulted. She found a bathroom—all black and white marble with a three-foot gold statue of some Greek or Norse god in the corner—and puked in the toilet. She couldn't help but laugh, wondering if her father had had his hands inside its marble tank at one time.

She wet a white linen hand towel and washed her face. She opened a medicine cabinet, found some toothpaste, smeared it on her teeth, and rinsed. As she was reapplying her Cherries in the Snow lipstick, someone banged on the door. "What are you doing? Having a fucking baby in there? Hurry up."

Whatever, asshole. Lottie was ready to argue, but when the door opened, she gasped. *Cory Jones.* Although he hadn't been in anything of note, Lottie was certain he was the Next Big Thing. Her heart fluttered, her mouth went dry. "Hi," she said. "Sorry."

He brushed past her and slammed the door.

Lottie Love, Chief Party Correspondent, stood outside the bathroom trembling. Getting a quote from Cory Jones, The Next Big Thing, would be a major coup. He was a bad boy who never spoke to the press, flashing the finger instead. If she could just nail a phrase from him, *Personality* would be ecstatic. Who knows? Vince might even promote her to associate bureau chief.

She stood in front of the door with her brand-new digital

recorder in hand, waiting and waiting. She phrased the questions in her head. "What do you think of the party? I love your work. What movies are you going to be in? Why the goatee?" She shuffled her weight from one wobbly leg to the other, her Payless stilettos scraping along the hardwood floor. Finally, the door opened and Cory emerged.

She breathed heavily and shut her eyes. "I'm Charlie. I mean, I'm Lottie Love, Chief Party Correspondent with *Personality* magazine? I know you probably don't want to talk to me and you don't have to. You can so just completely walk away right now and get back to the party, but it would be really the greatest, most fantastic thing in the world if I could get a quote from you. A sentence would be so perfect. Even half a sentence. How about a word or something?"

"Jeez, you talk too fast." Cory laughed. "I've never met someone who talks that fast in my life." He shook his head and started to walk away but halted in midstep. "My grandmother reads that shit wipe. It'd probably make her fucking day if she saw a quote from me in there." He ran his fingers through his greasy, highlighted hair. "What do you want to know? I think I must have missed a question or something."

Lottie cocked her head, smiled, and twirled a piece of hair between her fingers. "Umm," she said, scrunching her face as if in deep thought, but her mind was blank. Her heart caught in her throat. "Umm. I guess, like, how's the party? Are you having fun?"

Cory laughed. "Are you for real? That's the lamest question a reporter's ever asked me. Usually they want to know who I'm fucking. But believe it or not, I'm not with anyone tonight. I'm single and loving it." He smiled at Lottie, grabbed her hand that held the recorder, and pushed it in front of his face. He spoke into it. "That's why this party's so great. There's so many beautiful women here—the possibilities are endless."

His touch electrified her—she was beginning to think her trembling legs wouldn't hold up anymore. She had been too afraid to venture into his love life. Afraid he'd walk away and say nothing to her. But then Cory kept answering questions she hadn't even asked, acting as if she was an old friend.

As she stood there, Terri Max sidled up to Cory. Her new movie, *Detours and Dead Ends,* had just opened. Terri was a twenty-eight-year-old action star with a killer body who had already been divorced three times. With her last husband she had adopted an Uzbek baby girl, who dangled from her arms at Disney premieres and then vanished into the ether until the next big photo op. She and Cory had been photographed together constantly several months ago, but Lottie hadn't seen shots of the couple in weeks.

"Got a match?" she asked, ignoring Lottie while sticking out a Marlboro Light.

Cory grabbed Lottie's recorder. "I'll give you a light, but first tell this reporter girl, ummm . . ." He looked at Lottie.

"Lottie. Lottie Love."

"Yeah, tell Lori why this party is great, and it'll be in the next edition of *Personality.*"

Terri swatted at the air. "That rag?" Then her eyes grazed Lottie's breasts. "Amazing titties. Who's the architect? I bet it's Doctor Gene."

Cory stifled a laugh as Lottie's face reddened. "It's all me, thank you very much."

"Bullshit," Terri said. "Anyway, your rag did a story on me once and called it 'Talent to the Max.' They misquoted me about a dozen times. I used the word 'fucking' and they changed it to 'darn.' I said 'pissed' and they made it 'bothered.' Is that completely lame? Puh-lease. Jesus, Cory, give me a light or I'll have a complete and utter nicotine fit right here. I'll tell Lori some really ugly things about you."

Cory pulled a Zippo from a pocket of his ripped jeans. He dangled it in front of Terri. "Come on. Tell Lori how much you're in love with me."

Terri narrowed her eyes at Cory and clenched her jaw. "Okay. Okay. I wouldn't go anywhere near Cory because he has the smallest cock in the whole world! Now, light my fucking—I mean, darn—cigarette, goddamnit."

As Terri leaned over with a cigarette dangling from her mouth, Lottie peered at the back of her faded blue jeans, trying to read the label.

Terri swiveled toward Lottie and barked, "You're totally checking out my ass." She shook it at Lottie. "J-fuckin' Lo, eat your heart out."

"I couldn't be checking it out less. I was just trying to figure out the brand—for my story."

"James. That's all I own. I have a closet full of them."

Cory handed the recorder back to Lottie. "Here you go, Lois Lane. You know Terri was just joking before, right?"

"Was not," Terri yelled.

"Terri, tell her it's not true."

"It's totally true. I call it the gnat. That's why I dumped him."

"She's lying."

"Pull down your pants and prove it, gnat-boy!" Terri yelled, stomping upstairs.

Cory started to follow Terri and then stopped and turned toward Lottie.

"I so completely believe you."

"No, you don't. And you're gonna tell all your friends that I have a small dick. It'll probably be one of those items in your magazine where you don't name names but everyone knows who you're talking about."

"I promise I so won't."

Cory wasn't listening. He unzipped his pants.

"Please, I so completely don't need you to show me your thing."

"Terri is a complete headcase." He pulled down his pants.

"Oh my God, it's so not gnatlike."

"Print that, Lois Lane."

LOTTIE LOVE SPENT the entire evening in front of the bathroom. Everyone had to pee now and then, she reasoned. By the end of the night, Lottie had quotes from almost everyone who mattered. It was after 2:00 A.M. when she headed back to the office to write down her observations and quotes. She replayed her interviews, embarrassed whenever she heard her helium-saturated voice. As much as she tried to quash her Valley speak, it always trickled out, especially when she was nervous or excited—even after countless nights of practicing her diction, speaking in flat, even tones.

"OhmyGod, I love your body of work." Where did that phrase come from? "You are like the best actor in the entire universe, without a doubt." "OhmyGod, it's you. I love you!" "You were so completely amazing in *Dead Dogs* that I feel like you're still in character and going to poke my eyes out right now." Lottie covered her ears and fast-forwarded the recorder whenever her effusive vocals rang out.

She wrote a novella, omitting that she had never ventured five feet from the bathroom. Her fingers, still buzzing from celebrity, whirred against the keyboard in a dizzying frenzy.

It was literally a star-studded event in Bel Air when all the beautiful people turned out for a party celebrating the opening of the Hollywood chapter of Pet Rescue, a shelter for abandoned and abused animals! Celebrities in literally everything from tuxes and gowns to ripped jeans and T-shirts were there to show their support.

Sexy heartthrob Cory Jones, wearing vintage Levis, a Von Dutch hat, and a Jesus Is My Homeboy T-shirt that hugged his oh-so-buffed body, said he was solo. "I'm not with anyone tonight. I'm single and loving it!!! That's why this party's so great. There's so many beautiful women here—the possibilities are endless."

The possibilities seemed to end with couldn't-be-cuter Terri Max, starring in *Detours and Dead Ends.* She was wearing a black tank top and faded James jeans. "That's all I own. I have a closet full of them," the toned Max confided to me. Max

and Jones seemed to be literally thisclose with each other. Perhaps a reunion is in the stars? "I'm so horny," she confessed . . .

Lottie wrote and wrote until her fingers felt leaden and arthritic. From her windowless cubicle she didn't see the sun's forehead peek out. She didn't hear her colleagues lethargically trickle into the office. It was after 9:00 A.M. when Lottie, clutching twenty pages, realized that she understood what it must be like to be Judith Krantz, Jackie Collins, Ernest Hemingway! She had never been so inspired in her life.

Lottie could tell that Vince was pleased, even though her work was quickly whittled away to a few words underneath glossy photos by Matt Selig, one of the many *Personality* photographers on contract. "Decent reporting, Lottie. You got behind Cory Jones's pretty-boy facade. Good work."

"I'd love to be on the Chris Mercer team," she blurted out.

Vince smiled at the floor. "Thanks, Lottie, but you stick with the parties for now. In a few years you'll be ready to go to bat with the A-listers. In the meantime, read all the staff files, especially Mike Posner's. That's the best way to learn."

"Sure." Lottie forced a smile and turned quickly before Vince could see her rage. Was he really such a fucking moron? Clearly celebrities liked talking to her. Besides, she *had* read all the staff files.

Every piece a correspondent wrote—a file—was available on the computer system for everyone to read. If *Personality* was doing a cover story on Brad Pitt, about ten correspondents would be assigned to report on every aspect of his life—Jennifer, rumored love interests, movies, friends, beauty regimen, exercise, nightlife. Each reporter would send his file to New York, where a "trained" writer or team of writers would disassemble the files and somehow assemble a story. Reporters would spend days or sometimes weeks gathering quotes from people who worked on movies with Brad or saw Brad eating lunch at The Ivy or buying a

T-shirt at Fred Segal. Then they'd spend hours crafting a well-written file. In the end, they were lucky if a quote or two turned up in the finished product. The reporters who'd been in the L.A. bureau for more than five years had already given up—their files consisted of pages of quotes with no attempt at a narrative. Either way, Lottie wasn't impressed.

She went into her office and sought solace in her acid-pink Rolodex. Even though most of the world had Blackberries, *Personality* reporters liked to display bulging Rolodexes atop their desks. It was the journalistic version of "whose is bigger?"—a game Lottie knew she would win. She flipped the cards, admiring them. She knew it was just a matter of time before she amassed more contacts than anyone on staff—more than Vince, more than Mike Posner. She'd be the one to get Chris Mercer.

Chris Mercer. He was the *Now* Big Thing—as big as Leo after *Titanic*. But no one knew anything about him. There was a fan frenzy at the premiere of *Ark*, the movie in which he played a modern-day Noah, but Chris didn't show up. He just vanished. Paparazzi were staked out at all the hot spots, but they always wound up with pictures of Britney or Ashton or Paris instead. *Personality* hired an investigator who couldn't even find a home address.

There were theories. He's a recluse. He's got acute agoraphobia. He's single-handedly trying to reinvent the perception of actors—from stars to craftsmen. He's covered in acne that is camouflaged by makeup on screen. He was molested as a child. All this was pure speculation, most of it from oblivious outsiders like Vince and Bernie, the executive editor.

Lottie *would* get the scoop. She could see it now:

CHRIS MERCER REVEALS ALL, BY LOTTIE LOVE

If you asked her, Lottie probably wouldn't be able to say when she started to feel comfortable around celebrities. It was gradual. For months she stood right next to the bathroom, then near the bathroom, then in the foyer, then close to the door of the main room, then peering in the main room, then in the main room itself. Her hands still shook and her wobbly legs still threatened to collapse, but her stomach didn't somersault and spew its contents anymore. Like a child taking her first steps, Lottie finally pried her knuckles off the rim of the toilet and entered the kingdom.

Initially, she envied the other journalists who seemed to effortlessly mingle with celebs. They were brash. "Are you gay? Who are you sleeping with? How do you feel about your movie tanking?" She thought that with enough practice, she'd develop the Teflon coating necessary to be an ace reporter. But then she realized something: they weren't getting any of the answers. Their questions were greeted with icy stares, chilly rejoinders, silence, the finger. Meanwhile, Lottie, in her awkwardness, was harvesting pearls.

"I mean, I know you probably think I'm totally some psychotic fan, but I'm lit-rully the Chief Party Correspondent for Personality *magazine. Can you tell me what you're doing here? Are you having fun? By the way, I'm like such your biggest fan. Seriously, you couldn't have a bigger fan than me."*

And the stars would open their mouths.

IF BECOMING CHIEF Party Correspondent was Lottie's first big break, meeting Marlon Lang was the second.

Lottie was covering the premiere party at the El Rey for Marlon's debut movie, *Blind Love and Other Handicaps.* Vince wanted a few quotes for the magazine's party page. So Lottie squeezed herself into a tiny suede skirt and beige cardigan and expertly maneuvered through the party, talking to anyone whose face looked vaguely familiar.

"Hey, Reporter Girl," Cory Jones said. "Grandma thinks I'm a real actor now that I've been quoted in *Personality.*"

"I couldn't be happier that she liked it," Lottie said brightly, adjusting the buttons on her cardigan to keep them from bursting open.

Cory grabbed the guy next to him. "Hey, Marlon, have you met Reporter Girl?" He whispered something in Marlon's ear.

Marlon Lang turned and his eyes landed right on her breasts. They nearly popped out. He giggled. "Hey."

Marlon was gorgeous, with huge blue eyes, fat red lips, and perfectly mussed brown hair. And he was sensitive—or at least his character in *Blind Love* was. Lottie was sure the two were pretty similar. Marlon's celluloid equivalent relinquished his pro baseball career to travel around the world with the woman he loved, who had lost her eyesight when a baseball whacked her in the head.

"Hello," Lottie puffed out, breathlessly. "Oh my God, you were so brilliant in *Blind Love and Other Handicaps*."

Marlon ran his fingers through his gelled hair. "Thanks."

Lottie clicked on her recorder with a sweaty thumb. "Did you always know you wanted to be an actor?"

Marlon sucked in his lips and smiled. "My mom says I was performing from conception. I was named Marlon because one night my mom was watching *On The Waterfront* and I kicked during the scene when Marlon Brando says, 'I coulda been a contenda.'" Marlon jutted out his lips and spoke the line in a raspy voice. "I hope to one day be considered the Marlon Brando of my generation."

Lottie laughed, but realized from Marlon Lang's pinched expression that he wasn't kidding. She didn't get it. Why would anyone want to be Superman's big fat dead father?

After a few more minutes, Marlon excused himself. "I've really got to go mingle or I'll never hear the end of it from my publicist. But if you stick around, we can wrap up the questions in about an hour or so."

"Sure," Lottie said.

Lottie mingled too, chatting with frantic publicists who tried to pitch their B- and C-list clients to her. She let the flacks gab away even though their low-wattage stars had no chance of getting in the magazine—unless they committed murder, were killed, contracted a horrible fatal disease, or got arrested for shoplifting. It was difficult to concentrate on the conversations. There were too many actors milling about, distracting her. She couldn't help but turn her head or shift her eyes. The publicists kept droning on, though, probably accustomed to limited attention spans.

"So this Lem Brac calls me every day," said a publicist in a chocolate brown suit. "He desperately wants to write a story on Chris Mercer. But Chris isn't doing any publicity right now. He's focusing on his work. I keep telling him over and over, but still, every day, around two, he calls. It's completely annoying. He sounds like he's toasted, if you want to know the truth. I'm just telling you this because someone like that completely destroys the magazine's credibility."

"Oh, he's like the most pathetic man on earth," Lottie gushed. "He lit-rully does nothing there but go on long lunches."

Lottie remembered that when she first started, Lem, a fossilized British reporter who'd been at the magazine since it began, took her to lunch. He gave her this whole they're-not-your-friends spiel. He laid it on extra thick with a sappy story about some has-been actress from some dumb TV show who he fell in love with.

Do your job, Miss Love. But remember, they're not your friends. Never will be.

"Well, I wish he would stop calling. It's like, get a hint. Chris Mercer is becoming the biggest star out there." She smiled and handed Lottie a business card. "I'm Cyndi Bowman, CEO of Bowman Publicity."

Lottie pulled out a Lottie Love, Chief Party Correspondent, card from her Hello! Kitty wallet. "I would absolutely love to do a story on Chris. If there's any way, it would be so great."

The publicist, a woman about Lottie's age, scooped the card

out of her hand. "I'm afraid he doesn't feel *Personality*'s the right venue for him. He says it's too mainstream and too intrusive. Your magazine loves to take pictures of celebrities playing with their dog in their living room, but my clients want their privacy. They don't want their home splashed across a magazine for all the crazies in the world to see. You have no idea how insane the world is. *Personality* just doesn't appreciate a celebrity's right to privacy. But I have some other really, really great clients, real up-and-comers, who would love to be in *Personality*. I represent Scott Riatta, who plays bad boy Duke Dodge on *GH*. He's very involved in charities and is a real charmer."

As the publicist babbled on about the dregs of her clientele, Marlon reappeared.

"It was nice to meet you, Lottie," Cyndi said, planting a kiss in the air by Lottie's cheek. "Please, say hi to Vince Reggio for me. Is he still married?"

Lottie followed Marlon into an empty room with a sofa and two chairs. Lottie sat on the sofa, and Marlon pulled up a chair and sat across from her, his lanky body spilling off the seat. Without even a question to prompt him, Marlon began speaking.

"My motivation for *Blind Love and Other Handicaps* was that I was just coming back from a relationship gone bad. I thought this was my great love, but I guess she didn't feel the same way. Anyway, it helped put me in the place where I wanted to be for the role of Jake Blaze, a guy who won't commit to anyone because of some secret from his past. It was easy for me to find my comfort zone per se, because I was in pain at the time. I honed my craft in *Blind Love*. Of course, it helps when you have a fantastic director and a great cast. And Gregory Perry is an incredible writer."

Lottie nestled her chin in her palm as she stared into Marlon's deep blue eyes. She couldn't quite look away. Were those flecks of gold and orange?

"Are you dating anyone right now?"

"Nope. I'm completely single."

⋆★⋆

THE NEXT DAY, Lottie rewound the recorder to see where the interview ended and the seduction began. She realized it never had. Marlon had mesmerized both of them through talk of himself. In the middle of a monologue on preparing for his role as the misunderstood Jake Blaze, he invited Lottie to the Hotel Bel Air, where he was staying to promote his movie. He said he would love to have a drink or two and continue the interview in a more private place.

And Lottie agreed. Without even a thought, she said, "Okay. That sounds great." She convinced herself that there was no innuendo in either of their voices. She went with Marlon for the sake of the story. For the sake of *Personality* magazine.

Lottie's red convertible Cabrio (license plate: LOTALUV) trailed Marlon's black Cadillac Escalade. Her heart pounded; her head swirled as she thought about the craziness of it all. Marlon Lang! He was almost as cool as Joaquin Phoenix.

Just in case, she checked her black silk Kate Spade purse (she had found it tossed in a *Personality* closet after a photo shoot) for her diaphragm. Armed with her recorder and birth control, Lottie breathlessly headed for Marlon. When she entered the lobby, he was signing autographs for a few tourists.

Inside the suite, which was decorated with posters of Marlon from *Blind Love* (for the press interviews, he said, dismissively rolling his eyes), Marlon uncorked a bottle of Cristal and poured two glasses that fizzed and overflowed onto the floor. Lottie tried to capture much of the carbonation with her tongue as it slid down the long stem. She licked the glass while watching Marlon watch her.

"Cheers. To blind love—and lust with perfect vision," Marlon toasted as he lifted the glass high, weaving it through the air until it landed at his mouth.

"Cheers," Lottie said.

While Marlon checked phone messages, Lottie took out her recorder and held it awkwardly in her hand. Then, after a few exaggerated sighs, Marlon plopped down next to her on the sofa, their shoulders touching lightly.

"It's insane—all the offers that are coming in."

As he spoke, Marlon rested his hand on Lottie's knee. "There just isn't any good writing in Hollywood and I only work with substance. If the writing doesn't speak to me, then don't waste my time."

"I couldn't understand more."

Marlon's hand abandoned Lottie's knee and climbed up her leg slowly but confidently. Lottie felt the weight of his hot palm as it rubbed the top of her leg and traveled to her inner thigh. Her heart palpitated. The recorder fell out of her sticky hands and landed between her legs.

Listening to the replay, Lottie suddenly realized that she never uttered a word, even when Marlon's hand moved from her thigh farther up her short lace dress. "It's so great to be with someone I can talk to, who understands me in a way most don't," Marlon whispered. "I feel like you want to know the real me, not the famous me. That hasn't happened in a long, long time."

Marlon kissed her on the lips, hard and without hesitation, while one hand quickly—and dexterously—unbuttoned her tight beige cashmere sweater as if there was no possibility that she would reject his advances. Later, when Lottie became more experienced with celebrity, she realized that this was what turned her on the most—they didn't fumble with buttons or clasps. They never wavered.

As Marlon moved and pushed and thrusted, Lottie closed her eyes tight and imagined Marlon larger than life on-screen. *I am with Marlon Lang. Marlon Lang!* Over and over the words whirled in her head. *Marlon Lang is huffing and puffing over* me! The celluloid God. The teen heartthrob. *Tiger Beat* cover boy. The misunderstood Jake Blaze! Lottie opened her eyes and stared into the poster above her. His perfectly chiseled face, his full red lips, his ripped torso. Then she looked into his intense blue eyes, and she knew that most of the world—male or female—would kill to be in her place right now. That thought alone induced hot spasms, and she shuddered and sighed.

"Tell me I'm the best. Tell me I'm the best. Say it. Say it," Marlon moaned. She realized his eyes were fixed above her head, to the publicity poster of himself, shirtless and buffed and pouting.

"You're number one. Number one! Oh God, you're number one."

Marlon Lang Is Jake Blaze. Coming to a Theater Near You.

As she listened to the interview, she was surprised at how quickly it ended. In her mind, they had screwed for hours and hours, but the tape denied her this illusion. It was over in seconds.

"My God, he's like a high school virgin," her eavesdropping roommate had exclaimed.

But those seconds inexorably changed Lottie Love's life.

The electrifying feeling was incredible. Addicting. Lottie couldn't imagine herself being with anyone but a celebrity. Go ahead, call her a starfucker. She didn't care. In a few months, she had walked from the bathroom to the ballroom to the bedroom.

She would never take the service entrance.

LEMUEL BRAC DESPISED PUBLICISTS.

After more years than he could count, Lem had witnessed a complete metamorphosis in the business of celebrity journalism. When he was a fledgling reporter, publicists were people to have a few belts with after—or during—or instead of—work to nail a scoop. They slurred out secrets and scandals that eventually made their way into *Personality* magazine, thanks to Lem. He became the toast of the town. Whether celebrities loathed or loved him, they all wanted their profiles to be penned by him.

At one time, Lem could score one of the top tables at Spago or Morton's or Chasen's. He wasn't on the same rung as the Hollywood kings and queens, but he wasn't banished to serfdom either. Lem Brac was a duke of a small but important province that couldn't be ignored. The Hollywood royalty had to pay attention. In his ink-stained hands and gnarled notebooks, he held the keys to your kingdom. But he could also oust and replace you with a newer, younger, and more magazine-friendly king. Be nice to Sir Lem, show him respect, and you could live forever, or at least until syndication.

Then something happened. There was a change in command. The good ol' boy publicists he imbibed with were usurped by their daughters, who went from the office to Bikram yoga. Martini and steak lunches were déclassé. Salads and mineral water were de rigueur. Scoops were replaced by corporatespeak and icy silence. No matter how much he drank, they'd sit stone-faced and sober. "My client isn't ready to talk to the press." "My client is too sensitive." "My client is too big for *Personality,* but I have a soap star who is involved in many charitable organizations." "I've got to run. I have a six o'clock with my personal trainer." "Can't talk, but I'll give a return. ASAP. Promise." "We're going to take a pass, 'kay?"

These publi-sissies didn't see any genius in his Queen's English; instead they saw a stereotype: another drunk Limey. They'd seen his kind portrayed in movies dozens of times. He was a parable. He was their father, who stayed out all night drinking and screwing while teary-eyed Mom waited for a call from the police or the morgue. He was the reason they were in therapy. They knew all there was to know about Lemuel Brac—and they hated him.

One thing was certain: he needed a life preserver. Vince Reggio wanted him gone. This guy—arrayed in pressed linens, Good Humor–man whites, or Armani suits—with his electric beach tan, purged bowels, and quasi-televangelist hair, was always telling Lem how to do his job—and always in sports clichés.

"You've got to hit a few home runs for the team, Lem. This isn't the old *Personality* magazine—the bar's been raised, and you either jump over it or break your neck."

It was an insult. I don't want to raise the bar—I want to close it, Sir Lem would have replied back in the day. Instead, he bit his tongue, smiled, and nodded his head.

REGGIO RUMMAGED THROUGH his fruit salad with a fork, popped a melon ball into his maw and chewed, dabbing his mouth with a napkin.

"You know, the powers that be in New York have been wondering what you've been doing for us lately. There hasn't been a byline with your name on it for quite some time. Years, I'd say. I tell them that you're working on longer projects and industry contacts for the magazine. In other words, I cover your ass, but if they don't see more productivity from you, well . . ."

Reggio wasn't old-school. He didn't have what it took—that's why he was an editor. In Lem's eyes, editors were an inferior breed. But Lem could see that he was being set up for a fall.

"I know you've been trying to slam-dunk an exclusive with Chris Mercer. I told New York that you have some . . . contacts at his publicist's office. I actually said that if anyone can get us an interview with Mercer, it's our man Lem. I'm putting my credibility on the line for you. I explained that these things take time, but you know New Yorkers; they want everything yesterday. So?"

Reggio daintily plucked up an apple wedge with his fork. Lem smiled at him, oozing as much British charm as he could muster.

"Well, yes. Hopefully I'll have an answer soon. The chap is very well aware that we want to speak to him, but he's taking his time making a decision. I'll put in my call this afternoon. But mind you, my contact, Thomas Bowman, has retired and I'm dealing with his daughter. She's extremely green."

Vince stiffened. "Cyndi Bowman's a professional, Lem. I've dealt with her on several occasions. This is very important to us. I don't understand the holdup. Chris Mercer is so hot right now, but no one's gotten close to him. If we outrun our competition on this one and score a touchdown, it would really boost our reputation, especially among the younger audience. Our circulation is down. People are beginning to notice that we never interview the stars anymore, just their hair and makeup people. Don't take no for an answer. Turn negatives into positives."

"Yes . . . well . . . I'm perfectly capable of . . ."

"Besides, wasn't that your specialty? Getting elusive stars to talk?"

Lem coughed and cleared his throat. "That *is* my spe-see-al-it-ee." He spoke in accent overdrive while snapping his neck back. He pushed out a smile and then turned on the heels of his weathered Church's loafers.

His province was sinking deeper. This would be it for him. Lem needed a scoop to keep his job. At his age, he'd never get another gig in this town. If only Thom was still heading Bowman

Publicity, he'd have the interview wrapped up by now, with a book deal and a nice chunk of change.

To Lem, the problem with his adopted country was the absence of royalty. Without royalty, there is no concept of genuine, unconditional loyalty. With Brits, you have a monarch until death. Royalty can fuck a horse; it can proclaim its desire to be a lover's tampon; it can invent a religion; it can behead. Yet it's still around and the ever-subjugated Brit curtsies to it. In America, royalty is elected by the box office. Americans are fickle: they can elect and reject and elect again. They elevate celebrities to a pedestal and then sledgehammer them down. There is no such thing as real victory in this country. The best you can hope for is an endless supply of tenacity.

And despite what Reggio or the editors in New York thought, Lem was tenacious. Every day he'd scan the Hollywood magazines, searching for story ideas. He'd call his blokes at the British tabs and root around for scoops. But he knew nothing was true, and he didn't have the heart to pretend he believed anymore. *Yes, they divorced amicably. Of course they're the best of friends. Yes, he's a great dad. He'd rather play with his kids than act in a movie. Of course she's in the mental hospital because of exhaustion. Drugs? Never. They're in love—it's not a publicity stunt geared to their movie. Homosexual? Never!*

Every day after lunch, Lem would ring up Cyndi Bowman. Before he went on the wagon a couple of months ago, he'd guzzle from the bottle of Smirnoff's he kept in his bottom desk drawer. Now he just took a deep breath, then sipped his Starbucks.

"Bowman Publicity," the receptionist chimed. Bowman Publicity—Lem hated that. Ever since his friend the eponymous Thomas Bowman retired, his loving daughter had clipped his name as if trying to erase all evidence of the company's—and her—creator.

"Hello, this is Lem Brac *a-gain,* with *Personality.* I'm calling for Cyndi Bowman *a-gain.* Is she available?" Lem squeezed his eyes shut, for he knew what was coming.

A pause and then . . .

"I'm sorry, Mr. Black? Cyndi's in a conference right now, but I'll make sure she gives a return. Promise."

"Thank you, but I must remind you that you've *promised* every day this week. It seems the more promises you make, the less likely they'll be fulfilled."

"Miss Bowman's been extremely busy. She'll give a return ASAP."

"I'd really appreciate if Cyndi could *give a return* today. Please remind her that I was—am—a very good friend of her father, the founder of *Thomas* Bowman Publicity."

Lem seethed. Her father would die if he knew how utterly rude Cyndi was. Every day, Lem thought about driving up to Thom's Santa Barbara manse and explaining the situation. Thom Bowman had a rule: he always returned calls a maximum of two hours after receiving them. He prided himself on the principle. Ol' Thom could be out in the middle of a golf course, sipping martinis, and he'd return Lem's call before the next tee. That's how his empire was built. Cyndi was tearing it down.

FOR MONTHS HE had invited Cyndi out to lunch. When there were no more excuses, she huffed and agreed to meet him at Ivy at the Shore in Santa Monica. She was late, of course. Nearly twenty minutes. While Thom was jovial, Cyndi was sober. Her mouth seemed permanently sewn into a scowl. Perhaps it was a natural response to bad rhinoplasty. Her nose—like most of the population of nose jobs—was snipped too short and curled up too much, leaving Cynthetica with nostrils she could pick with a kneecap. Her eyes were pretty, he hated to admit. A deep blue and wide-set.

Lem desperately wanted to interview Mercer, but he couldn't let the desperation seep out of him. Once the black-rooted blond bimbo sensed that, it would be all over. Women have extremely sensitive radar for picking up a man's desperation, Lem knew, so he feigned indifference.

"They don't make them like your dad anymore. He was the best. A real character. It was always a pleasure to work with such a venerated icon."

Cyndi stared beyond Lem with half-shut eyes. Then she tucked her corn-colored hair behind her ears. "Well, I run the show now. My father's living in Santa Barbara and doesn't interfere at all with the business. Frankly, he's content playing golf and puttering around the garden. He's through with the business of publicity."

"Well, how about giving an old friend of your dad's an interview with Chris Mercer? He'd get the cover and an audience of close to forty million readers—that's quite a number at the old box office. I wouldn't even have to be that intrusive. Quite honestly, I don't need to describe every room of his house. Just a few nonthreatening questions. I'll ring up your father and tell him he made a wise choice passing the reins to you."

Cynthetica foraged through her Vuitton handbag and pulled out a tube of lipstick. While Lem played mendicant, Cyndi puckered her pencil-thin mouth and smeared on a fresh coat of Honey Nut Brown. She pursed her lips and checked her artistry in a pocket mirror, rubbing her tongue on a lipstick-stained tooth.

Cyndi dreamily stared past Lem, twirling her hair as she spoke. "Chris is a very sensitive actor. He hates publicity, truly hates it. If he had it his way, he'd just act. He doesn't understand why the world needs to know him. It actually makes him very upset. Chris became an actor because of a true love for the actual craft. He could do without the fame and fortune. He's a brilliant soul. He can joke one minute and then do Hamlet the next."

Lem tore into his rare New York strip sirloin while Cyndi poked at her garden salad. She quickly dunked a slab of lettuce into the low-cal vinaigrette on the side. She shook her fork and watched the dressing drip off.

"Chris is extremely cognizant of the fact that he's in demand. It's a feeding frenzy out there, bigger than anything I've ever seen, and I've seen a lot, believe you me."

Yes, and I've seen your mother change your shitty diaper, Lem nearly blurted.

Cyndi chewed her lettuce. Then she rolled her eyes and sighed. "Chris is calling the shots. He wants to handpick a writer to profile him. He's a man of great intellect. He reads and he writes—real prose, not fluffy magazine stuff—so he's looking for someone with excellent writing abilities and a keen insight into an actor's psyche."

Lem swallowed a piece of beef without chewing. If he were twenty years younger, he would have stared straight at Cyndi and said, "He must have been a good fuck, too." Instead, he gulped the remainder of his water and said, "Well, that's me. If you want an outside opinion, ask your father about Sir Lem."

Cyndi took a languid sip of her Pellegrino. "As I've already verbalized, my father's only thinking about his golf game these days—and movies. He loves old movies. And quite honestly, my father was from a different generation. He doesn't understand the celebrity paradigm of the new millennium. He kowtowed to the press, if you ask me. He thought a story in *Personality* was the measure of success, but I approach it differently."

"Oh really, Miss Bowman. And do tell how you've reinvented the art of publicity."

She didn't catch his sarcasm.

"My father would have been calling *Personality* months before anyone knew the name Chris Mercer. By the time Chris gained recognition, everyone would have been sick to death of him. People are screaming to know about Chris, and right now, we're enjoying the sound of mass hysteria."

"Your father did all right in his day."

Cyndi laughed and examined her nails. "I love my father to death, really. But, quite frankly, there's a whole new school of publicity out there. It's important that you media people get on the same page with us."

"Huh?" Lem swallowed the remainder of his drink. "What the

hell am I, bloody Rip Van Wrinkle?" Ambushed by the despondency in his voice, Lem burped out a quick laugh. "You can't even order beef tartar in this town anymore."

A tsunami of sadness rushed through him, but Lem wasn't about to lose his cool in front of the ice bitch. He forced out a weak smile and a fake laugh. "I miss my beef tartar," he said too loudly, smacking his lips and slapping his hand on the table.

Cyndi shot him a patronizing smile. "I'll tell you what. I'm strategizing with Chris next week and I'll mention you. At this point in time, that's all I can do. In the meantime, fax me some samples of your work so I can show Chris."

Imagine! A tryout for some moronic actor. *Shove it up your skinny ass,* he wanted to scream. Instead, he said, "Wonderful, wonderful. I'll get those over to you this afternoon. Thank you. Your father must be very proud of you. Actually, tell your father that Lem Brac said hello and that I think you're doing a brilliant job."

Cyndi motioned for the waiter to bring the check. When it arrived, she reached out for it while Lem tried to grab it away. "No. I won't have it," he said. "I invited you."

Cyndi smiled broadly, squinting her eyes and flaring her capacious nostrils. It was as if she was saying, *What a cute child, but you shouldn't have broken your piggybank for me.* Instead she said, "No. Please. No favors—no regrets. I'd feel better if I paid." Her icy voice prompted Lem's hand to leap off the check.

"Thank you very much," he croaked.

TWO WEEKS LATER, he still hadn't heard anything. Cyndi hadn't even had the class to return his calls—and he'd left one every afternoon since their horrid lunch date. After that lunch, Lem had given Reggio the thumbs-up sign, saying it seemed promising. Reggio had regarded Lem skeptically at first. But soon he was caught in the excitement. "Way to go, Sir Lem," he said, pumping a fist in the air. "You're off the bench and back out in the field. Now let's just finish the play."

Lem had actually been convinced that the minute Mercer saw his magnificent prose, he'd be dialing Sir Lem up himself. But there was nothing. Reggio wouldn't look Lem in the eye anymore. *You dropped the ball,* Lem could hear Reggio thinking.

And now it was a free-for-all, he was certain. Why else was Mike Posner being wined and dined by Bernie? Even Lot a Love waltzed into his office and announced that she was at a party chatting it up with Cyndi Bowman. "I lit-rully met every Next Big Thing. It was incredible. Cyndi told me that Chris lit-rully isn't talking to anybody. I told her we were, like, dying to do a story on him?"

As if that high-speed, squeaky-voiced, plastic bimbette was on a par with Sir Lem! There was nothing real about Lottie Love. Fake mammaries. Fake nose. Valley girl question mark lilt genetically encoded in her larynx. Lem couldn't take it anymore. The whole staff seemed intent on undermining him under direct orders from Chief Saboteur Vincent Reggio.

AFTER A LONG day at the office, Lem returned to his Beverly Hills apartment. The Sherman Oaks home had become his wife's decades ago, so Lem moved back to the West Side, to an impressive address and an unimpressive apartment. When he first arrived from Great Britain, Lem had been shocked by the concatenation of ugliness that constituted a neighborhood. His Moorish-styled condo was no exception. The name, Palm Oasis, was scrawled along the side of the building like some sash on a beauty pageant contestant from the Ozarks who'd never make it anywhere near the finals.

Safe at home, Lem grabbed a yellow legal pad and headed for the deck. It was less cluttered than his apartment, and the air was delirious with night jasmine. After the divorce, Lem had tried to rebuild a life for himself, and since his apartment was so small, he focused on his large wood-slatted deck. He had spent all his free time at nurseries picking out oleanders, verbena, bougainvillea, and cacti. He planted them in Greco-Roman-style clay pots, with gargoyles and Medusa's heads and cherubs frolicking about. He pruned and watered them and replanted them when they outgrew the pots. He strung tiki lights along the sides of his Popsicle-style fence. And it was a magnificent jungle. Yellow, purple, red, and pink flowers bloomed and rioted around him, their sugary scents wafting throughout the otherwise dank apartment. During the day, butterflies gamboled among the flowers. At night, publicists and agents mingled in the Lem-made jungle. They'd drink and bullshit until the wee hours of the morning.

Then sometime, a few years go, maybe even ten by now, maybe more, Lem stopped pruning. He wasn't exactly sure why or when. It wasn't as if it were a moment of revelation. One day he forgot, then the next and the next, until there was no point in trying to resuscitate his garden with water or fertilizer. He allowed it to quietly dehydrate and die. Now, the cracked clay pots were filled with dry bricks of dirt and a few straggly brittle weeds. The butterflies were long gone. So were the friends.

What a waste of time, Lem thought as he shook his head. But he still enjoyed sitting outside rather than in his cramped apartment. There was a stale, brackish smell to his place that he couldn't air out, even when he opened the windows and doors.

During his heyday, Lem had written a couple of modestly successful unauthorized biographies. Paul Newman, Katharine Hepburn, Farrah Fawcett, to name a few. It had been years and years since he wrote a book—Lem had lost the patience it took to nurture anything, it seemed. But he decided it was time to try again. This time, he would tell his own story. The truth. He was sick of all the lies, half-truths, and spins. He had a warehouse full of anecdotes that just needed to be pruned and watered, if only he could focus. So far he'd written two hundred pages. The yellow sheets of legal paper were stained with ink, wine, and vodka, and his handwriting was barely legible. A few years ago, he would have polished off the book by now. He did have a title: *They're Not Your Friends: My Years with Celebrity.* He began the tale with

Franny Blanchard, honing and tweaking it for months. His agent, Al Ziegler, had read the first chapters and loved it, but Zig died of a heart attack a few months ago. In his place was another Cynthetica, who'd probably want to see an outline and writing samples.

FRANNY BLANCHARD. HOW could someone who was part of his life for such a small amount of time still occupy such a big part of his memory? When Lem met Franny, she was a struggling actress who'd just landed a starring role on a new sitcom, *Lisa the Love Witch*. Their time together was full of promise. Franny Blanchard was full of promise. It was palpable to Lem. It radiated off Franny—energy and light bounced around her like lightning on a lake in a summer storm. She was beautiful, but it was something more than that.

He'd never heard of Franny, but he was already a star at *Personality* magazine when he got a call from a fledgling publicist named Thomas Bowman, who wanted to pitch him some stories.

"Sound great, Thomas. Let me grab your phone number and I'll get back to you—soon as my schedule clears."

Thom had laughed. "Listen, I wasn't born yesterday. You'll never call. You probably don't even have any intention of taking my number, do you? At this moment, is there any type of writing device in your hand?"

Lem smiled at his empty hands.

"Come on, my treat. I promise you won't be disappointed. We'll make it a quick lunch."

"Listen, *I* wasn't born yesterday either. Publicists don't know the meaning of a quick lunch."

But something about Thom Bowman appealed to him. Maybe it was the tenor of his voice—deep and gravelly, the voice of a man you could believe in. Maybe he seemed smarter than most people Lem had met since his move. Maybe he reminded Lem a little bit of himself.

They hit it off immediately. Both ordered numerous martinis and rare steaks with blood that dripped down their lips and formed puddles on their plates.

Thom was tall—about six-three—with movie-star looks. He had dark thick eyebrows, deep-set blue eyes, and a square chin. He had moved to Los Angeles years earlier to pursue an acting career.

"I love movies. Love 'em. Ask me anything, absolutely anything about movies and I'll know. I can recite dialogue from every major movie. *Casablanca. Gone With the Wind. The Wizard of* fucking *Oz.* The problem is, I don't recite it with feeling, with emotion, with empathy. I am an absolutely horrible actor, but I can sell ice to Eskimos. So I figured, if I can't be an actor, I'd sell 'em."

"Makes sense."

Thom smiled. "You think so? Good." Then he pulled out a headshot.

"This is Franny Blanchard. She's going to be huge. Huge. Isn't she gorgeous? You have to meet her. I'll call her right now. I'll have her stop by. You can see for yourself. This woman is something else. You'll see. Let me call her."

Lem laughed. "You're quite persistent. But I've gotta get back to the office. Deadlines."

Thom stared hard at Lem and smiled. "That's bloody bullshit. I know your magazine's schedule. Your deadlines aren't until Thursday. Come on; meet her. A quick drink. She loves strawberry daiquiris. She'll love you."

Lem stared back. "The truth is, the magazine only runs stories on actresses who *are* huge—not on actresses who are going to be huge, according to their publicists . . . or their mothers."

"Trust me. She's going to be enormous and then you'll be begging me. I'm giving you first crack because, well, I like you."

Lem guffawed. "Your audacity is incredible. Did everyone else turn you down? I'll tell you what, who else do you represent? Maybe I can work something out."

Franny Blanchard was Thom's only client. He'd just met her a few days earlier during an audition for *Lisa the Love Witch.* The casting director had told Franny she had the part and told Thom, "Don't call us. We'll call you." It had been rejection number 973. He was sitting in his broken-down Dodge Dart pondering his future when Franny asked for a ride home. It hit him then. He'd be her publicist.

"Okay. I'll meet her," Lem said. "I don't want you swinging from a noose on my account."

It turned out she was waiting in Thom's car.

LEM BRAC WAS thirty years old and too cynical to believe in love at first sight. But he met Franny and fell in love at the second strawberry daiquiri. She did, too, it seemed. For a few months, it was wonderful. He helped her rehearse. He'd type out his stories while she sat next to him reading scripts. He surprised her by convincing his editors to run a full-cover profile on this actress no one had heard of but whose series was about to air.

"Trust me on this one. She's going to be a star. We've got to catch her now before the competition does," he said.

"If you think she's going to be huge, then she's going to be huge. We trust your instincts, Lem," they said.

He even committed the cardinal sin of journalism—he let her read the article before he turned it in to his editors.

"I love it, Lem, but please don't quote my high school acting teacher. She hated me. 'Franny didn't show promise.' What the hell kind of thing is that to say?"

"It just shows how wrong she was and how far you've gone."

"It still hurts. Just because she didn't see it doesn't mean anything. And for my so-called best friend to say I was the class flirt, well, in Hollywood that means I'll blow just about anyone."

She unzipped his pants. He made changes. It was a hagiography if ever there was one.

★★★

"LISA THE LOVE Witch Reveals All" by Lem Brac. With a spell you were under her command. A few days after the story ran, she signed with a major agent. A few days after that, she signed a contract to play Lisa for a lot more money. A few days later, she landed a role in the next Clint Eastwood movie. And a few more days later, she dumped Lem Brac.

"It's too hard right now," she said over the phone. "I don't have time to give one hundred percent of Franny Blanchard to anyone."

"I don't need a hundred percent. How about fifty?"

She yawned into the phone. "We'll talk tomorrow. I've got to get some sleep."

"Let me come over. I'll tuck you in. I'll read you a bedtime story and then I'll go home. I need to see you."

Franny had laughed. "Oh Lemuel, you are naive. There are no bedtime stories in Hollywood, just movies to fall asleep to."

She had hung up. Lem knew she was gone for good. But it still shocked him the next day when he called the number and it had already been changed.

LEM WAS SNAPPED into the present by his trilling phone. No one called him at home anymore. It was probably a telemarketer. When he picked it up, he was surprised to hear an agitated Reggio.

"Any progress with Mercer? New York wants some news tomorrow."

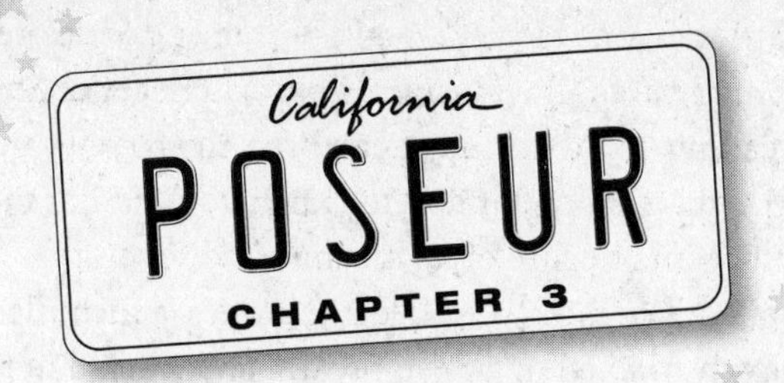

MIKE POSNER KNEW THAT MOST OF THE PEOPLE IN THE CONFERENCE room despised him.

He was twenty-nine. Handsome in a nonchalant kind of way. Talented. The heir apparent. Hell, he was Prince William of the Los Angeles bureau of *Personality* magazine. Big things were planned for Mike Posner. In case anyone doubted it, Vince Reggio announced it to all one hundred editors, writers, reporters, copy editors, researchers, and proofreaders assembled in the Los Angeles offices for three days of corporate seminars designed to unleash excellence in reporting, writing, and researching.

"Mike Posner arrived less than a year ago. Already he has amassed more sources than most seasoned reporters do in a lifetime. His scoops have made him a regular on *Access Hollywood, E.T., Extra, E.* If he were any more dedicated, he'd be pitching a tent in front of Jennifer Garner's house."

There were a few guffaws, a gentle roll of laughter, and some nervous giggles—the corporate laugh track, your reaction indicative of your power, ambition, or fear. There were smiles aimed at Mike, who sat at the head table next to Bernice Banks, the New York–based editor in chief. Bernie beamed and patted his back. Mike gave a quick grin and sipped at his water. *Gee, I'm just trying to do my job.*

"During this conference, we've covered reporting techniques, research gathering, and the intricacies of the *Personality* paradigm," Vince said as the staff nodded. Mike wondered if anyone knew what Vince was talking about. Bernie and Vince referred to the *Personality* paradigm constantly but had never defined it.

As if reading Mike's mind, Lem Brac cleared his throat and asked, "Would you be so kind as to expand on that for me? I must admit I've become unsure of its meaning."

The staff—even Mike—rolled their eyes and huffed. Bernie blinked slowly, sucked in a deep breath, and rubbed her temples.

"Vincent, would you mind enlightening Mr. Brac?"

Vince's eyes bugged out and he gulped some air. There was silence for a few moments. Then he said, "Well, Bernie, I couldn't do it justice. I'd rather you lobbed this ball."

Vince held his breath as he waited for Bernie. She smiled at him and he exhaled.

She cleared her throat. "Well, as *most* of you know, our stories all have the same format. The opening is a scene setter at the celebrity's home, which really gives an inside look into the celebrity. We want our readers to feel as though they're friends with Brad and Tom and Julia and Gwynie. So when a reporter scores an interview with say, Julia Roberts, the reporter must demand to go to her home to observe her routine. Be a fly on the wall. A great scene setter would be something like Danny cooking filet mignon while Julia plays with the twins. And we always love having dogs yapping away nearby. We love celebs interacting with animals. It makes them so human. Then follow this up with a really descriptive quote from Julia about why she's so happy with married life, et cetera. Domestic scenes like this make a good P.P. Then back that up with quotes from some thirds, which as we all know are friends, family, and coworkers. Third till you hurt and then third some more."

As Bernie babbled on, Mike wondered if she believed what she was spewing. Julia and Danny would never even speak to a *Personality* reporter, unless accosted by one on a red carpet. And then they'd only recite wardrobe details.

Mike flinched when he heard Bernie say his name.

"And now back to business. Mike will discuss an equally important but often ignored piece of the reporting puzzle: source cultivating. For without gathering and nurturing sources, there would be no *Personality* magazine. Sources are the lifeblood of our publication. Here, the art of sourcing is more important than the art of writing . . . Mike?"

Mike headed to the podium and shook Bernie's hand. He looked out at his audience. Many eagerly clutched pens, waiting for him to bestow wisdom. Lem Brac rolled his eyes. But what else was Lem going to do?

"When Vince asked me to speak on sourcing, I thought he was nuts. What do I know that you guys don't? Nothing. Building sources is like making friends. You gotta get these people to like you, to trust you, to want to tell you things. It helps when you can take 'em for lunch at The Ivy or drinks at Sky Bar . . ."

As he spoke, Mike watched Lottie Love scribble away. Working at *Personality* seemed like a day at the beach for Lottie. Half the time Mike expected her to have a big colorful towel in one hand and an inflatable raft in the other. She'd show up at the office spilling out of spandex, her skirts a patch of fabric highlighting muscular thighs and calves. She always smelled of cocoa butter. Lottie Love *was* California; to Mike, she personified the palm trees and orange blossoms and sandy beaches. This speech was for her. His eyes darted around the room, always landing on her to check if she was listening. After a few minutes, he realized she wasn't taking notes, just doodling. Her eyes were glazed, so he wrapped it up. Did he even stand a chance?

But even if he did, she'd eventually find out the truth about him.

AFTER HIS SPEECH, Mike was invited to lunch at The Ivy with Bernie and Vince. Mike sat in the leather backseat of Vince's spotless Lexus while Vince and Bernie sat up front. They all picked up cell phones and feigned importance by checking voice mails, assigning assistants chores, and leaving messages for publicists. Mike held his phone up to his ear, but he was really deciphering vanity plates. Since he had moved to L.A. it had become an obsession. Almost every car seemed to have one. Even Vince's read CR8TIF. Mike had to laugh at that one. Since his obsession began he had seen countless versions of "creative." KR8UFF, CR8IV, KR8OV. CR8OF. He wanted to scream out his window, NO, YOU'RE NOT! Especially to Vince.

"The reason I wanted to spend time with you is because I like your style," Bernie told Mike as they sat at a table in the back of The Ivy. "You've cultivated some great sources. Somehow you've gotten into Brad's inner circle. And Tom Cruise. Brilliant! The anecdotes about him running around with his kids were priceless. You captured him as a regular dad."

"Thanks."

"Did Vince ever tell you what the catalyst was for his promotion?" Bernie asked Mike. She patted Vince's shoulder. "He sat in dog shit for hours."

"Well, I . . ."

"Don't be modest, Vincenzo," she said, leaning in toward Mike. "He reported on Julia Roberts's wedding to Danny Moder. Of course we weren't invited, but Vince spent hours squatting in dog shit in Julia's neighbor's backyard. He watched the ceremony through the fence and got every detail. They had no idea. He even saw their first kiss as man and wife."

"God, the stench was awful. I had to throw away my pants."

"But you were willing to do it. That's what we need. People who are willing to lie in dog shit to get the goods."

She lifted up her ice tea. "To dog shit."

"Dog shit," they said, clinking glasses.

Speaking of shit, Mike knew that poor Vince had canceled his Friday high colonic for this meal. Every day at lunchtime, Vince marched out of the office, his face puckered with importance as if he were headed out for a meeting with a major Hollywood player. However, Lem Brac had clued Mike in. "Monday is his facial. Tuesday is his massage. Wednesday is the electric beach. Thursday is a manicure. Every other Friday is his high colonic—notice his gait changes on Friday. I'll tell you, the manicure is what I find the most offensive. I cannot tolerate a man with polished nails. It shows real lack of character."

As Bernie droned on about something or other, Mike nodded his head and furrowed his brow. He hoped to convey his I'm-hanging-on-your-every-word look. He also hoped she wouldn't ask a question.

"We need a circulation boost. It's a jungle out there with *People, Us, In Touch, Star,* and *The Enquirer* competing with us for the same stories. We're really taking a beating. Especially when you have these other rags paying huge amounts of money to sources. For us, it's really about journalism. That's the essence of what we do."

Mike remembered the stories Lem told at their first lunch. Last year, Bernie was so desperate to nail an exclusive on the Sebastian Brooks–Stephanie Winters wedding that the magazine paid $100,000 to the couple's favorite charity—PETA—so the bride's mother would give an interview spilling the details on the nuptials.

Then, a few months after the wedding, Bernie wanted to run an article on the glamour couple's home life. When they wouldn't cooperate, she found a shot of the couple posing on the red carpet. She had the photo department digitally alter it to make it appear as if they were standing in front of their Beverly Hills home, welcoming in a *Personality* correspondent. *Come on in! Let's take a tour,* they seemed to say. Reporters interviewed some hangers-on who had never even been in the couple's home but claimed to be close sources.

But journalism is what it's really about . . .

"We used to be the magazine everyone turned to for celebrity news," Bernie said, her face turning red as her words tumbled out faster and faster. "Now, people are turning to the quick fixes of *Us* and *In Touch,* which are essentially photos and cutesy captions. And then there's *Access Hollywood, Inside Edition,* and *Entertainment Tonight.* They can break celebrity gossip faster than we can.

Even *Nightline*'s landing the big star interviews instead of us." She shook her head and sipped some water. "That's why it's so important to get scoops."

"Absolutely," Mike offered.

"Not just any scoop. The scoop of the year. Even Diane and Katie can't get to him. I heard *Vanity Fair* begged him by offering story and photo approval, but he declined. I'm sure you know who I'm talking about." Bernie closed her eyes and clasped her hands as if in prayer. Mike noticed a piece of lettuce clinging to her front tooth. "Chris Mercer," she whispered breathlessly.

"Chris Mercer," Mike repeated, nodding his head. "Of course."

Bernie rubbed her hands together excitedly. "No one knows a damned thing about him. Not the tabloids; not the television shows. No one. If we could clinch an exclusive interview with him, well . . ." Bernie clutched the base of her hen's throat, breathed deeply, and shut her eyes. "Well, it would help us regain our place as the number one celebrity magazine. We would draw in a whole younger readership who loves Chris and wants to know more about him. He's hotter than hot."

"He's hotter than hot," Mike repeated.

"Absolutely! See, Vince, this guy *is* on the pulse of pop culture."

You're on the pulse of pop culture, Mike. You've cultivated some great sources, Mike.

It was much too easy to fool everybody. Ivy League graduates with their to-the-manor-born superiority but who were inferior in every other way. Hardworking, ink-stained, driven journalists who'd climbed their way up from fact checkers to editors. And all the colors in between. They all respected Mike. Hell, he lectured *them* and they took notes.

He was Mike Posner, the star celebrity journalist. A frequent guest on *E!*, *Access Hollywood*, *Entertainment Tonight*. Just the other night, he turned on the TV to see himself dissecting J.Lo and Marc Anthony. "My sources say they're soul mates." No one seemed to remember that a few months before he'd said the same thing about J.Lo and Ben. "My sources say that they are so in love. They are more alike than people realize."

Mike barely recognized himself anymore.

A YEAR AGO, Michael Posner, the only child of an accountant and an elementary school teacher, had abandoned New York City and headed to Los Angeles. Suddenly it didn't seem to matter that he had spent nearly half his life trying to get to the Big Apple. In a frenzied state, he packed up his apartment and drove across the country, hoping to achieve the dreams that eluded him in New York. A friend of a friend had a friend at *Personality* . . .

Mike had lived in Manhattan for less than a year when he decided to move. Before that, he'd paid his dues busting his ass at the *Rochester Tribune*. He had covered town board meetings where residents debated for hours the merits of a stop sign on Maple Lane, a crossing guard at the elementary school, a new fleet of police cars. His crime reporting consisted mostly of juvenile arrests for cow tipping and skinny-dipping with the occasional bank robbery or drug bust.

Every year since college graduation, he applied for a reporting job at the New York City papers. Every year, he'd get a rejection letter. Finally, after years of slogging through hicksville minutiae, Mike was hired by the *Daily News*.

The dream had always been alluring, but the reality was terrifying. He lived in a tiny studio apartment in an ungentrified part of the East Village. Mike would bolt upright in bed to the sounds of rats scuttling between the walls, a domestic dispute next door, or, worst of all, the phone's icy shrill. That was enough to induce a myocardial infarction. It would be an editor sending him to Harlem or the Bronx on a murder story. After years of being the best in Rochester, Mike had begun to believe it. But in the City, he was below average.

Each time he got an assignment, Mike tried to remain calm, even though he was petrified. Reporting for a major city tabloid was fucking frightening business. But he struggled to keep his face blank and his eyes narrowed so James Davenworth, his editor, wouldn't know how truly terrified he was. Mike knew Davenworth didn't think the skinny, dirty-blond, wide-eyed boy from the sticks had what it took. It was as if those years in Rochester had been turned into some kind of newsroom inside joke. "I'd rather have a City College graduate with no experience than some hick who thinks he's a hotshot," Davenworth bellowed out one day when Mike turned in copy a few minutes past deadline.

Then a stray bullet in Harlem killed little Joey Green. It was one of many little-kid-killed-by-a-stray-bullet-in-Harlem stories. Mike had been working on a series of articles—"Death of the Innocents." He had come up with the idea and hoped this would somehow elevate him in the eyes of Davenworth. "Hick," Davenworth would mumble under his breath while watching Mike's reaction when he'd tell him to head to Harlem for a murder investigation.

"Interview the parents," Davenworth commanded as he wrung out his fat, sweaty palms. "You know, the usual stuff. The parents-wanted-more-for-their-kid kind of story. Their dashed hopes and dreams. Can you handle that?"

Mike was in no mood for Davenworth's sarcasm that day, especially with the Posner Plan, his life map, slowly unraveling. His girlfriend, Liz, had dumped him a few minutes earlier, right outside the office. Actually, not just dumped him; she admitted there was someone else.

"What do you mean you think there's someone else? That's just you being paranoid. I haven't been with anyone," Mike said.

"*I* might have met someone else."

"You *might* have? Was this during an out-of-body experience?"

"I mean, I'm not sure if I met someone *significant* or not. But just the fact that I'm considering that I might have means that something's wrong with us."

"Look, if you want to screw someone else, don't try to make

yourself feel better, or less guilty, by pretending we had all these horrible problems. I know the real reason."

"I swear, Mike, it's not that."

"Yes it is. I know it is. It's always been it. You don't have to lie."

"It's not."

And then, as if on cue, his cell phone went off. Davenworth.

MIKE TRIED TO block out Liz. He focused on little Joey Green. Mike hated—absolutely hated—talking to the next of kin. He recited the mantra of his journalism professor at Ithaca College: They like to talk about it. They need to talk about it. You are a conduit between them and the rest of the world. They want to share their pain.

But this day, everything changed. Mike knocked on the peeling gunmetal gray door of apartment 7A. It creaked open. "Mr. Green?"

"Yes," a tall black man said, squinting his eyes at Mike.

"Hello, I'm Mike Posner, from the *Daily Ne—*"

"Not interested," the man boomed as he moved his body away from the door to close it.

Mike breathed deeply and continued in a soft voice. "I'm really sorry to be bothering you. I . . . I just wanted to talk to you about your son, Joey. We're writing an article on him and we'd like to get some insights from you. We want our readers to get to know him a little better."

The father was just a sliver behind the door. Then he opened it wider, rubbed his gray-speckled beard with his hand, and chuckled uncomfortably. "Joey?"

"Would it be possible for me to come in for a few minutes and talk to you about him?"

Joey's father narrowed his eyes and scratched the top of his shaved head. "Sure. Sure. You must be following his baseball career. You know, yesterday he pitched a no-hitter."

Mike winced and Joey's father caught it.

"You're not here about baseball, are you?"

Mike opened his mouth. Nothing came out.

And suddenly Joey's father's eyes bulged from their sockets. He screamed, "Oh my God, what's happened to Joey?"

Mike's heart pummeled so fiercely against his ribs that he thought they'd shatter. This guy didn't know.

"Honey, who's there?" a woman asked cheerfully. "Is that Joey?"

They didn't know. The cops hadn't told them yet.

"Shit . . . the cops . . . haven't . . ."

"Wait. What the hell's this about?"

"Joey? Where's Joey? OH MY GOD. JOEY! JOEY!"

Rivulets of sweat streaked down Mike's face. He opened his mouth, but a sound like a belch came out. His Bic dropped out of his nearly arthritic fingers. Somewhere glass was breaking. He heard a loud thud. Someone had passed out. He couldn't move.

"I'm sorry."

"Waaiiit. What the hell is going on?"

Joey's father lunged for Mike, but he was already out of reach. He bounded the stairs, three at a time. He couldn't see behind the veil of sweat that covered his face and collected in puddles at his eyes. When he reached the bottom, he leaned against the building and struggled for air. He knew he should go back. If he were a real reporter, he'd ring 7A's doorbell again. Hell, if he were a real reporter, he would have never run. Instead, his legs pushed forward, through the garbage-strewn streets. He bolted down Riverside Drive while the cross streets blurred past him. 125th. 115th. 90th. 75th. He stopped when he couldn't breathe anymore. He bent down, hands on his knees, and struggled for oxygen. He opened a few buttons on his blue oxford shirt and waved in fresh air with a hand.

He stood there, realizing that a degree in journalism from Ithaca, several years at the *Rochester Tribune*, and six months in New York had been in vain. Mike Posner was not cut out for this. He had run. And the cardinal rule in journalism was you never run.

"No one was home," he told Davenworth.

It was a stupid lie. Davenworth held up a story he had just pulled off the AP wire. A reporter had gotten there a few minutes after Mike to interview the family.

"The *Daily News* never runs away from a story. No matter what. Do you know how great the reaction to their son's death would have been for the article? It's called color, Mike. We live for moments like this. They're the purest moments a journalist can experience. Or maybe they don't teach you that in cow country."

"I just . . . I'll go back."

"Forget it. Carmody's already at the apartment, getting great stuff from the family and neighbors. Great stuff. She said the mother was so distraught she had to be rushed to the hospital. She may have had a heart attack."

"Uh-huh."

"Maybe you should reevaluate what you're doing here. Maybe you should determine whether you're cut out for this. This is what makes or breaks a career. Do you have the balls or not? Huh? Do you think Breslin or Hamill would have run?"

"But . . ."

"I think maybe I should have you write obits for a while until you toughen up, Mike . . . *Poseur*."

Mike Poseur. They were finally on to him.

Mike watched as red-hot flames danced and leapt around the Posner Plan. They devoured it in a quick flash of light.

"I quit."

It was the most impetuous thing he had ever done.

He had built a life around being too cautious. Even as a toddler, Mike would sneak up on dandelions as if they were land mines, his mother told him. "You never liked to be surprised," she said. "You always had to know exactly where you were going and what you would encounter before you got there."

Mike had disagreed with her assessment, but now he couldn't remember a time in his life where he didn't know precisely where he was heading. He went to nursery school to prepare for kindergarten to go to elementary school to head to high school to graduate from college to work at a local newspaper to write for the *Daily News*. And now, Mike was paralyzed. The dandelion was a Bouncing Betty.

Where to go?

As he made his way to the anonymity of the street, Mike suddenly thought about the things he had not done because he had been so consumed by the safety of the Posner Plan. He had never—even for the slightest moment—veered off course. He never bummed around Europe or followed the Dead or worked as a ski lift operator in Aspen. Actually, he never considered working anywhere outside of Manhattan because none of those places seemed to matter if you wanted to be the best. The rest of the United States is just fly-over country, right?

Then he remembered something. When he was a little kid growing up in the brutal cold of upstate New York, his mother would kneel alongside his bed, and they would say their prayers. For health, for everyone they loved to be happy, and for one day, California. His mother said that you walked out your door and pulled juicy oranges and lemons right from the trees in front of your Spanish-styled house. Palm trees stirred scents of citrus and jasmine through the air, she said. Everyone had pools.

"So let's pray that one day Daddy gets a transfer there. Let's pray for California."

Mike squeezed his eyes shut and forgot about health and happiness and prayed for California. If they moved to California, everything would be better. "California," he'd whisper, clenching his hands together. But instead of a transfer, his father eventually had a heart attack and died. Mike always believed it was his fault—he had prayed for California instead of his father's health.

Soon Mike became too cynical to pray for anything. But now, as he stood out in front of the citadel he had striven to breach for most of his organized, goal-oriented life, his thoughts turned to this forgotten prayer. Perhaps it was time to veer off course and follow the scent of citrus and jasmine and the rustling of palm trees. The dreams of his youth, before he became practical.

He and Mr. Cat would pack it up and head out to Los Angeles. A friend of a friend who worked at *Personality*'s New York bureau told him the L.A. bureau was hiring. He could get a job there easily, the friend assured him.

So he crammed his life into luggage—his clothes, his computer, his portfolio of articles—the whole time keeping one ear cocked to the phone, hoping for a last-minute job offer or Liz's change of heart. He called his cousin, Pete, who needed a place to live, and persuaded him to take over his yearlong lease. A few days later, he and Pete stuffed his beat-up Saab 900. Mike would have to drive with his head tilted.

There was no room for Mr. Cat.

And Mike knew that even if there were room for the frail, albino, old man of a cat with horribly matted fur, he probably couldn't survive the journey. It wouldn't be fair. Mike scanned his friendships to determine the appropriate place to leave Mr. Cat but came up empty. Mr. Cat was too frail, too nervous for his slacker friends who still thought they were in college. There was only one person who would be appropriate: Liz.

Just days ago, after they broke up, they had fought over Mr. Cat. Mike argued that the feline was technically HIS because it lived in HIS apartment. Liz said that maybe he had forgotten, but she had fed and brushed him and changed his litter box. Mr. Cat rubbed up against Liz's legs, not his. Mr. Cat meowed for Liz, not him. She was right, Mike knew. He couldn't even remember changing the litter box. But if she were leaving him for someone else, at least Mike would get the cat. He didn't relent.

"I had Mr. Cat at my place. He's mine. You can have supervised visitation," he had choked out before she slammed the door.

He said good-bye to Pete, propped Mr. Cat on his lap, and drove to Liz's redbrick apartment building on Bank Street. Mr. Cat purred quietly as Mike petted his warm, pear-shaped head. Mike felt his throat closing up on him and he breathed deeply. *Don't get emotional. It's only a fucking cat.* He had only wanted it because Liz had wanted it.

He carried Mr. Cat up the three flights to Liz's apartment. He concentrated on his legs climbing the stairs, the smell of lamb cooking in someone's apartment, a scratchy Muddy Waters record on a stereo. He knocked on her door, an idiot's smile plastered on his face. A guy opened it. "Huh," Mike said, his smile abandoning him as he leaned back to check the apartment number. "Did Liz move?"

"Ah, no." The guy stuck out his hand. "I'm Kyle."

"HI, MIKE," LIZ said. Then her eyes filled with excitement. "Mr. Cat!" She picked him out of Mike's arms and nuzzled him.

Mike felt as if all the oxygen had been punched out of him. "Mr. Cat is having difficulty adapting to my late-night bacchanalia. He's asked for a more stable environment."

She laughed, then studied him.

Mike sighed. "I'm moving to California and I don't think Mr. Cat could handle the trip. I was wondering if you'd take him."

"Mr. Cat? Of course, of course. California?"

"Yeah," he said. His eyes locked with hers, waiting, but she stared back at him silently, her eyes welling with tears. And he flashed back to that night, a few months ago, when they heard an anorexic Mr. Cat crying in an alleyway. Even though the feline had black rings around its eyes, ratty fur, and fleas, the woman who had decided she didn't love Mike picked Mr. Cat up and stroked his filthy fur.

The memory was enough, and Mike's eyes rimmed with tears. He concentrated on palm trees, beaches, orange groves, Hollywood parties. He wished Liz had been cruel or evil, but she had only been honest. She was in love with someone else. A straggly-looking guy with a wispy goatee. Another stray. He didn't look like much, but at least he didn't have Mike's problem. And who could blame her? Would *he* have stuck around?

Tears slipped out of his eyes and he shut them and pressed on his lids, trying to squeeze out the remaining drops. He wiped his face with the back of a hand.

"I'm sorry, Mike. I didn't mean for any of this to happen."

"I'm just going to miss that stupid cat." Mike swatted the air with his hands. "I've got to go. I've got a long drive ahead of me." He petted Mr. Cat's sunken cheeks. "You take care, Mr. Cat," he whispered. "I'll miss you." He kissed the top of Mr. Cat's head.

"I'll take good care of him, Mike."

"I know. I know. I'll send you a postcard."

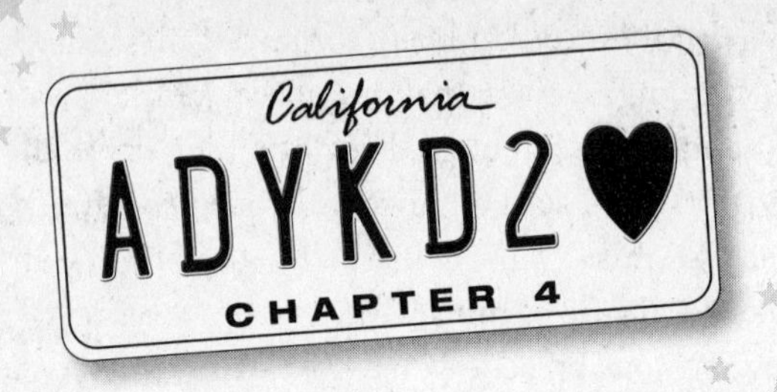

LOTTIE LOVE NEEDED HER OWN PLACE. DESPERATELY. SHE WAS almost twenty-three and sharing a semi-beach-adjacent apartment with an angry lesbian who wore a piercing that looked like a doorknob dangling from her chin.

"Your insane sponsor called again. Will you please tell her to get a fucking life?" her roommate sneered before slamming the front door to head to her inferior job as a production assistant on a movie with absolutely *no one* in it. So much for finding compatibility through roommatesearch.com.

Lottie had had six roommates during a two-year stint in her Santa Monica apartment. It wasn't her—it was them. Even though her therapist—a lipless, pinheaded woman with tiny teeth and huge gums—said Lottie had a classic Dr. Jekyll and Mr. Hyde personality that prevented her from having close friends, Lottie knew better.

"Why do you think you fluctuate from being charming and likable to being this other person intent on scaring people away? Is it your fear of intimacy?" Lipless asked her again and again.

Lipless was originally from somewhere in Middle America—Ohio or Iowa or Oklahoma, a place that began with a vowel—so she didn't understand. Los Angelenos are whimsical. People come and go—it's just the nature of the place. Kim, Roommate #1 and a good college friend, returned to Seattle after a year of auditions and no work. She's now teaching kindergarten. Renée, #2, became last year's January *Playboy* cover and moved into the mansion. Lottie saw her clutching Hef's arm—along with five other Marilyn Monroe wannabes—on the red carpet at the Oscars.

Okay, so Roommate #3 was a problem. But Lottie and Julie should never have lived together. Julie grew up with tons of siblings. They vacationed on kibbutzim. So she thought nothing of rummaging through Lottie's closet and stretching out her microminis and spandex camisoles or raiding the fridge and devouring Lottie's yogurts and low-fat string cheeses and Diet Cokes. As an only child, Lottie had never learned how to share. She'd write her name with a black marker on her food. She'd hide her clothes under the bed. It didn't matter. Julie would sit at the kitchen table dripping *Lottie Love's* Dannon Lite onto *Lottie Love's* Fred Segal tube top. After three months, Lottie couldn't take it anymore.

"I so hate to do this, but Tyler and I are going to try living together," she told Julie.

So Roommate #4 was her boyfriend, Tyler. They moved in together, after dating for three months, for all the wrong reasons (the departure of #3, the need to pay the rent, his nine-inch personality). Tyler, a director's assistant, was a complete slob. He never washed a dish, never took out the garbage, and never cleaned the toilet seat.

"I can't help it if I take atomic dumps," he'd say proudly.

She dumped him after a week.

Lottie lived on her own for two months before a vacant checking account mandated Roommate #5. Lottie had met Brooke at Pilates. One day, during fruit smoothies at Jamba Juice, Brooke mentioned that she needed a place to live. Lottie thought it was karma.

"I couldn't need a roommate more," Lottie said.

"I need to tell you something about myself. I hope you're cool with it." Brooke studied her for a few seconds. "I'm born again."

Lottie thought about this and smiled. How nonthreatening, she decided. She'd never have to worry about Brooke stealing a boyfriend or binging and vomiting all over the carpeting.

"I'm so fine with it—as long as you're completely fine with the fact that I couldn't be farther from being born again. I'm so like unborn in the worst sense of the word."

Brooke said she was fine with it, as long as Lottie didn't mind if she occasionally had some friends over to talk about religion. But soon Brooke started using their pad as Conversion Central. Sunday was Bible Study. Monday was the meeting for WAWOC—Women as Witnesses of Christ. Tuesday was Salvation Testimony night. Wednesday was Coffee and Fellowship night.

It didn't bother Lottie. She was usually out covering events for *Personality* anyway, so she rarely had any interface. Even when she was around, she found the meetings kind of entertaining. There was always plenty of drama. And she learned that most born-agains—at least in L.A.—had really sordid pasts, so there were some great stories, full of kink and drugs. It didn't even bother Lottie when Brooke tried to convert her. "Your life is meaningless and empty," she'd say.

"And I couldn't be happier about it," Lottie said. "You guys always seem to be crying."

"That's only on Salvation Testimony night."

But then after one Bible Study night, Lottie walked in on Brooke screwing Lottie's latest boyfriend. "I thought sex before marriage was illegal for you guys," Lottie yelled.

"The spirit is willing, but the flesh is weak."

"Well, get your weak flesh outta here."

"Accept Christ as your personal savior and forgive."

That night she went online and found #6, a man-hating lesbian who spent all her free time watching the Food Network because she got horny watching women cook.

Lottie decided to stay out of the kitchen.

SO THERE. NONE of it was really Lottie's fault.

Lipless didn't understand any of this. Instead she suggested that Lottie come more than once a week. "We need to begin intensive therapy and figure out what's at the core of Charlotte Love's personality fluctuations."

"Lottie."

Lottie understood the real reason Lipless wanted to see Lottie more often. The woman hadn't been laid in decades and Lottie's recent exploits aroused her. She wanted to know all the details about Lottie's job and the recent side benefits. Lottie imagined her therapist enjoyed telling friends, "I'm counseling someone who fucked Marlon Lang." To Lipless, Lottie was better than any soap opera.

Lipless lowered her half-glasses and stared at Lottie through eyes that were red rimmed from fatigue after too many years of listening to people's problems. "Perhaps you should reevaluate the qualities you're looking for in a man. Don't you want someone who's kind, sensitive, sharing? Don't you want someone who doesn't just take and take? Being with a celebrity should not be enough for you."

Lottie smiled weakly and nodded her head, making a note that this was *it* with this moron. She couldn't imagine being with anyone *but* a celebrity. She'd be better off saving her cash for her own apartment instead of wasting it on this useless therapy. Then she could scream, "YOU'RE NUMBER ONE" at the top of her lungs without a roommate pounding on her wall and cursing her out and telling her the next day that not every guy she bangs can be number one. What does a doorknob-wearing diesel dyke know anyway?

Besides, Marlon Lang really *was* number one. Lottie's could still feel adrenaline coursing through her body when she woke up after her first night with Marlon.

"So do you think you got good enough quotes from me? When's the photo shoot? If I sound stupid, make the grammar right," Marlon said as he uncoiled himself from Lottie and the sheets.

"Sure, but I may need to interview you some more," Lottie said, narrowing her eyes at Marlon as he emerged from the bed, naked and buff.

Marlon raised his eyebrows and smirked. "I have a lot more to say. Big things. Really big things."

"Oh, I know. I'm still aching from all the big things you told me last night."

"Do you think all the big things I had to say could get me on the cover of *Personality*?"

"It's possible. But I might have to hear some more big things first," Lottie said, surprised by her boldness. "My editor really trusts my instincts? I'm like so about to be promoted to an ABC—that's associate bureau chief, which is like lit-rully unheard of for someone my age. I'll talk to him today and tell him I think you're the Next Big Thing. I'm sure that will be enough to convince him. I like practically run that magazine."

Marlon grinned at her. "We'll do something again, soon," he said. "We have so much to, well, discuss."

He handed her a piece of paper with a cell phone number on it. Lottie smiled. Another card in her pink Rolodex.

MARLON CALLED THE next day. On their first official date, they ate at Katana (Ryan Seacreast stopped by to say hi) and drank at Sky Bar. They were whisked inside without waiting on lines. They were given a quiet table with an obsequious server. A hushed, reverent silence followed them, it seemed. "That's Marlon Lang," she heard them murmur, adding, "Who is *she*? An actress, probably." Cameras flashed at them. "Marlon, over here, over here," paparazzi yelled. "Come on, Mr. Lang, just a flash of those pearly whites, over here."

Lottie loved every minute of it. She felt as though she had accomplished something wonderful, although she didn't know what it was. No matter, the light was on her. People noticed her. She was having more fun than she had ever imagined.

But then *Blind Love and Other Handicaps* flopped. Marlon's acting was called "wooden and painful." "I'd rather watch paint dry than Marlon Lang act, because at least paint eventually dries—but Marlon Lang will never be able to act," the *L.A. Times* said.

"What do the critics know? They are all actor wannabes," Lottie said. "Did you ever read the reviews Marlon Brando got when he first started out? It makes your stuff sound like praise."

Lottie made this up. She had no idea what they had said about Brando. But Marlon was inconsolable. He smashed his fist into a plaster wall at Lottie's apartment. He picked up a wooden chair, lifted it over his head, and hurled it to the floor. It exploded into a pile of splinters. She cringed. It was her roommate's.

"You want to know the truth? Do you? I'm not named after Marlon Brando."

"Of course you are, everyone knows that. I even read it in the *L.A. Times.*"

"I made it all up. My real name is Arthur. Arthur fucking Mooney. Can you believe it? Maybe someone with a name like Artie Mooney should be a carpenter or a cabdriver. It's so ordinary. Artie. Little Artie Mooney with the asthma and the lisp. I thought I could show them all. Instead, I'm 'wooden.' I'm 'painful to watch.' I'm the laughingstock of Hollywood. One reviewer said I was as believable as Lassie playing Jesus Christ."

Marlon stared at Lottie as if suddenly remembering she was there. "Lottie, you've got to swear that you'll never tell anyone my real name. You better promise. Promise?"

"I so promise."

The next day, Lottie turned in a story on Marlon, the Next Big Thing. But it didn't matter; Vince wasn't interested.

"I admire your ambition, Lottie. But you've got to learn how to manage your time better. This guy doesn't seem to have staying power. He's just a flash in the pan. When you're in the business as long as I've been, you get these instincts. But hold on to your notes. If he dies of an overdose one day, you'll be in charge of the reporting."

That night Lottie cooked Marlon linguine with clam sauce, but all through dinner she kept hearing Vince's voice.

Flash in the pan. Flash in the pan.

She didn't expect to feel this way. She thought she'd be able to console him. Instead, she couldn't imagine having sex with him. How could she tell him he's Number One when his movie didn't even register at the box office? She hated herself for being so shallow. But she grew up knowing about the other side—where the light of Hollywood didn't reach. And she didn't want to regress.

Clam sauce dripped down Marlon's chin—a look that just yesterday Lottie would have found endearing, but today it repulsed her. He chewed with his mouth open, his tongue coated in a paste of linguini and saliva.

Flash in the pan.

"So when's the article coming out?"

Lottie squeezed her eyes shut.

Flash in the pan.

"What is it?"

Lottie kept her eyes closed while she tightly gripped the chair arms. "They're not going to run the article." She flinched, as if staving off a blow.

"Huh?" Linguine flew out of Marlon's mouth.

"My editor said he wanted to wait for your . . . well, next, umm, mov . . . ie. Then he'll run something on you."

Marlon stood up, grabbed his bowl of linguine and slammed it against the wall. Damn. Her roommate's bowl. Pieces of noodle stuck to the wall and shards of china were everywhere. "Even you don't believe in me. I thought you thought I was this great actor. Number One."

"I do. It so wasn't my decision. It's my editor's. I have nothing to do with it."

Marlon tugged a fistful of his greasy hair. "You probably told him that my name wasn't even Marlon."

Arthur "Marlon Lang" Mooney grabbed his leather jacket from the back of his chair and headed to the door.

"Don't go," Lottie said, but her voice sounded flat and unconvincing even to her.

Marlon turned toward Lottie, his face red and his temples pulsating. "How can I be wiff thumbone who doethenth think I'm great?" He shook his head violently and saliva slid out the sides of his mouth. He walked out the front door, slamming it shut.

DESPITE THE SPECTACULAR flameout, Lottie couldn't shake her celebrity fixation. The good simply outweighed the bad. Those seconds when Marlon was on the cusp of something big were thrilling; when his star fizzled, it was just time to move on to the Next Big Thing. And she had plenty of opportunities to meet qualified candidates. Soon she was a regular on the party circuit, nearly as part of the crowd as any of them. They'd stroll up to her with a quote and a smile, and Lottie Love fell in love nightly.

She dated soap stars (prime-time and daytime), supporting movie actors, sitcom stars, even the cute reporter from *Extra!* "You're Number One," she shrieked at each one. Sometimes it was for a night, sometimes it would last a little longer, but it would always end.

It was an education.

There was Tristan Keith, the lead in a new medical drama. Theirs was just a one-night stand, but God, was he beautiful. Definitely a contender for *Personality*'s Most Gorgeous Man of the Universe issue. He held her face in his hands and looked at her intensely, eyes brimming with tears. "I really had a great time, but I just can't see a future here. With my career getting hot, I just don't have the time or the energy to make a relationship work. Don't take it personally. If I were ready to get involved with someone, it would be you. You are a very special woman, Lottie."

"I completely understand," Lottie said, massaging the back of his neck.

She looked him up on the Internet and discovered that Tristan was "happily married" with two kids.

She added dozens of autographed photos to her collection: Adrian Brody, Orlando Bloom, Ashton Kutcher, Chris Klein, Tobey Maguire, Justin Timberlake. She also began lining the walls of her bedroom with photos of her conquests. Marlon and Tristan and Hunter and Chad and Ricky and Ken.

Then there was Ray Young.

Ray was the lead in a steamy nighttime soap opera, *Bel Air Belles.* Lottie was addicted to the show, which revolved around shirtless hunks and bikini-clad babes who lived in a perfectly coifed gated community. Everyone was fabulously wealthy. *Everyone* was having affairs. Ray played Lance Caine, the pool boy everyone wanted to bed. No one—except the viewers who tuned in at 9:00 P.M. Wednesdays—knew that the perpetually oil-slathered Lance was hiding a secret. For Lance was wealthy, too; he was just going through a rebellious stage. He cleaned pools during the day, rode a Harley and screwed women at night. But he was also heir to a huge railroad fortune. When the husbands of the women Lance slept with called him a bum, he'd smirk at the camera, sharing the Rembrandt Quick White irony with his viewers.

Lottie met Ray poolside at the Standard on Sunset for a party celebrating the show's top ten position in the Nielsens. Lottie interviewed the cast for a section of the magazine called "Fashion Focus," in which she reported on the latest trends. She talked to the women on their choice of blush or bracelets. She asked the men about watches and loafers. When Ray walked by, she couldn't help but wander away from a geeky B-lister who'd somehow managed to land a bit part on the show. She quizzed Ray about his vintage getup—frayed pale blue corduroys and an Alice Cooper T-shirt.

"I don't go to the trendy vintage shops on Melrose. I go to hardcore places, like the Salvation Army."

"I just have to tell you that I lit-rully love *Bel Air Belles,*" Lottie gushed.

Ray laughed. "You should go into acting. You're a good liar."

Lottie gasped. "I couldn't love your show more. I watch it like, every week. It is absolutely the best thing on television. Every time you get abused by one of those rich people, I cry. I mean litrully buckets of tears."

As they talked, Lottie discovered Ray was a Valley kid. He had lived in Encino and knew what it felt like to be an outsider. "I didn't want to spend my life looking in."

It was like hearing her own words being thrown back at her. "I've lit-rully been saying that for years," Lottie said. Then she suggested they go out to dinner to discuss the possibility of *Personality* naming him the Most Gorgeous Man in the Universe.

Ray eyes lit up and he smirked. "This mug? Don't make me laugh."

"Stop it right now. You so are. It's just a question of convincing the people in New York who still think like Warren Beatty is. I mean, my grandfather's hotter."

In the next few weeks, Lottie Love nearly became famous herself. A photo of Lottie and Ray walking arm in arm was splashed across *Star:* "Ray Young and His Main Squeeze." Lottie fought the urge to call up the writer and yell, "It's me, Charlie Love from Tarzana. Me." Instead she bought a bunch of copies of the magazine and ripped the articles out.

Lem Brac stuck his head in Lottie's office one afternoon while Lottie was daydreaming about Ray.

"Be careful, Miss Love," he said to her in that annoying English accent, which Lottie was convinced was fake. "Remember, they're not your friends."

Lottie didn't even acknowledge him. She picked up the phone and dialed her own number, checking the voice mail. There were two messages from Catherine, her sponsor. "Just checking in with you," she said. Even though Lottie hardly called her back, it hadn't deterred Catherine from phoning at least twice a day for the last six months. She knew she should return the woman's calls, but Catherine scared her. No one had ever been so determined to be a friend. It baffled Lottie.

LOTTIE WAS NEARLY euphoric when Ray invited her to the Emmys, especially since a month earlier Lottie had begged Vince to let her cover the event for *Personality.*

"You're still a rookie, Lottie. You keep practicing your swing and we'll put you in the big leagues next season. But talk to Mike Posner. He's in charge of putting together a team. Maybe you can do something."

Now she'd be inside with all the A-listers while Mike and his "team" would be stuck behind the velvet ropes groping for interviews. They'd be escorted into the parties with a publicist who'd walk them around as if they were dogs who might piss on one of the stars. Lottie was a guest. A guest of Ray Young, the Now Big Thing. Not only would she get into all the parties, she'd get inside the VIP rooms. She'd sit at the VIP tables!

Lottie planned to milk every minute of it. She called a publicist for Armani and explained the situation. "I'll be at the Emmys and would love to wear one of your gowns. Since I am practically in charge of the fashion section for *Personality*, I can like lit-rully guarantee that Armani will be mentioned in the column a lot. Plus, I'm attending the Emmys with Ray Young, you know, of *Bel Air Belles*, so I can guarantee that whatever you loan me will be very visible."

The woman on the other end didn't even pause. "Well, *Personality* magazine is a good friend of Armani, and you've been helpful getting our fashions out in the public eye. I know we can count on your continued support."

"That couldn't be more definite."

She also called Chanel, Versace, and Gucci.

A few hours later messengers arrived with entire racks of dresses for her to choose from. It was incredible. There was an ivory silk faille gown with two tiers of feathers; a seafoam green wrap dress, a black cap-sleeved silk satin gown; a nude strapless column dress with a draped bodice and back bow; a light green satin strapless dress; a bronze deep V-neck gown with a gathered waist; a slinky red corset dress with a plunging neckline; a pale blue satin gown with a mermaid bottom; and a nude dress adorned with teardrop-shaped crystals.

Mike Posner walked past Lottie's office just as the dresses were delivered. Damn. She had hoped most reporters would be out at lunch. He stared at her, and she stuck her tongue out at him. She knew it was immature, but that guy really bugged her. Would he rat her out for accepting free clothes? He fucking better not! Even though accepting gifts was openly frowned upon, everyone secretly did it. Even Vince accepted clothes, dinners, and hotel suites. But if she got caught, she'd be fired for it.

She also knew that Mike thought she was a fake. But he was so full of it, talking about this source and that source. What a waste of a cute face.

She shut the door to her office and spent the afternoon trying on the dresses before settling on a pale blue satin gown with a plunging neckline and cap sleeves. Very Nicole Kidman. She thought about calling Cartier to borrow some jewels, but decided to settle on the rhinestone and crystal costume jewelry she had inherited from her mother.

THE NIGHT WHOOSHED by in a blur of flashbulbs and shrieking fans. However, the highlight of the evening was perfectly clear. As they strode along the velvet-roped red carpet at the entranceway of Spago, Ray suddenly halted. Photographers snapped away, screaming at Ray, and he grabbed Lottie by the waist. He held her face in his hands and kissed her hard for what seemed like minutes. Cameras flashed so furiously at them that white lights danced in front of Lottie's eyes for the rest of the evening.

Inside, she sipped Cristal with some cast members from the show. They sat in a glass-enclosed fishbowl of a room in the middle of the restaurant, two beefy security guards blocking the entrance. Lottie kept her hand on Ray's knee while Lara Flynn Boyle and Jennifer Aniston chatted with him. "I'm addicted to your show," one of them said. For the first time in a long time, she didn't have to ask Jennifer or Lara or anyone who designed their stunning wardrobe. *She* was wearing a stunning wardrobe!

From the corner of her eye, she saw Mike Posner in a tux

standing by the bar outside the fishbowl. He sipped a beer and kept his tape recorder outstretched, as if he were interviewing a phantom. His eyes darted around, trying to find some kind of scoop, but there was no one near him—only publicists, network executives, and their spouses. She felt sorry for him as he scanned the fishbowl. He mumbled something into his tape recorder. Then his eyes locked on hers. He held up his hand and meekly waved, his fingers moving slightly. She knew he was hoping she'd give a big, generous sweep of her arms—COME ON IN! Instead, she smiled quickly and feebly and turned toward Ray, who was turned toward Jennifer. She could feel Mike still watching her. So she laughed hard, as if she were part of Ray's conversation.

After all, Lottie was no longer peripheral. She was with VIPs at the VIP table in a VIP room at a VIP party. So why did part of her feel as outside as Mike? She put her arms around Ray to obliterate these thoughts. He was still engrossed in another conversation.

THE NEXT DAY, Lottie and Ray appeared in midkiss on the party pages of *Variety* and *Hollywood Reporter* and the *L.A. Times.* And again, there was Lem, his ashen face at her door. "Be careful," he whispered. Lottie flared her nostrils and frowned in disgust, but he was already gone.

Vince stopped by, too. "See if you can get him to dig up any dirt on his costars."

It seemed like the perfect storybook romance—even though she wasn't screaming, "YOU'RE NUMBER ONE."

At least not yet. No sex. Just a few doorstep kisses. Lottie wasn't used to waiting, and it seemed nice and old-fashioned at first. After a while, well, she had needs, and she was hornier than she'd ever been. The kiss at the Emmys had been their most passionate, but afterward, Ray had the limo driver drop her off at her place.

Lottie decided to take action. A few weeks later Ray was hosting a party at his West Hollywood home for the cast and crew of *Bel Air Belles* and assorted industry types. This would be her first time at Ray's, and she wasn't going to leave. Lottie packed an overnight bag with lingerie, a toothbrush, oils, candles, handcuffs, and a week's worth of clothes. She tugged on a deep V-neck shirt that clung like Saran Wrap.

Ray's plantation-style home had a huge wraparound porch and a Dalmatian mailbox. When no one answered the door, Lottie pushed it open and was greeted by a neon green and orange parrot in a hanging wicker cage. "Somewhere over the rainbow," it squawked.

Lottie could get used to this place. The furniture was heavy mahogany, trimmed in studded leather, and the walls were decorated with posters from old movies like *Gone With the Wind, Cabaret, All About Eve, Some Like It Hot, The Misfits, Funny Girl, A Star Is Born.* The hardwood floors gleamed and the ceilings were high and beamed. Lottie began imagining herself moved in, cooking big dinners in the terra-cotta-tiled kitchen while Ray played tunes on the white Steinway in the living room. Ray's black-spotted Dalmatians, Scarlett and Ashley, would sleep at her feet.

Ray kissed her lightly on the cheek as she wandered into the kitchen. "I told you not to come," he said. "It's gonna be really boring."

"How could I not come?" Lottie said, inching closer to Ray's side.

But soon Ray was swept up in the role of host. Lottie tried to mingle, although without a digital recorder in one hand, she felt naked.

She walked from room to room, helping herself to white wine, shrimp, and dim sum. She watched the anorexic female guests give her what she called the estrogen salute. Their eyes took inventory of her Jimmy Choo's, her tight James jeans, her black spandex shirt, her makeup, and her hair, but they never looked her in the eyes. They scanned her slowly, without acknowledging her, and she scanned them back.

Lottie squeezed Ray whenever they ran into each other. "Can't you spend some time with me?" she said, knowing her voice sounded annoying and whiny. "Soon, soon," Ray replied. "I'm sorry, it's just been crazy here. I told you it would suck. I'll have someone walk you to your car. I don't even know who half of these people are, and they're all calling me Lance. Just go home. I'll call you tomorrow. Promise."

She kissed his cheek. "I know who you are," she said in a husky voice. She winked at him and brushed a hand on his crotch when a man with small glasses and a thin, angular face approached.

"You haven't introduced me yet to this charming woman," the man said, eyeing Lottie from the top of his wire rims. "Excuse Raymond's very rude behavior, but I'm Gregory Perry, a very good friend of Raymond's, or at least I used to be before he became Mr. Hollywood." He scooped up Lottie's hand and kissed it. "And who, may I ask, are you?"

"I'm Lottie Love."

"Lottie Love? What an interesting, alliterative name. You must be an actress."

His name sounded familiar to Lottie. "Are you an actor?" she asked.

"Heavens, no. I actually work for a living." He smiled at Lottie and shot a raised eyebrow sneer at Ray. "I write."

Lottie clasped her hands together, as if they had just discovered they were long-lost cousins. "So do I! I'm with *Personality* magazine? Who do you write for?"

"Mostly myself. But to make a living, I write for the masses." Gregory closed his eyes, shook his head fiercely as if it would rattle, and sniffed hard. "You may have heard of it—*Bel Air Belles*?"

Ray smiled uneasily and stuffed his hands in the pockets of his dark blue jeans. "You could say, or actually Gregory will say, that he created Lance Caine."

Gregory threw his hands up in the air as if commiserating with God. "COULD SAY? COULD SAY? Why, I gave birth to Lance Caine. I pushed him out of my loins. Believe me, it was a difficult labor. Lance Caine, the pool boy with a past. I gave Lance dimension and soul. You don't see that on prime-time soaps."

Gregory spoke loudly, flailing his arms in the air and punctuating his comments with a brittle laugh. He shifted his body to face Lottie directly and whispered boozily in her ear. "You know, I created Lance with Ray in mind. Don't tell him this, but there's no one else out there who could bring such perspective to the role. Ray is Lance and Lance is Ray; they're inextricable. Often I can't tell them apart. Both have their little dark secrets that make them so attractive to us. We all want to be the revealee. Right?"

Lottie laughed uncomfortably. "Oh, rully? Like tell me what Ray's big secret is."

Gregory smirked, looked directly at Ray, and squeaked. "Rully? Like it is so up to Ray. As if."

Lottie swallowed hard. It was a kick in her soul. She was back in school with her father's van rumbling down the street. She forced out a smile, but she could feel her eyes watering.

Ray furrowed his brows and sighed. "Stop trying to get scary on us, Gregory." He forced a laugh.

"What-uverrr, like you say, Mr. Big TV Star. I like, so wouldn't want to like, totally interfere with your wonderful publicity campaign." Gregory turned toward Lottie. "I hear your illustrious magazine may put Ray on the cover soon. OhmyGod, that would be like so, like, turiff. *Personality*'s Sexiest Man in the Cosmos. The masculine ideal. Every woman's masturbatory fantasy."

Gregory opened his eyes wide and scrunched his face at Lottie. "I need a drink. A really big, big drink."

"I think you've had plenty already," Ray called after him, but Gregory threw up his hands again and jerked his head back at the ceiling.

"There's no such thing as plenty. Excess is my God. Drink is my prayer!" Gregory curled his hands through the air in giant swoops before shooting Ray the finger.

"Nice. That was a line from our next episode." Ray eyed Gregory as he sidled up to the bar, then he turned toward Lottie. "Sorry about that. Gregory gets a little high-strung sometimes. You know these creative writer types. The guy's convinced that he invented me. He's brilliant, but disturbed."

"He couldn't have been any more disturbed," Lottie said.

Lottie stood there, not knowing what else to say, although she desperately wanted to continue the conversation. A tall, pretty woman with long blond hair walked up to them. "Hello, Ray. Have you seen Bryce around?"

"No. He's probably busy schmoozing someone, I'm sure. Have you met Lottie? Lottie, this is Tina." Then Ray walked away.

Tina gave her the estrogen salute and then nodded.

"I'm dating Bryce Korman," she began. "You know, Kent Plymouth from the show. He's in jail this week for rape. The accuser turns out to be insane."

"I thought so."

"Did you know all the names have meaning? They're not just these sexy names that someone just picked. For instance, Kent's last name is Plymouth as in Plymouth Rock, like in Mayflower old money, and Kent, as in Kent State, as in the end of innocence, or something like that."

"God, like anyone cares."

"It's just Gregory thinking he's so clever, but viewers don't give a shit."

"How about Lance Caine?"

"Hmmmm, Bryce told me once. Lance is a weapon. So it's something like his good looks are his weapons, but they're also his cane, or crutch, because he can get away with anything because of them."

"They both really mean cock," Lottie said

Tina laughed. "I'm so glad I met you. These parties always turn into business meetings. Bryce is desperately searching for someone who'll put him in features."

"Tell me about it. I haven't seen Ray for more than an iota of a second."

"Did you notice that you and I are the only women here who aren't working girls?"

"They're hookers?" Lottie laughed. "No wonder I felt so overdressed."

"Yuh-huh. And some of the guys, too. So are you Ray's *date*?" Tina laughed and made quotes with her fingers.

"*Girlfriend.*"

Tina studied Lottie. "Oh . . . Well, anyway, Bryce pretends I don't exist. Bad for the image, he says. His publicist has people thinking he's seventeen years old and a dating machine, but he's thirty-three and we've been together for three years. I guess that's too boring for the teenyboppers out there, but it kills me when I read articles where Bryce says stuff like, 'I'm single, but looking for the right girl.'"

Tina folded her arms and eyed the crowd, searching for Bryce. "And I'm so good to that man." Then she narrowed her eyes at Lottie. "So what do you do?"

"I'm Chief Party Correspondent for *Personality* magazine."

Tina's eyes widened and her mouth opened as if suddenly realizing something. "Oh my God, I had no idea you were with the press. Please, please don't print that stuff I told you about Bryce being thirty-three. It would totally ruin his career. He would absolutely kill me. Please."

"It's like such not a big deal. I won't say a word."

"Everyone on the show lies about their age. They're all about ten years older than they say they are. Before he got the part, Ray had to get plastic surgery to get rid of the bags under his eyes. He's like almost forty years old. So if you write about Bryce, you'll have to mention that about Ray."

"Ray? Forty? Bags under his eyes? I so don't believe you."

"Don't tell him I said anything, okay?"

Tina hugged Lottie. "I hope I get to see you more. These parties are always about business, so it's nice to find someone to talk to who isn't an actress or a hooker. Usually, I end up smoking cigarettes by myself outside, just to have something to do. I don't even really smoke. Well, I'm trying to cut down. Anyway, I'm going to find Bryce. I'll see you later, okay? I really want you to meet my Bryce. I'd love for the three of us to get together. You like to party, right?"

"I couldn't like to party more."

Lottie stood there alone, wondering what to do. Then she had an idea.

LOTTIE'S HEELS ECHOED in the quiet street that was lit only by a dazzling half-moon, as opalescent and wide as a Hollywood smile. She walked a few blocks, breathing in the menthol air of the eucalyptus trees lining the path to her red convertible. After grabbing her duffel bag, she headed back toward the house. Suddenly a car skidded to a stop next to her.

"Lottie Love!"

Lottie's heart sank. She recognized the voice immediately. She turned toward it.

"Oh, Catherine? What are you doing here?"

"Lottie, I'm so glad I found you . . . I called your roommate and she told me where you were. Call me psychic, but I just got this feeling tonight that you needed me. And I can see I'm right. I can smell the booze from here. Let's get out. Now."

"Catherine, you are lit-rully taking this sponsor thing way too seriously. I couldn't be better."

"Too seriously? I'm trying to save you, Lottie Love. Don't you understand?" Catherine's eyes welled with tears. "Lottie, don't you see, you've come so far. Don't fall like this. I'm here for you. Come on. Let's go to your house. We can talk."

"Catherine, leave me alone."

"Listen, right now you might hate me. But someday you'll thank me for this. Trust me, I was the same way. I was worse. I'd do anything for a fix. You've only been going to the meetings for a few months. You're not ready to be around alcohol yet."

"You couldn't be freaking me out more."

"You're stuck with me."

Catherine got out of the car and stood in front of Lottie, arms akimbo.

Lottie sighed. "Okay, okay. You're right. A cinch by the inch. Hard by the yard. Yadda yadda."

"Okay, let's go."

Lottie opened the door to Catherine's car and was about to climb in when she stopped, as if just remembering something.

"Let me just say good night to Ray and return his duffel bag," she said. "He'll freak if I just take off. That man couldn't be more possessive."

"Okay. Let me go in with you."

Lottie nodded. "Okay." She feigned deep thought. "You know what? This is something I so need to do myself. I couldn't need to prove I can do it more. You know, be around booze and just walk away. It's an important step."

"It's too big of a step, too soon. I'm coming with you."

"I'll tell you what. Let me go in and if I don't come out in five, you come looking for me." Lottie closed her eyes, inhaled, and rubbed her temples. "But I think I can do it."

"Okay. I'll be waiting right here. And if you're not out, I'm going to yank you out of there."

Lottie ran into the house, locked the front door. She headed up the stairs, then stopped, and went back down. She found Ray's bodyguard chugging a beer and hitting on a hooker.

"There's a crazy fan outside," Lottie said, acting as flustered as possible.

"What?" The bodyguard slammed down his beer.

"Yeah. She's pretending to be an AA sponsor or something. She says her name's Catherine and that a spaceship landed in her backyard and these aliens got out and told her to bring them Ray Young. She's insane."

"Thanks for the heads-up," the bodyguard said. He turned toward the hooker. "My job is twenty-four/seven. I'll be back."

LOTTIE RACED UPSTAIRS.

She opened a bedroom door. Inside, sitting on the edge of the bed—fully clothed—were Tina and Bryce.

"Sorry," she whispered, backing out.

"Lottie, come in. I want you to meet Bryce. I was just telling him about you. Isn't she pretty, Bryce?"

Bryce looked at her without saying anything.

Tina stared at Lottie through glassy eyes. "I was just going to send Bryce downstairs to look for you, but you found us instead. You ready to party?"

"I'm trying to find Ray. Have you seen him?"

Tina patted the mattress. "Why don't you join us? We can all talk."

"I should really find Ray."

"Oh, stay. Don't be a party pooper. Ray's not going anywhere. He lives here."

"Well, okay." Lottie walked toward the canopied bed and sat next to Tina. "I mean, it's so weird. I seriously spent less than two minutes with him."

Tina combed her fingers through Lottie's hair. "I know, honey. It's all right." She stood up and gently kissed Lottie's cheek.

"Oh baby," Bryce groaned.

Tina pulled Lottie's face close to hers and kissed her lightly on the lips.

Lottie turned toward Bryce. He was suddenly naked on the bed, his arms resting behind his head, his legs splayed, his penis enormous. Tina sat back down, patted the mattress, and looked up at Lottie.

"Oh my God, you are so joking, right?"

"Lottie, we couldn't be more serious."

"I mean, no. I'm so not gay or bi or whatever."

"I'm not either," Tina said, stroking Lottie's cheek. "I'm fun. I'm free. I'm comfortable with me. Let's have some fun. You've got amazing breasts, by the way. I wanna get mine done, too."

"They're real."

"Yeah right," Bryce said. "Can I check?"

"You completely cannot. That is so fow-ull."

"I don't believe you."

"They couldn't be more real." Lottie felt dizzy. "I have to get out of here now." She turned toward the door.

"They're fake!" Bryce yelled.

Lottie turned around, lifted up her shirt, pulled down her bra, and quickly flashed a tit. "Real!" she yelled before slamming the door.

Lottie was about to go back downstairs when she heard a familiar voice by the front door.

"I don't know what you're talking about. I need to find my friend. I'm her sponsor. She needs help."

"Listen, I know all about you and your little spaceship. I'm calling the cops."

LOTTIE OPENED ANOTHER door and realized it had to be Ray's bedroom. And what a bed it was! It seemed to be on steroids. The frame and headboard were gigantic logs that looked as if they had been rolled in by Paul Bunyan himself. To get into bed, Ray had to hoist himself up on a three-step ladder—the mattress was at least five feet off the floor. Behind and above the bed were mirrors. Behind the nice boy, let's-not-rush-this image was a kink!

Off the bedroom was another room, which Ray had converted into a closet. Lottie realized that it was the size of her bedroom. There were at least one hundred pairs of jeans arranged according to shade—black-blue, navy blue, faded blue, powder blue, white blue. In shoe racks on the floor there were at least twenty pairs of peroxide-white Nike sneakers. There was also a poster for *Bel Air Belles* featuring Ray shirtless and brooding. WILL THE REAL LANCE CAINE PLEASE STAND UP, it read in fat red letters.

Lottie got to work.

She zipped open her bag and pulled out her lacy black Retail Slut lingerie, with the price tag still on it. She held it up, admiring its curves and plunges and translucence. Then she pulled out aphrodisiac candles she had bought at an aromatherapy shop at the Beverly Center. She arranged and lit the candles on the Paul Bunyan nightstands, draping a red silk handkerchief over the lamp next to the bed.

Lottie undressed and reapplied her makeup in front of a mirror framed by oversized lightbulbs. (She couldn't help but notice that a basket next to the toilet held teen magazines with Ray's face on the cover.) The Varilux bulbs were so strong that Lottie felt especially anemic and inadequate under their relentless glare. She brushed on extra dabs of blush and thickened her lashes with Maybelline dark black vitamin-enriched mascara. She applied two coats of Cherries in the Snow lipstick. Then she stared at herself. Not bad. She pulled on her negligee. Then she fluffed up her eyebrows and dabbed the sides of her lips with an index finger.

Lottie pranced around the bedroom, sucking in her stomach, pushing out her breasts, and puckering her lips. All those hours at the gym, sweating at kickboxing, spinning, Pilates, and weight-training classes, had paid off. She was almost as skinny as those hookers downstairs. Another few weeks and she'd nearly have those six-packs she'd been crunching toward.

Lottie halted in midflounce when she heard voices outside the door. As the knob began to turn, she panicked and quickly searched the room for an answer. Should she dart under the covers and look seductive? Maybe it was Catherine.

As the door opened a few more inches, Lottie dove underneath the bed.

A shaft of light swept across the floor and quickly disappeared as the door quietly shut again. There were four feet right in front of Lottie, two of which she recognized as Ray's Clorox-white Nikes. The other pair of feet was clad in scuffed black Doc Martens.

"You know what? I'm sick and tired of your drinking. It's gotten way out of hand lately, and I spent this whole evening wondering what the hell you were going to say to embarrass me this time." Lottie recognized Ray's voice. He sounded as if he were straining to squash a scream.

"Oh, puh-lease, Mr. Uptight. I'm just having a good time. You used to know how to do that before you became the It Boy. Relax." The words were slurred and spongy.

"Relax? Relax? Don't you know that things are completely different now? I can't relax. The minute I'm off guard, I get written up in the gossip columns. You know the threats I've been getting from some of them. There's no such thing as relaxing anymore. You can't possibly understand the pressure I'm under."

"Pressure. A year ago you were moaning because you'd walk down the street and no one gave a fuck. Now, you have your little hordes of giggling fans following your every move and you hate it. You're making more money than you've ever dreamed of. And you complain."

"You can't understand."

"Hah!" the voice cackled. A fist banged into a table. "I'm sorry. I feel like it's all my fault. I mean, without me, you'd just be some waiter at California Pizza Kitchen with a name tag that says, 'Hi, I'm Ray from Encino.' I created Lance Caine for you and now you seem to fucking hate me for it. You're out to hurt and belittle me because of it. I propelled you to stardom and you resent me."

Ray burped out a fake chuckle. "Now who's being an actor? Don't be so melodramatic, Mr. Inflated Ego. Without my talent, that piece of shit show would have been off the air in a week. I carry that show with its half-assed actors and lame writing."

Lottie watched as the Doc Martens jumped up and landed with a thud. "Lame writing? A few weeks ago, you called it brilliant."

"Yeah, because I knew if I even tried to tell you the truth, you'd go over-the-top insane. I can't believe some of the shit I'm spewing out. What the hell is 'Call me a bum if you want, but I clean pools, while you're busy making everything dirty'?" Ray snarled. "What kind of dreck is that? Next season, my agent promised that my contract would give me script approval. If I even decide to do a next season."

"Great. Fine. All of a sudden you're an actor and a writer. The piano thinks it can compose a concerto. Not only is Lance Caine a pool boy, but he's a real fucking Renaissance man. Michelangelo, why don't you fire your head writer and write the series yourself, you self-centered asshole."

It was quiet, and then Lottie heard body-heaving sobs mixed with the sound of someone choking on mucus. Then there were grunts and snorts. Lottie watched the Doc Martens move toward the door.

"Hold on a minute," Ray said, his voice softening. "G, stop crying. I would never get rid of you." Lottie watched Ray's white Nikes step toward the Doc Martens. Their toes were practically touching.

"Do you really hate my writing?" Gregory sniffled.

Ray sighed, laughing quietly. "No. I love your writing. Remember when Lance said, 'How can you know me, when I'm too afraid to know myself?' That was brilliant. I felt like you were speaking just to me."

Gregory blew his nose. "I was. You know I only write for you. You're my, well—I know it sounds cliché—muse. I just wish I could shout it from the Hollywood sign."

"So do I, but we can't."

"I know. I know. You don't know how hard it is for me."

There were more sniffles followed by the *phttt* of lips on lips. Lottie cowered underneath her little log cabin with her heart pounding and her brain scrambling to decode the unseen. There was the rustling of cotton, the tugging of belts, and the pulling of zippers. There was moaning, panting, and the sloshing of saliva. The scuffed Doc Martens climbed the ladder followed by the Clorox-white Nikes. There was a thud overhead, more moaning, and then the sounds of the springs wheezing as the mattress banged into Lottie's head.

Lottie squeezed her eyes and held her breath. "That feels so good, baby," one of them sighed. "Ohhh, yeah. That's nice." Her face flushed while her stomach turned somersaults. Lottie felt like crying, but she was too scared to give herself away. The bed rattled and jerked. Lottie crouched down lower while bodies writhed and heaved above hers. A fucking beard! What a jerk she'd been, believing that he didn't want to rush her.

No more actors, ever, she resolved, knowing somewhere that it was like the empty promise of an alcoholic.

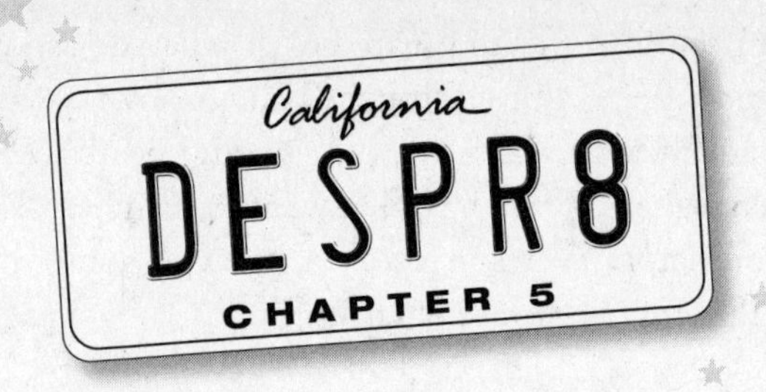

WHEN LEM RANG UP CYNDI FOR THE HUNDREDTH TIME THAT month, Boyd, the new receptionist, told him he would have to go through Jonathan Swerling's office.

"And who, may I ask, is Mr. Swerling?" Lem asked, his accent on full throttle.

"Mr. Swerling represents Ms. Bowman. He is *her* publicist."

Lem's mouth unhinged. "What do you mean," he shrieked, sounding like a Valley girl. "What in bloody blazes does she need a publicist for? She *is* a publicist!"

"Mr., umm . . . Back, if you need to get in touch with Ms. Bowman, you must fax a request to Mr. Swerling, who will pass it on to Ms. Bowman. He'll call you back with a yay or a nay."

"Is this some sort of game? I must go through a publicist to speak to a publicist? I've never heard of anything quite so absurd. Besides, Ms. Bowman knows precisely why I'm calling. I'm not sending off any bloody fax. If you could kindly tell her to, as you assistants so eloquently put it, give a return? I'd appreciate it."

Boyd coughed. "I'm sorry, sir. I was advised that any inquiries from the press must first be handled by Mr. Swerling's office. B.P. must cater to our celebrity clientele before we can help the press."

Lem spoke through his teeth in a low, drained tone. "Let me tell you something, Boyd. That company was founded by Thomas Bowman, a man who would return any phone call within two hours, no matter what, even if it was from little walleyed Suzy Cheese Cake looking for a summer internship. If Thomas Bowman knew what was happening to his beloved company, well, he'd have an aneurysm. A publicist for a publicist! Even Kafka couldn't have imagined this."

Boyd ahemmed into the mouthpiece. "Sir, Mr. Kafkar isn't my employer. I have another call on line two that requires immediate attention."

Lem listened to the moaning of the dial tone as if waiting for an explanation. In slow motion he placed the phone in its cradle. Holding his head in his hands, he squeezed his eyes shut. Sometime, maybe while he was stumbling around Wilshire Boulevard, the entire world had changed. His garden had been invaded by weeds until it was reduced to a collection of chipped coffins filled with charred dirt and skeletal remains of flowers. The butterflies were dead.

Lem was frozen. He needed this interview more than anything. Any day, Reggio was going to thank him for his services but explain that while he hated to do it, he had no choice. This was a new age of journalism, and Lem just wasn't making his contributions to the *Personality* paradigm. He'd tell Lem that he hoped they could still be good friends. Hell, he'd even give him a recommendation. If there's anything he can do, just ask, he'd say while averting his eyes. Then he'd have security escort Lem from the building.

Lem's hands shook. He wanted booze so badly he could taste it.

He took out his ink-mottled yellow legal pad and began working on *They're Not Your Friends*. If he was going to get fired, he might as well do his own thing. Since he had stopped drinking he'd been writing every day. Perhaps he could actually finish this book. Lem wrote frantically.

Still not assimilated in the world of high-tech journalism, Lem preferred pen to keyboard. His fingers were rendered leaden by the computer. He'd delete entire stories by just one press of a key. "You have to learn to save your stories every few minutes," Reggio would say, shaking his head and rolling his eyes. But instead of adapting, Lem stopped writing for *Personality*. He couldn't understand how a computer was considered a technical advancement when it could obliterate prose with one aberrant touch. He'd rather scrawl away with his Bic and real paper. He loved the feel of the pen between his fingers and the sound of the tip scraping away at the page. It somehow seemed primordial, as if he were a Java man scratching at the wall of a cave.

AFTER FRANNY DUMPED him, Lem had changed forever. He couldn't stop thinking about her and the life he had imagined for them. He circled her block in his car for hours. He wrote long, effusive letters that were never mailed. For a few months Franny had allowed Lem to peer into a window of a life he didn't know he wanted. Then she moved on and left him wanting more. Soon she disappeared into the security of celebrity. She moved into a fortress. She had a bodyguard trail her. She showed up at events with an entourage. Lem couldn't even try to get close.

One day, while sipping martinis at a party in Brentwood and staring at the door praying for Franny to walk through, Lem had had a revelation. He understood that his life would never be the same because of Lisa the Love Witch's spell. He had spent his days—and nights—consumed with thoughts of her for more than a year with no end in sight. He watched repeats of her mind-numbing show religiously. He didn't even think about women except as a comparison to Franny. This had to end.

"You need a wife," Thom Bowman said. He handed Lem a martini. Bowman had become Lem's best bloke. He'd also quickly transformed himself into the hottest publicist in town. After Franny's article ran, every television star was clamoring to be represented by Thom Bowman Publicity.

Although Lem never discussed it, Thom seemed to understand Lem's obsession.

"Move on. Find a woman like my sweet Marjorie. Find a woman whose career is wife and mother, not actress. Franny Blanchard couldn't love anyone but Franny Blanchard. She's brought a lot of men grief and sadness. She's a user. You're not the first, believe you me."

"Couldn't you have warned me?"

Thom's eyes locked with Lem's. "Warn you? This was only business, ol' boy." He let out a brittle laugh. "She's Hollywood trash. I wanted you to write an article, not fall in love."

It seemed to Lem that Thom played matchmaker to alleviate some nagging guilt. One day, feigning serendipity, he introduced Lem to his new intern. She was an absolute beauty who had nothing to do with show business. "I'll tell you, Sir Lem, if I were single, I'd throw a spear at her," Thom confided. "She's wife material. She reminds me of my Marjorie. When I found out she was from Merry Ol', I had to hire her, just for you. Let's just say she's my little get-well present to you. This will take your mind off the Love Bitch."

Lem was smitten with the raven-haired intern. And Patricia was enamored by Lem's talent and charisma. She thought he was a genius (probably partly Thom's influence, Lem knew). In short, she worshipped him, and he couldn't resist the adulation. After a year, they married.

At first he believed she was his cure. Her love for him had tamed him. With a gold band on his finger, he would never need to stray, he convinced himself. He'd rush home from work to be with her, cutting his parties and pub crawling to a minimum. They bought a house in the San Fernando Valley, with plans to fill it with children.

So, was he trying to sabotage himself when he started staying out late again? No. He figured he'd get it all out of his system before the egg was in the nest. He still had a few wild oats to sow before becoming completely domesticated. And the Valley was so boring.

But Lem could never have just a few drinks. And alcohol blotted out his vows of fidelity. Soon he found himself waking up in strange rooms. He'd dress quickly and rush home. He'd speed along the 101 freeway—a shaft of moonlight following him like a conscience.

Patricia always pretended to be asleep. The next morning both would pretend nothing had happened, although Lem was certain she knew. Live in Los Angeles long enough and you learn to act, regardless of your profession.

She'd clean his alcohol-stained shirts and ignore the perfume smell on the collars. Each time Lem stumbled home in the middle of the night, he'd promise himself that it was the last time. But the next night, half intoxicated by booze, half intoxicated by the image of himself holding court at Morton's or Chasen's, he'd be back at his old tricks. He still kept one eye on the door. It was, after all, Franny's fault. Each conquest fueled his need for Franny. Thom had been wrong about marriage quashing any desire, though he couldn't admit it to Thom; no, he couldn't handle Thom's disappointment.

He knew he had to stop or his life would be ruined forever.

One night after work when Patricia wasn't home yet, Lem decided to destroy anything that reminded him of Franny. He opened a closet in his den and took out a large cardboard box bulging with all the articles he had written for *Personality.* He rummaged through it. There was Olivia Newton-John, Bill Cosby, Madonna, Michael J. Fox, Sylvester Stallone, Michael Jackson, Billy Crystal. Then he spotted her in the morass of celebrity faces—Franny Blanchard staring back at him with her piercing eyes. It was the article he had written a few years earlier. Her coy smile seemed to know something he didn't—something he desperately wanted to decode.

He stared and stared. Underneath the stack was a white silk scarf he had taken from her. He inhaled and caught a faint whiff of her perfume. Chanel No. 5.

He grabbed the scarf and the stack of magazines and headed out the den, down the hall toward the garbage cans outside. But somehow he got sidetracked. The smell of her on the scarf was too powerful, too full of promise. He had every intention of exorcising their home of the Love Witch. Instead, he tossed the magazines onto his sofa.

He stared at her face. Her full, thick lips. Her mane of blond hair. He breathed in Chanel No. 5. He slowly unbuttoned her skirt, pulled off her stockings, tugged at her black lace underwear, while crying out for her.

"Franny! Franny. Franny."

"What?!!"

Lem blinked his eyes. Franny had disappeared and Patricia was staring over him, her jaw dropped and eyes wide.

Lem felt the blood rush to his face. "I was just nap—"

Patricia swept her hands along the sofa and the magazines flew across the room, some smacking against the walls before tumbling to the ground.

"And here I was just going to tell you . . ." Patricia covered her mouth and turned. Lem heard her heels clicking quickly against the terra-cotta-tiled floor.

"Tell me what," he yelled after her. "Tell me what?"

The front door slammed. Patricia had reached her threshold. She'd put up with the boozing and even the cheating, but whacking off to this false goddess was too much. And Lem knew the minute she left that she was gone from his life. She came back a few days later and told him to pack up and leave. He pleaded with her to let him stay, but she just shook her head. He said he'd go into therapy or marriage counseling, whatever it took. But Patricia just stared past him through glassy eyes.

"You'll always be in love with her," Patricia said. "Perhaps if she were a real live flesh and blood person, I could even live with that. But she's only a magazine cover. She's only gamma ray molecules. I refuse to compete with that for the rest of my life. I want a better life for my . . . for me."

"I love you. I didn't realize how much until now. I'm begging you. I'll change."

Patricia hissed. "Don't ask me to live a life of regrets. Look what that's done for you."

Lem stood there, slack jawed. He slowly walked out the door. After driving around in his Citroën for hours, he stopped by Thom's Brentwood home. Marjorie answered the door with booze on her breath and a baby in her arms. "With a spell everyone's under her command," she said before slamming the door. Then Lem checked into a twenty-five-bungalow motel with a big blue neon vacancy sign flashing out front. The "V" and the "A" and the "C" were broken so only "ANCY" pulsated and buzzed in the cool night. Then the newly single Lemuel Brac called in sick for a week. Bad stomach virus.

Lem spent seven days blitzed out of his skull. Lounging by the motel's leaf-choked pool one day, he watched a father play with his children. He'd throw them into the air and they'd squeal with delight as they plunged into the water. And Lem Brac knew that he'd lost his chance for real true happiness. He sobbed quietly, realizing for the first time that no one had ever loved or understood him better than Patricia. He chugged his Smirnoff's to forget this. Then he pried the ring off his finger and tossed it into the water. In the midst of the kids' splashing, it barely made a ripple before sinking to the bottom.

"I'm back," he said to his reflection as it danced and then dissipated in the chlorinated depths. The children stopped splashing and stared at him. "I'm back," he whispered, knowing that he was unequivocably gone.

LEM SHOOK HIS head, put down his pen, and started rummaging through his office for a bottle of booze he might have stashed somewhere. His hands trembled as he imagined the cool vodka rushing down his throat. It had been months, but the ache for it hadn't dulled one bit. He didn't find anything so he sat back down and took a long breath. Then he called Jonathan Swerling, publicist to the publicist. He was busy advising a client, Lem was informed.

"Please tell him that Lem Brac called. It's a matter of extreme urgency that I speak to Ms. Bowman today." Lem exhaled. "I hate to tell you this, but we're about to do a story on Chris Mercer without his cooperation. We've already spoken with several co-stars . . . and high school acquaintances."

The lie—a veiled threat since most actors were complete losers in high school—was bound to get him a call back, and maybe, just maybe, he could scare them into an interview. Celebrities were terrified by high school classmates who knew them at their acne-covered worst.

"I'll make sure Mr. Swerling receives your message. Thank you for calling." His clipped staccato mimicked Cyndi's receptionist, Boyd. For all Lem knew, maybe it even was Boyd, and the publicist's publicist was a ruse to impress.

LEM TRIED TO write but couldn't concentrate. It was hard to focus when his life seemed so precarious. If only the phone would ring. But even if it did, it wouldn't matter. Lem had to be, as Reggio loved to say, *proactive*.

He left midday so there was no traffic. Two hours later he was in front of Thom Bowman's enormous estate in Santa Barbara. Lem felt nervous. He hadn't visited Thom since he retired—when was it? Two or three years ago now? He had called a few times, but Marjorie, Thom's wife, always answered. Lem would instinctively hang up. Lem knew Marjorie detested him for cheating on Patricia. But her hatred was so fierce that Lem was certain there was more to it.

He wondered why Thom had never called him. He remembered being pissed out of his mind at Thom's farewell party. He had given a slurry toast. Cyndi had been there, shaking her head the whole time. Had he offended Thom in some way he didn't remember? Maybe it was just retirement. Lem understood that retirement was this vortex healthy men were sucked into, skinned and deboned, and eventually spooned out as corpses.

As he rang the doorbell, he prayed Marjorie wouldn't be home. The door slowly opened.

"Lemblac?" Marjorie slurred out. "Did shue ever hear about calling?"

"Nice to see you, too, Marj," Lem said, smiling. Not even three and she was bombed. "I was in the neighborhood and . . ."

"Thom's sch-ick. Ish not a good time."

As she went to close the door, Lem pushed at it. "Marjorie, just a few minutes. I desperately need to see him . . . for old times' sake."

"That's reason enough to deny ax-chess," she said, shaking her head. But she moved away from the door. "Come in, but I don't know who you'll being shee. The Great Osh."

"Great who?" Lem asked, but Marjorie had turned and was weaving down the hall. She nearly knocked over angelic Hummel figurines as her hips ricocheted off walls and tables. She stopped in front of a cherrywood-paneled door and opened it.

"Thom, visitor," she said quickly as she continued zigzagging down the hall. Without turning around, she said, "Make yourshelf comfoshoble."

Lem headed in. The room was dark, lit only by a movie projector. But no movie played. There was just a blank white screen. Thom was jotting notes from behind a cherrywood desk.

"Thom Bowman!"

Thom stared quizzically at Lem for a moment. Then he smiled, stood up, and, with outstretched arms, bear-hugged Lem, nearly lifting him off the floor.

Lem laughed almost giddily. "Thom, old man, that's quite a reception. I was beginning to feel friendless in the land of L.A. How are you doing?"

"I can't complain—no one will listen," Bowman began as he had ever since Lem was but a fledgling American. Lem's heart leapt—for the first time in a long time, something sounded familiar. Thom Bowman was the salt of the earth. The best friend he'd ever had.

"Thom Bowman! You have no bloody idea how great it is to see you. No bloody idea. Everybody, all of the land of plastic fantastic, misses you. *I* miss you."

Thom cackled in that huge, boisterous laugh of his. It was contagious, and Lem couldn't help but burp out a whimper.

Thom slapped Lem on the back. "This is the beginning of a beautiful friendship."

"Yes . . . well. I guess we haven't been keeping in touch very well."

"What we got here is a failure to communicate."

Lem laughed. "I suppose so." He looked at Thom. "*Cool Hand Luke*. Bloody wonderful movie. Paul Newman in his finest hour. You know, I was reminiscing about the time we met. How different life was then."

Lem waited for Thom to say something, but he didn't. He just stared at Lem, as if overcome by his visit. Then he smiled and opened his mouth.

"Life is like a . . . box of chocolates. You never know what you're gonna get."

Lem laughed. "*Forrest Gump*, eh? Most overrated movie, in my humble opinion. Give an actor the role of a dim-witted imbecile and he knows he'll get that statue. Tom Hanks at his pandering worst."

Thom chuckled, cleared his throat, and continued his Tom Hanks impersonation. "You wouldn't believe me if I told you, but I could run like the wind blows. From that day on, if I was ever going somewhere, I was running."

"More Forrest?" Lem cleared his throat and pointed to the white movie screen. "Is that what you were just watching?"

Thom nodded. "Stupid is as stupid does."

"Guess so." Lem squinted at Thom. But his friend's face registered nothing. "How's the old golf game, old buddy? Christ, I'm slaving away at *Personality* while you're swatting a putter. There's something wrong with that picture, especially since I'm smarter and better looking than you, buddy."

Thom cackled again and stared at Lem. "Who are you?"

Lem laughed and put his arm around Thom. "You're nuts, old boy. But it's great to see you. Bloody great."

"Get your stinkin' paws off me, you damned dirty ape."

Thom guffawed. Lem's arm flew back to his sides.

"*Planet of the Apes.*" Lem nearly choked on the words. What in bloody hell had happened? What had retirement done to Thom? Lem stared hard, looking for light in Thom's eyes. He tried to smell his breath. Could Thom be as blitzed as the Mrs.? He checked the desk for an empty glass. All he saw was a small bottle of some kind of medicine. He peered at the label. The Cure. He tried again.

"You miss the business, Thom? You miss it at all?"

Thom coughed. "Leave the gun. Take the cannoli."

"Aha," Lem said. "Thom, what the fuck's going on? Are you putting me on?"

Thom stared vacantly at Lem. Lem waved his hands in front of Thom's face. He snapped his fingers.

"Thom, Thom, are you there? Are you pissed out of your mind on Bloody Marys? I know how much you like those in the afternoon. Remember you used to say a Bloody Mary wasn't a drink, it was an appetizer? Remember? Remember?"

"Of all the gin joints in all the towns in all the world, she walks into mine."

Lem's heart hammered away and he felt dizzy. His face blazed and his mouth dried up. What the fuck had happened to his friend?

"Thom, Thom, you wanna know the goddamned truth? These bloody fucking four-flushers want me out of there. I need a bloody break. I need your help. One interview. I can be Sir Lem again. They'll leave me alone. Talk to your daughter. Thom, Thom. Please. This isn't a game. I'm trying to save my life. Please, don't quote movies. Please don't leave me now."

Again, silence. A long silence. Another vacant stare. It was like speaking to a dead man. Lem turned away and stared at their silhouettes on the empty screen. Thom was nearly a head taller then Lem. Finally, Thom cleared his throat. Lem prayed for his friend to be there.

"Who are you?"

Lem grabbed Thom by the collar. "Thom, it's me. Lem. Lem Brac. Come on, old buddy."

"They're not going to lick me! I'm going to live through this, and when it's over, I'll never be hungry again."

Lem's heart flopped in his chest. Thom wasn't drunk. Usually the guy slurred his words after a few rounds, but nothing like this. "Thom? Thom, what is this?"

Thom's voice became louder and louder until it boomed.

"Forget it, Jake. It's Chinatown . . . Plastics . . . Pay no attention to the man behind the curtain. The great Oz has spoken . . . Go ahead, make my day . . . Dave, this conversation can serve no purpose anymore. Good-bye."

"You're right," Lem whispered. "Good-bye." Then he slowly opened the door and headed out. He turned and looked at Thom. He wiped his eyes with a finger when he realized everything suddenly had gone blurry. He was crying.

MIKE RENTED AN APARTMENT IN STUDIO CITY, WHICH WAS RIGHT at the rim of Hollywood but part of the San Fernando Valley. Studio City's Ventura Boulevard was lined with ersatz antique stores, twenty-five-room motels with big neon signs, and restaurants that, for some reason Mike couldn't figure out, were mostly Thai. Thai Spoon, Thai Kitchen, Sate Grill, Bangkok Noodles, Pad Thai House, House of Thai, Thai Delite. They all specialized in minimalist decor with framed embroidered elephants, faded black-and-white headshots of unknown actors raving about the cuisine, and institutional fluorescent lighting, which gave them an ice-rink ambiance. And there was always the requisite murky-watered aquarium with bloated goldfish gasping for aerated water but breathing out good feng shui for everyone.

Mike's street off Ventura was a place where stucco condo complexes were lined up like building blocks. They looked exactly the same, more like medical centers than home sweet home. It was Legoland with names like Hawaiian Breeze, Sunnyside Hills, Paradise Palms, The Riviera, and Monaco Gardens—all written in slanted script on pale pastel facades. The roofs were bedecked with corrugated terra-cotta tiles, but instead of the desired effect of Mediterranean elegance, they looked more like Howard Johnson kitsch. Where was the California his mother had told him about?

Mike had discovered that Studio City was the dwelling of choice for bit players, strugglers, and hangers-on, all vying to be PLYRS, ACTRS, AKTRSIS, and, most important, YUNG. Mike decided that these were people who, from a wide angle, seemed okay and sometimes even beautiful, but zoom in and they were loaded with rips, tears, frays, wrinkles, and pockmarks. Collagen and Botox distorted their smiles and bloated the skin where their cheekbones once stood; pumped-up lips like bicycle tires flapped out words as if perpetually anesthetized. Plastic surgery permanently shocked their eyes and swallowed their expressions, so it was hard to discern whether they were happy, sad, or just praying for the Big Break.

A real estate agent with a license plate that read ICSALES lived next to Mike. On the other side was a twenty-something blond woman with a dog named Root Canal. When Mike first heard her yelling her canine's moniker, he assumed she was in some kind of dental distress. One day when Mike was lounging at the pool, enjoying the November sun, Root Canal and his owner plopped in a chaise next to him, even though there were twenty empty chairs around the pool's perimeter. The owner introduced her poodle.

"I know. I know. It's a strange name. I was dating this hot dentist who couldn't commit to me. I either wanted a dog or a husband so when Dentist Donald wouldn't stand up to the challenge, I bought my little poodle here and named him Root Canal. We met over one. Donald said I had a great mouth. Very Julia Roberts with a hint of Cameron Diaz, he said."

"Aha."

"After we broke up, I thought about changing Rootie's name, but it didn't work. Typical. The jerk—not Rootie, D.D.—stayed with me long enough so that I couldn't change Rootie's name without confusing him."

The dog sniffed Mike's hand.

"My name's Amber. Amber Pepridge."

"Hello, Amber. I'm Mike Posner. "

"You staying here for a while?"

"I guess."

"Really? Because no one stays in Los Angeles for long, and if you're living in Studio City, it's an even shorter stay. Actually if you're in an apartment in Studio City, you've probably left already; it's just your energy that's still here. I'm probably having a conversation right now with your psychic residue."

"Maybe *I* am. Maybe you've already left."

"No way. I'm not leaving till my energy's up on the big screen. As you probably guessed, I'm an actress. We all are, aren't we? You have to be, right? You sort of have that Leo DiCap thing going with that slender build and maybe a little Matt Damon meets Matthew Perry bone structure. I'm not sure who else you are though." She squinted as she studied him. "Who do I look like?"

Amber Pepridge spoke as though she was a beauty pageant contestant explaining to the world how she'd save the children in Ethiopia if only she was crowned Miss USA. Her gesticulations were grand and sweeping, and she enunciated each syllable and punctuated each sentence with a long, radiant smile. She eyeballed Mike the entire time.

"I don't know," he said.

"Well, as I said, I've been told I have a Julia Roberts mouth with a hint of Cameron Diaz. Meg Ryan's eyes. And I sort of have Marisa Tomei's cheekbones. I had a casting director say that Sarah Jessica Parker is in my hair. So, who reps you?"

"Nobody."

"Nobody? You need representation."

"I'm not an actor."

"You're kidding? I don't think I've ever met anyone in this building who wasn't trying to be an actor."

"That women on the other side of me—she's a real estate agent."

"Yeah, sure she is. I don't think she's sold a house yet, but if you turn on your TV in the afternoon, you'll see her on her cable access show. *Reel Estate*, I think it's called. She talks about celebrity houses for sale."

Rootie jumped onto Amber's white plastic chaise. "Hello, baby. Hello. How's my little baby?" Amber said as she petted him. "Rootie just had his balls clipped, but you couldn't tell, I bet."

"Well, no."

"I didn't want to do it, but Rootie was humping everything in sight. Wall-to-wall jism, forgive my bluntness. My audition clothes were ruined. I lost a really good role on a sitcom cause I had a Monica Lewinsky–esque stain on my dress. It was humiliating. The casting directors were laughing hysterically during my audition. I thought I got the part."

Amber shook her head. "So we compromised. I fixed him, but I had the doctor insert Neutricals."

"Neutricals?"

"Plastic balls."

"Your dog has plastic balls?" Mike ducked his head to check Rootie's plumbing.

"My animal psychologist said dogs suffer self-esteem problems after their balls are, well, ripped off. Imagine how you'd feel? So my doctor inserted these plastic balls."

Amber studied Mike. He knew what she was probably thinking. *He looks like a tourist.* After a lifetime in the frozen tundra that is upstate New York, he'd never had an actual summer wardrobe and didn't know precisely how to dress for the desert. Today, he was wearing a long-sleeved shirt even though it was probably almost eighty degrees. But it was cold this morning. After nearly a year he still couldn't figure it out.

"I should make you dinner sometime. You're the first person in the building who actually unpacked his suitcase. Everyone here's waiting for the Callback. They're packed up and ready to go on location anywhere. Most of us have been living here temporarily for years and years."

"Sure," Mike said, knowing it would never happen. Los Angelenos lacked follow-up skills.

"So what do you do?"

"Well, I write for . . . *Personality*." He said it slowly, knowing Amber would be extremely impressed.

"You're absolutely fucking kidding me. That's my favorite magazine EVER."

"Yeah, well . . ."

"You must have a lot of friends in the industry."

"Well . . ."

"You know anyone who'd be interested in auditioning a talented actress looking for her big break? Here's my card. If you think of someone you know who wants someone who can do comedy and drama, tell them to call me. When I become huge, I'll mention you in all the articles. I'd never forget those who helped me on the way up; I guarantee it."

Mike studied the card. Amber Pepridge: Actress, Singer, Entertainer.

Amber was beautiful and hot. And she wanted Mike. Well, she wanted what she thought Mike stood for. If he said, "I'll see what I can do. Let's go to your place and look at your portfolio," he'd be getting laid in about ten minutes. But Mike would never do anything about it. No, he couldn't risk being the laughingstock of the building.

HOW TO PUT IT? Mike had a lot in common with Root Canal. He was, well, not well endowed. Actually, small. Laughably small. Nubby. God, it was so embarrassing. When he lost his virginity, his girlfriend didn't even know it. "Are you in yet? Where are you? Come on, Mike. Is something wrong? Is it me? You're not attracted to me. Are you? What is it?" He ran out of the room. He never dated. Liz had been his only real girlfriend. She fell in love with him because he wasn't like the other guys who just wanted to get in her pants, she said. Little did she know how desperately he wanted to be like the guys who just wanted to get in her pants. When he finally told her, she was too smitten to care. And he figured he'd marry her and never have to deal with the embarrassment again. Instead, she dumped him. Probably because of it. Of course because of it.

Lady killer. His friends back east thought he didn't have a girlfriend because he was screwing hordes of chicks.

Ace reporter. His editors thought he was the best-connected writer at the magazine.

Mike Poseur. He didn't know who he was anymore. A pin-dicked guy who couldn't get laid if his life depended on it. A mediocre reporter who discovered that being the best required a whole lot of lying.

WHEN MIKE STARTED at the magazine, he was told to write a story about Brad Pitt and Jennifer Aniston. He assumed he'd sit down and interview them.

"Are you kidding? They hate you," Brad's publicist said.

"Me? They don't even know me."

"Your magazine. It's too intrusive. They won't talk to you. Ever. Your magazine said it was doing a story on Brad's movie career and instead you just wrote about all the women you assumed he nailed. Of course it was all wrong. And then you had to dig up his high school classmates. And some reporter staked out his parents' home."

Mike panicked. He'd moved his whole life to Los Angeles and already he was failing. Then over lunch, Lem Brac explained.

"We never talk to the celebrity. We talk to friends of friends. We talk to hairstylists and assistant directors. Look at the credits for the movies they're in. Find the people at the bottom rung. The assistants to assistants. They'll always talk. They'll tell you everything you need to know. Even if they don't know a thing themselves."

But most of them didn't return calls. He remembered the first person who actually spoke to him. It was a hairstylist's assistant who had wrapped Brad Pitt's hair in foil. The conversation went something like this:

"I don't know anything."

"You must know something."

"I spent about ten minutes helping my boss put underlights in his hair. Brad read the newspaper the whole time. We didn't talk."

"Underlights?"

"Well, it's this procedure where instead of . . ."

"Never mind. Think. You must know something about him."

"Well, his hair looks great with underlights. He has the most amazing smile. He's just gorgeous. Radiant."

"That's really great stuff, but what about his marriage? We need stories about Brad and Jennifer. What are they like together?"

"I saw them together on *Access Hollywood.* They seem happy."

"That's a start. What else?"

"Well, I heard from one of my friends that they are so in love. But he probably read about it in your magazine."

"Great, great. What else did he say?"

"I think that's it."

"Come on, come on . . ."

"Well, I think he overheard Brad talking on the set one day. He was gonna make dinner for her. But I'm not sure."

"Really? See, that's something. You remember what kind of food?"

"Well, I think he likes Italian food. My friend saw him eating spaghetti on the set, I think. But then again, I read in your magazine that they're both really into The Zone."

Mike was ready to dismiss the whole anecdote. But then Vince banged on the door. "Get anything yet? We're having a meeting in ten."

Mike couldn't be mediocre anymore. He couldn't relive the *Daily News* experience. He had to be the best. Suddenly, he heard himself in the meeting.

"I have this great source. A good friend of Brad's. I promised I wouldn't use his name. He says they're homebodies. They love spending evenings in, cooking for each other. They take turns.

Sometimes they'll cook together and make elaborate meals for friends. Just last night Brad made Jennifer this enormous Italian dinner. Seafood pasta, a salad. Every now and then they go off The Zone."

Vince clapped. "Great stuff!"

In an instant, he was no longer Mike the hick from Rochester.

Soon he began developing other "sources." No one questioned him. The key was to write things celebrities wouldn't get upset about. Fluff and puff. Tom Cruise hugging and playing with his daughter on the set of a movie. Demi Moore's friends talking about what a doting mom she is. Julia Roberts telling a "good friend" how in love she is with her husband. Innocuous, positive stuff. Stuff that no one would suspect was a lie. Stuff that even the celebrity might believe happened or, at least, wished happened.

It was too easy.

ONE DAY MIKE and Lottie were assigned to collaborate on a story.

"Show her the ropes. She's green, but there's something there," Vince had confided. "Teach her the art of sourcing."

"Sure thing, Vince."

There had been rumors that the great romance between Sebastian Brooks and Stephanie Winters had fizzled. They hadn't filed divorce papers yet, but allegedly the action/adventure film stars were living apart. Mike made some calls.

"They're just so busy with their careers." "Sebastian just can't commit to one woman." "Stephanie's still got some wild oats to sow." "He needs someone more down to earth." "She needs someone more sophisticated."

"She's completely obsessed with Dustin Hoffman."

"What? So, are they having an affair?"

"Affair? With who?"

"Dustin Hoffman."

"With Dustin Hoffman? Gross! That's her baby!"

"Her baby?"

"They named their *baby* Dustin Hoffman. Anyway, she's a great mother. And Sebs is jealous. He doesn't like sharing the spotlight per se."

"Sebastian is a natural dad—Stephanie hates competing with Dustin Hoffman." "They're from the opposite sides of the track." "They're still in love." "They'll be back together in a week." "They hate each other." "They'll never speak to each other again." "It's all a publicity stunt."

It was then that Mike realized that *Personality*'s reporting techniques were very similar to the children's game of Telephone. In the game, something is whispered from one ear to the next until the last kid in the chain blurts out a hysterically distorted rendition. "They still love each other" becomes "thistle of easy over."

At *Personality*, reporters interviewed what was tantamount to the last person in Telephone. Key grips, boom operators, casting directors, and set designers were all quoted as sources, even if their contact with the celebrity was as minimal as a few dabs of pancake makeup on a movie set a few years back. That's why it was so easy to lie. "We haven't seen each other in years" becomes "a source close to the subject."

Actually, the reporting at *Personality* was exactly like the game of Telephone—except the last kid in the chain was deaf.

VINCE CALLED LOTTIE and Mike into his office to discuss their progress.

"This is huge. Huge. We want to be the first to report accurately on their breakup, before the divorce papers become a matter of public record," Vince said, narrowing his eyes and clenching his jaw. "This is the kind of breaking news story that we do best. Bernie is wetting her pants. So, do you have anything?"

Mike stared at Vince, but he could barely concentrate; the smell of cocoa butter emanating from Lottie's pores was intoxicating. He shifted his eyes toward her as she beamed a smile at Vince.

"My sources say they're trying to work it out," Mike said, sucking in his cheeks.

Lottie glared at him. "*My sources* say it's officially over."

Mike gave Lottie a quick smirk and then smiled at Vince. "I heard they wanna make it work, for Dustin Hoffman's sake."

Lottie sneered at Mike. "My sources say Stephanie doesn't want anything to do with Dustin."

"My sources say Stephanie's a great mother."

"Mine say she sucks."

Mike was so turned on he could have played verbal volleyball all day.

Vince cleared his throat. "It seems your sources are at odds." Vince nodded at Mike, as if saying, *I know whom to believe.* "We need more. And we still need a *Personality* paradigm scene setter. Anything on that front?"

Mike thought quickly. Should he just make it up? A quick scene.

The two of them at The Ivy? After all, every celeb loves being noticed at The Ivy. Chances are they were there recently. *A lot of whispering.* Celebrities are going to whisper, right? *They looked sad.* They always look kinda sad. *They didn't finish their meal.* They never do. Too many fat grams. *She ate a salad.* That's a no-brainer. *He left a big tip and signed some autographs.* What? Like he's gonna argue? *She had big sunglasses on and was aloof.* Aren't they always? *A witness said she'd been crying.* Blame the witness for inaccuracies. Maybe it was the sun in her eyes.

Mike could see the lead:

> **There's trouble in paradise. As Sebastian Brooks and Stephanie Winters recently dined at The Ivy, their moods seemed somber. They were whispering. Stephanie picked up a tissue and wiped her eyes.**
>
> **"They seemed to be breaking up at the table," said a source who wished to remain anonymous. "Stephanie barely touched her salad. Sebastian tried to console her, but it was no use."**
>
> **This was in sharp contrast to their appearance at the Oscars . . .**

"My source says Sebastian's staying at the Chateau Marmont," Lottie said.

Vince smiled at Mike. "Well, it's a long shot, but why don't you check it out."

Lottie stamped her foot. "Hey, it's so my lead."

"You can come," Mike offered.

"I so don't believe this," Lottie said.

"Excellent idea, Mike. Why don't both of you go? Lottie, you can learn a lot from this guy. We need that scene setter, Mike."

"LET ME SEE what I can get," Mike said in the hotel lobby, in a voice a few octaves deeper than usual. Lottie grunted. He ambled up to the desk clerk. "Hello, sir," he boomed, feeling the heat of Lottie's gaze on his back. "I'm Mike Posner, with *Personality* magazine."

"The hotel is not interested in subscriptions, young man," the vulture-faced clerk deadpanned.

Mike reddened, but he managed a smile. "I'm sorry; let me clarify that. I'm a reporter with the magazine. We're working on a story on the actor Sebastian Brooks. I understand he's been staying here for the last couple of days. Can you confirm that?"

The desk clerk had big bat ears and pink translucent skin wrapped tightly around his sunken face. He snapped out a laugh, like a snake spitting venom, without changing his sepulchral expression.

"Obviously, you must be very new at your job, Mr. Posner," he said, while his beady blue eyes shot hate daggers. "We don't give out any information on our hotel guests. But, off the record, I wouldn't waste my time here; try another hotel. No one by that name has checked into our establishment."

Mike's face burned. He turned around slowly, waiting for Lottie's disgusted expression to greet him, but she was already gone. Typical, Mike thought. She was probably on to some other lead. He went outside, but her red Cabrio was still parked by the valet stand. Mike decided to check the bar.

It was still early in the evening, but the dimly lit bar was already filling up with hipsters in frayed jeans, vintage graphic tees, and artfully mussed hair. He saw two women wearing tight Cookie Monster T-shirts. He chuckled silently. Just last week, Lottie had written a file about how Sesame Street tees were suddenly all the rage.

In its midst was Lottie Love, plopped at the bar, sipping something frothy and leaning toward the bartender as if he were dispensing great wisdom. Mike had been making a fool of himself while Lottie was at the bar drinking margaritas and flirting.

Mike stood next to Lottie.

"OhmyGod," he heard Lottie fawn. "You must get like so many celebrities in this place. You must be like almost a celebrity yourself."

The bartender ran a towel through a wineglass and gave a knowing smirk. "Yes. I suppose all the big names come through here. I'm famous for my martinis. I favor a lemon peel over an olive. Just the peel—not the juice. It's a subtle difference, but it gives the drink a completely different identity. And everything, even a martini, wants its own identity."

Mike stifled a laugh.

"Rully? That is so completely fascinating."

"Now it's trendy to ask for sour apple martinis and wild cherry martinis and shit, pink bubblegum martinis, but trust me, there's going to be a backlash for a simpler martini with a subtle flavor."

"I'm so impressed! I will so have to try one before the end of the night," Lottie said, thrusting out her boobs. Mike took a stool next to her and cleared his throat, but she slit her eyes at him and then looked away. "Excuse me," the pompadoured bartender said as he headed to the end of the bar to take a drink order.

Mike glared at Lottie. "Nice work, Lottie. You're supposed to be helping me. Instead you're flirting with Fonzie over there."

Lottie stuck her top teeth over her lower lip and crossed her eyes. "Duh, hullo Mr. Desk Clerk, whose mouth is sewn shut except when he sucks on his manager's dick. I'm from such a major magazine and even though you'll get fired if you tell me who stays here, I'm like the nicest guy ever, even if I just fell off the turnip truck in Rochester."

Mike opened his mouth, but nothing came out. "Okay," he finally said. "Okay, Lottie Love. Let's see you work your charm. But I bet you'll get less than I did. The guy downstairs said Brooks didn't even stay here. And, for the record, I was living in Manhattan."

"Puh-lease, let me give you a dollar so you can buy a clue. No one in Hollywood uses real names. Now stop talking to me or else the bartender will never ever come back here . . . or do you want to run away from *this* story? I hear you're good at that."

Mike's heart caught in his throat. "What? What are you talking about?" His voice shook.

"Oh, nothing. Nothing at all, Mr. Sourcing Expert."

Mike grabbed her arm. "I mean it, what are you trying to say?"

"I mean, what do I know? I'm just a stupid Valley girl. *Like ohmyGod. Fer sure.*"

Mike pivoted on his stool and took a long, deep breath. So Lottie knew about the debacle in New York. He exhaled and concentrated on the rows and rows of liquor bottles lining the shelves behind the bar. From the corner of his eye, he watched Lottie dangle a cigarette out of the side of her mouth. Within seconds the bartender was back, holding out a torch of light for Lottie, even though smoking was outlawed in L.A. bars. While his heart pounded away, Mike held up a few dollars to order a Sierra Nevada Pale Ale, but the bartender ignored him.

Mike continued to look straight ahead, although he cocked his ear toward Lottie.

"So do you have any favorite celebrities that come in here?" She spoke in a husky, velvety voice.

"Ben and Matt. They're always nice. Salt of the earth. They were here a few days ago . . ."

Lottie took a long, slow drag of her Marlboro Light. She puckered her lips, and the smoke funneled up toward the ceiling. She took another labored drag, the tip of her cigarette glowing a bright orange ember. As if suddenly remembering Mike, she twisted her lips and blew smoke right into his face. Mike coughed weakly as she swiveled her chair back toward the bartender. He breathed in deep. God, she hated him. He could use a beer.

"What about that actor who's in all those action movies? You know, oh, he's really cute. I mean, he's so not as cute as you, of course. But you kinda remind me of him. You have the same biceps. Oh, what's his name?" Lottie contorted her face as if trying to pinch out a factoid. "Sebastian Brooks?"

The bartender smiled knowingly and winked. "He's actually a big fan of my martini with a lemon peel." He leaned in. "Sebs was here every night last week drinking them, one after another. He can really pound them down."

"Wow," Lottie said, batting her black-mascaraed eyelashes. "I'm such an enormous fan of his. What's he like?"

The bartender exhaled and scratched his forehead. He smiled widely as if he were a professor bestowing wisdom on an eager pupil. "Well," he whispered, leaning over the bar toward Lottie. "Let's just say he had more than his share of my martinis."

"Was his wife with him? She's beautiful."

The bartender took a deep breath, leaned closer to Lottie, and whispered as if sharing this information actually caused him great pain.

"Looks like there's big trouble in paradise for the poor guy. I spent the week acting like his personal therapist. Shit, I should have charged him, considering the elephant bucks he makes. Fifteen mil a picture is what I heard. Outrageous."

The bartender shook his head while rubbing his thumb and forefinger against the sides of his mouth. "Turns out Stephanie was yanking the wank of the producer on their latest movie. Sounds like the entire crew knew about it. The guy's not the brightest candle on the cake, if I do say so myself."

"That couldn't be more tragic. They seemed so incredibly happy. The perfect couple."

The bartender raised his brow, smiled knowingly at Lottie, and again shook his head from side to side. "If there's one thing I've learned from this job it's that nothing is what it seems. I have the richest actors, the most powerful directors, big-time movie producers getting sloshed in here nightly and crying on my $9.99 Gap T-shirt."

The bartender ran a hand through his mousse-enervated hair. *What a crock of shit just to get laid,* Mike thought.

The bartender droned on. "When poor old Brooks found out, he left the movie without finishing it. He says he's going to be sued by the producers for megabucks. He was here every night last week, drinking martinis and falling asleep at the bar. You missed it, two nights ago, he got up on the bar and sang 'Love Stinks.' He stripped down to his boxers."

The bartender swabbed the top of the bar with a towel. He raised his eyebrows and sucked on his cheeks.

"If there's one thing you learn when you're a bartender it's that there's no such thing as a perfect couple, especially in LaLa land. There ain't no such beast. No such beast a'tall."

Mike coughed into his hand to quash a laugh.

"Well, that's too bad," Lottie said in the middle of a tobacco exhale, which she again directed at Mike. Then her eyes looked past Mike in horror. She twisted her arm and dramatically checked her watch. She spoke quickly. "Your stories were so completely fascinating that I totally lost track of time. I couldn't be more late."

"You're leaving?"

"Yeah, I . . ."

Suddenly a pretty woman with long brown hair, bright red lips, and a determined glint in her almond-shaped eyes grabbed Lottie's arm.

"We need to talk."

"Not here," Lottie said through clenched teeth.

"You shouldn't be here. You're not ready. Remember, you have a disease, Lottie."

"I'm just doing my job, Catherine."

The woman surveyed the bar. "Your job description requires you to drink margaritas?"

"It's nonalcoholic."

"Yeah, right. You know, when I signed on to be your sponsor . . ."

"I know. I know, but not here." Lottie turned to Mike and stuck out her tongue. Mike grinned. So Lottie Love was an alcoholic. She knew one of his secrets, but now he knew hers. He watched as her friend pulled her out of the bar.

"Too bad. All the pretty ones are nympho party animals in their early twenties and Twelve-Steppers by twenty-five," the bartender said. Then he looked at Mike. "Hey, you wanna drink?"

"No, thanks," Mike whispered, still staring at the door even though Lottie was gone.

MIKE WATCHED AS LOTALUV peeled out of the lot. He handed his ticket to the valet and waited. "Are you Mike?" the valet asked. Mike nodded his head. "A hot chick left a note for you." He handed him a piece of paper.

Thanks so completely much for teaching a rookie the ropes.

~LL

Mike crumpled the piece of paper into a ball and threw it onto the Pepsi-can-and-newspaper-strewn floor of his car. Tomorrow he'd find his own anonymous sources. A good friend. A costar. Whatever it took. As long as he kept it fairly innocuous. Was Tom Cruise going to complain? "Why did Mike Posner write that I'm a doting father? It's a lie." No, Mike knew there was a foolproof way to lie. Tomorrow he'd find a friend who'd be in shock. Who'd talk about a party where Sebastian and Stephanie were so happy.

"They seem so much in love. I can't believe it. Why just last week, Sebs told me . . ."

Mike drove along Sunset to the 405. Even at 9:00 P.M. there was traffic on the freeway. He idled, waiting to see what the snarl was about. Sometimes traffic halted for the most inane reasons. They called rubberneckers Lookie Loos out here—and Lookie Loos were a different breed of driver. They'd brake to contemplate a stalled car, or a cop writing a ticket, or a flamingo-pink sunset. Californians seemed perpetually in a fog, their eyes never quite focused or familiar with the terrain they passed daily. Once, a truck transporting huge ceramic amusement park bears stalled and overheated on the other side of the freeway. Traffic was snagged for over an hour as each driver studied the truck's inventory as if it were a spaceship filled with aliens. Then there was a time when a truck carrying toilet paper spilled its contents. Instead of plowing over the rolls, drivers navigated their cars between the toilet paper as if each roll was a land mine. Sometimes, traffic was schizophrenic—it clogged and then dispersed for no apparent reason. Mike would search the sides of the road for an explanation for the jam and its sudden release, but there would be nothing. And rain—forget it. Californians reacted to rain the way the rest of the world reacted to mortar fire. If it's drizzling out and you need to take the freeway to your destination, you might as well stay in bed.

Mike crawled onto the 101, thrumming his hands against the wheel as if somehow that motion would unclog the artery. Up ahead, he saw the reason for the snarl: there were bright white lights illuminating the lavender sky. Helicopters whirred overhead. In a big lot beneath the helicopters a giant insect chased a crowd of people who seemed to be screaming and falling onto one another. The freeway was like a drive-in theater as drivers gawked at the movie-in-progress. Would it be next summer's blockbuster? Mike watched the giant insect as it kicked its legs and then flipped into the air. Science fiction meets martial arts most likely means box office gold, Mike figured. A car behind him honked, and Mike jolted up in his seat. He had been so busy watching he hadn't noticed traffic moving ahead of him. He hit the accelerator and craned his neck toward the insect.

***

IT TOOK MIKE close to an hour to travel the eleven-mile trek home. It was nearly ten, and he was hungry and in need of several beers to drown out thoughts of Lottie Love. He parked his car and found a seat at the counter of Jerry's Deli. Mike liked Jerry's because it reminded him of delis in New York. The walls were filled with posters advertising Broadway plays. Mickey Rooney and Anne-Margret in *Sugar Babies.* Julie Andrews in *Victor/Victoria.* Yul Brenner in *The King and I. Showboat. 42nd Street. Annie. Cats.* The ceiling was strung with a roller coaster of klieg lights clamped to metal bars, casting off yellow, blue, red, and green glows. Mike also liked Jerry's because he could eat alone at the counter without feeling like a loser. He hated sitting at a table and staring across at an empty chair. He also hated eating at a bar, where the mood of desperation mixed with expectation was as thick as the grease on the french fries.

Mike quaffed a Heineken and chewed on a corned beef on rye slathered with bright yellow mustard. He ordered another beer and then another as he listened to the nonsensical din of conversation around him. He stared at the posters as if hoping to be transmogrified back to New York when he blinked his eyes. He missed the guys in the newsrooms in Rochester and NYC. He missed Liz. He missed Mr. Cat. And though she was only a few miles away, he even missed Lottie Love.

A FEW DAYS later, Mike was sent to cover the Pediatric AIDS charity picnic. "There's a good chance Mercer will be there, and you can talk him into an interview," Vince said, nudging him. "Mingle. Interview some celebrities for our party page. Talk about the latest fashion trends. Lottie will be there. You can have her assist you."

The Pediatric AIDS picnic was an annual event where anyone with $1,000 to spare could mingle with fame. It was a petting zoo of celebrity. Wearing HERO baseball caps, celebrities manned booths while ordinary folk lined up under the guise of wanting to play games like Ducky Dash, Hoop-er-roo, Frog in a Bucket—even though what they really wanted was to shake a hand and have a picture snapped with Jack Nicholson, Robin Williams, Drew Barrymore, Heidi Klum, the cast of *That '70s Show,* the cast of *The O.C.*, the cast of *ER*. Grown men waited more than a half hour to pump Jack's hand and smile for the camera. They beamed lovingly at Jack, who grunted out a quick smile as the camera clicked.

"We'll get you out of here real soon, Mr. Nicholson. Thanks for being such a good sport," his publicist said. "Now people, give Mr. Nicholson some space. Mr. Nicholson needs some space, people."

"I'm your biggest fan. I really love your body of work."

"You're the best, Jack. I love you. I've seen everything you've done."

Seeing celebrities up close always reminded Mike of being a little kid and catching a glimpse of Mickey Mouse at Disney World. There was nothing real about Mickey, and if you looked hard enough, you could see human eyes peering out from the mask. It seemed impossible that Jack or Julia or Tom or Nicole could actually exist off screen, unless as a person in costume—another Disney attraction.

"Hey, Jack. I'm Mike Posner, with *Personality* magazine," Mike blurted out. Jack snarled and walked away. An assistant ran up to Mike and breathlessly said, "Don't you know? Jack never talks to the press. He has two rules at these events. He never takes off his sunglasses for photos, and he never grants interviews. We're just lucky he's here today, what with his schedule. He makes time for the kids."

No sign of Mercer, and he was getting nothing while Lottie flipped her hair back and chatted with Robin Williams. "Oh, you are so like the funniest man alive," she squealed.

It had to be nearly a hundred degrees out. Sweat cascaded down Mike's face as he scanned the crowd of celebrities ambling along the sprawling lawn of some media mogul who donated his property every year for this event. Stars of megawatt caliber, right in front of him, but Mike didn't even know what to ask. Their faces were a tabula rasa, and Mike felt no connection whatsoever to them. It was like trying to make small talk with that costumed Mickey Mouse. "So, how's Minnie? Do you feel rodents get a bad rap in Hollywood?" Lottie flitted about, easily conversing with some greasy-headed guys whose photos had been in the pages of *Personality.* Mike headed down the sloping lawn to the awning-topped bar. He gulped one Sierra Nevada after another, until the beer, coupled with the searing sun, left him slightly dizzy.

He was beginning to feel like a full-fledged goober, aimlessly shuffling about, notebook in hand, not knowing what to do or what to say. He headed to a table piled high with Spago pizza and grabbed a piece with mushrooms on top. Then he wandered around the periphery of the tent where the celebrity-manned booths were scattered. Lines for the hottest celebrities—Jack, Robin, Heidi, Drew, the cast of *The O.C.*—snaked along the tent and down a green sloping hill.

Lottie, probably intoxicated and therefore friendlier than ever, bounced up to him wearing mangy cutoff jean shorts, a very, very tight hot pink tank top, and Uggs that ended at her calves. "I've lit-rully talked to almost every single A-list celebrity here. Chris Mercer's publicist told me he's a no-show. He's busy filming . . . What have you done?" Mike opened his mouth, but she continued, "Don't even bother with anyone from the WB. I've talked to everyone. I've gotten some incredible stuff. Adam is soooo cute, but what's with the facial hair? I told him that he looks much, much better without it. I swear he was so completely hitting on me."

Adam? Mike had no idea who she was talking about. He occupied his mouth by cramming in pizza. "Well, it looks like there's no work left for me. Who haven't you talked to?"

Lottie grabbed Mike's beer and took a long sip.

"Are you supposed to be doing that?" Mike asked. Lottie shot him the finger. Then she pointed to the ring-toss booth. He squinted his eyes but had no idea who the celebrity was. Mike made a note to get out and see more movies.

When he reached the booth, he stood a few feet back. In Mike's distorted vision, the celebrity appeared blurry around the edges, so Mike narrowed his eyes and focused. Then he scanned his brain's index for movies and television. Nothing hit him. He turned his head to make sure Lottie had flitted away, but she was staring up at Mike, arms akimbo, watching him intensely, as if she knew he had no clue what he was doing. She wanted to see him run away. Instead, Mike moved closer to the booth.

"It's always a pleasure," the celebrity boomed, smiling broadly and patting a girl on the back. "Keep watching the show." Then he turned to Mike. "Do you want me to sign something for you?" He reached out for Mike's reporter's notebook.

"Hey, he cut in line," a child's tinny voice chimed behind Mike.

"Yeah. Wait in line like the rest of us."

Mike pulled his notebook closer to him. "I'm Mike Posner, with *Personality* magazine."

"You wanna interview me or something?"

"Sure," he said. "So, ahh, why are you here?"

"Well, Chas Notto just died of the disease. So I feel like I understand, on some level, what these people are going through."

Mike's eyes blurred as he scribbled the quote in his notebook. "Was Chas a good friend?"

Silence.

The celebrity's beaming smile collapsed into a frown.

"Huh? What?" He turned to the short, thin, bald man standing next to him. "He doesn't know who Chas was."

"Of course I know who Chas is . . . was. I was just wondering if you were good friends."

"YOU DON'T KNOW WHO CHAS IS!" The short, thin, bald man—most likely this guy's publicist—roared as spit flew out of his mouth.

A murmur rippled through the teen and tween crowd. "OhmyGod, he so completely doesn't know who Chas was."

"Du-uh."

"Live in a cave much?"

"Chas Notto is . . . was a *character* on Raymond's show, *Bel Air Belles.*" The bald man spoke in a rapid gunfire staccato. "It was only the most important story arc of the season. Do you even know what you're talking about? I keep telling the magazines not to send anyone our way unless they've done their research. Quite frankly, it's an insult. And it makes your magazine look very unprofessional."

"Hey, he butted," the chorus of kids continued.

"I was next."

"No, I was."

The publicist glared at Mike, demanding an explanation. Then he squeezed Raymond's shoulder. "You have to be living in Siberia not to know about the Chas Notto story arc."

"I was next. I was next," the kids continued.

The publicist—like all publicists—was a man with no distinguishable facial features. His remaining hair was dirty blond, and his eyes, nose, and mouth were soft and nondescript, as if his face were the host of a convention on banality. If you looked straight at him, you couldn't describe him, and once you turned away you could no longer recollect him.

Mike realized that this was why the two had chosen each other for their symbiotic relationship. With his looks, presence, and power, the celebrity is the shark. The publicist, on the other hand, is the insignificant pilot fish, eating the crumbs that fall from the shark's mouth while guiding the shark through the murky waters of fame. By associating with a man whose features are as formless as cottage cheese and whose personality is as bland as melba toast, the shark/celebrity's jagged dark features appear more striking and beautiful, his charisma more charismatic. In return, the publicist/pilot fish swims so close to the shark that he comes to believe he is the dangerous predator. He watches the other fish eye him with fear and awe and he forgets who he really is. All he knows is that he is no longer a tiny crumb-eating pilot fish. He is a shark!

"This is Raymond Young," the publicist whistled through his teeth. "He plays Lance Caine, the misunderstood pool boy with a past on the hit drama series *Bel Air Belles*. Helll-oooh! It's only the number one show on the network, and Raymond's the breakout star of the series."

"I don't have time for this," Ray huffed. "I'm here for the children."

Ray Young. He looked familiar. Then Mike flashed on the Emmys. This guy had been Lottie's date!

The publicist took a deep breath and massaged a kink in his neck as if to emphasize that this conversation was causing him undue stress. "Raymond has been working eighteen-hour days for the last few months. This is the first day he's had off in ages, and look what he's doing. Helping others. If I were you, I'd tell my editors to do a positive, inspirational-driven story on Ray."

Mike wiped the sweat from his face with the bottom of his polo shirt. "You might be on to something there," he said.

"I know I'm on to something. You wouldn't believe what wonderful things Raymond does. He visited this one girl who was dying of cancer, and, I swear, he cured her. She went into remission. That's a story for your magazine. Look, I'm doing all your work for you. You should put me on retainer. I'll show all of you how it's done."

"Come on, I was next. I was next. I can't wait any longer. Ray! Ray! I love you, Ray. I love you so much. I'd die for you, Ray. I mean it. I mean it. If God said you must die so Ray can live, I'd give my life."

The publicist threw his arms out as if embracing the pleading fan.

"Now, I must get back to the fans. That's why we're here today," he said, sweeping his arms toward the phalanx of photo seekers behind Mike. "I'm glad you had the opportunity to talk to Raymond. He rarely gives such extensive interviews. You should be very grateful."

Mike laughed. The pilot fish had no idea that it was he, and not the shark, who had done all the talking.

"OhmyGod, I'm next. I'm next. I'm going to be sick," someone squealed. Mike took a step back as a sixteen-year-old girl threw her arms around Ray, tears streaming down her face as her body convulsed. "I love you, Lance. I love you so much. I . . . OhmyGod, I can't believe it's really you. I'm with Lance Caine!"

MIKE WALKED DOWN the undulating hill toward another refreshment stand. His body felt numb, and his legs were rubbery as he treaded over the grassy berm.

"Mike?" someone yelled. "Mike." He kept walking, pretending he heard nothing. He was sure it was Lottie checking in with him. He needed another drink before he dealt with Lot A Love.

"Mike?" He realized it wasn't Lottie, for the voice had no San Fernando Valley question-mark cadence. But what other woman would call out for him?

Mike swung his head around and scanned the shorts-wearing, lemonade-sipping crowd weaving in and out of the white tents. The booze and sun had taken its toll. His sight was cloudy and his neck felt numb. "Mike." The husky voice practically tapped him on the shoulder. He turned around and there was a pretty brunette woman with familiar eyes in a lime green sundress dotted with bouquets of flowers. Mike squinted to readjust his eyes. He noticed a few other guys looking at her and pointing. She must be an actress.

"Hello, Mike. My name's Catherine Lavery. I saw you the other night . . . with Lottie."

"Oh, right. You're her . . . friend."

Since Catherine was standing at the apex of a sloping hill, Mike had to crane his neck up toward her. He strained to meet her gold-flecked blue eyes. She reminded him of someone he knew, but he couldn't place it.

"I know this isn't really my place, but I'm worried about her.

She made such progress, but I think she's . . . well, slipping. That's why I'm here, to check up on her."

"What? You paid a thousand dollars to spy on Lottie?" Mike said.

"Not exactly. My friend's the caterer. She let me come with her as long as I promised to help clean up after. Anyway, I know I probably shouldn't be talking to you about this, but, well, you seem like a nice guy. I just wondered if you could keep an eye out for her."

She grabbed his hand briefly and Mike felt a warm rush. Maybe someone as caring as this Catherine would be able to overlook his inadequacies.

"Sure."

"Thank you, Mike. When Lottie told me how much she hated you, I knew you had to be a good person."

"What? She hates me?"

"Don't take it personally. She hates all good people right now. She just wants to be around enablers."

They exchanged business cards.

"I'll help any way I can," Mike said. "Maybe we can talk about this over dinner?"

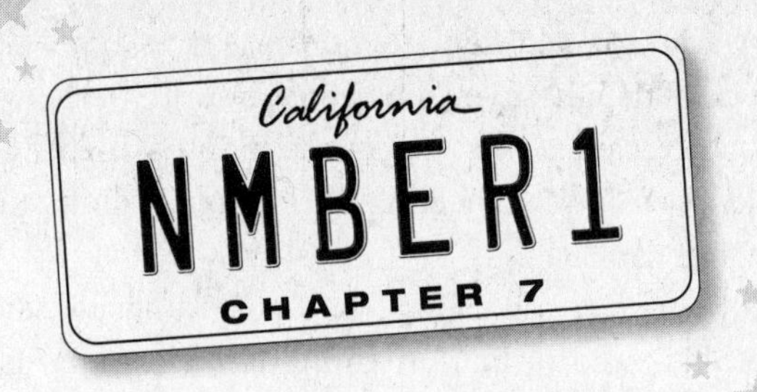

SHE TOLD HER THERAPIST THE STORY. WHEN RAY STARTED TO snore, Lottie slithered out from underneath her log-cabin shelter, collected her stuff, and raced into the cold Los Angeles night wearing only skimpy lingerie. Catherine, of course, had been waiting for her. She followed her home and made her a cup of hot chocolate. She even helped Lottie hang the *Bel Air Belles* poster she'd stolen from Ray's closet. *Will the real Lance Caine please bend over?*

"I couldn't be more sorry about the alien thing," she told Catherine.

"Forget it. I've done a lot worse under the influence."

"I doubt it. I've never met anyone like you. Sometimes you seem too good."

"I'm not. Trust me. My own father can't stand me."

"Yeah, right." Lottie laughed. "My father's Hank Love Plumbing. You know, *We'll make your pipes sing*. The van with the smiling man in the white outfit painted on it. When I was born, he wanted to paint me next to him."

Catherine smiled. "That's sweet."

"That couldn't be more embarrassing."

"Not at all. At least your father acknowledges you. My father has erased me from his life. I haven't seen him in years."

"What an asshole."

"I don't know. I think I must have done some screwed-up things to make him hate me so much."

Lottie stared hard at Catherine, wondering what this woman

could have done to make her father despise her. Catherine seemed like the type of daughter you'd want to show off to the world, not disown. Lottie realized that in her six months at AA, Catherine hadn't said a word in the meetings. Lottie really didn't know anything about her.

"I did all my revealing a long time ago," Catherine said. "I hate public speaking more than anything. It makes me sick to my stomach. I'd only get up there if someone forced me. Now I'm just there for the camaraderie."

Lottie thought about telling Catherine everything, but she was really enjoying her company. She imagined even Catherine would have her limits. She could handle Lottie's aliens and bar hopping, but the truth would be too much.

Instead, she loaned Catherine a pair of flannel pajamas and popped up some Paul Newman no-butter corn. Then they flopped on the couch to watch one of Lottie's all-time favorites, *Four Weddings and a Funeral.*

"I love Hugh Grant," Catherine said.

"I couldn't love him more." Lottie smiled so hard it hurt her cheeks. She couldn't remember the last time she'd had a girls' night.

SHE TOLD LIPLESS everything. That is, everything but the name. "It's this actor who couldn't be more on the hottest show on television. But that's really all I'm going to say."

Lottie's therapist pursed her thin, bloodless lips and sighed. "How does this make you feel, Lottie?"

"Well, like I said, it was pretty uncomfortable and kind of like, tacky. I still have this huge bump on the top of my head. I seriously almost passed out. How embarrassing would that have been?"

"Lottie, do you feel used at all? Do you feel taken advantage of?" Then Lipless paused, jotted down some notes, and with a wide-eyed smirk, said nearly breathlessly, "Now who did you say this actor was?"

Nice try. Lottie smiled smugly and tossed her hair back. Not everyone could be in the inner circle. Maybe Lottie should barter with her. Tell Lipless that she'll tell all for twenty free sessions or something.

"I just don't feel like very comfortable about revealing any more than I have. I lit-rully haven't told anyone, except . . . a friend. Even my editor doesn't know, and this would like be such a major scoop for the magazine. I am so not kidding. But how would I look? How totally psychotic is that? Hanging under a bed like a crazy person?"

"I understand, Lottie, but remember everything you tell me is confidential. Nothing leaves this room. I could never betray a patient's trust. Now, who was it? Come on, you can tell me."

Lottie decided she should be charging Lipless instead of the other way around.

LIVE! WEDNESDAYS AT 5:00 P.M.: LOTTIE LOVE REVEALS ALL ON THE NEXT DR. LIPLESS

Her therapist breathed deep. "Okay. Okay. I don't have to know," she said, wrinkling her face in disappointment. Then she smiled sweetly and cooed. "But if you ever want to tell me, you know I'm here for you. Remember my motto: If you want to heal, you must reveal." She smoothed out the front of her tan linen suit and coughed into her hand to regain composure. "Let's see if you can try something for our next session? Okay? I'd like you to go out with someone who isn't an actor. Can you do that?"

"Can't you just prescribe Wellbutrin?"

Her therapist squeezed her hands together on her lap as if pleading. "Just try. Let's see what happens and we'll talk about it next week."

"I'm not sure if I'll do it."

But perhaps her therapist was right. Lottie had been dating actors exclusively for nearly a year now, and what had it gotten her? A night hiding under a bed. A few flings. A case of crabs.

She knew her coworkers called her a starfucker behind her back. The women in the office were jealous of her, and the men—even the married ones—were pissed because she wouldn't do any of them. They imitated her by jutting out their chests and sticking out their asses. She couldn't help it if she was a 38C or that proper posture gave her a J.Lo booty.

But in L.A., being a starfucker is neither an insult nor a compliment. Lottie, like most people born and bred there, understood that. The transplants from the East Coast and Middle America acted so above it. But given a chance, they were dying to screw some famous ass, you betcha. As Lottie saw it, the mother pimps the daughter off to a successful oncologist and everyone pretends it's some fairy-tale union. Nobody calls her a doctorfucker; instead she's a princess in a white dress. Lottie made all her own choices, and they still called her a slut behind her back. Whatever. Who cared what a bunch of no-name idiots thought?

But maybe, just maybe, she was ready for something a little more meaningful. Maybe, dare she say, she was ready for a relationship.

But she didn't know any nonactors except for the people she worked with. Most of them were married or too old, except that new guy Mike, who definitely had the hots for her. But even though he was older than she was, he seemed much younger. He was cute, but something was not quite right. His face was too boyish—his eyes bugged out sometimes when he spoke, and at other times his heavy lids made him look drowsy. So he either seemed wide awake or half asleep, but never just normal. He was like one of those Claymation characters from the Sunday morning cartoons she had watched as a kid. All big eyes and innocence, and that always translated into lousy in bed. Lottie had a feeling the guy was hung like a mosquito. And she was almost never wrong when it came to guessing penis size. Those guys gave off an aura. Mike had this forced cockiness about him.

Mike bragged about being a big-shot reporter in Manhattan, but she knew he'd only done that for a few months because he couldn't take the pressure. He was really a hick from Rochester, and even though he tried to fight his hickness, it was all over him. He looked like he was opening his big dopey eyes for the first time. He even tried to impress her at Bar Marmont with his pitiful newspaperman skills, but he had just humiliated himself and she ended up getting the story. A hick is a few links in the food chain below a Valley girl, Lottie understood.

But she tried dating nonactors anyway. She dated a waiter at Chateau Marmont, but he turned out to be a struggling actor. So was the teller at Bank of America, the mechanic at Texaco, the deliveryman from Chin Chin, her dentist, even the lawyer with Universal. She went out a few times with a pilot and liked the idea of him in a cockpit, navigating a plane. After a few dates, he confessed he really wanted to be a movie star. The next day he quit his job and became an extra in a Tom Cruise movie.

There. Enough was enough. She'd proved it to herself; and now her therapist would have nothing to say. Lottie could teach that lipless bitch a few things. She'd tell her, "There are two kinds of people in the world: stars and those who want to be around them." Lottie Love was not going to spend her life around the latter. No way! Everyone in the world wanted to be a star, so why even waste time on anything but the real thing? She thought about how her elementary school principal fawned over the action actor and dismissed her father. That was not going to happen to her—ever.

But Lottie knew she was getting up there. She was still young enough, but by thirty, she'd be ancient in a town obsessed with youth. She was no dope. When her mother was Lottie's age, Lottie was already three. Eventually she'd have to get in a relationship that lasted more than a month or two.

How did she get to be old enough to be seriously called a woman? She wasn't exactly sure when that happened. But it was like wearing makeup: one day you play with your mother's blush and eyeliner. A few years later, you wear it defiantly to school, even though it looks more like a clown's mask. And then, without warning, it's expected of you—because without it you look dull and anemic. And you secretly wish you were six again, when the compact and lipstick case on your mother's bureau were like passports into exotic lands that you would never be old enough to enter.

LOTTIE'S FINANCIAL SITUATION was also a bad subject. When Vince Reggio told her that she was no longer an intern and he was putting her on staff, she was so excited that she forgot to ask about money. Besides, he acted like he was doing her a big favor. Finally, after she thanked him like she was some homeless person he had handed a dollar, he said with a broad smile, "Don't you want to know how much we're going to pay you?"

"Oh, right, of course," she answered, sounding confused and disheveled.

"Thirty-five thousand dollars to start—and we'll evaluate you after a year." Vince beamed at her like she had just won the door prize at some game show.

But Lottie was ecstatic. She had gone from making no money to having a real salary! Lottie finally felt appreciated.

All that changed when she discovered how much Mike was making.

She'd been in Vince's office discussing the parties she was reporting on that week when Vince's phone rang. While Vince took the call, Lottie inventoried his mahogany desk. There on top of an avalanche of press releases and movie invitations was Mike's contract. Contract! Vince hadn't handed Lottie any such official document! And it said his salary would be seventy-five thousand dollars. What a crock! All that money for a guy who hadn't even heard of *Bel Air Belles* or Marlon Lang or Sebastian Brooks or Ray Young. He was completely lame! Lottie wanted to slam her fist on Vince's desk and tell him that this was an outrage! Anger coursed through her veins and blinded her.

Every day since then she'd thought about it, how Mike's worth was more than double hers. She couldn't afford her dump of an apartment without a roommate. She couldn't pay off her debts. She cobbled together a wardrobe from Loehmann's, Express, and the *Personality* fashion closet. Every day she considered marching into Vince's office and telling him he'd made a big mistake. Lipless said it was Lottie's own fault for being nosy. She had no right to snoop around. But wasn't being nosy her job? Vince should appreciate her nosiness.

"*You're a real reporter, Lottie,*" he'd say. "*We can't keep anything from you.*"

Lottie Love was pissed. She could barely even look at Mike, with his newborn chick eyes that seemed to be looking at the world for the first time and begging for help. Every time she saw the Hick, anger festered in her. Mr. Hot-Shot New York Reporter—what crap! He couldn't keep up with her, and he knew it. But Vince had no idea. In Vince's Gerber Baby brain, she was a big-breasted bimbo and the Hick was the ace reporter.

AFTER SHE GOT the scoop from the Bar Marmont bartender, Lottie floored it all the way back to the office, where she wrote up her report. At the top of her article, she scribbled:

Note: This is from Lottie Love.
Mike Posner will send his report up separately.

THE TRUTH ABOUT STEPHANIE WINTERS AND SEBASTIAN BROOKS

By Lottie Love,
Chief Party Correspondent

According to sources who are thisclose to the couple, Stephanie Winters began having a lust-filled affair with a producer on the set of the couple's recent movie, so ironically titled *Til Death Do Us Part.* The oh so hunky Brooks has been literally drowning his sorrows at Bar Marmont, where he had been totally living for the past two weeks and ordering many, many martinis with lemon peels in them. Last Saturday, he stripped down to his boxers and sang "Love Stinks" for the bar.

"He's a very talented singer, and the women went wild," said a source.

According to my extremely exclusive source, he left his latest movie without completing it. The sexy Winters is living with the producer, who is going to sue Sebastian for not finishing the movie even though he is sleeping with Sebastian's wife. But that's Hollywood. Movies come before love. "Looks like there's trouble in paradise for the poor guy," my close source says. "He is such a mess."

Lottie couldn't wait for Mike to get reamed out for shirking his responsibilities. She expected Vince to call her into his office and confess, *"Lottie, we aren't paying you nearly what you deserve. You're the best."*

Vince would see her as she saw herself—as their mouthpiece. *Lottie Love: She makes their words sing.* It didn't get any bigger than *Personality*. It didn't get better than Lottie Love, Chief Party Correspondent. Seasoned with a year's experience, Lottie understood celebrity. And she helped the world—the fat, bored, lazy world sprawled on a Barcalounger with the remote in one hand and Doritos in the other—understand them.

Instead, her hard work went unnoticed—as usual. The next day, Sebastian and Stephanie's publicist announced that after a brief separation, the couple who had tied with Brad and Jen as *Personality*'s Happiest Couple of 2004 was back together.

"We have been so busy working that we neglected the things that are really important to us. We have decided to take a much needed vacation," the Happiest Couple announced through a press release.

After a few desperate and breathy calls from Cyndi Bowman about her clients' privacy, Vince decided to drop the entire article. "Sometimes, we have to take the high road." He smiled dreamily, most likely thinking of the favors Cyndi promised if the story didn't run.

Yeah, and sometimes you have to get laid, Lottie thought.

"SEE WHAT HAPPENS when you try to be devious?" Lipless droned. "It always backfires on you. Now, if this money issue really bothers you, why don't you talk to Vince about it? Tell him you feel you're worth more. Tell him about your contributions, and see what he says. Don't come across hostile. Approach this in a friendly manner."

Despite all the bad advice Lipless had given her, Lottie decided to try it. And of course, it backfired. "As with all the other correspondents, you'll be reviewed at the end of the year. We'll make a determination then," Vince said, picking up the phone so she'd get the hint that the subject was dropped. Lottie stood there, her mouth hanging open.

"End of story, Lottie." Vince began dialing a number.

"But . . . but, I like feel I've done a really good job here."

Vince exhaled, rolled his eyes, and then flashed a steely grin. "Let's see how the end of the year pans out and then decide. We'll see how many scoops you clinch for the home team, okay? Until then, don't drop the ball." He looked back at the phone and finished dialing. Lottie spun around and tore out of the office. Didn't they get it? Gerber Baby, the Drunk, the Hick, Fat-Ankled Bernie. Lottie Love was better than any of them!

LOTTIE SCHEDULED A LUNCH with Cyndi Bowman. They met at Kate Mantilini's, a big, chaotic, barnlike restaurant on Wilshire. Cyndi was sitting at a booth underneath black-and-white photographs of sweaty boxers in midpunch when Lottie arrived. She was on her cell phone but gestured for Lottie to sit down while she finished the call.

"I can't believe how unprofessional you are," Cyndi huffed into the phone. "We've had to do all the work. You should be cheering to have this kind of access to such a major, major star. Instead, *we* picked the location for the photo shoot. *We* had to arrange hair and makeup, and you're not even buying the clothes for her! Quite frankly, I'm about to have a complete meltdown over this whole article. Period. I don't want to talk about this anymore."

Lottie watched Cyndi's lips flex and made a note to find out the name of her lipstick.

"What?" Lottie watched as Cyndi's eyes nearly popped out of her skull. "That is completely ridiculous. She is twenty-seven and that's final. I won't have you writing that she is thirty-three despite what her mother told you. Her mother is wrong! Completely wrong. What does her mother know anyway—they've been estranged for years . . . I'm not even having this conversation with you . . . What? . . . If you print that she is in her thirties, I'll shut down all access by your magazine. You'll never interview another one of my clients again. She is twenty-seven! Two-seven, get it? Got it? Good. This conversation is officially over."

Cyndi punched the End button with a bloodred fingernail and threw the cell phone on the table. "These journalists. We get them an interview with one of the biggest, hottest celebrities on the planet, and instead of kissing our ass, they want more and they want to print things that just aren't true." Cyndi shook her hands in the air as if she was wringing a writer's neck. "Anyway, I don't want to bore you with my mundane problems. Just another day in the exciting life of Cyndi Bowman. By the way, you look so good and thin. You're practically anorexic."

"I wish. I feel as fat as a house next to you. You're emaciated," Lottie gushed. "You so completely look Third World."

After they ordered identical Chinese tofu salads with low-cal vinaigrette on the side, Cyndi handed Lottie a thick white envelope. "I've put together a package for you with all my up-and-coming clients. If you ask me, they're all worthy of cover stories. So, take a look when you have a chance, and see if you can get *Personality* to do some articles on them. They're all going to be like the Next Big Thing. My advice to you is to catch them now, while you still can, because believe you me, they're going places.

They won't want to have anything to do with *Personality* in a few months."

They munched on their roughage.

"So how's Vince Reggio doing?" Cyndi asked, curling a piece of hair around her finger. "By the way, you've got vinaigrette all over your chest."

Lottie grimaced and began rubbing her camisole with water. Why hadn't she brought a cardigan?

Cyndi's phone trilled. "Ugh," she sighed, rolling her eyes and shaking her head. "Don't ever run your own company. It's more trouble than it's worth, believe you me." Cyndi jabbed a button and put the phone to her ear. "Hullo," she sighed, sucking her cheeks. "Oh, God, what is it this time? Oh my God, no. FUCK. No! Jesus. Okay. I'll be there right away."

Cyndi poked the End button and tossed the phone down. She buried her head in her hands and roughly rubbed her temples with her fingertips. "Fuck," she snarled. Then she stabbed her fork into a chunk of baby greens.

"Is everything okay?" Lottie asked.

Cyndi held up a finger and chewed on the lettuce. Then she chugged down some ice tea. "My father," she said into the glass, staring at her brown lipstick stains. She drained the remainder of her drink. She rested her head in her hands.

"Oh, is he interfering with how you run the company?" Lottie groaned, twirling a strand of auburn hair. "Don't even get me started. My father is Hank Love. You've probably seen his trucks barreling around town? I mean, how could you not? Talk about completely humiliating. He's got these humongous billboards of himself on both sides of the truck. He wanted to paint me on the side, too, but my mom talked him out of it. I'd be in therapy like every minute of my life instead of every other minute."

Lottie leaned into the table, a breast resting on her dish. "I think you're doing such a fantastic job. You guys are amazing. You have like every Next Big Thing. And you have Chris Mercer. I'd do anything to do an interview with him."

Cyndi raised her finger to the waitress to summon the check. "I'm going to have to go now." She hoisted another batch of lettuce to her mouth.

Lottie studied her. Maybe she should start dressing in stylish professional suits like Cyndi, who was wearing a taupe Calvin Klein jacket and skirt with an ivory silk shirt underneath. All of a sudden Lottie felt ridiculous in her clunky shoes and stained spandex shirt and little swatch of a waist-tied pleated skirt. She had felt sexy when she left her home this morning, but now she realized she needed to overhaul her wardrobe. Maybe she and Cyndi could go shopping together at the Beverly Center. As soon as she finagled that raise.

Cyndi swirled out a signature on the receipt. She gulped her iced tea and cleared her throat. "I don't want to freak you out or anything. But that was my secretary . . . my father just died."

Lottie choked in the middle of a gulp of her iced tea. "OhmyGod," she shrieked. "I'm so sorry."

Cyndi pursed her lips, running a thumb and forefinger along their rims.

"Are you okay? Can I do anything? Maybe you shouldn't drive in your condition."

Cyndi smiled, reached over, and squeezed Lottie's arm. "I'm fine," she said. She pulled out her lipstick and slowly smeared it on. She sniffed dramatically.

"I've just got to go. Head to Santa Barbara and have a good cry. I'm so completely numb right now. Maybe it will hit me when I get there. Maybe not. It's hard to tell. No, I'm sure once I get there, I'll be bawling like a baby. I'll be inconsolable. I better go now or I'll start to lose it."

As she spoke, she waved the tube of lipstick through the air. Honey Nut Brown, Lottie noticed.

Cyndi stood up and Lottie followed her. "I feel like I should like do something for you," Lottie said. "I'm like so on the verge of crying just thinking about how you must feel."

"No. I'm fine," Cyndi said, leaning in with a hydrofoil kiss.

"What you can do for me is read the packet I gave you. Get some of those actors in *Personality*."

"Okay," Lottie said as she gave Cyndi a quick hug. "If you need anything, just call." She tilted her head at Cyndi, narrowed her eyes, sniffled, and pinched her face in sadness. "I'm, like, soooosoooooo sorry."

BACK AT THE office, Lottie ran into Lem at the fax machine. He was staring at its buttons trying to figure out what to press, listlessly clutching his cup of Starbucks. From the back, he looked sad and vulnerable. His gray hair was cut to the base of his head and stubble was growing out along the top of his neck where the barber must have shaved it. Lottie felt sorry for Lem Brac. He seemed like the kind of guy who'd been run over by the world. She remembered him saying at a few meetings that he was good friends with Cyndi's father.

Should she tell him?

"Umm . . . Lem," she said softly.

Lem turned and squinted at her, as if trying to place her. She realized she hadn't really spoken to him since their lunch when she first started. She'd never really looked at him before. There was something familiar about those eyes. She suddenly felt like she knew him.

"Yes, Miss Love?"

"I don't know how to tell you this, but Thom Bowman is . . . ah . . . dead?"

"Thomas Bowman? Dead? Thom. Dead. Dead?" Lottie noticed that his bottom lip started quivering. "I just saw him. Just the other day."

Lem stared beyond Lottie as his eyes misted over. "Thomas," he said. "He was one of the last of the real men. A true friend. My only friend. He's the one who told me to always remember that they're not your friends."

Lem's papers fell out of his hands and drifted to the floor, but he didn't seem to notice. Lottie saw the cover page—*They're Not*

Your Friends by Lem Brac, it said. Maybe Lem was scamming them all, working on a book while getting paid to do nothing at the magazine. Maybe he wasn't such a loser.

Lem cupped a hand to his mouth and stared intently at something beyond Lottie, but when Lottie turned her head to see what it was, nothing was there.

Lottie felt foolish standing there, but she didn't know what to do. Like a zombie, Lem picked up the papers and then staggered back to his office. Lottie considered following him and asking if there was anything she could do. But, truth be told, Lottie didn't want to set foot in that dim, creepy room filled with pictures of has-beens unknown to Lottie Love, who was aware of all Big Things.

Besides, Lottie already had a plan. She'd head to Santa Barbara for the funeral. Maybe if Cyndi saw her there, supporting her through her grief, she'd hand her an exclusive with Chris Mercer. She'd attend the funeral, tell Cyndi that she'd lost her mother a few years ago and understood her pain. Then she'd have the rest of the day to soak up the sun. She'd convince Vince to let her expense a hotel there. After all, she was Lottie Love, Chief Party Correspondent. And she was highly underrated.

AN ENDLESS ROW OF OLEANDER ADORNS THE MEDIAN OF THE Camino Real freeway heading into Santa Barbara. As Mike's Saab whooshed by, the flowers danced in his turbocharged wake. With their white petals they resembled waves foaming and tumbling into a gray asphalt ocean. A few miles down the freeway, as Mike passed signs advertising fresh strawberries, seedless grapes, and juicy avocados, their color switched to candy pink, then flaming red, and then back to white. Lem remembered he once had a few oleanders perched in Greco-Roman urns on his deck. Those, too, were dead.

Mike and Lem were headed to Thomas Bowman's funeral at the Prince of Peace Presbyterian Church in Santa Barbara. Even though Mike had never met Thom, he had agreed to drive to the service. Vince had suggested that Mike go with Lem to represent *Personality* magazine. Lem knew the rumor was that Cyndi Bowman's biggest client—Chris Mercer—might show up.

Despite the motives, Lem was pleased that Mike was behind the wheel while he watched the flowers riot from the passenger side window. Even though they were only a few miles outside Los Angeles, it felt like another country. Lem stared out as they zoomed through dusty towns dotted with RV parks, spa stores, and satellite dishes. These towns disappeared, and soon they hit outlet shops and malls disguised as Spanish villas.

Adidas. Calvin Klein. Ann Taylor. Bass. Chico's. Hugo Boss. Izod. Casual Male Big & Tall. Nike. Maidenform. Bass. Sports Chalet. Baby City. Marshall's. Babies-R-Us. Chili's. Toys-R-Us. The Gap.

Old Navy. Friday's. McDonald's. Olive Garden. Carl's Jr. Taco Bell. El Pollo Loco. Coco's.

"We've hit the real oasis in the desert," Lem mused. "The consumer oasis. Shop till you drop. Drive your family out to the desert and buy some shirts at the Ralph Lauren outlet. Drive home, feeling fulfilled and satisfied with the money you saved. A real Polo shirt for a quarter of the price. Then you realize the buttons are missing, the stitching is off. The color isn't fashion forward."

Mike laughed. And Lem began to think that Mike was an all-round good bloke, although he had an annoying habit of pointing out every vanity plate they passed.

"SOCCRMA. Isn't that cute," Mike said while thumping on the wheel of his car. "LNDLRD. Oh, God. That person wants us all to know he owns property, even though he drives a piece of shit Hyundai. Look at that Porsche. It says TOY4DR. God, that's just about the worst I've ever seen."

"HME4SLE. Oh, home for sale. Gee, I wonder if that's a realtor, duh . . . 7HANDICP. Yeah, I bet. Oh, and look at that one—EST8ESQ. Well, we're all impressed."

There were STAR2BS, GR8M8S, and 12STPERS. Some guy in a Chevy pickup LUVCUBS. Some girl in a Honda Civic LUVGSUS. Some woman in a silver Jaguar LUVHUBE. Mike noticed them all.

POOR MIKE STILL wasn't getting laid. Lem could tell the minute he opened the car door to an avalanche of newspapers and magazines crammed onto the passenger seat. Good-looking guy, too—*the kind of looks women go for,* Lem thought. With his innocent wide eyes, disheveled tousle of hair, and wrinkled khakis, he looked like he needed to be taken care of. But Mike was too uptight. Sometimes these Americans just didn't know how to have fun. Mike probably couldn't get his John Thomas up unless he thought he was in love. Noble, but naive. This was Los Angeles. Lem realized shortly after leaving his mother country for the city of silicone that out here, love didn't translate very well off-screen.

In Hollywood, a person needed to recover from a fatal disease or an apocalyptic-style disaster to realize that he was in love with the beautiful woman he couldn't stand a mere ninety minutes earlier. When the credits started rolling, you wondered for a second how those two would survive now that there were no more ax murderers or typhoons or metastasizing malignancies. But then the lights switched on and the ushers opened the doors and you were back outside, hoping for an incurable ailment, an avalanche, or a plague so you, too, could find true happiness.

"So Thom Bowman was a good friend of yours?" Mike asked Lem after they had traveled in silence for several minutes.

"Yes. One of the best. This guy was a class act. Not like the people running the show now. You have to take a crap for them so they can analyze it and determine if you're worthy of a few minutes in their celebrity's presence. Thom loved the press. He understood what we needed and he accommodated us. He got me some big interviews. And if you left a message for him, ol' Thomas Bowman was certain to get back to you within two hours, not a minute later. Two hours on the nose, no matter what. It was a policy he lived by."

Lem cleared his throat while Mike fumbled with the air conditioner.

"Thom was the only person I completely trusted. There are very few people you can trust in this town, I'm sure you're discovering this. For years, Thom begged me to work for him. He even talked about making me a partner, putting my name on the firm and everything. But I turned him down. I thought I had to be loyal to my craft or something. What bloody horseshit!"

"So, do you regret it?"

"Well, Michael, I always doubted my decision, especially when the tide changed at *Personality* and that jetsam named Vincent Reggio washed ashore. But then I got a whiff of that bloody daughter ol' Thom sired. I think I would have killed myself or slit her throat and hung her out a window if we had had to work together. Have you met her?"

"Yeah. Bad nose job and nightmare personality. Great legs, though."

Lem laughed and shook his head. "Poor Thomas. I don't know how a guy like that could have a daughter like her, but he did. Thom was too busy running shop, I guess." He looked out the window. "Look to your left."

Mike turned his head. There in her red convertible VW with the top down was Lottie Love. Her auburn hair was blowing behind her and her mouth was wide open, shouting lyrics to some song Lem was certain not to recognize. As if sensing their gaze, she turned her face toward them, her eyes hidden behind amber-tinted Fendi wrap sunglasses. Mike recognized them from a story Lottie had written a few weeks earlier. She tossed a cigarette stub out the window, flashed a smile, and accelerated.

"LOTALUV," Mike said, squeezing the accelerator.

"What's she doing heading our way? There must be some big celebrity bash in Santa Barbara. A party for the Next Big Thing, no doubt."

"Not quite," Mike said slowly. "She's going to the funeral."

Lem gasped. "You must be bloody joking."

Mike hiccuped out his nose. "Oh, according to Vince, Lottie's becoming titty buddies with Cyndi Bowman. She told Vince she thought it would really help her efforts if she attended the funeral, paid her respects, played good mourner, and then groveled for an interview with Chris Mercer. She thinks of Cyndi as her new best friend."

"Lovely. Absolutely lovely."

"She even convinced Vince that she needed to spend the night in Santa Barbara. She's staying at the Biltmore."

The freeway opened up on the shimmering Pacific, where craggy hills garnished with yellow wildflowers slid into the ocean. Lem watched as tiny boats cut a white swath of foam through the inky glass and surfers paddled out on their boards. On the shore side, they passed signs advertising antique shops and farm-fresh fruits and vegetables.

"Get off at this exit," Lem said sharply.

"Isn't this too soon?" Mike followed Lem's directions, but they didn't lead to a church. Instead they were in front of a cart topped with a big hot dog that read SURF DOGS. They got out of the Saab.

"What are we doing here?"

"These are the best hot dogs in all of California." Lem ordered a Surf Dog with onions and sauerkraut. "Please don't tell me you're a vegan. I loathe all people who feel superior to us carnivores and yet inferior to pigs. Every now and then one must poison oneself with nitrates and pig entrails."

Mike slathered his dog with ketchup and mustard. They sat at a picnic bench next to a small garden filled with purple and orange ice plants and paddle cacti.

"My deck used to have . . ." Lem shook his head and cleared his throat. "We found this place years and years ago. I've never been here with anyone but Bowman. If you follow the path behind the railroad tracks, you'll find a sea lion rookery. I'm told there are hundreds frolicking on the beach there. Supposed to be quite spectacular."

"You haven't seen it?"

"It's a hike, ol' boy. Nearly a half mile from here to the ocean. Besides, we were always heading off for libations somewhere. Or we were already staggering by the time we got here."

Mike glanced at his watch. "We only have a couple miles left and the service is in over an hour. Let's go find the sea lions."

"As I said, it is quite a hike. Quite a hike."

"Come on, the only time I ever see the ocean is in movies."

The next thing he knew, Lem was swallowing the end of his dog and following Mike on a narrow dirt path toward the rookery. "Come to think of it, I don't believe I've ever seen a sea lion before," Lem said as he peeled off his blazer. "Except on the telly. I'm told that you can't get too close or the mothers get scared and they'll abandon their babies on shore. I'd hate to have that on my conscience. Did I mention that it's quite a hike?"

Lem huffed as they treaded through a field of overgrown grass and yellow wildflowers. They crossed railroad tracks before reaching a rocky promontory overlooking a horseshoe-shaped piece of shore littered with what looked like slabs of rock.

Mike shielded his eyes with a hand and scanned the beach as he panted. "I don't see anything. Maybe they're all mating."

"Look harder," Lem said excitedly when he realized that the rocks were actually moving. "Those aren't bloody rocks! They're sea lions," he squealed, surprised at the enthusiasm in his voice. "Bloody sea lions all over the bloody beach!"

Lem nearly leapt off the edge of the precipice to gawk. The sea lions were stretching their sleek bodies, rolling along the sand, splashing in the foamy water.

"I had no idea there'd be so many. They're absolutely marvelous. And huge. They're as big as elephants."

He watched them, mesmerized by their big eyes and round, innocent faces. They reminded him of children romping on a beach. Why hadn't he had children? Lem thought about the man with his kids at the motel years and years ago. Even then, Lem felt that it would never happen for him. But why? He had been young. He could have changed. A childless life is a life with no purpose. Even the sea lions know that. Lem looked over at Mike, who was sitting on a rock, staring down at the creatures. Lem judged the guy for having newspapers on the seat of his Saab and not living life to the fullest, when he'd done the same thing himself. But Mike had his whole life in front of him. It was too late for Lem.

"Don't let the flowers die," Lem whispered.

"Huh?"

"Just always take care of the important things—the things that make you happy—because it's easy to neglect them; and then, one day, they're no longer around. The flowers die and the butterflies disappear, and one day you realize that you haven't been happy for quite some time because of it. Nothing is better for your soul than a garden full of butterflies."

"Hey, Lem, I'm sorry about your friend," Mike said softly.

"Good friends are a rarity, that's for sure."

"I haven't made one friend since I've been out here," Mike said.

Lem tapped Mike's head. "Nonsense. What am I?"

Smiling, Mike checked his watch. "Hey, so much for this love-fest, we're gonna be late."

"Okay, son," Lem quietly said.

Son.

THEY EXITED IN downtown Santa Barbara. Lem read aloud directions while Mike navigated through the eucalyptus- and palm tree–shaded streets until they arrived in front of a small Spanish-style chapel with a turreted terra-cotta roof. A sign encased in glass at the front of the church's patch of emerald lawn read, "To love a butterfly you must care for a caterpillar." "Everyone's a writer," Lem grumbled while shaking his head. Then he fixed his hair with a comb that was missing half its teeth and tightened his red-and-blue striped tie. He popped three BreathSavers in his mouth.

Nearby, Lottie was standing by her car, applying some shade of brown lipstick while staring at herself in the driver's side mirror. Lem caught Mike peeking at her breasts, which were ballooning out of the otherwise surprisingly conservative black suit.

"She's quite proud of her prow," Lem whispered. "I think you two would make a cute couple. Maybe you have more in common than meets the eye."

Mike jerked his head back and narrowed his eyes at Lem. "Yeah, right," he said, pursing his lips. But Lem couldn't help notice that the boy's face turned red at his suggestion.

Lem headed toward Lottie.

"Would you be so kind as to accompany us, Miss Love?" Lem said with a gallant swirl of his hand. "Mr. Posner and I would greatly appreciate it."

Lottie raised her lips into a smile and just as quickly slammed them into a frown. "Thanks. But I like promised some of Cyndi's coworkers that I'd wait for them. We so want to like be a kind of united front for her. I mean I was like lit-rully there when Cyndi heard the horrible news."

LEM AND MIKE sat toward the back of the church, watching the circus of demi- and pseudocelebrities vie with the coffin for attention. There were women in big hats and impenetrable sunglasses dramatically weaving tissues through the air. There were perfectly coiffed men in black Armani, their eyes scanning the church for the A-list pews. Lem imagined each slipping an usher a couple of bills to be closer to the casket. He laughed at the thought, and then the organ wheezed a dirge while the Bowman family dragged themselves down the red-carpeted aisle. Lem caught a glimpse of a black-bedecked Cynthetica in an umbrella-sized hat with what looked like mosquito netting in front of it. She held a cluster of tissues to her nose and leaned on her mother.

Lem craned his neck and realized he didn't know anyone. The church was filled with faces he had never seen or no longer recognized due to surgical alterations or botulism paralysis. Lem's eyesight blurred as tears fogged his vision. He didn't know if the tears were for Thom or himself. He felt as much in that casket as his dead friend.

Lem was lost in his thoughts when he saw Cyndi stride up to the podium sans headpiece. She cleared her throat, dabbed the corners of her eyes with the tip of a tissue. She smiled weakly. She pulled a piece of paper out of her jacket pocket and methodically unfolded it right into the microphone, where it crackled as if the church were on fire.

"My father, Thomas Bowman, taught me everything I know," she began, her mouth practically inhaling the microphone. "Thomas Bowman was the best in the business. I grew up knowing that about him, and I wanted to be just like my daddy. That's all I wanted in life, to be like my hero, my father."

Cyndi breathed deeply, blotting her eyes and placing a red-nailed hand at her throat as if gasping for air. "I promise to live up to his memory." She pounded her fist lightly on the podium like some anemic revivalist. "I want to carry the torch my father lit so proudly. Thomas Bowman is dead. We will all mourn him. But his name will live on eternally at Bowman Publicity. He will be forever immortalized through the celebrities he so brilliantly represented. He may not have a star on the Hollywood Walk of Fame, but he deserves a little piece of every star."

The sniffling congregation erupted into earsplitting applause. Cyndi covered her face with her hands, and her body convulsed with sobs. The crowd applauded and applauded. Lem wondered if they'd ever stop.

AFTER THE SERVICE, about two hundred mourners headed to Thom's. The gathering was held outside on the interminable green lawn tucked between an ostrich farm and a horse stable. Lem's eyes immediately gravitated to the white tented bar, which was set up next to what appeared to be a tribute table. The table was littered with framed photographs, but Lem was too far away to see all but one. In the center of the white-linen tablecloth was an ornate gilt-framed shot of Thom flanked by Arnold and Maria. Lem knew that Thom had met the two on a few occasions but didn't know them well at all—certainly not well enough to warrant a space at his tribute table, let alone the focus! The handiwork of Cynthetica.

Guests ambled up to the Bowmans to pay their respects. Another American tradition Lem couldn't understand. In England, he and his mates would get bloody pissed after a friend died. Then they'd slur out stories to illustrate what an all-round good bloke and horrible bastard the deceased was. They'd mourn him and then determine that it was a damned good thing ol' Nigel was dead or they'd kill the asshole themselves. Instead of crying, they'd curse him while nursing a hangover. There was no time to grieve when you were rushing to the loo to puke.

Lem went to the bar and ordered ginger ale. As he passed the tribute table he scanned each photograph. Every celebrity in the history of celebrity seemed to be on display, but there were no photos of him. Lem Brac hadn't even made the cut in the retrospective of his best friend's life. He shook his head sadly.

Lem slogged through the wet grass toward Marjorie Bowman.

But suddenly his eyes veered right and landed unexpectedly on her.

After all those years of searching for her, perhaps his eyes operated on instinct. No matter, there she was, standing in the middle of a cluster of the bereaved, a ribbon of pink against the endless black fabric of mourners. In one hand, she clutched a clear drink with a lemon perched on the rim. The other hand gestured lightly like a butterfly riding a warm breeze. He watched her from the corner of his eyes—his heart throbbing in his throat—as he moved closer to the family. She was still beautiful, still captivating, still heartbreaking. After all these years, all the anger he had felt for her disappeared with the slightest wave of her slinky wrist as she gestured to the mesmerized crowd. After all these years, she was still Lisa the Love Witch.

Lem's leg twisted awkwardly in the grass and part of his ginger ale tumbled out, landing right in his crotch. It looked like he had pissed himself.

"Mr. Brac. Mr. Brac."

Lem turned to see a very tall thirty-year-old man with thick eyebrows and box-office-gold good looks smiling at him. If he had been drinking, he'd think he was hallucinating. It was as if he had just landed in the country and was meeting Thomas Bowman for the first time.

"It's me. Tommy Bowman." He hugged Lem.

Lem held the guy's shoulders and studied him.

"Tommy! Tommy! My God, it's been more than ten years. You look just like your father. Where have you been?"

"A place called Cody, Wyoming. Not very glamorous, but beautiful, and as far away from this as possible."

"You're a veterinarian? Your father was very proud."

"My dad always made fun of me; he said I wasn't dealing with the real world. But I always felt my clients were much more human than any of his. I mean, look around. You're probably the only person who kept in touch with him. You were probably his only real friend, but he didn't even realize it. He bought into all of this."

Lem's voice trembled. "Sadly, we lost touch." He shook his head. "I wanted to call him desperately. I did. But I always felt uncomfortable. It's a horribly insignificant excuse."

"I'm glad you're here. You're the only friend of my dad's I liked." Tommy looked around. "My dad said you were always better than the rest of them, but he said you never thought you were good enough." He loosened his tie and stared out past Lem. He continued, more to himself than Lem. "I know I should have been here more. At first I thought he was just a little absentminded. He'd forget things like car keys and where he left his golf clubs. Mom tried to hide it from us, too. She'd always make excuses. I remember being in the car with him, and he couldn't figure out how to get home. Mom said it was because of all those years he spent in limos. I knew it was a lie, but it was easier to accept than my responsibility."

"Responsibility?"

"Despite how much I hate it here, I should have moved back."

"Ab-sho-lutely," a voice boomed behind them. It was Marjorie. She put her arms around Tommy and squeezed him tightly. "But I'm just glad my baby boy's here now. And I'm never going to let him leave."

Tommy swallowed hard. "Maybe I'll just convince Mom to move to Wyoming with me."

"That will be the goddamned day. They don't have salons there. I'd be getting my hair cut by the guy who sheeps shears." Marjorie let out a tiny laugh that sounded like a finch's chirp. "Shears sheep."

"Mom, you shouldn't be drinking," Tommy said.

"I just had some of The Cure, to help me calm down. Cyndi swears by it." She squeezed Lem's hand. "Kids. When did the roles reverse? Anyway, I'm glad you came," she said. "Poor Thomas.

Poor, poor Thomas. He couldn't tell me he shit his pants, but he could recite every line from *Gone With the Wind*. If I wanted to pretend we were having a meaningful conversation, I'd actually be Scarlett." Marjorie shook her head. "I don't know what happened. The doctors said his brain was gone, but his body was healthy. I thought he'd be with us for years and years to come. And then boom, facedown, right at his desk."

Marjorie looked off into the distance and shook her head and turned toward Tommy. "Where's Shin-di? She should be with us." She looked at Lem. "You know, when she was eight years old, she announced to Thom and me that she would no longer like to be referred to as Shhhyn-thia, thank you very much. She said, 'My name is Shin-di. And it's C-Y-N-D-I. Please make a note of it.' She even put out a memo and made copies of it for her classmates. Can you imagine? We thought it was just a phase, but she seems very much rooted in that name now. She's become that name, if you can become a name."

Marjorie's pupils were tiny dots, and her eyes were glazed. Her breath was horrible, as if some kind of rodent had burrowed in and died by her tonsils. Lem figured she was probably on some kind of doctor-prescribed drug designed to cure mourning.

"Yes, I suppose so," Lem politely whispered. He wondered if Franny were still holding court behind him.

Marjorie brought a drink to her mouth, but the tilted glass missed her lips and the liquid landed with a splat on the grass. She didn't seem to notice. Tommy grabbed the glass out of her hands and put his arms around her. Tears streamed down Marjorie's face, and she wiped them with gnarled fingers. Lem couldn't help but notice the condition of her hands. They were overrun with ropy veins that coiled around her knuckles, which looked like roots about to burst through the age-spotted soil of her hand. Her fingers were nicotine stained, and her nails were thick and corrugated with bright pink polish that had begun to peel, revealing a milky undertone.

"I'm going to tell Lem who's here," Tommy said. "Okay?"

Marjorie shook her head.

"You know, that's part of the reason I had to leave this place. Everyone thinks you can hide things or rewrite the truth and it all goes away. But it doesn't. It's no different than lying."

"Is that what you tell the cows?" Marjorie hissed.

Tommy stared hard at his mother. "Mommy, please."

Her voice softened. "Okay. Okay."

Lem caught another glimpse of Franny as she fluttered down the sloping lawn. She seemed to sense, without looking, that heads were turning toward her with each step. But she stared ahead at the horizon with what Lem imagined was a half smirk on her face. Then she stopped, slid her pink sandals off her pink-toed feet, and casually held them by the straps in her left hand. She tossed her hair back and arched her neck, allowing a shaft of light to caress her. She floated down the remainder of the lawn, her tiny wrists leading the rest of her, while the crowd craned their necks to watch. No matter what, Franny Blanchard would always be a legend. She was stealing Thom Bowman's only show.

Lem cleared his throat. "I know Franny's here. I saw her."

"With a spell you're under her command," Marjorie angrily spit out. "And weren't we all, in some way, under her command?"

Tommy looked hard at Lem. "Not her. Patricia. Your ex-wife."

JUST AS TOMMY approached with Lem Brac's ex-wife, Lottie appeared, thrusting out her breasts. They all stood there silently for a moment until Lottie spoke.

"Hi. I'm Lottie Love, Chief Party Correspondent for *Personality* magazine."

"Hi, Lottie. I'm Tommy Bowman. Chief vet for the greater municipality of Cody, Wyoming."

As Tommy and Lottie flirted, Lem and Patricia faced each other.

"Hello, Lemuel," she said.

"Patty." He leaned in and kissed her on the cheek. His heart was a grenade in his chest.

"How are you?" Patricia whispered.

"Fine. And you?"

"Can't complain."

She was beautiful. He stared at her and wondered what their life would have been like if he'd forgotten about Franny. Would they be living in the Valley and sending their children off to college? Or would he have messed up in some other way?

Patricia was divorced and had three children.

"You know, my husband is smiling somewhere right now. He loved the idea of you two." Marjorie looked at them and shrugged. "I'm in mourning. I'm allowed to be obnoxious."

They talked some more, about jobs, about travel, about the things that didn't really matter. Occasionally Lottie would eavesdrop, in a very subtle way that impressed Lem. But she was probably shocked to discover that Lem Brac had a life outside of the caricature she imagined him to be: recovering alcoholic limey on a downward spiral.

Marjorie leaned in. "Patricia, show Lem your gorgeous children."

Patricia shook her head and narrowed her eyes at Marjorie. "No. Not today."

"Not today? Nonsense." Marjorie grabbed Patricia's purse.

"Marjorie!"

She rummaged through the purse and opened up a wallet. Patricia tried to snatch it as Marjorie shoved it under Lem's nose.

"There's Allen and Simon," she said. "They call me Auntie Madge."

"They're beautiful, Patricia. You must be very proud."

Patricia's eyes blazed. "Marjorie, please."

Marjorie tsked. "They're adorable. Fifteen and sixteen now. I always wished I had more children. But my two keep me challenged."

Marjorie turned to another photo. She looked up at Lem and smiled. "And that's Cathy. Isn't she a beauty?"

Lem nodded. "She's lovely," he said without really looking. But Marjorie kept the picture right under his nose. He hated Marjorie for being so cruel. What was she trying to do? Show him how good life could have been if he had followed Thom's plans? He wanted to scream out, YES, MARJORIE, I BLOODY FUCKED UP MY LIFE. YOU DON'T HAVE TO SHOW ME. I KNOW. I KNOW! I LIVE WITH IT EVERY DAY.

Then something struck him. Cathy was beautiful. But there was something so familiar. He struggled to place it. Was she an actress? Was her father a famous actor? Those eyes. There was something about those eyes.

And the voice in Lem's head was like a punch.

MIKE WANDERED OUT of the funeral festivities. It had seemed ridiculous to him, all these people pretending to be upset as if they were on some sort of cattle call for mourners. "More tears, people," he could hear a director bray. "Come on, I need despair. I don't see enough sorrow!"

Mike threw his blazer into the backseat of the car, pulled off his tie, and rolled up the sleeves on his powder blue oxford shirt. The beach was only a few blocks down from the Bowmans'; he just followed the smell of the ocean. When he moved to Los Angeles, Mike envisioned spending weekends at the beach, but he never seemed to have the time. He'd been to the ocean maybe twice. As some Hollywood publicist had once predicted, he'd seen more of the Pacific in movies.

It was another beautiful day, and the sun's rays spilled across the water, flashing and glinting like diamonds against the inky blue surface. Mike shaded his eyes and squinted out at the Pacific. A breeze slapped at his clothes. Mike wiped sweat off his face with a sleeve, gazing at the surfers dressed as sleek sea lions who bobbed in the water, waiting to ride the crest of a perfect wave.

Mike wondered why he didn't take advantage of being out here and learn to surf.

But when he thought about it, Mike couldn't even imagine himself as a surfer. He couldn't even body surf without the waves vacuuming him up and sweeping the bottom of the ocean with his ass. Mike felt overwhelmed with sadness. What the hell could he really do well?

Pretend. Pretend nothing was wrong.

As his eyes moved from the surfers to the shore, they landed right on Lottie Love. There she was, sitting up on a bright red towel and rubbing Fred Segal suntan lotion on her arms. Her fingers glided along her biceps, then moved to her legs and eventually her exposed, taut abs. After she had massaged her stomach, she tilted her head back and ran her red-tipped fingers along her throat. Lottie eased facedown onto her towel while her fingers bent backward to untie her acid green bikini top. She slid it off, exposing her naked back. Mike sighed.

He removed his loafers and socks and trekked along the sand, watching children laugh as their sand castles were swallowed by the ocean. Without thinking about it, he wandered right to where Lottie was sprawled out. He stood over her, staring at her tanned back marred only by a small tattoo on her left shoulder blade. Mike bent over to get a closer look. It was a red heart with LOVE written in bloated letters underneath.

With her rippled back and a bubble ass stuffed into a tiny bikini, Lottie had a great body, a body that was meant for the beach. Mike imagined that she had emerged from the ocean's foam rather than from the loins of a plumber. He closed his eyes and the smells of coconut oil, citrus, and palm trees bombarded his nose. This was California, he knew. Right here. He imagined his hands slathering coconut oil on her back, her thighs, her chest. With his eyes closed and the smells and sounds of California rushing through his veins, he felt as if he were a child, imagining this place and wondering if his prayers would ever be answered.

THE FACT THAT BERNICE BANKS PICKED THE MOST GORGEOUS Man in the Universe for *Personality* drove Lottie Love berserk. Bernie was old, and she dressed in prissy suits with pleated skirts that fell way below her elephant knees. She was so out of touch that when the magazine ran a photo of Bernie next to some celebrity in its publisher's letter, the art department would concoct a trim, computer-generated body, digitally paint on a stylish outfit, and stick Bernie's head on top. They even airbrushed out a spare chin, Lottie had heard. Bernie reminded Lottie of a biology teacher who sat in front of the class explaining sex in a manner that implied all her firsthand knowledge had been gleaned from a textbook. *The penis is inserted into the vagina . . .*

Unlike Bernie, Lottie had her finger on the pulse of Hollywood. She was young, hip, and vibrant. Her hot pink Rolodex was filled with more contacts than anyone else at the magazine. She *knew* who the Next Big Thing was. And chances were, she'd dated him. Maybe even slept with him. She'd impress Bernice with her knowledge of the Industry, make her realize how invaluable she was to *Personality*! And before long, she'd be earning three times her salary and probably have a new title, like Associate Bureau Chief and Party Editor. Lottie could hear the conversation:

"Shame on you for paying her this pauper's salary, Vince. Give the girl a raise immediately. We don't want to lose her."

Bernie, who was based in New York but seemed to spend most of her time in sunny L.A., sat at the head of the conference table with Vince on one side and Peg, the perky deputy bureau chief, on the other. Next to Peg was Ben Walsh, one of the five—or six, Lottie had lost count—associate bureau chiefs and a celebrity autobiography writer. When she had started, Lem had told Lottie that Ben was the only person qualified to write someone else's autobiography because he had no discernible personality of his own. Lottie thought he had one, but it seemed to be one enormous mean streak. The only time he talked was to criticize some reporter's work. "That guy's a hack," he'd sneer. If he was in a chatty mood, he'd pull you aside and bad-mouth everyone on staff. When Lottie first started, she had felt almost privileged to be taken into his confidence. Then she learned that he was calling her a starfucker behind her back.

No one could figure out how someone so vile could somehow charm a celebrity. In his latest as-told-to book, this one on the Olson twins, he devoted an entire chapter to their first period. Lottie couldn't believe how detailed it was—from them doubling over with cramps to practicing with tampons to their sophisticated views on becoming women. And Ben wrote about it all in the voice of the twins. She couldn't imagine anyone talking to Ben about anything, let alone being on the rag. He admitted that he "occasionally massaged quotes because celebrities were so inarticulate." Rumor was he did more than that—he invented his quotes—but the Olson twins liked his prose so much, they didn't complain.

Next to Vince and Ben were the rest of the associate bureau chiefs, followed by Mike Posner and the senior staffers. In Lottie's first days she had plopped herself in any old chair during a meeting. When Vince had arrived (ten minutes late, to make his entrance), he had glared at Lottie. Later she learned the seating arrangement was based on a meritocracy. Her seat was all the way at the other end, next to Melissa, Vince's assistant.

Bernie went around the room, learning names of new employees and making small talk with the veterans. Lottie knew it would be another ten minutes before Bernie lumbered down to Lottie's end of the table. Lottie took the time to admire her new outfit. A tan linen pantsuit from Calvin Klein and octagonal-shaped Armani eyeglasses, even though her vision was twenty-twenty. Very professional, very Cyndi Bowman. Maybe buttoning up a bit would force Bernie and Vince to take her seriously. Lottie was ready to show them all that she was a force to be reckoned with. Just last night she had proved it at her weekly I'm-a-Lush meeting.

"HELLO, I'M LOTTIE Love, and, well, as most of you know, I'm an alcoholic."

"Hi, Lottie!"

"There isn't a day that goes by that I don't think about drinking? I see a bottle of vodka and I can feel the sensation of the booze going down my throat. I imagine it and sometimes, I swear, I lit-rully start to feel buzzed. It's like a phantom buzz. But it's never good enough, and soon I need the real thing. My whole body just craves it. It's this horrible ache in every fiber of my being."

She searched for him. He was in the third row, right behind crazy Joe. When she first attended meetings, Joe had been newly married and clean and sober for three years. He gave pep talks at the conclusion of the meetings and was a sponsor for at least ten people. He'd always say that if he could do it, anyone could. "I'm living proof you can do anything," he'd say with an enormous smile. Then he went on some weird health kick, and soon afterward his addictions came hurtling back. Now he was a wreck. His wife had left him. He'd lost his job. He sat there twitching and shaking. He was proof that you couldn't really do anything. Lottie quickly looked away from him and back to Chris. He nodded his head in what she imagined was a mix of understanding and sympathy for her.

After the meeting, she searched for Chris. She watched as he yelled after Joe. Joe had been almost out the door, but he stopped. Chris walked toward him, his outstretched hand holding a wad of cash. With a dramatic sweep, he handed Joe the money and shook his hand. Lottie felt a lump in her throat. Poor

Joe. Couldn't Chris have been just a little discreet? Couldn't he have waited until Joe was out the door? Do actors always have to be performing?

But the lump melted as soon as Chris approached her. Just as she knew he eventually would.

"Hello, Lottie. I'm Chris Mercer." He stuck out his hand and she shook it. "I just wanted you to know that what you said was so eloquent. It's like you were talking about me."

"Really? Sometimes I couldn't feel more alone," she said. The truth was she had found out online that he'd given almost this exact quote to some obscure European newspaper.

"Well, you're not alone. I know I don't know you at all, but ever since you started coming to these meetings, I feel like I know you really well. It's like you're my long-lost sister."

Sister? She didn't want to be his sister.

"Really. You couldn't be more sweet."

He pulled out a card. "This is my cell phone. Call me when things are too hard to take. My only request is that you don't give this out to anybody. I'm gonna be going into hiding at the Chateau Marmont for a few weeks to prepare for a role. I'm an actor. If you need to call there, ask for Johnny Malibu. Here, I'll jot it down for you."

He grabbed a pen from his pants pocket and scribbled. Lottie smiled, thinking about tucking the card into her bursting Rolodex.

"Call me anytime you need help. Or even if it's just to talk. I know exactly the place you're at."

SHE SMILED AT the memory, the modest "I'm-an-actor" comment. The flirtatious "Call me anytime." Now she was in a conference room facing a group of people who thought they were so superior to her. But not one of them would ever have a conversation with the likes of Chris Mercer.

Suddenly Bernie was staring right at Lottie.

"Hello, Bernie. It's good to see you again," Lottie said, beaming at her.

Bernie squeezed out a half smile and squinted her eyes. "And you are?"

Lottie had been introduced to Bernie nearly a half-dozen times by now, but the woman always forgot her. Purposefully, Lottie was certain. Who'd want to remember someone who reminded you of how ugly you really are?

But Lottie knew that introductions were everything, even if it was the sixth introduction. So she imagined she was Cyndi. She paused for a few seconds, looked Bernie straight in the eye, and boomed, "I'm Lottie Love . . . Chief Party Correspondent."

Bernie gasped, bugged out her eyes, and held a hand to her breast. "Chief Party Correspondent?"

"Yes. That's me," Lottie said proudly.

"Now *that's* a fun job I wouldn't mind having." Her voice oozed sarcasm while the room tittered. "Do we actually pay you to go to parties?"

More laughter.

Lottie's faced burned. Fun? Like Lottie waltzed around a ballroom sipping champagne and feasting on caviar. Fun? She'd like to see Bernie—or any of them—clomp around, trying to work a crowd. That bag acted like anyone could do Lottie's job. It took a knack and talent and an understanding of celebrity you couldn't glean from an employee manual. And here they were laughing at her. All of them. They all made double what she did and she worked harder and longer than any of them! *Maintain composure,* Lottie told herself.

Lottie cleared her throat and said between clenched teeth, "Actually it's lit-rully such hard work." She stared squarely into Bernie's squinty eyes and beamed a quick, full-tooth smile.

With a voice dripping condescension, Bernie said, "I'm sure it *literally* is, Miss Love." Again, she pinched her cheeks and rolled her eyes for her little audience of frightened journalists. "I'm sure it is. But let's all get back to business, shall we?" She looked right at Lottie as if waiting for a response, so Lottie nodded.

"Now, as you all know, our Most Gorgeous Man in the Universe issue is always a top seller. But that's only if we have the right man on the cover. We can't have Brad Pitt or Tom Cruise on the cover again, although I wish we could." Bernie breathed deep and sighed loudly. "And Ben was perfect when he was with J.Lo. She really upped his sex quotient. But, quite frankly, I never thought that relationship had what it took to go the distance."

"Absolutely, Bernie," Vince piped in. "He's a salt-of-the-earth guy still very much of his backstreet Boston roots. She's high maintenance and desperate to disengage from her past."

Lottie had to laugh. These people had never even talked to J.Lo or Ben, and they were discussing them as if they were all best friends.

"Well, let's have a Gorgeous Man think tank right now," Bernie said.

"Robert Redford. I still think he's the sexiest, no matter what," Veronica Sullivan said, as if she knew sexy. *Puh-lease,* Lottie thought. The woman wore long floral dresses that smelled like mothballs.

"Oh my God, he's like older than my father," Lottie burst out, shaking her head and smiling at Bernie as if they had some secret understanding.

"Harrison Ford. He's gorgeous and sexy and appeals to a broad spectrum of our readership," someone piped in. "Focus groups show our audience loves him."

Lottie burped out a throaty laugh and tensed her brows. "Could anyone be so much more boring? And, please, what's with that earring? It's not fooling anyone, Harry. You're still OLD."

"Arnold. He's the thinking man's sex symbol. The sexiest governor ever. And maybe he'll run for president one day."

"Have you seen him in a bathing suit lately? He has saggy breasts," Lottie snapped. From the corner of her eye she saw

Vince shake his head at her and purse his lips. Lottie didn't care—she wanted to make an impression on Bernie.

Bernice crossed her arms. "Well, Miss Love, since you've vetoed every suggestion thus far, do you have anything to add to the mix?"

When Lottie had received the memo announcing Bernie's visit to discuss the Most Gorgeous Man issue, she imagined what Cyndi Bowman would do. She prepared. She devoured newspapers and magazines for attractive celebrities. She analyzed the posters in her office and bedroom, and, most important, she perused her pink Rolodex. Lottie stood, slowly put on her new eyeglasses, and slid out a piece of paper from a manila folder. She cleared her throat, paused, and scanned the room. "I've done some research and compiled a list of possible candidates for the Most Gorgeous Man in the Universe issue."

Again, Lottie cleared her throat, paused, and scanned the room. For some reason, her eyes settled on Mike Posner, who was smirking at her. She thought about how he had stood over her at the beach. He thought she didn't know he was there, but she felt his presence the whole time. Why did it excite her? There was no way she could like a hick like Mike. An *overpaid* hick.

Remember, this is a performance, Lottie. And you were born to be an actress, she told herself. She thought about the applause at her lush meeting.

"Marlon Lang. I'm so cognizant of the fact that his movie, *Blind Love and Other Handicaps,* didn't do very well at the box office, but at this point in time, he's still so on his way to being the Next Big Thing. I heard he's in negotiations to star in a *Titanic*-type movie. Cory Jones. He's working on a book of poetry. He's lit-rully such a Renaissance man. I also think Raymond Young would be like a perfect choice. He's the misunderstood pool boy from *Bel Air Belles.* He's going places. And my inside sources tell me that he is about to sign a mega-huge deal to star in a movie about a misunderstood lifeguard . . ."

Bernie cleared her throat and threw up her arms. "None of these people are big enough. They don't have cover caliber."

"Well, my sources tell me that they're the Next Big Things in Hollywood."

Bernie harrumphed. "We're not interested in the Next Big Thing. *Personality* magazine is interested in the Now Big Thing."

Lottie cleared her throat. "But if we focus on the Next Big Thing before they're the Now Big Thing, we'll be on the cutting edge. We'd be ahead of our competition. "

There was a gasp. No one—not even Vince—dared argue with Bernie. Bernie's face pinched. She drilled Lottie with her eyes.

"Those boys seem better suited for magazines like *Tiger Beat-off* and *Teen Cream Dream*."

Bernie cackled. Vince cackled. The staff tittered.

Lottie exhaled and tried to stay focused. She remembered a slogan someone had said at AA: Don't be interrupted from your goals by external forces. So Lottie stared straight at Bernie as if none of the others were in the room. "Well, I was saving this for last, but how about Chris Mercer?"

Bernie laughed. "Well, that's the obvious choice, but he won't talk to us."

"Well, I discussed this with him last night."

"Really? *You* discussed *this* with Chris Mercer." Bernie leaned into the table, not quite knowing whether to believe Lottie or not. She looked at Vince. "Vince?" Vince shrugged his shoulders. Bernie turned toward Lottie.

"And? And? And? Were you able to convince him to do a sit-down with us?"

"Well, yes . . . just about . . . I'm almost there."

Bernie stood up. Her eyes shot daggers at Lottie.

"Almost? Almost?" She boomed like an actress onstage. "When you get a rare opportunity to talk to Chris Mercer, there's no room for almosts. You either clinch the interview or you fail."

"Well, I couldn't be closer to clinching. It's just a matter of . . ."

"Sorry, Lottie, that's just not good enough for *Personality* magazine. Right, Vince?"

Vince nodded his head.

"Well, I mean, I couldn't be more closer to clinching."

Bernie flipped a hand through the air. "I don't even know what that means." She looked past her to Mike. "What would you have done?"

Mike coughed quickly and his ears turned red. "Well . . . well, I probably wouldn't have left until he agreed to something. Anything. Even if it's just a half-hour lunch."

"Great suggestion, Mike. Lottie, you should have called Mike immediately for advice."

Mike smiled weakly.

Lottie could see white heat pulsing in front of her eyes. She shut them, but the furious white light flickered inside her head. She hated that everyone listened to Mike's bullshit as if it were gospel. Her head blazed. She could barely see, barely breathe.

And then Mr. Hyde suffocated Dr. Jekyll.

"Puh-lease, you've so got to be kidding me. If anyone could make it happen, it's me. Not Mike. He's a phony. You all make more money than I do and none of you knows anything. I'm the only one with real access."

The words slipped out. Lottie had heard them in her head for weeks now, but she never thought she'd actually say them. Her mouth hung open as if the words had shorted her out. Bernie and Vince stared at her, their eyes wild and their lips clamped down as if stapled to the inside of their mouths.

Vince coughed to loosen his constricted vocal cords. "Perhaps if you have such a low opinion of your colleagues, you should find a higher calling than our out-of-touch, poorly paying magazine." Vince spoke through his teeth in a slow, steady voice.

Lottie's mouth remained agape. She didn't know what to say. She couldn't agree with Vince—after all, this job was her life. She couldn't disagree; she'd look weak. She shut her eyes and tried to imagine what Cyndi Bowman would do in such a predicament. But Cyndi wouldn't be stupid enough to have a boss. Cyndi Bowman was in charge. With no alternative, Lottie grabbed her notepad and stormed out the door.

LOTTIE HAD relished the trade up from her corkboard cubicle to a real office, albeit one without windows. She compensated for the lack of a view with posters of Billy Crudup, Ryan Phillippe, Brad Pitt, Stephen Dorff, Marlon Lang, and Raymond Young. She bought a small refrigerator so she didn't have to share the mold-infested communal one. She shopped once a week at Pavillion's next door to fill it with Diet Pepsi, frozen yogurt, and carrots. This was her home away from home. She raced inside and slammed the door. She couldn't even imagine giving this up. It was her life. Lottie Love *was* Chief Party Correspondent. That was how she had come to define herself. There was nothing left to say.

Lottie dialed Chris's cell phone. She got his message. "It's me. Emote!" She didn't pause to consider how ridiculous that sounded. She thought about leaving a message but hung up as Lem stuck his ashen face into her office.

"My advice is to march right into Reggio's office, act contrite, say you got emotional, and then promise it will never happen again. Speak in sports jargon, if you can. Say you fumbled the ball, but you want to play for the home team. I'm certain you'll be able to salvage your job if you do your best at humility. If there's one thing I've learned over the years . . ."

Lottie banged her head on her desk and groaned. "I know. I know. Fucking-they're-not-your-friends. Puh-lease. I so don't need you to tell me anything you've learned over the years. It hasn't helped me once, and, ah, HULL-OH, it hasn't helped you either."

Lem stumbled backward as if he'd been socked in the stomach, Starbucks spilling from his cup to the floor. He leaned on the door frame for support. "I was just trying to help, Charlotte."

Charlotte. Nobody but nobody called her Charlotte. Charlotte was a loser from Tarzana. The white lights flickered again.

"The name is Lottie. And for your information, I'm about to interview Chris Mercer. Me. Not you. Not Mike Posner. Me."

"Okay, Miss Love. I was just . . . well, never mind."

An hour passed. Lottie figured it had blown over. She and Vince had both said things they didn't mean. Lottie took out a salad and a Diet Pepsi from her refrigerator and ate slowly, trying to forget about the disastrous morning. While she gnawed on romaine, she imagined Vince and Bernie at lunch right then discussing her. *"You know, she's young and headstrong, Vince, but that's what we need here,"* Lottie heard Bernie saying. *"She is underrated. I think she's justified in asking for more money."*

Vince would reply, *"You're absolutely right. There is no one better than Lottie Love, Chief Party Correspondent. You should see who she's gotten to talk to us."*

Lottie was replaying the conversation when Vince stepped into her office and shut the door quietly behind him.

"Hello, Vince," she gulped, trying to appear secure.

Vince stood in front of her, arms crossed, eyes squinted, brows furrowed. "Lottie, I'll make this short. I'd like you to pack up your things and get out of here, ASAP. Your services are no longer necessary at *Personality* magazine."

"What? I . . . I . . . I . . . don't . . . I don't want to leave."

"I'm afraid the ball's not in your court. You give me no other choice. How dare you embarrass me, Mike, and the entire team in front of Bernice? How dare you use that public forum for your own personal grievances? Considering your talent, *Personality* magazine has been more than generous with you." He paused, letting the words sink in. "I want you out of this office in an hour. If you're going to give me problems, I'll have you escorted out by security."

Lottie's lips trembled. She swallowed hard to quash the cauldron of sobs bubbling in her throat. "I'm sorry," she croaked. "Just give me another chance."

"Sorry doesn't even begin to erase the black mark you've put on this bureau and me. I have no other choice then to terminate your association with *Personality*. Bernice actually demanded it." Vince spoke like a cyborg—his words were completely drained of expression and inflection.

"But . . . but I'm meeting with Chris Mercer. I could do a great interview. I'm really good with people. I'm a people person. I'll get an exclusive for the magazine. Chris Mercer wants to speak to me. No one else. He requested *me*. Me. I could make it happen today."

Lottie watched Vince, waiting for his demeanor to change with the news of her scoop. But he stood at her door, his back straight as a pole, his neck craning upward as if her words were nothing more than the annoying buzz of a mosquito. She knew that in Vince's eyes, she was already dead. There was just this little inconvenience of the body.

Her time at *Personality* flashed before her in a dizzying whirl. She saw Marlon, Adam, Adrian, Cory, Raymond, Jason, Ian, Tom, Tristan, Brad, Ashton, and Leo appear like snapshots before her eyes. The parties, premieres, and award shows zoomed by in a dizzying frenzy. Lottie couldn't leave *Personality*. Without it, she might as well go back to Tarzana. She might as well be Charlotte Love, daughter of Hank Love Plumbing. *She'll Make Your Pipes Sing.*

Lottie felt like screaming. Blood throbbed at her temples. Her arms and legs trembled. "Please, Vince. I didn't mean it. Please give me another chance. I . . . I . . . fumbled the basket, but I'm batting for the home team. I'll . . . score a touchdown with Chris Mercer. I . . . I . . . promise."

"Please let's make this easy, Lottie. Bernie thought that a party correspondent was a frivolous job anyway. And then . . . well, I do know about the dresses you borrowed for the Emmys."

"What are you talking . . ."

Vince shook his head. "Lottie, please. I was going to overlook that breach of ethics, but it seems impossible now. Bernie knows about it, too. Please. I have nothing further to say."

Dresses. The Emmys! She should have known! Mike was somehow involved!

Vince slowly turned around and walked out, his arms rigid at his sides, his eyes staring straight ahead. Lottie closed her eyes and put her head in her hands. Again, she saw the faces of the entire year race past her—Cory and Marlon and Ray and Chris—until they narrowed and collapsed into one another, somehow turning into Mike. Mike, the only one who would have said something about those dresses! Lottie opened her eyes to destroy the apparition.

There was a knock on the door. Lottie jerked her head up expecting Vince to be there, telling her he had made a big mistake. *It was the heat of the moment, but I realize how invaluable you are to the team.*

"Lottie Love?"

It was a bespectacled, squat black security guard.

"I've been asked to escort you off the premises. Your possessions will be boxed and shipped to your home address." The guard pushed a walkie-talkie to his mouth and mumbled something into its static.

"No!" Lottie yelled. "I want to pack my own stuff. This is *my* life. I want to take down my posters and pictures. I don't want anyone else touching my things. It's all mine. I don't trust anyone else."

"I'm sorry. I'm just doing what I'm told. Please cooperate and make it easy on the both of us."

"No," Lottie snapped. She stood up on rubbery legs as she began racing around her office, unsure of what to do. She pulled too hard at her *Bel Air Belles* poster, and it tore right down the middle of Lance Caine's perfectly chiseled face. Lottie jerked her head angrily toward the security guard and flared her nostrils. "See what you made me do?" she barked.

"Please. You're just making this difficult for yourself. I'll take care of everything for you."

"If I left this to you, I'd never see my things again. Everyone wants them. Everyone. And do you have *any* idea what I had to do to get these?" She swept her hand across the room.

The security guard wore a navy blue blazer with a badge, and EARL was embroidered in light blue slanted script on his jacket pocket. He mumbled something else into his walkie-talkie and slowly walked toward Lottie. "Come on, let's be adults here," he whispered. "Let's not make a scene."

Lottie shook her head.

"Please, Miss Love. Don't do this to yourself. Let's just walk out of here nice and calm."

Lottie's heart pounded, but she felt strangely disconnected to the events. It was as if she were watching some psycho lose control. It couldn't possibly be Lottie Love, Chief Party Correspondent. She was gobbling up popcorn and staring at the screen as an actress unraveled. If she really wanted to make it interesting, she'd pull out a gun right now. Instead, she glared at fat Earl. "I'm not leaving and you can't make me."

"Come on, Miss Love," he said softly. "Let's get out of here."

Lottie looked past Earl and saw that the entire office had assembled outside her door. As she glared at them, they quickly shifted their eyes while their mouths hung open like idiots. Taking a deep breath, she grabbed a few framed photographs of herself with various members of the cast of *Bel Air Belles, Everwood, That '70s Show, The O.C.* As she stared at the photograph of Justin Timberlake with his arms around her waist, she began to cry. Soon her body was quaking with sobs. She gasped for air. Earl moved closer and put his arm softy on her shoulder.

"There, there. It's not that bad," he cooed, his hot breath hitting the side of her head.

"It *is* that bad," Lottie choked out, as tears seeped down her cheeks. "It *is* so that bad."

"If you don't want them to see you, we can take the service elevator."

"No," Lottie snapped.

With a hand lightly touching her back, Earl guided Lottie toward the door and whispered, "Miss Love, you are the most beautiful and talented one in this place. Don't give these people a show. That's what they want, a show, because then they'll feel better about themselves. But we're not going to let them. Pretend it's Oscar night and I'm escorting you into the Kodak Theater. You're dressed in a fine gown with a diamond necklace and earrings that sparkle like your eyes. Come on, Miss Love. Let's walk along the red carpet while these bystanders watch us with envy, silently praying that we'll trip and fall. But we won't because you're too beautiful, too magical for that."

Lottie wiped muddy tears with her fingers, keeping her head cocked as she shuffled along so she wouldn't have to see any reporters' eyes. She stared at the metal mouth of the elevator. She mirrored the look she had watched actors give her as they breezed along the red carpet at premieres while she stood on the other side of the velvet rope shouting questions. They seemed to always look ahead at something that wasn't there, with eyes that were perpetually unfocused. Lottie managed to squeeze out a half smile.

Earl stooped over and whispered in her ear. "I'm fifty-five years old, and I've lost plenty of jobs in my day. Plenty. Let me tell you, it's going to be okay. Remember, it's only a job."

For the benefit of the crowd assembled near the elevator bank, Lottie cackled as if Earl had said the funniest thing she'd ever heard. She took a deep breath. "It's not only a job—it's my life, my whole entire life." Lottie's voice began as a whisper and petered into a few decibels below a murmur, until her trembling lips moved without any sound.

To keep herself from crying again, Lottie imagined that she was outfitted in a red Armani gown, heading into the Oscars while her fans begged for a photograph, some eye contact, some acknowledgment that they did indeed exist in the same realm as she. But Lottie Love was too beautiful and elegant and too good for them so she stared straight ahead, thinking only of the award she was about to receive.

And the Oscar goes to . . . Lottie Love.

But then her eyes slipped away from the elevator and accidentally landed on Mike. He was watching her. She stepped into the elevator with Earl and a seething red hate coursed through her body. She was not a movie star; she was only Charlie Love from Tarzana.

It wasn't until the elevator landed at the lobby that she realized she'd left behind her most prized possession: her Rolodex.

AFTER A FEW DAYS OF UNEMPLOYMENT, OF FIRST MOPING AND then pampering herself with facials, manicures, massages, and yoga, Lottie had a revelation: she didn't need *Personality* or Vince or Bernie or any of them. She had been wasting her time breathing polluted office air and working for pennies. It was as if God himself had orchestrated the firing to remind Lottie that she was bigger than *Personality. Reach your potential, Lottie Love!* She had a more important agenda than Chief Party Correspondent.

"One day, I just decided that I'd had enough of that horrible place. I was so like totally stagnating there. It just didn't allow me to express myself creatively," she told Cyndi Bowman over apple martinis at Lola's.

"Bravo, Lottie Love. Bravo. You empowered yourself."

"I so did."

"No offense, Lottie, but I really don't understand why anyone with even half an intellect would want to work at that rag."

"You couldn't be more right."

"*Personality* just looks for the negative. The writing is horrible, and its audience is pure trailer trash. It never focuses on the positive things celebrities do."

Cyndi reached across the table and, with both hands, squeezed Lottie's wrists. "*Personality* is perfect for a loser like Lem Brac."

"And Mike Posner. He's such a fraud. He just makes things up, but everyone believes everything he says. His word is gospel there. He can do no wrong. It couldn't be more disgusting."

With each word, Lottie became more and more animated, until

her hands were a blur, sawing and hammering the air. Red-faced and exhausted, she sunk in her chair, sighing as she patted down her hair.

Cyndi leaned her head toward Lottie and smiled. "But he is kinda cute."

"Cute? That's revolting. Mike Posner is so not cute . . . You think he's cute?"

Cyndi smiled. "Let's talk about you. How can we empower Lottie Love?"

Lottie blinked as if suddenly remembering where she was. For a moment she had been back at the elevator, arm in arm with fat Earl.

"You could not be more right," Lottie said, slapping her hand on the table. "I need to become . . . empowered."

Cyndi foraged through her Murakami bag and pulled out her Honey Nut Brown lipstick. She smacked her lips together and blotted them with a napkin. "The reason I invited you for a drink was, of course, to see how you're doing since you made your big escape." Cyndi patted Lottie's arm. "And, of course, you're doing fine, just as I suspected."

Cyndi paused and scrunched her face at Lottie, as if she were about to pinch out some great news she'd been constipated with.

"Now that you're a free woman, I wanted to offer you a chance of a lifetime: How about coming on board at Cyndi Bowman Publicity? My business is expanding daily. My staff puts in eighteen-hour days, and I'm literally working round-the-clock—twenty-four/seven. It's never enough. There's so much to do. Our client base is growing and growing."

Cyndi began ticking off a list with her fingers. "We need someone well connected. Someone who's a people person. Someone who understands celebrity. Someone with your Rolodex." Cyndi nodded her head at Lottie, paused, and added, "Cyndi Bowman Publicity needs someone like Lottie Love."

Lottie felt a jolt of warmth race through her body. Her heart galloped wildly. Already the offers were pouring in! Cyndi stared at her, waiting for a response. But Lottie forced herself to remain silent. And speaking of her Rolodex, she'd called Melissa, the office assistant, a dozen times about getting her stuff. Fat Earl lied just like she knew he had. No Rolodex. No files. No Brad Pitt poster.

"I don't expect an answer right now," Cyndi said, her velvety whisper suddenly metamorphosing into an icy staccato. "But, in my opinion, it would be the biggest mistake if you didn't jump on this offer. This is a much better side to be on. And what better place to work than the best? You'll still be able to write. And I encourage my staff to be creative in their press releases. It's not like *Personality*, where everything is rewritten. Of course, I have to tweak things a bit, but I try not to quash a writer's personal style . . . I love writers who use lots of exclamation points. I hate writers who use the word 'said,' when there's plenty of other options, like 'exclaimed,' 'extolled,' 'announced,' 'annunciated . . .'"

Lottie nodded. "I couldn't love exclamation points more."

Cyndi stared at Lottie. "The best part about it is that you'll be on the other side. You'll be the manipulatrix instead of the manipulated. And it's an all-woman staff. We look out for one another, and we're all the best of friends. I like everyone to bond. It's actually mandatory. We all go to Kundalini yoga together Thursday nights."

Lottie thought it sounded nearly too good to be true. She'd still be on the inside—even more so. Celebrities would put their complete trust in her. She'd create and promote their image. She'd hold strategy sessions with Leo and Brad and Tom and Joaquin.

"Lottie, Brad Pitt is on line one. He needs some advice. Lottie, Johnny Depp is on line two."

She wouldn't have to grovel for interviews and quotes, but she could make Mike and Lem and Vince beg.

I'll take it, she nearly shouted, but she choked back the words. After all, she wasn't born yesterday.

"It sounds like so completely fahn-tas-tic, but the last few days have been like so lit-rully crazy. The phone has been going hysterical, and I need a couple of days to sort this madness out." Lottie breathed deeply.

Cyndi narrowed her eyes and knitted her pencil-thin brows. She sighed loudly, while her Honey Nut Brown lips remained taut. Then she flashed a steely grin.

"Well, we'll see," Cyndi chimed, raising her voice in tinny fulsome merriment. "My phones are ringing off the hooks, too, Lottie. There are a lot of people who would do anything to work at the fastest-growing publicity firm in Los Angeles. I mean *major* executives from *major* studios who are willing to give it all up and take a pay cut to work for me. I thought I'd give you the first shot, but . . . if you're not interested . . ."

Lottie's eyes widened. "No. I am like so completely interested. I couldn't be more interested."

"So, why can't you jump on it, Lottie?" Cyndi asked, drumming her fists at the air. "What is Lottie Love so afraid of? Has your time at that rag turned you against publicists?"

"It is so not that." Lottie's voice was more high pitched than usual.

"So then, go for it. Car-pee diem. Seize the day. Do something proactive for Lottie Love."

Lottie's heart stampeded up her throat. She gulped hard and exhaled. "OhmyGod. Why not? When do I like begin?"

MIKE CHECKED HIS WATCH. EIGHT O'CLOCK. HE'D BEEN SITTING at his desk doodling for hours. Finally Vince's door slammed shut. Then Vince did his bed check around the perimeter, determining who was among the truly dedicated. Mike had even seen Vince go into darkened offices and touch lamps to check if they were still warm. Vince poked his face into Mike's office.

"Mike, go home. Get a life."

Mike laughed. But truth was, if you wanted to get ahead at *Personality* you weren't allowed to get a life. This was your life. The later you stayed, the better—even if you were actually burning CDs rather than the midnight oil.

Mike listened to the *ting* of the elevator. The office was officially empty. This would be easy. Why then did Mike feel a little nervous?

LAST NIGHT HE'D been on his first date since Liz. He and Catherine went to Stella's on Melrose. They sat underneath a bougainvillea-covered trellis and ate pasta and never ran out of things to talk about. Catherine was smart and caring, the type of person he didn't realize existed anymore—at least in Los Angeles. He knew she'd had some problems with booze, but she hadn't touched a drop in years. There was something safe about Catherine. She didn't stay out late. She didn't get drunk and rowdy. Plus, she probably didn't sleep around much, which meant maybe he wouldn't seem so inadequate. She was an interior decorator. She was working on two houses in Bel Air, but she'd put a lot on hold while she tried to cure Lottie Love.

"Lottie's an amazing person. I've never heard someone speak so honestly about her addiction. When she talks to the group, this surprising vulnerability comes out. She spends so much of her life hiding it from the world. But when she shares herself, you see her goodness."

"I think I understand," Mike said, but he didn't. Who was this Lottie Love she was talking about? Only someone special could see goodness in Lottie Love. He didn't tell Catherine about the Lottie Love who'd humiliated him in front of his coworkers.

"That's why I won't quit. She keeps pushing me away, but I'm going to help her every way I know how. If someone didn't do it for me, God knows where I'd be today."

Mike searched for a flaw. Catherine had pale skin, blue almond-shaped eyes, and the reddest lips he'd ever seen. She almost looked familiar, as if he'd known her for years. He smiled as he watched a group of guys stare at Catherine and whisper. He was with the best-looking woman in the place. This woman was too good to be true. Maybe this was someone he wouldn't have to lie to. He looked into Catherine's eyes and thought, *This woman can save me. I can be good again.*

"You can't be this good," he said.

"Trust me, I'm not."

"So tell me what's wrong with you before I start to really like you," Mike said.

Catherine looked down at the table. "You don't want to know."

"I do."

She took a gulp of her water. "I'm gonna change the subject quickly. You think you could do me a little favor?"

"Anything."

"Lottie's devastated that she left her Rolodex at the office."

Mike stopped chewing. "Her Rolodex?"

"Yeah. It meant everything to her. You have no idea. Everything she knows is on that thing. She was promised all her stuff would be sent to her. But so far, nothing. You think you could get it for her? I completely understand if you say no, but, well, I just thought I'd ask . . ." Catherine touched his arm. "You just seem like someone I could ask. I hope I'm not imposing. I mean, it is rightfully hers."

Mike stared into Catherine's eyes. And he believed it when he said, "Sure. No problem. I'll do it."

MIKE WAITED A few more minutes. He went into Melissa's cubicle. The tiny space was crammed with cat memorabilia. There were small porcelain cats, beanbag cats, stuffed cats, and photographs of Melissa and her cats. Bumper stickers covered her corkboards: KISS A CAT. FORGET MEN—ADOPT A KITTEN. HONK IF YOU'RE A CAT LOVER. WHISKERS FOR PRESIDENT. ALL I NEED TO KNOW I LEARNED FROM MY CAT. GOT PUSSY? Melissa had the mailroom guy fired for sexual harassment, yet she had a GOT PUSSY? bumper sticker in her office.

Mike had been locked out of his office so many times now that he knew exactly where the master key was. Melissa hid it in the soil of her cactus plant. She'd do it right in front of Mike. The man-hating cat lover didn't think she'd have to worry about that wide-eyed kid from the boondocks. Mike smiled. He grabbed the key. A few needles pricked his fingers.

Mike's heart galloped crazily as he twisted the key in Lottie's office door. He glanced right and left. Then he opened the door. He felt as though he was entering a teenager's inner sanctum. A bare-chested, long-haired Brad Pitt, circa *Legends of the Fall*, stared disapprovingly at him. Someone named Marlon Lang looked really pissed. Ashton Kutcher seemed oblivious to all of it.

There on her desk was her hot pink Rolodex. Glinting and fat. Ten times thicker than his. Mike grabbed it, shut the door, and headed for the elevator.

HE RIFFLED THROUGH the Rolodex as he sipped a Sierra Nevada at Houston's. There was a message from Catherine on his cell phone.

"Hey, Mike. I had a great time last night . . . Not to bug you, but any luck with Lottie's Rolodex? The girl's going nuts. She wants to break into the office, but I'm afraid they'll have her arrested. Let me know. Thanks."

Mike hadn't stopped thinking about Catherine. He wanted to see her again. And part of him really wanted to call and be a hero. He'd stop by and hand it over. She'd thank him, they'd talk, and who knows? He felt she'd never laugh at him.

But the Rolodex was incredible. He knew Lottie Love had access, but home numbers of A-list celebrities? It was like reading a diary. Marlon Lang got three stars. Ray Young was "gay as a kite." There were asterisks and exclamation points next to Ashton Kutcher's name, whatever that meant. Ben Affleck got three stars. Matt Damon one and a half. Sure, he wanted to give it to Catherine, but he had to Xerox its contents first. Besides, didn't he owe it to himself after what Lottie did to him?

Mike glugged his beer and shook his head. If he deceived Catherine, wouldn't he ruin any chance of a real relationship?

He ignored his trilling cell phone. A few minutes later, he checked the message. It was Catherine again.

"I think Lottie's been drinking. She said she's going to head over to the office tonight and sneak in. If you have any luck, please let me know. Sorry to keep bugging you, but she's scaring me."

Catherine sounded upset. Did he really need the Rolodex? *No,* he told himself as he started dialing Catherine's number while thumbing through the Rolodex. It fell open to Mercer, Chris. There was his card with a phone number.

Scribbled underneath was: alias Johnny Malibu, Chateau Marmont.

Mike clicked the phone off. So Lottie hadn't been bullshitting about Chris Mercer after all.

"Hello, there, Mr. Posner."

Mike quickly tossed the Rolodex into his briefcase.

"Hi, Lem . . . Uh, you just get out of the office?" Mike hadn't even bothered to check Lem's office. He just assumed the old Brit left at five every night. What did that guy do, anyway?

"Yes. I'm desperately trying to pry open the muse's mouth. But she utterly refuses to speak to me."

Lem's eyes were on Mike, waiting for something. Mike downed his Sierra Nevada and nodded at the bartender.

"Your finger's bleeding." Lem pointed to Mike's hand, where a few cactus bristles poked out.

Mike shrugged his shoulders. Then he turned toward the bartender. "I'll take another. How about you, Lem? Can I get you anything?"

"Unfortunately, the only ale I drink these nights is ginger. It's been a hundred eighty-two days and five hours since my last real drink."

"Shit, why do you come here?"

"I like to torture myself." Lem smiled. "Actually, I was walking by and I saw you in here, so I thought, why not? I'm a big boy. I can sit at a bar without a drink. I think." Lem stared hard at Mike. "It's a shame about Lottie Love."

"I guess."

"She had a lot of great contacts at the magazine. Vince pretty much pimped her out. Bernie just couldn't handle looking at her. She's everything Bernie wishes she could be."

"You know, she's an alcoholic."

Lem raised his glass and chortled. "Lottie Love? I know alcoholics intimately and she's not one of them."

"You're wrong."

"I know . . . I know. Your sources say . . ." Lem laughed.

"What does that mean?" Mike gulped hard. Was Lem on to him?

"Nothing, really. It's just that we all rely so heavily on sources that no one really knows the truth. That's why I stopped writing."

Mike closed his eyes while the beer massaged his brain cells, leaving him feeling elastic and relaxed. He rubbed his eyelids. When he opened his eyes, Lem's bore into him. Mike wished the guy would leave him alone so he could figure out a plan.

"So, Mike, are you happy at our most shallowed halls?"

Mike thought about this. "Well, I wouldn't say I'm happy. I'm just not miserable."

Lem swilled his ginger ale. "It's all so tedious, isn't it? Today I was asked to look into the impending divorce of two actors. Why? Why? What's the reason, the masses want to know? They want bloodshed and tears. *Personality* demands we dig dirt. But more often than not, it's mundane. Relationships end. People get bored with each other. The blood no longer rushes to the extremities. But that's never good enough. So we interview people who have no idea." Lem took a breath. "I got into this business to find truth. Do you ever feel that lying's our real commodity?"

"What do I know? I'm a hick from Rochester."

"You're a star right now, Mr. Posner. But remember, stars fade or fall, but they never shine forever. Those celestial bodies lighting up the darkness right now are already dead. Their agents haven't had the nerve to tell them."

"Cheers," Mike said, guzzling the rest of his drink. "To Marilyn Monroe."

"Now let me ask you a personal question, Mr. Posner. If I may."

There was a long pause. Mike gulped down his beer. Had Lem seen Lottie's Rolodex?

"Do you have a girlfriend?"

Mike exhaled. "No. Not now."

"Well, have you been . . . with anyone recently?"

"Let's bitch and moan about the job. Let's talk about our ambitions, or lack of."

Lem shook his head. "Sex and ambition are inextricable. Once you give up on sex, you've given up on life. Trust me."

Mike laughed into his beer. Then he gulped the remainder. "Sex has given up on me."

"Nonsense. You're young, handsome. You've got it all."

"You don't know the half of it—literally."

Lem's rheumy eyes looked past Mike and out toward the door. Then he blinked, as if staving off some ghost. He smiled.

"I've wasted a lot of time. I've spent an entire life on an apparition. And the person who mattered most, I didn't even see. I didn't even know she existed."

"What are you talking about?"

Lem snapped his head back. "Don't mind me. I'm talking nonsense. I saw a memo on Vince's desk. They're going to start cleaning house. I don't know what I'll do next. I don't want to fail. If only I could get Chris Mercer." He sighed and closed his eyes for moment. "Michael, you're young and in touch. Can you . . . I hate to sound desperate, but, well, can you help me?"

Mike held his breath. "I wish I could, but it sounds like Cyndi Bowman won't let anyone near him." He checked his watch. "Listen, I've gotta get going. You wanna lift or anything?"

"I think I'll stay here a while longer and torture myself. I have many more hours before I head into the arms of Morpheus."

MIKE DROVE DOWN Wilshire, passing the art deco apartment buildings and hotels dotting Westwood and Beverly Hills. He turned on Doheny until he hit Sunset. He drove past a tattoo parlor, a cluster of restaurants with a smattering of patrons dining alfresco, a few clubs with lines beginning to form along velvet ropes, billboards for movies he'd never heard of, a statue of Rocky and Bullwinkle. Then he was in front of the Chateau Marmont.

Michael, can you help me?

Lem's voice echoed in his head. The guy scared him. Talentless and lost. He was everything Mike prayed he would never be.

How could he help Lem when he had to save himself from becoming Lem?

He picked up his phone and dialed her number as if he were dialing 911. Relief washed over him when her machine picked up.

"Catherine, it's Mike. I had a great time, too . . . Listen, I haven't been able to find the master key, but I'm working on it. Tell Lottie not to worry. I'll have her Rolodex real soon."

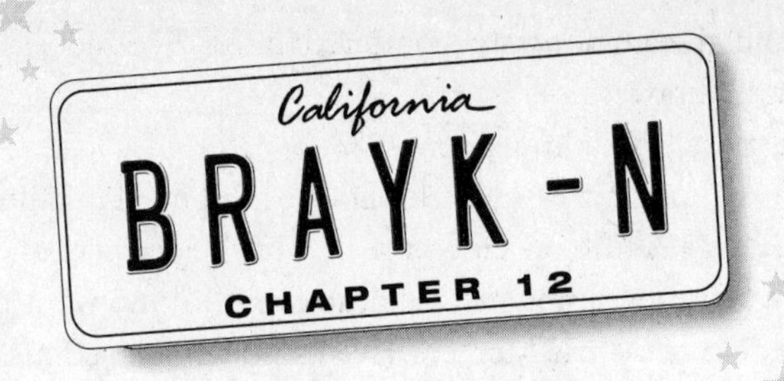

"IDENTIFICATION PLEASE."

"Gee, where is it? Let me see." Lottie smiled and thrust her boobs out at the security guard working the lobby. He didn't even look up.

"I can't allow anyone inside the premises without proper identification."

"I so completely understand." Lottie licked her lips. Then she rummaged through her purse and found her *Personality* ID card. She smiled. Maybe it would still work. The security guard studied her with a slight snarl. Then he ran her card through a scanner. He looked from the scanner to her and back again. He smirked. He was enjoying this little power trip. She knew what was next.

"Sorry. I can't allow you to enter the premises."

"What?" She bugged out her eyes and clutched her chest. "There's got to be some kind of mistake."

"There's no mistake." He sucked in his cheeks.

Lottie's toothy smile evaporated. She slammed her fist on the counter. "You have got to be fucking kidding me."

"Watch your language. This is a professional office building," he hissed. Then he paused, stared hard at Lottie, and grimaced. "My computer shows you were terminated."

"Listen, where the hell—I mean, heck—is Earl?"

"Earl?"

"Yeah, fat Earl. He promised he'd send all my stuff and he hasn't. I need to speak to him."

"Earl? Oh, Earl."

"Isn't that what I said, oh, about an hour ago? Earl!!! Fat Earl."

"You can see Earl tomorrow at one on channel seven."

"What?"

"He got a role on *General Hospital*."

"What? I don't fucking believe it."

"Well, believe it. He was never about security anyway. He didn't do anything here except rehearse his lines."

"That fat asshole liar. Jesus, my life sucks." She shut her eyes and shook her head. "Please, just let me in. I need my stuff. Come on, two seconds. Please. Please."

He scanned her and frowned. "Sorry, honey, no can do. You're going to have to leave now. Take it up with management tomorrow."

The security guard looked past Lottie and smiled.

"Working late, Mr. Brac?"

"Hello there, Robert. I just had a few ginger ales at Houston's and forgot some notes. I swear I had a better mind when I was soused. Be right down."

Lem headed toward the elevator.

"Now that's a man to know," the security guard said to Lottie. "That guy has more class than anyone in this building. And he's seen it all."

But Lottie was already at the elevator.

"HEY!" he shouted after her.

"Lem, Lem, you think I could ride up with you? I just want to collect my stuff. They promised me they'd send my stuff. Please."

Lem looked toward the security guard. "It's okay. She's with me."

ONCE INSIDE THE elevator, Lottie felt awkward. She hadn't been alone with Lem since lunch her first week on the job when he'd ordered some silly drink called a Roy Rogers and told her, "They're not your friends."

"Earl, the security guard, promised me he'd send all my stuff, but I found out he was just rehearsing lines."

"Isn't that all we do here? Rehearse lines from a script we think we understand."

"Huh?"

When the door opened, Lottie felt relieved. She headed toward her office. Lem went to his. She still had her key.

She surveyed her room. Brad and Tom and Ashton and Marlon and Tobey and Cory stared down at her. "We missed you," they seemed to say. "Welcome back." Lottie opened her file drawers and emptied their contents. She stood on tiptoes as she slowly untacked Brad Pitt.

"I thought you could use this."

Lem stood at the door holding a cardboard box.

"Thanks."

"I keep this on reserve. Every day I think I might have to collect as many valuables as I can and leave," Lem said. "Here, let me help you."

As Lem carefully removed Brad Pitt from her wall, Lottie was suddenly embarrassed by how juvenile her office was. No wonder no one respected her. She turned away and tossed the contents of her desk into the box. Then it hit her.

"MY ROLODEX!"

"What?"

"My Rolodex is gone. Someone took my Rolodex. You have no idea what was in that thing. Everything. My entire life. Everything, everything, everything. Shitshitshitshitshit. I don't believe this."

"Are you certain? Maybe it was . . ."

Lottie saw a look of realization pass over Lem's face.

"What? What? Who took it? You know, don't you?"

"No, I don't know. Maybe it was just moved. Perhaps it's in one of your drawers."

Lottie opened and shut drawers, but nothing. She looked up at Lem.

"It was him."

"Him?"

"Mike. Mike Posner."

"There, there, Lottie. Let's not jump to any conclusions."

"Conclusions? You want a conclusion? Mike stole my Rolodex because he's a complete talentless hack. God, I hate him."

Lem chuckled.

Lottie's face flushed and her heart pounded. She picked up the cardboard box and banged it on the floor. "I guess I am funny to you. I'm just a stupid Valley girl. LikeohmyGod. And Mike's this big-shot ace reporter. Why would he want dumb ol' Lottie Love's Rolodex?"

Lem swallowed hard. "Charlotte Love, that's not why I laughed."

"*Lottie*. Only my father calls me Charlotte."

"I think it's a beautiful name," Lem said. "Charlotte was my favorite Brontë."

"Huh?" Lottie huffed. "Well, I hate it. It reminds me of my disastrous childhood."

"I'd gamble that your childhood wasn't nearly as awful as you think." Lem smiled. "Anyway, I wasn't laughing at you."

"Yeah, right."

"Miss Love, I laughed because there's no reason for you to hate Mike Posner."

"He's a fraud."

"That's only because he's not as lucky as you are."

"Lucky? What? You think things just come easy to me?"

"'Lucky' might not be the appropriate word. Let's say you are more fortunate. You have more talent."

"Yeah, right. That's why they fired me."

"I'm a big fan of Lottie Love's oeuvre," Lem said, smiling. Then he leaned and whispered, "I recently started reading all your party stories."

Lottie rolled her eyes as if this was the silliest thing she'd ever heard. "God, why?"

"What better way for an old has-been to become informed?"

Lottie snorted out a cynical laugh.

"I was absolutely amazed by the truths you are able to uncover. You really get these people to reveal. Quite honestly, I didn't think it was at all possible. But somehow you bloody well do it—and brilliantly. They speak to you about love and sex and breakups and insecurities. I can't quite fathom another reporter who could unearth those juicy morsels. It's all so wonderfully refreshing."

"You must be the only one who actually reads my files. The editors just turn everything into photo captions."

"It doesn't matter. What matters is that you can do anything. And deep down you know that. Mike Posner is stuck right now—he doesn't trust himself because he doesn't believe."

"The people who lie the best do the best. I don't even know who I'm supposed to be or what I'm supposed to do anymore."

"That's only because you define who you are by the job you have and by the people you . . . know."

Lottie wiped away a tear and laughed. "You meant screw."

"Whatever are you talking about?"

"You were thinking 'people you screw' and then you stopped yourself."

"I was thinking no such thing, but if you can read my thoughts, you are even a better reporter than I imagined." Lem laughed. "Just don't sell yourself so short."

Lottie tried out a small smile. "You really think I'm good?"

Lem handed her a tissue from the box on her desk. "Excellent. But it doesn't matter what I think. What anyone thinks. Charlotte—excuse me, Lottie—has to know it."

"Sorry about the other day. I was having a rough time." Lottie blew her nose and smiled. "I wish I'd gotten to know you better when I worked here."

"Well, to be honest, up until recently I was too drunk most of the time to get to know anybody. I'm an alcoholic." Lem paused. "See, you must be an excellent journalist. You know, I've never said those words out loud before."

Lottie thought about this and giggled. Then she broke out into near convulsions of laughter.

"You know what? I'm not an alcoholic. I haven't said *that* out loud before."

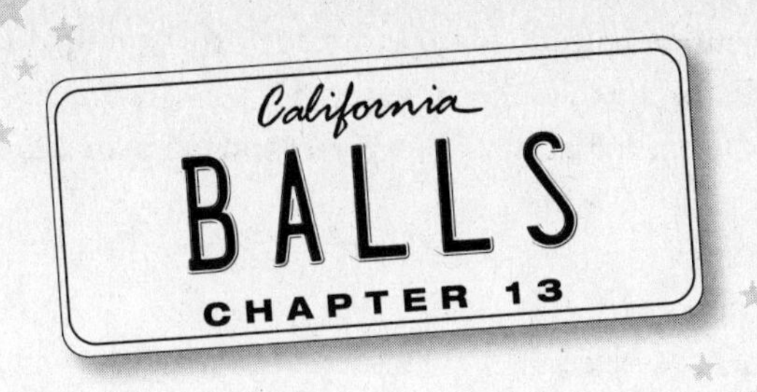

MIKE LAY ON A PILLOW, EYES SHUT, HEAD THROBBING, TRYING to summon the events of the previous evening. It wasn't too long after he walked into the dimly lit Bar Marmont that the frayed rope in Mike's mind ripped from the undercurrent of beer and gin. He had felt the snap, indicating that his synapses were marooned and therefore his brain was officially closed for the evening. He was essentially a body without a command center. He could no longer be responsible for his actions. And without a boss to tell him it was time to go home, his body obliviously continued on.

When he tried to hoist himself off the bed, it was as if someone had clamped a vise to his skull. He flopped back down, struggling to capture the flotsam and jetsam of last night's events off the flooded shore of his consciousness.

AT BAR MARMONT he had ordered a few martinis from a hermaphroditic waitress in a kimono. Fake butterflies with blue and gold wings adhered to the ceiling like specimens in a science lab. There were the usual suspects—boys in their I'm-in-the-industry uniform: thrift-store corduroys, goatees, thick black-rimmed glasses, and hair moussed and gelled and threatened into that just-out-of-bed look. Girls in skimpy belly shirts and low-riding Juicy Coutures.

Mike remembered surveying the bar. He closed his eyes as the buzz from the white-water rapids rush of booze encompassed him. He could feel the room—the First Auditions, the Developments-in-Progress—whir around him. He remembered thinking maybe he could pull a Lottie Love by flirting with Vampira, a waitress with black lips, teeth cut into fangs, and white powdered skin.

"Hey." He smiled at her. "I love that tongue piercing. Is it hard to talk?"

"To you, yes."

Hick. Hick. Hick.

"I hear Chris Mercer's staying here."

Silence. Vampira rolled her eyes and moved to the other end of the bar. He flashed money and she returned. He ordered another martini, with a lemon peel. "What about Johnny Malibu?"

Vampira eyed him suspiciously.

"Oh, so you do know Johnny?" she said, her voice softening.

"Yeah, I'm here to see him."

"Well, you should have told me. I thought you were a tourist from Nebraska or something." She laughed. "I'll take you to him."

She handed him the martini and then moved from behind the bar and escorted him up a path that led to a garden, where a beefy guy in jeans and a T-shirt stood. Vampira whispered something in the guy's ear. Mike thought he was about to get thrown out. Instead, the guy told Mike to follow him down a row of bungalows. He pointed to one and knocked on the door. "Someone for Johnny," he said. He walked away.

Mike didn't know what to do. He'd never expected to be right at the doorway to his biggest scoop. He wasn't prepared. He stood there for a few seconds, wondering if he should just walk away. He remembered Joey Green.

Hick.

The door swung open.

"The more the merrier," a shirtless Chris Mercer said, smiling as he chugged a beer. Then he looked at Mike. "Who the hell are you?" He turned his head toward someone in the room. "Hey, when I said invite friends, I meant female friends. Duh!"

"What are you talking about," said a woman as she moved toward the door. Her lipstick was smeared and her hair was disheveled. She looked at Mike sleepily.

Then her eyes bugged out.

"OhmyGod, I know you. You're with *Personality* magazine."

Bad nose job. Great legs. Cyndi Bowman.

"What? How the fuck did you get in?" Spit flew out of Chris's mouth as he spoke. "I'm gonna have the whole fucking staff fired." He looked at Cyndi. "Maybe I should fire you, too."

"Oh, Chris," Cyndi moaned.

He pushed her aside and moved out the door. Mike was surprised at how short the legendary Chris Mercer was. Mike, at five feet ten, had about four inches on the guy.

"What do you want? You want me to say this is my girlfriend, 'cause she's not. Okay? Far from it."

Cyndi's face contorted. Mike would have sworn she started to cry. But then she smiled. "I'm his publicist. We were strategizing."

"Yeah, but you wanna see us fuck so you'll have a story for your magazine? An exclusive. Is that what you want? Is it?"

Chris tossed off his shoes, undid his belt, and tugged on his pants. Mike stood there, his mouth like the Grand Canyon.

"Chris, stop it. Remember what I told you about losing control."

"I thought you liked it when I lost control," Chris sneered. "That's the only time you get any."

"Stop."

"No. Let's give him a story. Okay? Come on, Cyndi, get naked."

"Chris!"

Chris threw his underwear at Mike's face. Then he shoved Mike.

"WHAT ARE YOU FUCKING WAITING FOR? ISN'T THIS WHAT YOU WANT? Up close and personal with Chris Mercer."

He lunged again and slipped his hand into Mike's pocket. Before Mike could stop him, Chris pulled out his tape recorder. He pressed the buttons.

"Testing, testing, one, two, three. I am Chris Mercer. I am Chris fucking Mercer. Isn't that cool? I am actually Chris Mercer. I am so fucking rich and powerful and you are dogshit."

He rewound the tape. Then he hit Play. "I am Chris fucking

Mercer . . ." As the tape replayed his message, Chris stuck out his tongue and licked the recorder while grabbing his crotch. "Look at me. I'm fucking myself."

He hurled the tape recorder into the air. It shattered as it hit the ground.

Mike stood frozen as two security guards rushed in. They each took an arm and heaved him into the street.

MIKE REALIZED THEN that his ass was still sore. He rubbed it.

A wave of nausea swept through his entire body, and he bolted naked from the bed into the bathroom. He crouched on the floor, heaving into the toilet. As he washed the sweat and puke off his face, it suddenly hit him. The towels were too soft and pastel! Mike studied the bathroom in horror. It was his bathroom—same position of the toilet, the tub, the medicine cabinet—but something was different. There were frilly pink curtains on the window. Designer shampoo in the shower. Fragrant soap in the soap dish. A hair dryer. A curling iron. Someone had invaded his home and redecorated!

Mike opened the door to the bathroom and returned to the bedroom. It was his bedroom—at least it looked like it—same size, same windows, same closets, just more frilly. Mike's stomach somersaulted. He must still be dreaming. Or had he become someone else? Someone who liked pink floral comforters and matching pillow shams and curtains. Someone who had a collection of stuffed bears, arranged in size order.

Someone with a poodle.

A poodle? There was a poodle curled up on top of the bed, eyeing Mike. A poodle who yipped when he barked. He sounded like he had no balls.

No balls.

NO BALLS!

"**MY-I-IKE, I MADE** you breakfast."

Mike rushed to the kitchen.

"You were so romantic last night. You just pushed at the door and then barged right in here," his neighbor said. Mike couldn't remember her name. She smiled while whisking. "I sensed chemistry the first time we met. I know you were, well, slightly buzzed last night, but it was really romantic in a rugged kind of Richard Gere or Harrison Ford way."

Mike shook his head, too stunned to speak. *Cookies,* he thought. It was a name that reminded him of cookies. Ginger snaps? Chocolate chip? Keebler? Fig Newton? Graham?

"Well, I'm sorry."

"Don't be embarrassed. I thought it was very charming. They say that the truth comes out after a few drinks anyway. You seem like a pretty repressed guy, at least in your sober life."

Rootie nuzzled Mike's leg. Was that soft clicking the sound of colliding plastic balls?

His neighbor scooped up the sizzling omelet with a spatula and set it on a plate.

"Have a seat. This is for you. Remember I told you that my goal was to become a vegan? Well, ta-da . . . I'm a vegan. I'm adhering to the same macrobiotic diet as Gwynnie and Madonna. I'm thinking of becoming a Kabbalah, too, you know, to get some spirituality in my life."

Mike stared at the omelet in front of him while his stomach flipped. He poked at it with a fork but couldn't bring it to his mouth. He was too tired and too dehydrated to move. "Listen, I should get going. I didn't mean to barge in on you."

"Yes, you did—or at least your more uninhibited self did."

Mike rubbed his temples. He eyed her, wondering if she had learned the truth about him.

"It was two in the morning, and I thought someone was trying to break in here. I was scared out of my mind and just about to call the cops. Then I looked out the peephole and there you were, practically ramming the door in with your shoulder. So Rootie and I let you in. Right, Rootie? You seemed harmless . . . enough."

His neighbor sat across from Mike, sipping on a mug of green tea. *Oatmeal? Toll House? Sugar? Mallomar?*

He waited for a comment, a laugh, some indication.

"You were great, by the way."

Great? Mike Posner? He wished he could remember. Something. Anything.

Pepperidge Farms! Amber Pepperidge Farms!

Amber trotted into her bedroom. Mike snapped his fingers at Rootie. As the canine licked Mike's hand, he lowered his plate for the dog. The dog headed for the plate, sniffed it, groaned, and turned away. Mike tossed the pseudoeggs into Amber's Justin Timberlake garbage can, hiding it underneath an empty Tropicana orange juice carton.

When Amber returned, Mike realized everything about her was heart shaped. Her lips. Her cleavage. Even her face, framed by honey-blond hair. He bet she dotted her *i*'s with little hearts, just like Lottie. Her *o*'s were probably heart shaped, too. Her boobs were enormous and disproportionate on her thin five-foot-four-inch frame, creating a heart-shaped body. Maybe Amber would be famous one day. Then he could say she said he was great.

"I'm sorry. I really don't remember much . . ."

"Well, I mean, we didn't do that much," Amber said. "I'm not a slut or anything—especially with a guy who's drunk."

Amber wrapped her arms around Mike and kissed him on the lips. Mike squeezed his eyes shut and kissed her back. They fell onto the couch, and soon Root Canal was on top of Mike's back, licking his ear. They kissed and kissed. In the middle of a kiss, bile traveled up his intestines and into his throat. He pulled his lips from Amber and swallowed hard. Amber grabbed his crotch. Was it his imagination or was she rooting around trying to find it?

"Mike—eee."

"Amber . . . I've got to . . ."

"Mike? . . . Mike?"

Mike jumped off the couch and out of the apartment, breathing deep and swallowing hard. He fumbled with the keys to his place, opened the door, and puked in the kitchen sink. He remembered that on the way to the funeral Lem had told him not to let the tools rust. He should tell Lem that his tools had not only rusted—they were defective.

LITTLE JOEY GREEN and now Amber. Mike *Poseur*. He spent so much of his time running away from his inadequacies. It was just a matter of time before they all chased him down. Mike closed the blinds and lay in bed. Someone knocked on the door, but he ignored it. He left a message with Melissa, saying he was sick. He checked his messages at the office. The first was from Catherine.

"I guess Lottie broke into the office last night and the Rolodex was already gone. She's crazed." There was a laugh. "She thinks you took it. But I told her there was no way. Anyway, maybe we can get coffee later this week?"

The second message was from Cyndi Bowman.

"Call me ASAP regarding Chris Mercer."

Fuck you, Mike thought. Fuck Chris Mercer. What an asshole. Mike was glad he'd never have to interview the guy. He wasn't worth the ink. Stars fade or fall, but they never shine forever.

His home phone rang. Mike screened.

"Hello, it's Cyndi Bowman, Bowman Publicity."

Cyndi Bowman? Calling him at home? In a voice desperate to conceal complete and utter fear?

He couldn't resist. He picked up the phone. "This is Mike," he grunted.

"If you plan to divulge an iota of your evening to the press, I'll have so many lawyers up your ass you'll . . . you'll . . . you'll be sorry."

"Yeah, well, tell your client or boyfriend, or whatever he is, that he owes me a tape recorder."

"You were trespassing." He could practically hear Cyndi's teeth unclenching. She was rabid. "Remember, if anything gets out, I'll make sure no celebrity will have anything to do with you or your magazine."

"Yeah, if it gets out that you're humping your client . . ."

"We were strategizing." She paused and cleared her throat. "I know what you're thinking. You better think twice." She shrieked into the phone, "Get it. Got it? Good."

Mike could practically feel her hot spit on his face.

"Cyndi, I . . . I . . ."

"I know what we have to do. I practically invented this game. If I give you access to my client, I want you to guarantee last night won't be mentioned to . . . umm . . . Vince Reggio or anyone."

"Well . . . huh?"

"I'll give you an hour with him. An exclusive, 'kay? But I don't want any mention of last night in the article, or there will be major problems. Major."

"Okay."

"As long as we're on the same page, I'll get the wheels in motion," she said.

"Okay." Mike shrugged his shoulders. What the fuck had just happened?

"And I'll send you over a new tape recorder ASAP."

When they hung up, Mike pumped his fist in the air. When it hit him that this was something Vince would do, Mike froze in midpump.

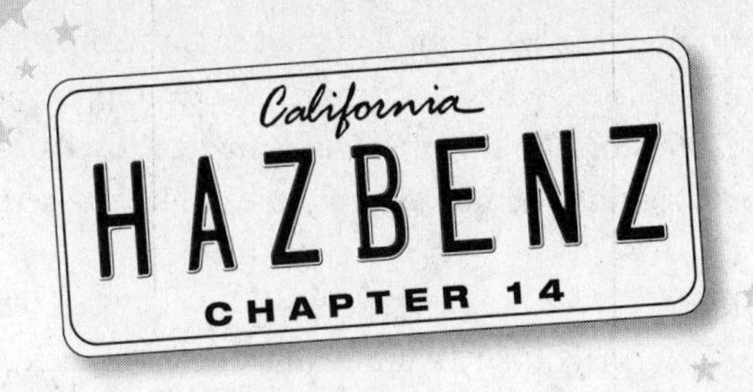

ON LOTTIE LOVE'S FIRST DAY AT HER NEW JOB CYNDI GAVE HER A list of the clients she would represent. Lottie stared hard at the names, but none sounded familiar. One thing was certain: these were not the Next Big Things.

"You've been given a list of some of our older, more established client base," Cyndi began.

Lottie laughed. "You mean the has-beens."

Cyndi tossed her head back and clucked, smoothing her Agnes B. blazer. "No, Lottie." She spoke as if Lottie were a disobedient child. "They are the bedrock of C.B. Publicity. They founded this company, and we owe them a big debt. You may think this is an insult, but it shows the kind of faith I have in you."

Lottie laughed again. "You couldn't be more brilliant at being a publicist, but this is Lottie Love you're talking to. These people are losers."

"Lottie, the truth is, yes, these people haven't had press in a number of years. But if anyone can get them ink, it's you. I don't feel comfortable giving this assignment to anyone else."

Lottie rolled her eyes. She hadn't been there but a few hours and already she was beginning to loathe the Cyndi Bowman.

But she wasn't going to let it get to her. Lem Brac had told her she was good. *You have talent,* he said. *You get these people to reveal.* Nobody had ever said anything like that to her before.

She smiled and clicked on the television in her office. One of the perks at Bowman was that everyone had a TV to keep up with pop culture. She flipped around, trying to find something interesting while she studied her lame clients. She tapped her brand-new kitten heels on the floor. She adjusted the fuchsia camisole peeking out from her demure wrap dress. Then she spotted a familiar face.

Fat Earl.

He wore a security guard's uniform as he stood next to a frazzled woman pointing a gun at him. Lottie turned up the volume.

"If you come any closer, you'll be a corpse," the woman screamed.

Fat Earl smiled, walked toward the woman, and tugged the gun out of her hand. As he looked hard at her, the camera zoomed in on him. Then he spoke.

"Don't give these people a show. That's what they want, a show, because then they'll feel better about themselves. But we're not going to let them. Pretend it's Oscar night and I'm escorting you into the Kodak Theater. You're dressed in a fine gown with a diamond necklace and earrings that sparkle like your eyes. So, come on. Let's walk along the red carpet while these bystanders watch us with envy, silently praying that we'll trip and fall. But we won't because you're too beautiful, too magical for that."

"What the hell?" Lottie yelled at the TV.

Fat Earl seemed to smile right at her. She couldn't believe it. He'd probably be the one walking down the red carpet to receive a Daytime Emmy. Shit! Fat fucking Earl had duped her. She had actually believed him.

She clicked off Earl and hurled the remote across the room. Then she scanned her client list. Okay, she'd deal with it for a while (after all, she needed the money), but then she'd demand better clients. These were fucking corpses. Lottie felt like marching into Cyndi's office and saying that the best solution would be to stuff them in caskets and bury them beneath six feet of dirt.

Then her eyes caught a name that looked vaguely familiar. Frances Blanchard? Next to the name, Cyndi had scribbled, *Meeting, today at two. See me.*

Frances Blanchard? How did she know that name?

She opened up the file. So this woman was once a star who warranted a lot of press, and Lottie Love had barely heard of her. The file bulged with every single story, brief, and blurb that had ever been written on Franny Blanchard. She found a bunch of articles with Lem Brac's name and began to read and read.

She was near tears when she finished. Lem wrote better than anyone she'd ever read. His stories were rich with detail and filled with emotion, without relying on exclamation points. He wrote simply, but she could feel what it was like to be Lem Brac and in love. Her heart hurt when she finished. She couldn't believe someone this talented had seen talent in her. Could it be possible that she was actually good at something besides thrusting out her boobs?

Lottie was certain that everything she'd ever gotten in life was because of her body. She had won the internship at *Personality* because she stuck her chest out in her professor's face. She scored most of her interviews because she flirted and teased. She had been a joke at *Personality*. They had called her a starfucker behind her back. She was the office's comic relief.

But Lem saw something in her. Lottie couldn't stop thinking about him. It was like having a crush, but different. It was more like the crush she had on Dr. Bernstein, the guy who'd operated on her nose. It wasn't like she wanted to do him—he was way too old. But he had, in some ways, healed her, made her feel worthy. She kept thinking about ways to run into Lem so she could feel healed and worthy again.

Franny Blanchard was someone Lem had believed in once. Lottie had to meet her. She had to get Lem to interview Franny again. Maybe he'd find out what he'd been looking for all these years. Or maybe, just maybe, Lottie could get them to rekindle whatever it was they once had.

Lottie laughed. She was beginning to sound like a Hollywood movie.

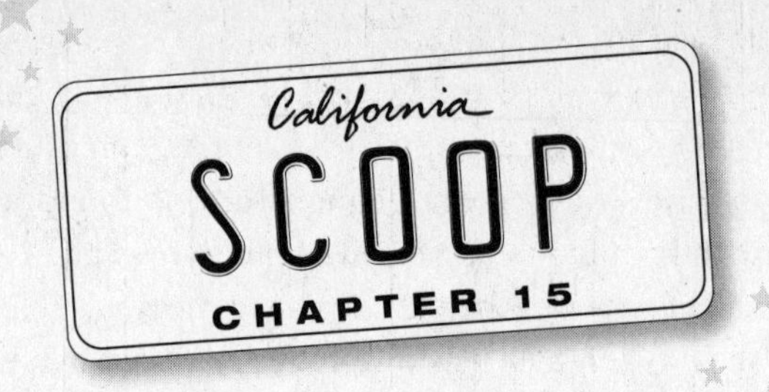

LEM PUSHED OPEN THE DOOR. HEADS SWIVELED AND FACES clenched in disapproval as he scrambled for a seat. "Sorry, traffic," he mumbled. Reggio frowned, cleared his throat, and turned his head back toward Bernie.

Bernie was still in town. Lem should have known—this May had been exceptionally rainy in New York, and Bernie needed some sunshine. But she manned the helm of the conference table as if the reporters actually needed a dose of snarls and insults to sustain them. She was a haystack of a woman with a shrunken head on linebacker shoulders. *There is nothing worse than a woman with no discernible neck,* Lem thought.

"I have some good news and some bad news," Reggio said, staring at a sheet of paper in front of him. "Let's get the bad news out of the way, shall we?" He glanced at Bernie, who nodded. "As most of you have heard, someone stole the master key. We searched the office to see if anything was taken, and it appears as though Lottie Love's former office has been picked clean."

There were gasps. *Shit,* thought Lem. Should he confess? Or be silent? Either way, this would somehow come back to haunt him. He could feel it, and the certainty of this feeling settled in his chest like a slab of lead.

Bernie cleared her throat. "I don't think we have anything to worry about. My gut reaction is that Ms. Love managed to sweet-talk her way into the building and left with her trinkets," Bernie said, heaving out her chest on the words "sweet-talk." "But still, everyone should check to make sure important files weren't taken. Ms. Love seemed very agitated regarding her termination."

There was something else. Vince Reggio was about to explode with his good news. It must be a promotion, Lem imagined. Americans love adding adjectives in front of job titles. It made them feel important, even though the tasks remained the same. To American ears, Executive Vice President in Charge of Bureaucratic Rigamarole sounds more impressive if there's a "chief" prefixed to it. Americans! It's no longer politcally correct to call a team the Redskins or the Braves, but a bald, bloated guy sitting behind a desk in a tie is a chief. *What an insult to Native Americans,* Lem thought, certain that an Indian would much rather be associated with a kid storming down a field with a ball in his hand than a fraudulent suit droning on about paradigm shifts.

Reggio cleared his throat and boomed, "Okay, let's move on to more pleasant news. Drumroll, please."

Bernie playfully rapped the table with her swollen knuckles. Reggio chuckled.

"Our intrepid reporter Mike Posner has scored an exclusive with . . . ta-da . . . Chris Mercer."

There were more gasps. Reggio flapped his hands together and the rest of the office joined in. Then he gave the thumbs-up sign.

"Good going, Mike. Do you want to tell us how you hit the ball out of the park?"

Mike knitted his brows while his ears turned bright red. "I, um, pretty much ran into Chris. It was . . . luck."

"Elaborate, Mike. Don't be so modest. We all want to learn your tricks, even I. Everyone can improve their skills," Bernie said, sucking in her cheeks. "Tell them what you told me."

Mike shrugged his shoulders.

"Okay, I'll do it for you. One of Mr. Posner's many, many sources gave him a tip. Chris Mercer has been holed up at the Chateau Marmont under an assumed name for weeks. Mike has been staking the place, hoping he'd catch the big CM. He found his bungalow, knocked on the door, and Chris answered. As simple as that. You see, people—Mike didn't get lucky. He didn't just happen upon the Merce Man. His tenacity finally paid off. There is no such thing as luck in this business. Luck equals tenacity plus opportunity."

While reporters scribbled this in notebooks, Lem glanced at Mike, who quickly averted his eyes.

"Please, Mike, tell us more," Bernie said.

"Well . . . I just was . . . lucky."

"Okay. I'll speak for you," Bernie said. "Mike said he was with *Personality* magazine and we wanted to do a story on him. Well, Chris said he wanted absolutely nothing to do with our magazine. He said it was not cutting edge enough, too mainstream. Mike goes, 'Chris, who are you kidding? Mainstream is your audience. *Personality* brings you forty million potential moviegoers. How's that for mainstream?' He said he never thought about it that way. And Mike said, 'Well, you should,' and walked away. About five minutes later he was begging Mike for an interview."

Bernie stared lovingly at her golden boy. Then she scowled. "That's what we need—more investigative journalism. You should all take a cue from Mike and do some real digging. Cultivate sources who'll tell you where A-listers are hiding. A lot of you are getting lazy; you know who you are. A lot of you kowtow to celebrity. You've got to be tough and pushy. Mike is relentless. He doesn't take no for an answer. He gets in their faces, and he gets results. Thank you, Mike."

"Sure," Mike said with his head down. Again, the room applauded.

"Well, that's all, team," Reggio said, slapping his hands together. "Let's hustle and break some records today! And I advise all of you to take a moment out of your day to congratulate Mike and get some pointers from him." Reggio pumped his fist in the air and laughed. "That is, Mike, if you're not too busy muckraking."

Lem looked at Mike, who sat there grinning as he bounced a

pen against a yellow legal pad. Soon Bernie was at Mike's side, and he stood to shake hands. They looked like two war correspondents just returned from the trenches.

So his suspicions were confirmed. Lottie was right. Mike had stolen the master key and Lottie's Rolodex. Then he sat at a bar while Lem yammered away about how desperately he needed to interview Chris Mercer. Right there, Mike was hatching a plan. And then he left, knowing exactly where he was heading. Leaving Lem all alone.

"There was this one time, I staked out Sinatra for weeks," Lem heard Bernie bellow. "He wouldn't give me the time of day. Finally I yelled to him, 'Hey, old blue eyes, I'm not asking you to fly me to the moon, but the best is yet to come if you let me interview you' . . ."

After the meeting, Lem took a walk along Wilshire. He stopped in the Starbucks down the street. When he quit the booze, he started relying on caffeine. He hated to admit it, but he enjoyed the whole Starbucks "experience." At first he'd fought it. How could anyone spend a minimum of three dollars on a cup of coffee? But then he decided there was something poetic about it. People queuing up at the door of this corporate behemoth, weary, desperate for a jolt, and struggling to somehow be different.

No black coffee for me, they silently scream. I'm an individual, Goddamnit! I'll take a grande vanilla latte no foam with two percent milk. I'll have a tall decaf mocha valencia with vanilla soy, no whip. How about a skinny venti iced chai latte?

Nearly three months ago, when he first started frequenting Starbucks, he'd stare at the menu in complete bewilderment. Couldn't he just say small, medium, or large? he'd ask. The "barista" would look at him in disgust. But now Lem Brac was an expert. In fact, he had waged a silent challenge. Every day he'd order a different drink and use as many words as possible. He delighted in this newfound language.

Today he decided on "grande caramel macchiato with two percent milk and light foam."

He walked down the street back to the office, sipping his ten-word concoction while wondering what the hell had happened.

He'd thought that once he stopped with the booze, he'd be able to get back on track. But all he could think about was vodka. Despite his intellectual amusement, the macchiato couldn't hold a candle to Smirnoff's. Last night, Lottie had talked to him about Alcoholics Anonymous. Maybe that's what he needed, although he always thought those programs were for wimps. He was a loner. He could do it on his own, right? Well, maybe he couldn't.

Preoccupied, he wandered into the *Personality* building. As the elevator door closed, a hand pushed it opened. Mike jumped on. When he saw Lem, his eyes bulged. He was a trapped rat. There was silence. But Mike Posner was never one to handle silence really well. If they were in a car, he'd be reciting vanity plates.

He cleared his throat. "Lem, I guess I scammed them pretty well. The truth is, I just happened to run into the guy. I was pretty loaded, but I had to give them a story. You wanna know what really happened? It's pretty crazy . . ."

"No. From appearances, it seems you scammed me as well."

"What? Come on Lem, I wouldn't scam you." Mike huffed out a laugh. His eyes followed the elevator light as it crawled from number to number.

"After you left, I ran into Miss Love," Lem said. "I helped her pack up her office. She was very upset." Lem's eyes bored into Mike's. "It appears someone made off with her Rolodex."

Mike's eyes popped like one of those squeeze dolls. "It wasn't me."

"I didn't accuse you, Michael," Lem said, smiling and shaking his head. "All the rules have changed. When I started in this racket, a reporter would never, never steal a story from another reporter. No matter what."

Mike's eyes blazed.

"Steal a story! Steal a story?" His voice cracked. "What the hell are you talking about? Chris Mercer? That was never your story and you know it. Vince was just amusing . . ."

Lem flinched. "Of course you're right. You hit the ball out of the park; now you better run the bases and score your touchdown . . . Please, Michael. You did a great job with Reggio and Bernie in the meeting, but I've been around far too long."

Mike stared at Lem, his eyes burning. "I stole nothing. Nothing." He spoke in a flat, low, trembling voice. "Not the story. Not Lottie's Rolodex. I don't need to."

Mike froze with his fists clenched and his jaw slack, while taut knots at his temples pulsated. To Lem, he resembled a child considering whether or not to have a tantrum. He stood there, frozen in place, his wide eyes darting around. Lem was suddenly overwhelmed with sympathy for the guy who would someday probably fire him. The elevator *ting*ed and the door slowly slid open.

"Of course you didn't. You're a star, Mike Posner. A star. Don't forget it."

HE HAD WANTED the interview more than anything since he saw those eyes. If he could earn the respect of his colleagues, maybe he could earn hers. Maybe he could stay sober for her.

Since the funeral, that photograph had haunted him. Those eyes. He thought he was crazy. Maybe it was the sea lions. Maybe it was calling Mike "son." Maybe it was Thom's death.

He ignored it for a few days. But then he helped Lottie pack up her office and he felt the need kick in. He was back at the motel watching the father splashing around with his kids. He'd always wanted to be a dad. After helping Lottie, he realized he could still be of value.

That night he scanned his old photo albums. There was Lem Brac as a baby in a cradle, in a pram, nestled between his mum and dad. There were those lips. The reddest lips he'd ever seen. And those eyes. His mother's eyes. Almond shaped.

Patricia's daughter, Cathy, had *his* mother's eyes.

Lem Brac was a father. Why hadn't he known? He could understand Patricia's motives. Why let her daughter discover her father was a drunk and a philanderer? But Thom Bowman? How could he have kept such a secret from Lem for all those years? Why?

He had rung up Marjorie Bowman the day after the funeral. She was resting, so he spoke to Tommy.

"You should really talk to Patricia, not me," Tommy said. "I can't tell you anything."

"It's true. Isn't it?"

"I don't know anything. You should just talk to Patricia."

LEM SLUMPED AT his desk. To distract himself, he studied the press kit Lottie had messengered over. In it was everything that had ever been written about Franny, including his stories. Lottie said they moved her, and she wished she had gotten to know him better when she worked at *Personality.* Lem allowed himself a small smile. Lottie Love, the girl who looked the fakest, was actually very authentic. He hoped she allowed herself to fall in love, get married, and have children one day. He hoped she didn't keep the passenger seat crammed with old newspapers.

There were also samples of Franny Blanchard's product line called The Cure—Homeopathic Remedies to Promote Health and Well-Being. Why does every has-been feel the need to either write children's stories, à la Jamie Lee Curtis and Madonna, or come out with an invention they'll hawk on 3:00 A.M. infomercials, like Suzanne Somers and Victoria Principal? Lem read the labels on each bottle. Calm. Health. Strength.

CALM. With ingredients to promote serenity, CALM relaxes your muscles, your body, your mind, your soul.

He remembered the same bottle on Thom Bowman's desk. It was the stuff Marjorie had the day of the funeral. Calm. He needed to feel calm more than anything.

Lem twisted the cap off and took a few sips. He rubbed his temple with an index finger. Then he breathed deeply and shut his eyes.

Suddenly a familiar sensation rode through his body. He hadn't felt this way in, oh, six months, but who's counting? If he had known herbs could make you feel so good, he would have taken them years ago. Lem brought the bottle to his mouth and glugged it.

It wasn't enough.

LEM FIXED HIS hair with a nearly toothless comb and checked his reflection in a dust-covered pocket mirror he kept in the top drawer of his desk. Every time he looked at himself, he was shocked. Any trace of that young reporter with promise had disappeared from his features. His skin was raw and craggy. His nose was riddled with broken blood vessels. His blue eyes—once piercing and full of adventure—were yellow around the rims and runny, just like raw eggs. This was not the face of a man anyone could ever fall in love with. This was not the face a daughter could be proud of. The alcohol he had chugged daily had blotted out his features and left him puffy and frayed, as if he were out of focus. Booze was like a squatter who had erased any trace of the former inhabitant. Sir Lem had packed his bags and moved out long ago. The Lush resided here now; and while he had been away for six months, The Lush would always return.

He could no longer deny the squatter. Who the hell had he been fooling? His appetite was ravenous. Lem's hands trembled as he grabbed his wallet and headed toward the elevator.

Lem walked right past Bernie as she called her golden children to lunch.

"VINCENZO, MIGUEL, Orso awaits," she bellowed, brushing past Lem without so much as a nod of recognition. Why did certain people feel the need to address others as foreigners? It was a mystery to Lem, but he didn't really give a rat's ass.

THE SLIDING GLASS doors whooshed open and the frosty air inside blasted through Lem. It was nearing the official beginning of summer, and Pavillion's was decked out accordingly with stacks of striped chaise lounge chairs and rubber floats, a cylindrical plastic tube filled with brightly colored beach balls, a display of barbecue grills, and a cluster of rangy palms already wilting outside in the fluorescent sun. Lem moved past this frivolity to the liquor section, where he grabbed a bottle of Smirnoff's.

"Jennifer—Serving You Since 2004" read the cashier's name tag. "Hello, and how are we today?" She was cheerful and perky, the official personality of the city.

Lem smiled back. Jennifer—Serving You Since 2004 still had the right to be jovial. According to her name tag, she'd only been at the gig for a few months; so most likely, she was still optimistic about her acting career. Only in Los Angeles did the best-looking specimens ring up and bag groceries. They were blue-eyed, chiseled-cheeked, pouty-lipped, buffed-bodied confections of hope as they rehearsed lines while scanning toilet paper, tampons, and toothpaste. They chattered across aisles about the latest audition horror story, interrupting their tales to ask a customer if he preferred paper or plastic. But their level of enthusiasm diminished with each year of service. When your cashier has been serving you since 1995, you better check your receipt for errors. With each bagful of groceries, a dream recedes farther and farther down the conveyor belt.

Jennifer—Serving You Since 2004 smiled as she handed Lem his change and a receipt. "Thank you and come again," she sang. "Now you have a nice day!"

Lem looked into her eyes. She was so innocent, so full of hope, so full of have-a-nice-days. And he felt so very, very sorry for her. He reached across the conveyor belt and grabbed her gently by the shoulders.

"Jennifer, don't forget your dreams. Don't ever forget your dreams. Promise me, promise me." His voice sounded foreign to him. Was he slurring?

Jennifer stared at him, wide-eyed and frightened. "How do you know my name?"

"What's the problem?" a customer growled. "Miss, should we get a manager?"

"Where's the manager?"

"GET THE MANAGER!"

"Manager to cashier seven. Manager to cashier seven."

Lem let go of her. He grabbed his bag and headed for the door. A pain shot through his chest. It was like a hot knife chiseling away at his very core.

In the garage elevator, Lem was transported to the building's bowels and his waiting Citroën. He sat behind the wheel, unscrewed his Smirnoff's, took a swig, licked his lips, and sucked in a deep breath. He sat quietly as the vodka trickled down his parched throat, cooling the poker in his chest. Lem took a few more sips, until the pain finally subsided and he basked in the dark tranquility. But the mossy subterranean silence was interrupted by the stomp of heels against concrete. Lem watched in the darkness as "Miguel," "Vincenzo," and Bernie giggled and climbed into Reggio's glinting white Lexus.

When the only trace of them was the carbon monoxide fumes dangling in the air, Lem shut his eyes and rested his head back on the car seat. Just as Franny had predicted, he felt calm. In his muscles. His body. His mind. His soul. And soon he was asleep, dreaming of running into Franny's waiting arms. With a spell you were at her command.

WE'LL MAKE YOUR PIPES SING!

Sparkling teeth in a mouth as big as a slice of watermelon. Chalk-white jumpsuit. A wrench in one hand, a plunger in the other. A wave of unnatural jet-black hair.

There was her father, larger than life on the side of his truck—parked right in front of Franny Blanchard's sprawling Tudor. Her heart raced. Please, let it be one of his employees—Dale or Eric or Matthew—she silently begged. She squeezed her eyes shut. When she opened them she quickly looked at the license plate. No numerals. The original. Fuckfuckfuckfuckfuck.

"Isn't that your father's truck?" Cyndi's smirk said shiteater-shiteater. *Your daddy's a shiteater. Na na na na na.*

"Yes, it is!" Lottie answered as if Cyndi had said, "Isn't that your father's billion-dollar yacht?"

Their appointment was at two, but they'd gotten there ten minutes early. Lottie didn't really see the point. She knew they'd be waiting at least twenty minutes before Franny would see them. Celebrities had a knack for being busy doing nothing. The more successful the actor, the longer you waited. And publicists, existing on one of the lowest rungs in the Hollywood caste system (sandwiched between journalists and personal assistants), were forced to sit there, glancing at their watches and smiling, as if it were a gift to wait.

Franny's personal assistant, a woman with even bigger breasts than Lottie, ushered them into the house.

"Hello, Amber," Cyndi sang. "This is Lottie, the newest addition to the Bowman family."

"Hello." Amber surveyed Lottie's breasts. "You guys are early."

The assistant escorted them into Franny's enormous living room, which featured vaulted ceilings and Mexican tiles on the floor. There were two huge white leather couches, Ionic-columned floor lamps, an oversized glass-topped table sporting fat legs carved with gods' heads, and intricate gargoyle wall sconces with bright, white-lit eyes. Even though it was late May, a fire crackled loudly in the mammoth white-brick fireplace while vents furiously pumped cold air above it. *Franny is proficient at wasting time, energy, and money,* Lottie thought. Over and around the fireplace were portraits of Franny during her Lisa days. Lottie studied one: a silkscreen portrait shaded by acid pinks and green.

"That couldn't be more of a bad imitation of Andy Warhol," Lottie whispered.

"That *is* a Warhol," Cyndi huffed and rolled her eyes.

"Well, I never thought he was that great anyway."

Lottie sat down on one of the two white sofas. When she looked across the room, Lem's *Personality* cover story stared back at her—enlarged to six by eight feet and encased behind a colossal rosewood frame of Corinthian columns as thick as tree trunks. It seemed to hang precariously, and Lottie was sure that if a fly alighted atop its pediment, the entire stucco wall would crumble under its enormous weight. Lottie studied the face. Even though the same photograph had been in Lem's office, she'd never really looked at it. She realized that the eyes, like the *Mona Lisa*'s, caught every angle of the room. "*Personality*" was printed across the top of the photograph and near the bottom it read LISA THE LOVE WITCH REVEALS ALL.

Glass shattered somewhere upstairs.

"OH GOD! OH GOD!" a female voice shrieked.

Lottie bolted up as her heart raced. "What's going on?"

"I have no idea," Cyndi said.

Amber entered with a tray of water. "Everything's fine," she chimed as she set the tray on the coffee table. "Franny will be right with you."

"What was that noise?" Cyndi asked while reapplying Honey Nut Brown.

"Well, umm . . . nothing."

"Nothing?"

"Trust me, it's nothing." Amber giggled. "Happens all the time."

"DON'T STOP. DON'T EVER STOP!" a female voice commanded.

Then Lottie heard a familiar voice.

"Oh God, Franny. Oh God. Oh God. You're the best. Franny, Franny. Oh, Franny . . . you're number one!"

You're number one?

Lottie's face turned crimson. She stared hard at the floor as if it were in deep conversation with her. She plugged her ears. This was the last thing she wanted to hear. It was like incest by proxy. *You're number one?* She suddenly remembered something. When Lottie was a kid, her dad would sometimes get stopped by women—on the street, in restaurants, movie theaters, stores—who'd say, "You're number one" while sucking in their cheeks. Lottie could never understand why this infuriated her mother. Shouldn't she be happy all these people thought her husband was the best plumber around? Now she realized it was never about plumbing. It was about making Daddy's pipe sing.

She had to get out of there. Cyndi cleared her throat, but Lottie couldn't look up. What do you do? What does Emily fucking Post suggest when your father's upstairs screwing a skanky aging star? Maybe it wasn't so bad. Maybe Cyndi didn't realize it was Lottie's dad. Maybe she thought her father was fixing toilets in some remote corner of the house.

"Oh! Oh, oh, Hank!!!! HA-A-ANK."

"FRANNYFRANNYFRANNY."

Amber giggled. "OhmyGod, she's so getting his pipes to sing."

Cyndi laughed so hard she nearly hyperventilated. She waved

a manila folder in front of her face as if this would somehow calm her down. She took a deep breath, wiped her eyes, cleared her throat, and eyed Lottie. But Lottie continued to stare at the floor. She could practically see each molecule in the terra-cotta. There was another thud. Pound pound pound.

Amber whispered, "This morning, she tossed an entire bag of rice down the toilet, just to have an excuse to call him. . . . Gross." She paused. "Let me put this DVD on for you."

The assistant pressed some buttons on the remote and Euro-trash-techno-pop blared through the speakers, blotting out the commotion upstairs. A silhouette of Franny filled the screen.

The camera panned Franny's naked but strategically shaded body. It finally settled on her dimly lit face. "We are all works of art," Franny whispered to the camera while slowly thrusting her neck back. Then her hand pulled a chain suspended from the ceiling. Franny was doused by a shower of bronze paint. She arched her back as the paint coated her. She massaged the color into her flesh as if she were soaping herself.

Franny was transformed into a bronze statue, ready for any lawn in Los Angeles. She faced the camera again. "I *am* a work of art." Even Franny's pubis was coated in bronze.

"I am the canvas and I am the paintbrush. I am art. I am the artist."

The fifty-something woman on the plasma screen was still coated in bronze paint, but now she was writhing on a blank white canvas. She gyrated her hips, smearing bronze onto the canvas. Then she propped herself up on all fours and crawled along the periphery like a bedraggled cat. She tugged at her bronze-matted hair with her bronze hands and then ran her fingers through it, chin out, eyes closed, and mouth slightly opened. Euro-techno beats segued into Vivaldi's "Spring," then Gershwin's "Rhapsody in Blue," Enya's "Watermark," a discofied Beethoven's Fifth, even Ludacris's "Blow It Out." Franny meditated on the canvas—followed by sessions of tai chi, ballet, and yoga—for an interminable sixty minutes.

How could Lem have spent all these years being in love with

such a vapid, vain woman? Could she have been different back then? Was Lem just as stupid as most men? Or maybe Franny represented every failure he had ever had.

Lottie was almost asleep when Cyndi jumped out of her seat and bounded toward the door as if the house was on fire.

"Hello! Hello!" Cyndi sang as if the most incredible person in the universe had just entered. Lottie stood up. As she shook hands and told Franny what a pleasure it was to meet her, Lottie heard the familiar rumble of the plumbing truck as Hank Love headed to his next appointment.

Franny was dismayed that she had been relegated to the new girl on staff.

"Cyndi, now that you've signed Chris Mercer, you're getting too big to handle me, aren't you?"

"It's not that at all, Franny darling. Lottie arrived straight from *Personality* magazine. She's extremely well connected. She's already nailed you an interview with the magazine. Who knows? Maybe it could be a cover." Cyndi's face exploded into a plastic smile. "Now, if you'll excuse me, I'll be outside returning some calls. I'll let you get acquainted." Cyndi smirked. "I'll bet you two have a lot in common. More than you know."

God, now she definitely despised Cyndi Bowman.

"IT'S A PERFECT match since I'm known as a healer." Franny prattled on about her homeopathic elixirs, and Lottie struggled to keep her eyes open. "Unfortunately, people take better care of their cars than their insides. I'm hoping I get herbs into the mainstream and change that. Mind you, even though The Cure doesn't have FDA approval, it's safer and more healing than any over-the-counter or prescription drug. It's a shame people don't take herbs seriously. It's like herbs are medicine's silly hippy-dippy cousins. But when The Cure hits the market next month, it's going to change the health of this country."

"Aha."

Franny spoke endlessly about the products in The Cure line,

her infomercials, her craft, her past, her present. Finally, after what seemed like hours, Lottie talked to her about the upcoming *Personality* article. She studied Franny's face when she told her Lem Brac would do the interview.

"Lem Brac," Lottie repeated.

"Uh-huh," Franny said blankly.

"You remember him?"

"Lem Brac? I don't know him," Franny said. "Should I?"

Lottie nodded toward the framed photograph on the wall. "Yes, you do. He did that story."

Franny snorted. "Honey, I've been interviewed so much during my lifetime, after a while, every face is a blur."

Lottie studied Franny. Was the woman lying to her? She thought about all the guys she'd fucked in the last year. She could recall every moment with each one. But maybe she was just a dizzy blur to them.

Of course she was.

Lottie persisted. For Lem. When she had packed up her office, Lem had told her about Franny, even reminiscing about their first kiss on the Santa Monica carousel.

"You rode the carousel at Santa Monica Pier. It couldn't have been more romantic." Lottie looked at Franny, but her face remained blank. "You kissed while the horses went up and down. The guy in charge told you lovebirds to get off, but you wouldn't. You two kept kissing. So you rode around for like an hour without paying. All these kids were hooting and hollering."

Franny smiled and nodded her head. So she did remember, after all.

"Lottie, is it? This happens to me all the time," Franny said, waving her hand through the air. "Men paint these weird fantasies about me and they start to believe them. This Lem person may have interviewed me, but I didn't go out with him, and I definitely didn't ride a merry-go-round with him. Did he say I fucked him on the horse, too?"

"No," Lottie whispered. "No. He didn't say that." Why did she feel as if she'd just been insulted? Or could Lem be so far gone he didn't know what was real?

"Well, anyway, I need the press, so I'd be happy to meet with him. But please explain that I have a man in my life, and he satisfies me intellectually, emotionally, and sexually." She grinned goofily. "He . . . makes my soul sing."

Lottie cringed. Cyndi reentered the room.

"I assume you two are getting along famously," she said. "Listen, kiddos, I'm going to have to run. Chris Mercer's gonna be interviewed by *Personality* magazine, and I have to get him ready."

"On to bigger and better things," Franny said snottily.

"I thought you said he was too big for *Personality,*" Lottie blurted out.

Franny gasped.

"WHAT? And I'm not?" Franny grabbed her chest. "Just get old Franny Blanchard anything. How about an exclusive interview with a Pennysaver?"

Cyndi glared at Lottie. "I never said such a thing about *Personality.* It's got the highest circulation rate of any celebrity magazine in the world."

Franny stormed out of the room.

"That was real professional, Lottie," Cyndi hissed.

"Oh, Cyndi, I'm so sorry," Lottie nearly choked on the words. "It's just that you seem to loathe *Personality.*"

"Well, it's a long story," Cyndi said. "Anyway, they've got this reporter there who's brilliant. He found out where Chris was staying and what his alias was. I thought I was the only one who knew that."

"So who's the reporter?"

Lottie braced herself. She knew the answer before Cyndi Bowman said:

"Mike Posner."

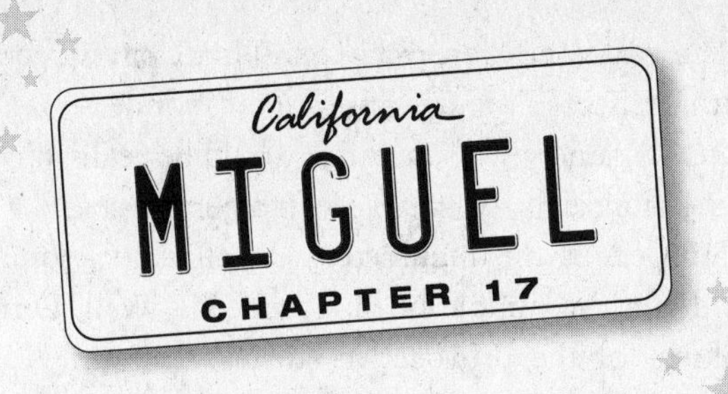

MIKE WANTED TO HIDE UNDER THE TABLE AT ORSO EVERY TIME Bernie called him Miguel in front of the Mexican busboy. Instead, he smiled as if Bernie was the wittiest person he'd ever met—as if it was an honor to sit across from her and Vince as they waited for him to spout forth scoops, gossip, anything. He squeezed out as much bullshit as possible, knowing they knew less than he did.

"I heard Julia and Danny are planning a trip. A second honeymoon, to escape from all the press," he heard himself say. "My sources believe this marriage is going to work. They are really in love. Julia talks about him nonstop, and she loves being a mom." Mike took a sip of water to shut himself up. The less he knew, the more he prattled on. If he kept it up, he'd be assigned a cover story on the couple.

"Great stuff, Miguel," Bernie said. "I think we should start a round-up cover story on celebrities who make their love work and how. Let's see: there's Julia and Danny, Antonio and Melanie, Michael and Catherine . . . What's new with Demi?" Bernie asked, then shuddered. "I hate how they keep referring to her as a well-preserved forty-year-old. You'd never hear anyone talk about Tom Cruise or Brad Pitt that way. Men are just hitting their peak at forty. If a woman looks good, she's 'well preserved.' Horrible."

Mike nodded his head as he stuffed some prosciutto-and-Parmesan thin-crust pizza into his mouth. He couldn't afford to talk anymore or he'd be assigned another cover story: Hot Men, Well-Preserved Women.

Bernie stared dreamily. "We really need a good circulation

booster. Hopefully the Mercer story will help, but we could really use a death. Princess Di and John-John did wonders for the magazine. I hate to sound ghoulish, but it would be really nice if some young, beautiful celebrity would die in a fiery wreck."

Vince tugged at the moussed and gelled lock of hair that swooped down the middle of his forehead. "Well, Bernie, we'll keep looking for the provocative stories." He smiled. "And, of course, we do have Courtney Love's obit written."

Bernie nodded her head and chuckled. Then she turned toward Mike. "Miguel, is everything coming together for the big interview tonight?"

"Sure."

"Positive? Because this thing has to happen tonight and then go straight to press or it's my well-preserved ass in a sling. We don't normally operate this close to deadline, and the suits in New York are a bit concerned—especially since our backup cover is on celebrity dieting again. They don't think it has legs. They think we're beating that one to death. But I told them if Mike Posner says it's going to happen, it's going to happen. End of story."

"I just talked to Chris's publicist." Mike looked from Bernie to Vince. "It's a slam dunk. Guaranteed. I'm meeting him tonight at a celebrity charity party. They promised me an hour alone with him plus access to some of his friends."

"Great. Have some write-around material available, just in case. Make sure you get as much as possible about his disease. People love that stuff."

Disease? Shit, Mike still hadn't done any research. He figured he'd ask the basics. Dating. The craft. Family. But disease?

"If you could get him to talk honestly about his alcoholism and recovery, it would be a real exclusive for the magazine," Vince said. "Except for a few vague blurbs, he's never really opened up. Call me the minute it's over and let me know how it went so edit can write the headlines ASAP. We've got to get this done tonight."

"No problem."

Now it made sense. No wonder they'd been so willing to talk to Mike. They were afraid he'd mention that Chris was blitzed out of his skull the other night.

Bernie cleared her throat. "I see it as something like: 'Chris Mercer. His acting. His addiction. His A-list girlfriends.'" She turned toward Vince. "So, Vincenzo, do you think we should press charges against our former employee Ms. Love? You know, what she did was trespassing and theft. That Rolodex was *Personality* property. This is our very own *Personality*-gate."

"Well, we don't know for certain . . ."

Bernie clucked. A piece of ravioli flew out of her mouth. "Ha! We don't know for certain! Oh, puh-lease. I'll tell you, my gut says that we should press charges. That girl is trouble." She looked hard at Mike. "Do you know what we discovered today? Lottie Love was attending AA meetings to get close to Chris Mercer. Passing herself off as an alcoholic. That's how she met him." She shook her head. "Disgusting."

"Really?" Mike said.

"If the *L.A. Times* gets that, we'll never get our credibility back. This is a total breach of journalistic ethics."

Vince looked gray and sweaty. And Mike could tell the guy had known all along. He remembered that Lem had told him some stories about Vince's ethics. A few years ago, when the magazine was covering more hard-news stories, Vince had told a reporter to pose as a grief counselor at Columbine High to get colorful first-person accounts of the shootings there.

"Anyway, we have to let her know we mean business. Because of her, we have to get every office lock changed. It's going to cost the company hundreds."

Mike touched his pants pocket that held the master key. He couldn't believe he'd forgotten to put it back. And he'd even managed to lose the Rolodex. Where the hell could he have put it?

Bernie turned toward Vince. "So, have you looked at the video yet?"

"Not yet. I thought I'd wait for your go-ahead. You know how this could look if someone gets wind of it, especially 'Page Six.' They think we're paranoid enough as it is."

"Well, screw them and let's find our criminal."

Mike looked up from his pizza. "Video?"

Bernie smiled coyly at Vince. "Vincenzo is our very own Columbo."

"Huh?"

Bernie looked at Mike and laughed. "Is *Columbo* before your time? I keep forgetting how young everybody is getting. Peter Falk played this detective on television. He acted scatterbrained, but he always solved the—"

"I know who Columbo is," Mike said as casually as possible. "But what video?"

Vince looked around the restaurant as if to ensure that no one was eavesdropping. He leaned in toward Mike. "During the last few months, we've had some things stolen from the office. At first it was petty stuff—invitations to various parties, free CDs publicists had sent us to review, black-and-white celebrity headshots." Vince sipped his water. "But last week, two framed photographs disappeared and then a radio. My gut was that it was the guys in the mailroom. So, just the other day, I had a surveillance camera installed in Melissa's pencil sharpener to catch our thief in action. It's activated whenever anyone walks by after hours."

Mike coughed out a piece of proscuitto. He gulped down his water.

"Isn't Vincenzo brilliant?" Bernie flashed a huge grin. "He couldn't have planned it more perfectly. We'll be able to nail Lottie Love. There's no way she can deny it . . . Mike, you look pale. I hope that thing you're eating didn't give you *E. coli.*"

The restaurant started spinning. Mike guzzled more water. He heard Bernie whisper, "Sebastian Brooks just walked in."

"He's with an entourage. Is anyone there your source? That stuff you got on Sebastian was pure gold. I loved him dancing in his underwear to 'Love Stinks.'"

Mike couldn't get the whirring and buzzing to go away. He felt like he was choking. His heart pushed up his throat. He swallowed more water.

"He gets my panties wet, excuse my bluntness. I'd love to do a profile on him," Bernie said. "Mike, you think it could happen? Mike? . . . Mike?"

He felt sick, like any moment he might spew his pizza right in Bernie's face. How could he have been so stupid? He should have known he was never alone in that place. Christ, it was like working for a prison. They probably had cameras in the crapper, too.

"Mike, I think one of the guys just smiled at you. It must be your source. Don't look. I don't want you to blow your cover," Bernie said. "Oh, that Sebastian has a great tush. He is sooo cute."

Bernie cooed. She was considered a no-nonsense leader who wasn't impressed by celebrity, but Mike had heard from Lem that she drooled over the ones she liked. She'd follow her favorites at parties and then beg for an autograph when she thought no one was looking. She'd promise cover stories if they posed with her, and she'd stand there while the camera flashed, squeezing out a look of indifference. The photo would eventually find its way into the publisher's letter, as if mingling with celebrity were all in a day's work for her.

"Miguel, you *have* to get us a profile."

"Yeah," Mike croaked out. "I mean, I don't know. My source says he needs some time . . ." Mike massaged the back of his neck. "He and Stephanie just ended it for good last week. He's not ready for a relationship right now, anyway."

"That's great stuff, Miguel. Great." Bernie winked at him. "But he will be back in the dating world, and we do want to be the first to get an exclusive on the new woman in his life. We don't want to read about it in *The Enquirer*."

Fuck. Just when things were going so well, he had to blow it. The story of his life. Liz. Little Joey Green. Even Amber. Probably Catherine. He was just a hick from Rochester. He never should have left. He didn't have the right immune system for this place or this job. It wasn't in his DNA. He should have stayed at the local paper. He'd be editor in chief by now.

"Vincenzo, should we tell Miguel what we caught on tape the other day? Or is it a little too risqué for our boy from the boondocks?"

Hick. Hick. Hick.

"Well, you'll have to do the honors, Bernie."

Hick. Hick. Hick. Hick. Hick.

Bernie leaned in again. "The other day, a few DVDs were stolen from Melissa's in-box, so we decided to take a look at the film to see if we could nail our culprit." Bernie paused, shook her head, and leaned even closer. Mike could smell the plaque on her teeth. She giggled. She took a sip of water, started laughing, and spit some up. She wiped her mouth and turned toward Vince. "Vincenzo, help me." She burst into a fit of laughter.

Vince leaned in toward Mike. "We have twenty minutes of Melissa . . . well . . . I mean . . . she was . . ."

Bernie guffawed. Ravioli flew out of her nose.

". . . pleasuring herself with one of those stuffed cats," Bernie roared. She leaned her head right on the table as her body shook with laughter.

Vince smirked and shook his head.

Bernie thrust an index finger into Mike's face. "See, I told you it was too much for him. Look at him! Look at him!"

"Mike?"

"Mike, are you okay?"

Mike exhaled and shut his eyes.

"You don't need to look at that tape."

Bernie glugged her water, wiped her eyes, and took an enormous breath. Then she crinkled her eyes at Mike.

"Mike, what is it?" Vince said.

He should just tell them. So what, they fire him? He didn't need this shit. These people were assholes.

He looked hard at them. His heart skittered.

"Well . . . well . . ." He exhaled. "It's just that it might be really embarrassing."

Bernie guffawed again. "Not as embarrassing as Melissa getting head—excuse me, tail—from Hello! Kitty," she bellowed. The entire restaurant stared at her.

Mike closed his eyes and swallowed. "Forget it."

"Mike, what are you getting at?"

Her eyes bored into him. He gulped hard. Then the words just spewed out of him.

"It's just that he's been with the company for so long."

"Who? Who's been at the company? Who?"

"It just that . . . well, can't you just talk to him? I'm sure he'll tell you everything. He didn't mean anything by it. He's a good guy."

"Lemuel Brac? Lemuel Brac?" Bernie boomed. Heads turned again.

"Mike? Lem Brac's been stealing from the office?" Vince asked incredulously.

"No! Of course not. Well, I mean, well . . . he was only helping Lottie. He let her in the building. You can ask him about it. He'll tell you everything. He didn't do anything."

There, that wasn't so bad. Maybe Vince wouldn't review the images. His heart relaxed a bit. The room shifted back into focus.

"Not so bad? Not so bad? He aided and abetted a trespasser!"

"Well, I mean, she was only taking *her* things."

"Her things? Anything she did while at *Personality* magazine is the sole property of the magazine. Mike, why didn't you tell us sooner?"

"Well, I . . ."

"This is grounds for dismissal."

His stomach somersaulted. "But . . . but . . . I didn't."

Bernie laughed. "Not you, Miguel, Lem Brac. I've wanted to get rid of that piece of English deadwood for years now. Some of the older staffers consider him venerable. They always fought me on it. But now I have the proper ammunition." She rubbed her hands together.

"But he really didn't . . . Don't fire him."

Bernie's eyes narrowed. "She probably screwed him, didn't she? He's the crypt keeper, but that wouldn't stop that little slut. I don't know what all these men find so appealing about her. I guess it's the fake tits. Isn't it? Men always love big tits. Real or not. Vincenzo? Miguel?"

Vince and Mike exchanged helpless looks. Mike bit into his pizza. He chewed but couldn't swallow.

"Just talk to Lem."

"Actually, Vincenzo, he does have a point. Let's see if we can talk to Lem about this. Get him to retire on his own. I'd rather not have the papers find out that we bugged the office. 'Page Six' would have a field day with that. And the old-timers in New York would yell entrapment. They'd think we were trying to frame Lem."

"Whatever you say, Bernie."

"Once again, Mike, you seem to know everything. What would we do without you?"

Mike smiled. Vince looked hard at Mike as if seeing him for the first time.

COLDPLAY'S "A RUSH OF BLOOD TO THE HEAD" BLASTED FROM Mike's radio as his Saab snaked around the tortuous roads that sliced through the dehydrated, dusty mountains of Mandeville Canyon. He was headed toward Ferris Wheel of Faith, a celebrity charity event for sufferers of Crohn's disease and ulcerative colitis. Chris Mercer, whose cousin had some kind of inflamed bowel problem, was one of the celebrity hosts. Mike would interview Chris, rush back to the office, and churn out the story.

He drove past castlelike homes featuring turrets and redbrick moats, Spanish villas with corrugated tiled roofs, Swiss chalets with stained-glass windows, Chinese pagodas, English Tudors, Southern plantation estates. It's a small world after all—especially when you had a ton of money and lived in Brentwood.

Mike wheeled through a secluded gravel street where flag-waving valets directed him to a stretch of land overlooking an endless cacti and yellow wildflower basin. As he parked his car, his cell phone rang.

"Mike Pos—"

"Where's my Rolodex?"

"What?"

"Listen, you asshole, you couldn't have my Rolodex more. And I want it back. NOW! If you don't give it back, you'll be sorry."

Mike felt light-headed. "Who is this?"

"You know who this is. It's Lottie Love. You have my Rolodex, and I want it back."

"Lottie, I don't know what the hell you're talking about."

"Okay. Fine. Be that way."

"Lottie, I really don't know what—" But the phone went dead.

Mike had an idea where it was. Amber's. But he hadn't had the nerve to call her since she had rooted around in his pants. Besides, what did it matter? What was Lottie Love going to do to him that he hadn't already done to himself? He couldn't stop thinking about how he'd betrayed Lem, the only guy who'd befriended him this past year. Who had Mike Posner become, anyway?

LIMOS WHISKED GUESTS up the mile-long windy road to the mansion. Mike headed toward an idling one. He jumped in and smiled at the woman next to him. It was Mira Sorvino. The limo driver looked at him through the rearview mirror.

"You have your invite?"

"Sure."

"Can I see it?"

Asshole, Mike thought, as he pulled the crumpled card out of his pocket. He held it up for the driver.

"That's a blue invite," the drive huffed. "The limo's for VIPs with gold invites. You'll have to wait for the shuttle."

"But you're going up anyway. What does it matter?"

"I'm sorry, it's the rule."

Demoted, Mike had to wait half an hour for the shuttle to crunch up a gravel driveway and deposit him near a walkway illuminated by candle-wielding bronze lions.

Mike looked around. The mansion was an homage to every architectural style. It was as if the owner—some producer Mike hadn't heard of—couldn't make up his mind about what he wanted his house to be. So it became a little bit of everything: a tiled Mediterranean roof with a Swiss chalet slope, a piled fieldstone facade, an arcade of Doric columns festooned with spiral scrolls, and a sweeping Southern-plantation-style porch, complete with a wicker swing set, chairs, and a pissing-boy fountain with the water flying into a leaping fish's mouth. Despite the view of the yellow-colored foothills, the place had almost no windows, save for a few dark slits that gave the house a permanent case of ennui. The oversized front door was a slab of dark wood intricately carved with gargoyles, angels, and some Greek and Roman gods. A dozen busts of chalky-white demigods wearing laurel leaves ornamented the edges of the roof.

The enormous lawn was littered with bronze and silver statues. There was a prebloated Elvis, his bronze mouth molded into a croon and his hands locked on guitar strings as thick as cables. There was Marilyn, her skirt billowing, her bronze face staring blankly ahead through wide, vacuous eyes. There was a beaming Dorothy in pigtails carrying a smiling Toto in a woven bronze basket. On the next tier of the sloping lawn was Barbra, her hands clasping a microphone, her face pinched in song, a silver tear suspended on her left cheek. James Dean scowled nearby with a cigarette dangling from thick lips. His hair was like the bow of a ship.

With a lawn like this, in any other part of the country the producer would be considered trailer trash. Here he's brilliant. Mike flinched, realizing this was something Lem would say.

"RECTUM. ANUS."

A woman's voice boomed through the P.A. system. "No one likes to use these words. No one ever wants to believe that the star of *The O.C.* or *Everwood* or *The West Wing* sits on the potty. So, repeat after me. Because if we can get you guys to admit it, the world won't feel so ashamed. Okay. Everybody . . . I *have* a rectum . . . I *have* an anus . . . I make bowel movements. I am a healthy person! Everyone. All together."

Yelling "I have an anus" were actors Mike vaguely recognized. Everyone at the office, with the exception of Lem, could rattle off the names of the Now Big Things and the Next Big Things, in both TV and film. But Mike still had no idea. He looked around for Chris Mercer and Cyndi Bowman. He checked his watch. He still had an hour before the interview. He went to the bar and ordered a Sierra Nevada.

Mike stood at the periphery, slowly sipping his beer and staring at the black mountains silhouetted against the lavender sky. They seemed so close and so alive that Mike felt if he ran to the edge of this producer's property, he could pet them and feel their steady breath and the warmth of blood stirring inside them. The moon, transparent behind a screen of silver clouds, looked like the tiniest feather drifting languidly above the festivities—a feather that could be knocked across the sky by a faint sigh of one of these craggy black behemoths.

Los Angeles is all about scenery.

Beautiful women brushed past him, giggling and chattering excitedly. He surveyed the crowd and eyed Chris holding court at a nearby table. He stood in front of his admirers, leaning his left arm on a leg that he was casually resting on a wicker chair. Mike stared. Chris, despite being an asshole (and quite short), was unbelievably handsome, with jet-black hair, deep-set violet eyes, a square chin, angular cheekbones, and lips that *Glamour* would describe as cherry red and pillowy. As he spoke, weaving his hands through the cool air, the rest of the table leaned in, hanging on each word. Then they laughed, loudly, their heads jerking back in appreciation. Chris shoved his hands in his pockets, nodded at the table, spun on his heels, and continued on to the next batch of admirers. He moved slowly, as if to heighten the anticipation of the crowd he was heading toward. "Hey, Mercer, over here." "Yoo-hoo, Chris!"

Mike felt smaller than ever before as he stood there, enveloped in the sublimity of the mountains and celebrity. Lem had been right all along, hadn't he? When the two had gone out to lunch when Mike first started, Lem told him not to become friends with any of them. When Mike said he didn't intend to, Lem disagreed, even though they had just met. Trust me, you do want to be their friends, he had said.

Mike lifted his glass in the air. "To Lem. You know more than I gave you credit for." On Monday, maybe he could make it up to Lem somehow.

He noticed a stunning blond, probably a model or an actress, watching in amusement.

"I'm really not that crazy," he said. Then he brought the drink to his lips and sipped.

"That's too bad, because I am." She laughed.

Mike tried to think of something witty to say, but his brain shorted out on him, and he stood there mute, overwhelmed by her shiny hair and perfect face and tanned legs.

"I'm Julia."

"Mike."

"Hello, Mike. Are you an actor?"

"No. A writer."

"Really? Movies?"

"No."

"Television?"

"No."

"Documentaries?" She cringed and started to pivot away.

"Magazine."

She turned back toward him and smiled.

"Oh. Which one?"

Mike loved this moment. Everyone—unless you were an enormous star—was impressed with *Personality*. Practically the entire country had grown up with it, devouring pages about their favorite celebs. And it was always doubly fun to tell an actress, because for a brief moment he could pretend the possibilities were endless.

"*Personality*."

A pause. A glint in her Caribbean blue eyes.

"Ohhhh. *Personality*." She moved closer to Mike. "I'm an actress. I'm starring in a pilot."

"Oh, really? What's it called?"

"*Sin Gals*."

"Singles?"

"No, Sin *Gals*. It's about single girls who, well, become prostitutes. It's *Pretty Woman* meets *Friends* but with a lot more humor." She flashed a smile. "So what do you think, Mike? Do you think it will be picked up?"

"Absolutely. Sounds better than watching a bunch of doctors or cops or bachelors."

Julia laughed. "It hasn't been picked up just yet, but it's only a matter of time. Gregory Perry, the creator, is a brilliant writer. There's so much crap on television these days. If this isn't picked up, I swear, I'll . . . I'll . . . become an accountant."

Mike laughed. "That's pretty drastic. Let me refill your drink. What's your pleasure?"

"Whips, chains, leather." Julia giggled.

Mike smiled.

Julia raised her hand as if she were a student hoping to be called on. "Actually, I must confess, that's a line from the pilot. Not bad, right? I think this series has hope."

"So do I."

"I feel like a Bellini. That's if the bartender has fresh peaches. If not, I'll have a margarita with Patron and fresh lime juice."

Mike returned to the bartender, a stocky bald guy whose eyelashes fairly dripped with mascara. "Peaches," the bartender asked, shaking his luminous blue-veined head. "Is it for *someone*?"

"Well, I'm not gonna put it in my gas tank."

The bartender frowned and shook his head as if Mike were a complete idiot. "To put it in plain English, what is the name of the person it's for?"

"Julia."

"Julia? Julia Roberts is here?" the bartender demanded as his eyes scanned Mike's face. "Wait a minute. I read in the trades that she's filming in Europe. So what's this Julia in?"

"*Sin Gals*."

"Oh. That hasn't even been picked up," the bartender said, his voice deflating. "Like I said, there's no peaches. Can I get you something else?"

Mike ordered Julia a margarita, wondering if the bartender would have torn through the yard, slithered up trees, and shook them for peaches had Mike mentioned a more stellar name. At least in Rochester, where no one had heard of a Bellini, where Bud Light ruled the bar scene, everyone was treated the same. *What am I doing at a party like this?* Mike wondered. He was suddenly overwhelmed by homesickness.

It ended fast. When he returned to Julia, a cluster of gorgeous women waited for him.

"Julia says you write for *Personality,*" they chimed at once. "You should do a story on me."

"You? Why you? You haven't done anything but bad theater."

"Bad theater. I guess you're forgetting about all those guest appearances on prime-time shows that I beat you out of. Ha!"

"Please, no one remembers guest appearances. You've got to be a regular to make it count."

"Or have a recurring role, like I did all season on *Malcolm in the Middle.*"

"Hey, you guys, I was here first. Mike and I were having a nice conversation."

"So? It's not like you're with him. And even if you were with him, I wouldn't care. I would do him in front of you."

"Guess what, Mike? I get to die next week on *ER*. And not just like in the first few minutes. I linger for like half the show."

"So what? You still die."

"Yeah, you know what that means. You can't come back."

Mike smiled. Guests eyed him, wondering if the guy surrounded by a bunch of beautiful women was someone. He checked his watch. Only a few more minutes before he was supposed to meet Cyndi and Chris in front of something called the Colossal Colon. He scanned the lawn. There were people milling about what looked like a giant worm. Must be the colon, he decided.

"Listen, I've gotta go interview . . ." A long pause. "Chris Mercer."

"Wow! What's he like?"

"Well, don't leave without saying good-bye."

"We'll be waiting for you."

"Hurry back."

"Can I come too?"

MIKE ARRIVED AT the giant worm/colon just as Cyndi Bowman was exiting it. She gave him a quick smile, then extended her hand as if they had never met before.

"Cyndi Bowman," she said. "Chris should be here any second." She pointed toward the colon. "You should check it out. You can walk into it and see what hemorrhoids and fissures look like up close."

"It's just something I'm not that curious about."

"Okay. Just hang then. Chris'll be here any second."

A few more minutes passed. Mike scanned the lawn but didn't see Chris anywhere. His cell phone trilled.

"Mike Posner."

"Where's my Rolodex?"

"I don't have it."

"Okay then. Be that way. You couldn't be more sorry."

Mike laughed. "Doesn't that mean I shouldn't be sorry at all?"

Silence. Mike pressed the Off button as Cyndi eyed him. She hummed nervously as her eyes skittered across the lawn. She checked her watch.

"He should be here momentarily. I saw him just a little while ago. This really isn't like Chris at all. Probably someone with colitis is talking his ear off." She leaned in, giggled, and whispered, "He shouldn't be much longer. Those people have to take a crap every five seconds."

ANOTHER HALF HOUR. Mike watched as Cyndi canvassed the lawn, castigating assistants on her cell phone. "You find him now or it's your ass." She'd press keys and speak. Press keys and speak.

Mike's heart pounded and he felt light-headed. A waiter with a tray of champagne sauntered by, and Mike grabbed one, guzzled, and grabbed another. Cyndi marched toward him from the lawn. "We're locating him right now," she said. She forced out a quick smile while her eyes looked past Mike.

Suddenly there was a tremor of sighs, and Mike raised his head, scanning the crowd for the epicenter of the starquake. It had to be Chris. Mike looked around. It was someone else Mike didn't recognize.

His cell phone rang.

"Hello?" he exhaled into the phone.

"It looks like the star reporter won't be interviewing Chris Mercer after all."

CLICK.

"Lottie?"

He took off, running around the lawn searching for Lottie Love. She must be somewhere watching these events unfold and having a really good laugh. His eyes darted over the tables, the bars, the tents, everywhere. He banged on bathroom doors. Then he raced around again, covering the periphery, nearly knocking over Courteney Cox. He took another champagne. Where the fuck was she?

He spotted her at the bar. Long auburn hair. Michael Stars black camisole. Earl jeans. A cigarette dangling from her mouth.

"Lottie!" He grabbed her shoulder.

She jerked and grimaced. "Do you mind?"

Just another Lottie Love clone in a sea of Lottie Love clones.

She was nowhere. Chris was nowhere. Cyndi Bowman marched toward him.

Was she talking to him or into her headset? He could never tell. He hated those headsets—everyone thought they looked like the Secret Service or Britney onstage, when they were really just greeters at The Gap.

Cyndi looked right at Mike and crinkled her face into a pained smile.

"Well, of course I understand."

"What do you understand?" Mike asked.

"Some things must be a priority . . ."

"What's a priority?"

Cyndi stuck an index finger out at Mike to silence him.

"Well, Christopher, you do what you have to do . . . Absolutely . . . Absolutely. Well, thanks so much. We'll talk tomorrow . . . Or stop by. Anytime."

She dropped her index finger and squeezed out a grimace.

"So, it looks like this thing won't be happening tonight, 'kay?" She spoke in a singsongy voice and squeezed out an "I'm suffering from colitis" smile. "Call me tomorrow to resched."

"WHAT? I CAN'T RESCHEDULE. THIS NEEDS TO HAPPEN RIGHT NOW. YOU GUARANTEED THIS. GET HIM ON THE PHONE."

White dots of fury flew in front of Mike's eyes. Cyndi frowned.

"You don't need to raise your voice at me. I'm sorry for the misunderstanding."

"MISUNDERSTANDING? There was no misunderstanding. You fucking—"

She stuck out her hand like a traffic cop. "Okay, you so do not need to use vulgarities. As a journalist, you know that sometimes situations arise that are beyond our control."

"As a publicist, you're supposed to fucking make sure this interview happens."

Cyndi took a deep breath. "It will happen. Just not tonight, 'kay?"

"No, it's not 'kay." Mike spit it out like a curse. "It's not 'kay at all."

"Well, it's beyond my control." Cyndi pulled her hair back and sighed, as if she needed to regain composure. "As you know, Chris is a recovering alcoholic and it's a daily struggle," she said. "Anyway, he just got a call from someone he sponsors who had hit bottom and needed his help. That's the kind of guy he is. He'd drop everything to help an alcoholic. Everything."

She prattled on, but Mike stopped listening. *Lottie Love.* Somehow Lottie had screwed this up for him. Lem was right. Stars don't shine forever. His barely blinked.

He gasped for breath. He struggled to speak calmly. "Cyndi, please. If I can't talk to him in person, at least get him on the telephone. I need something. Call him up."

She squeezed out another fulsome grin. "No can do. He specifically asked not to be disturbed."

"This is bullshit. Bullshit. Where the fuck is he?"

"There's nothing I can do, o-kay? I'll confab with him in the A.M. Promise!" She nearly sang.

"LET'S TALK ABOUT COLONOSCOPIES," the hostess yelled into a microphone.

Mike stared hard at Cyndi. "This is bullshit. I'll get all of Chris's high school classmates on the phone. I'll talk to his neighbors. I'll find his enemies. I'll do this without you or him. And you'll hate it. I'll write about the other night. Everything."

Cyndi threw up her hands. "I guess you'll do what you have to do. But I know your deadline is in . . ." She checked her watch. "Like a half hour, and it's already bedtime in Jersey, his hometown." She smiled.

Mike bit his tongue and clenched his fists. "You're a real fucking bitch. And . . . and . . . you should sue the doctor who gave you that nose."

"MIKE!" JULIA FROM *Sin Gals* yelled out to him, but he ignored her. He wandered across the lawn, leaned against the Barbra Streisand sculpture, closed his eyes, and tried to calm his palpitating heart. He took deep breaths.

He called the Chateau Marmont.

"Chris Mercer, please."

"I'm sorry . . ."

"Okay, Johnny Malibu."

"I'm sorry . . ."

"I know that Chris Mercer—or whatever he's calling himself

these days—is staying there. I need to talk to him right now. Right now! It's an emergency."

"I know it is. And I'm sorry. There's nothing I can do to help you. Perhaps you can write to his fan club."

Click.

MIKE BANGED A fist into Barbra. What the fuck to do? He studied his cell phone, trying to figure out how to break the news to Vince. Then it occurred to him.

He pressed a button to reveal the last incoming number. He dialed it.

It rang and rang.

He redialed and redialed. Finally, it picked up.

"Lottie! Lottie!" Mike screamed into the phone. "Talk to me. Right now."

No one answered. He heard a panting sound.

"Lottie. I know you're there. Talk to me. Fucking talk to me."

No answer. Silence. And then panting. Then something that sounded like squeaking. *ErrEErrEErrE.*

"Answer me!"

Then more breathing. Heavier and heavier. Squeaking. Grunting. *ErrErrErrE.* Moan. And finally he heard Lottie Love's voice.

"Yes."

"Lottie!"

"Yes . . . yes. Yes. YESSSSS!"

"Lottie. Listen to me right now," he screamed.

"Oh, yes. Oh, yessss! YOU'RE NUMBER ONE. CHRIS MERCER, YOU ARE NUMBER ONE!"

"HEY, MAN. YOU OKAY?"

Lem sat in the back of a cheddar-colored cab en route to Franny's. He sipped Smirnoff's out of a paper bag. A white-hot poker chiseled away at his heart.

One hundred something days blown.

"You okay?" the cabbie repeated, eyeing Lem through the rearview mirror.

"Quite," Lem said. Actually he wasn't. His chest felt leaden, and he had trouble catching his breath. He rolled down the window and breathed in the smoggy air. Then he rested his head on the seat back.

"Nice neighborhood, dude," the cabbie said. Lem closed his eyes. What was it with these Americans, he wondered. They are all so bloody afraid of silence that they beat it up and strangle it every chance they get with talk of neighborhoods or license plates. No doubt this guy was another struggling actor. Marlon Lang, the ID on the glove box read. Poor Marlon, with his straggly hair and mangy goatee. This guy didn't have star quality; the best he could hope for was the part of the annoying cabdriver. Marlon—Driving You Since 2004.

"Lotta money here. Not too shabby." Marlon clicked his tongue and shook his head. "I wouldn't mind a crib up here. It'll happen. One day. I'm not a cabdriver, really. I'm an actor. I'm preparing for a role. An action adventure. I play an alien disguised as a New York City cabdriver. Chris Mercer kills me."

"You too?"

"Huh?"

Lem laughed a little too hard.

THIS MORNING, besides being hungover, Lem was in trouble. He knew it almost as soon as he walked into Reggio's office.

"Franny Blanchard is interested in a where-are-they-now treatment. I thought our *Personality* readers would find a profile on Franny to be a good read. She is quite a legend. Still has a lot of fans out there," Lem said.

The other day Lottie had told him she now represented Franny Blanchard. She asked him to intervew her. Lem realized that if he wanted his daughter in his life, he'd have to deal with the past. And that meant more than throwing away a bunch of old magazines. He'd meet with Franny. He'd figure out what had been real and what had been an illusion.

But Reggio looked dazed. His Good Humor–man linens were wrinkled. His hair was disheveled and gel-less. "Blanchard . . . Blanchard," he mumbled, scanning his brain's pop-culture repository. "Ah, Lisa the Love Witch. She doesn't interest me. Just another faded actress who's desperately struggling to have the limelight shine in her face. That is, as long as her public is wearing rose-colored glasses."

"I think her fans are still interested to know what she's doing."

Reggio rested his head in his hands. "Lem, not today. This is a really bad day for me. Mike Posner dropped the ball with Chris Mercer."

"Mike? I'm sure that wasn't his fault. You know how these celebrities are."

"He didn't have any backup. He had no thirds, no write-around. And I just got reamed out by Julia Roberts's publicist. Mike's source gave him some erroneous information."

"I'm certain he can explain . . ."

Reggio massaged his temples and looked at Lem as if suddenly remembering he was there. "You're quick to come to Mike's defense," he muttered. "Especially considering."

"Considering?" Lem squinted his eyes and studied Reggio.

Reggio ignored Lem and picked up his phone. "Melissa, Lem Brac is in my office. Could you send Bernie down here?"

"All this for a where-are-they-now on Franny Blanchard?" Lem laughed nervously.

"Lem, Bernie and I need to speak to you."

"About what?"

Vince shook his head but didn't say anything. He eyed the door while tapping a pen on his desk. Then he sat erect and smiled broadly. He nodded as Bernie entered. She looked past Lem right at Reggio.

"Craziness," she boomed. "Craziness, craziness. All is craziness. But we pulled it off. The second installment of celebrity diets. You should see the proofs. The photos are beautiful. And yours truly managed a pub letter about my battle with the bulge." She grabbed a slab of fat from her stomach as she spoke. "I think I've just located an entire battalion." She chortled. Then she looked solemnly at Lem.

"Lemuel." She nodded at the floor.

"Bernie."

"I suppose Vincenzo has explained the situation."

Reggio coughed nervously.

"Actually, he has not," Lem said.

"Have a seat," Bernie said as she plopped onto the couch. Lem sat down across from her. The poker stabbed at his heart.

Bernie cleared her throat. "Lem, it has come to our attention that you gave a terminated employee access to our offices."

Lem relaxed and smiled. "Oh. Right. I was finishing up some odds and ends. Lottie stopped by to collect her belongings. Security wouldn't let her in, so I walked up with her."

Bernie looked hard at him. "And you don't see a problem with that? Lemuel, this is someone who is no longer with the company. Someone with a serious gripe. Someone who could cause serious dam—"

"She just came in to collect her possessions. She wasn't really out of my sight."

"Oh, I'm sure she wasn't." Bernie smiled slyly. "But somehow she did manage to steal the master key. I'm certain she was planning a second break-in."

"She didn't take the master key. I was with her—"

"Well, someone stole the master key. This is going to cost the company a lot of money, thank you very much, Lemuel."

Lem looked past them, concentrating on the pressed-wood entertainment center in the front of the room. The cabinets were empty, save for a television, a DVD player, and a few trophies. Those golden trophies looked like dusty Mormon temples. They had been on the shelves for as long as Lem could remember, but he had never really looked at them before. As Lem stared, he realized the winged gods perched on faux marble stands were swinging tennis racquets, baseballs, and golf clubs. These were not awards for journalism, as Lem had believed all those years. Instead, these were someone's athletic awards—probably poor Reggio's Little League trophies. He grinned. Bernie eyed him.

"I'm glad this is all so amusing to you," Bernie said. She looked at her watch. "I've got a conference call to attend to." She looked at Reggio and nodded. "Vincenzo, you handle this."

Reggio twitched nervously as she stomped out. He stared at his desk.

"It's been a stressful twenty-four hours and everybody's nerves are frayed," Reggio said.

"I was just trying to help out a colleague."

"A *former* colleague," Reggio said through clenched teeth. "We have no choice in this matter, Lem."

"No choice?"

"Lem, let's not do this. Okay? We're all adults. I'm going to have to ask you to resign."

Lem laughed. "After all these years, you're going to fire me because I let some kid collect her Tom Cruise posters?"

Reggio sighed and shook his head. "I'm not firing you. You're resigning. Lem, you'll get a nice package. Take an early retirement. Play golf."

"I don't . . . play . . . golf," Lem scoffed.

"Well, Bernie's cleaning house. They just hired a news editor who's going to want harder-edged stories. James Davenworth from the *New York Daily News.* And you haven't been pulling your weight for quite some time. We could say you're working on bigger projects. A book. Whatever you want us to say."

Lem stared at the trophies. He squinted to read them. Vincent Reggio: Team Spirit. Vincent Reggio: Most Dedicated. Vincent Reggio: Most Improved. Vincent Reggio: Hardest Worker. That translated into Vincent Reggio: No Athletic Ability Whatsoever.

This made Lem laugh. Insanely. He doubled over. His body rattled and he wheezed, groping for breath. His stomach cramped and his chest tightened. Lem wiped his moist eyes with a beige shirtsleeve. He struggled for composure, the hinges of his jaw twitching. When he looked up, Reggio was staring.

"Lem, this is extremely serious."

"Vincent," Lem gasped. "Vincent."

"What's funny?"

"Everything. You. These trophies. This place. If you want to fire me, fire me. Don't use euphemisms. Don't say I'm off to work on projects or that I'll be serving in a consultant capacity or that I'm moving to the upstairs office. Say I was fired. Yell it. Scream it. Put it in a fucking goddamn memo. Lem Brac was fired."

Reggio winced. "I was trying to be kind."

Lem jerked his head back. "Kind? Kind *Vincenzo.* Don't insult me by assuming I'm not as clever as you. You and Bernie and the rest of the new establishment don't want to raise the ire of the old guys on staff. The guys who remember Sir Lem. It has nothing to do with kindness. Nothing. Just remember, one day you're gonna get old. One day you're going to be offered a consultancy position or an office upstairs or nebulous projects."

Reggio closed his eyes and rubbed his temples.

"Call it what you like. In two weeks, I want you out of here."

"Reggio, you are a truly dangerous man," Lem said. "A coward. An untalented coward with power."

Reggio glared at Lem while his temples pulsated. He opened his mouth. The guy who spoke in sports metaphors but who couldn't throw a ball didn't know what to say. So instead, Reggio did what he always did when under stress: he picked up the phone and pretended to dial a number.

BACK IN HIS office Lem drained the remainder of his bottle of Smirnoff's and opened a second. He called Marjorie Bowman.

Her son, Tommy, answered.

"I want to meet her."

"Who?"

"My daughter."

There was silence. "I don't know anything. But Patricia's visiting my mom. Hold on."

"No . . . wait." Lem's heart beat crazily. "Tommy, don't."

"Hello?"

It was Patricia. Lem opened his mouth, but nothing came out.

"Hello? Hello? Is anyone there?"

"Patricia."

"Yes?"

"I want to meet her."

There was silence.

"Have you been drinking?"

"No. I mean, yes, but not much. That's it. I'm sobering up. It's not like the old days, Patricia. I went cold turkey for months. I just want to see her. Cathy."

Again, there was a long silence. Lem heard what sounded like sniffles.

"I don't know what you're talking about," she said.

"Yes, you do. Please, Patricia, I know I don't deserve the truth, but I can't deal with any more lies. Please. I saw. She has my mother's eyes. She has my mother's eyes."

"No, Lem. Please. Please leave Cathy alone. Get help. Go to AA."

"But I just want to—"

"Lemuel." Patricia's voice was suddenly gruff. "Cathy . . . has had a rough time of it. A really rough time of it. If you saw what she went through, you'd understand."

"So it is true."

"Leave her alone. She's had her own problems. She doesn't need yours."

"Problems? What kind of problems?"

"Lem, please."

"Patricia, what kind of problems?"

"Substance abuse." There was a long pause. "She had problems with substance abuse. She's recovered now, thank God. But you have no idea what she went through. It was an absolute horror."

Another long pause.

"God, it's me, isn't it? She inherited that from me. I haven't even met her and I've only been a bad influence."

He hung up the phone. What had he been thinking? He'd never make a good father. Even as an absent father, he was horrible.

LEM SNAPPED BACK to the present as Marlon whistled. "What a street," he said. To avoid any more inane conversation, Lem opened the file Lottie had given him. Yesterday he'd read all the articles he'd written on Franny and had been impressed. He'd forgotten what a great writer he had been. He shuffled through the articles again. They traced an all too familiar path: a smattering of press follows a star on the rise. Then, in her heyday, every major publication spits out tons of blathering praise. Photographs of Franny with Travolta, Eastwood, Stallone, Arnold. Then the decline, with a few sightings and a few mentions about movies of the week. Then nothing. And now, infomercials. A few product lines. Whatever it takes.

An envelope fell from the folder onto the cab's floor. He recognized Thom Bowman's slanted penmanship. It was addressed to Franny Blanchard.

Marlon whistled again as they pulled up to Franny Blanchard's manse. "Nyyy-ice," he said. Then he turned his greasy head around to face Lem. "Hey, man, anyone famous live here?"

"No." Lem's tongue felt thick and spongy when he spoke. "Not anymore."

He exited, slammed the cab door, and tossed a $20 bill through the front window. Even though he'd been in America for decades, he still paid cabbies English style.

Then he stood in front of Franny's house and slowly read the letter Thom Bowman had forgotten to send.

LOTTIE LOVE SAT IN LIPLESS'S OFFICE TRYING TO EXPLAIN WHY she felt so horrible. But she couldn't get the words out.

"What is it, Lottie?" Lipless asked.

"I need help," she said. "I am lit-rully an awful person."

"What did you do that makes you feel this way?"

"I . . . I . . . I . . ."

"Come on, Lottie. You can tell me. You can tell me anything."

It was too much for her to say. Maybe she'd call Lem. Maybe he could help her.

"We can just sit here," Lipless said.

So she did. At a negotiated rate of $50 an hour, it was an expensive silence.

"Maybe next time you'll be ready to talk."

Lottie imagined Lipless's mind racing with possibilities. *What has my little starfucking patient done this time?*

WILL LOTTIE LOVE REVEAL? TOMORROW AT NOON.

"I screwed the hottest star in America to get back at this guy who stole something that is really valuable to me. I hate myself. I thought I'd feel great. I mean, isn't this what I always wanted? But I can't even look in the mirror."

WHEN LOTTIE ARRIVED at the office, Cyndi was exceptionally chirpy.

"Look over the Franny Blanchard material. Isn't Lame Lem heading there later today to interview her? What a morning! I've been trying to get Chris Mercer on the phone, but he's MIA. By the way, a new batch of Franny's The Cure arrived. It's on your desk. You should try Calm. It really works wonders. Trust me."

Lottie didn't bother to turn on her office lights. She sat in the darkness and retrieved her messages. Catherine had called to check on her. Lottie felt sick. Catherine had been the only real friend she'd ever had. But it was a friendship founded on lies. Lottie almost wished she really were an alcoholic just to keep Catherine in her life.

Her intercom beeped. Cyndi's voice filled the room.

"Make sure Lem Bric-a-brac runs that story on Franny Blanchard ASAP. I just found out he's retiring in two weeks. We don't want Franny to wind up in some slush pile."

"That's gotta be a mistake. Lem so wouldn't retire."

"I just spoke to Vincent Reggio. It's probably just a euphemism for getting fired, but Vince is too classy to say it. Anyway, Franny needs press. So ride his decrepit ass."

Poor Lem. She knew they wanted him out of there, but what had he done to get himself fired? She called Vince's assistant, Melissa.

"Don't ever call here."

"What?"

"If they know I'm on the phone with you, I'll be outta here so fast."

"Please, Melissa, you couldn't be more drama queen. Just tell me why Lem was fired."

"Du-uh! Maybe for letting you in the office."

"What?"

"Like you didn't know."

"I didn't."

"Lottie, seriously, everything you touch turns to shit. No wonder your father's a plumber."

"What are you talking about?"

"Think about it. Poor Marlon Lang, Lem Brac, and I even heard Mike Posner cursing you out. You're poison, Lottie. You ruin people."

"Fuck you, Melissa," Lottie said as she slammed down her phone.

But as the phone traveled from her ear to its cradle, Lottie had a revelation: it was true. Lottie was poison. She never helped anyone. She just took and took, and she didn't care about the consequences. She knew Lem could get in trouble, but she didn't think about him. All she thought about was her Rolodex, her posters, her files. Herself. And then there was Catherine. Lottie had found out later they had called the cops on Catherine at Ray Young's party. She already had some sort of record and could have gotten in a lot of trouble. And Marlon. She couldn't even look at him when his movie flopped. She had sabotaged Mike and used Chris Mercer.

Lottie broke the number one office rule: she bawled right at her desk.

Cyndi knocked on her door.

"Oh, honey. You okay?"

"Yeah. I'm getting it together like right now." Lottie sniffed hard.

"By the way, I finally located Chris Mercer." Cyndi sucked in her cheeks. Had he told her? Lottie stiffened.

"I know that was completely unprofessional," Lottie said.

"What are you talking about?"

So Chris hadn't told her. She exhaled. "Oh . . . I mean, my crying at the office."

"Forget about it. Someone's always crying here. A good cry is like an orgasm," she said. Then quickly added, "Guess what?"

"What?"

"You're never gonna believe it."

"What?"

"He's . . . in love," Cyndi chirped.

"Oh. Who?"

"Chris Mercer. Who do you think I'm talking about? I've never heard him like this. The press will have a field day with this especially if it's . . ." Cyndi seemed lost in thought. She smiled. "Anyway, we have to keep it quiet for as long as possible . . . Lottie, are you okay? You look white as a ghost."

"I'm okay."

"Well, back to the grind." She skipped out.

Shit. Shit. Shit.

Was Chris Mercer in love with her? Isn't that what she'd always wanted? An A-list celebrity? A few days ago she would have been ecstatic. Instead, she felt miserable. Another relationship founded on lies. Another person she'd poisoned. When they were screwing the other night, she couldn't think about anyone but Mike Posner. She was filled with such rage. And Chris thought she was having the biggest orgasm of her life, when she was really acting for Mike.

An actress. Despite what she promised her mother, that's all she'd ever been. An actress playing a journalist. An actress playing a publicist. An actress playing a star's arm candy. An actress pretending she didn't belong at the service entrance.

She took a deep breath. She thrummed her fingers against her computer, scanned her office. Her eyes landed on Calm. She opened the bottle and gulped some. It tasted sweet, like butterscotch. She swilled some more. Then she rested her head on the desk.

It worked! Lottie felt more relaxed than she had in a long, long time. Almost light-headed. Slightly buzzed. She wiped her eyes and blew her nose. The room hummed. She giggled. She took another sip. This stuff was good! She guzzled down some more, hiccuped out a laugh. Eyes closed, she relished the buzz. Then she picked up the bottle and examined the label. *Franny Blanchard's The Cure: Calm. Manufactured by Curandero, Tijuana, Mexico.* She squinted to read the ingredients. Passiflora incarnata, fresh skull cap, kava kava root, artemesia vulgaris, humulus lupulus, rowanberry, pure grain alcohol.

Pure grain alcohol.

A few months ago this would have meant nothing to her. But because of her Big Lie, she knew everything there was to know about alcoholics. She thought about crazy Joe, the guy from AA.

SHE BARGED INTO Cyndi's office.

"Come on, just a hint," Cyndi cooed into the phone. "Why are you being like this? If you can't tell me, who can you tell? You have to tell me if we're going to work out a media plan . . . Aha. Oh, really." Cyndi voice turned chilly. "Well, I hope it works out."

As Cyndi slammed down the phone, Lottie realized something: poor Cyndi was in love with Chris Mercer.

"It's some lush he met at AA," Cyndi snarled. "Jeez, the press will have a field day with this one. I mean, talk about a relationship starting off on the wrong foot."

Lottie nodded. She felt sick.

"What is it now, Lottie?" Cyndi said angrily. "I've got a pile of work here."

Lottie sniffled as her heart pounded. For a second, she forgot why she was there.

"Lottie?"

"I tried Calm."

"Isn't it great? I can't get enough of it."

"It's got grain alcohol in it."

"No wonder I feel so good all the time." Cyndi waited for Lottie to say something. "So, ah, is there a problem?"

"Well, it's just that we're promoting this in our press releases as an all-natural nonaddictive thing, and it couldn't be further from the truth."

"So?"

"I know this guy, Joe. He was a recovering alcoholic and doing great. He hadn't touched the stuff in like five years. Then he started this big health kick. Vitamins and herbs. Anyway, it turned out some herbal drink he was taking had alcohol in it. He couldn't stop himself. Now he's a total mess."

Cyndi sighed. "Okay, thanks for that interesting bit of news. And what precisely does that have to do with me?"

"Well, it's just that we should mention it has grain alcohol—"

"Lottie, please. We're not hiding anything. People should read the fine print before taking any type of medicine or stimulant."

"Did you read the fine print?"

"Well, I don't need to, Lottie. I'm not some raging alcoholic."

"I've gotta get outta here," Lottie said as she turned toward the door.

"I need you in the office. Chris Mercer is coming by. We must work on a media plan for his alleged love life. I'd like your input. This will be a tremendous learning opportunity for you."

"I can't. I have to find Lem. I have to tell him about the pure grain alcohol."

"Lem? So what? What's Lem Brac got to do with anything? Our job is to protect our clients from the press, not the other way around."

"I don't want something else to be my fault."

"Lottie, that's not part of your job description. Have you read the Bowman mission statement? We get clients publicity. You know, I completely hate Franny Blanchard, but I'm able to put that aside and do my job."

"This is different."

"No, it's not!" Cyndi shouted. "It's just something else about Franny we need to ignore. Just like your father fucking Franny. You think that's a big deal? Huh? Well, welcome to my world. I grew up with it. She was fucking my father right under our roof while my mother was having one of her nervous breakdowns in the next room. I heard it all. My dad and her always reciting movie dialogue. God, I fucking hate *Gone With the Wind*."

"Cyn, I'm sorry, but—"

"But what? I'm a professional here. You think I want that woman anywhere near me? But she's a client and I'm doing my job." Cyndi closed her eyes and breathed deeply. "So don't worry about whether or not a journalist is reading the fine print. Okay?

It means nothing to us. What's happened to you anyway? It's like suddenly you have this total conscience."

Lottie smiled.

"Maybe I do," she said.

"Well, we don't need that here."

"Okay." Lottie smiled again. "Then I quit."

HE'D BEEN IN LOS ANGELES FOR A YEAR, BUT HAD NO IDEA WHERE to go or who to talk to. He drove slowly along Ventura, staring out at the pink and blue ribbons of neon, the Thai restaurants, the vegans with placards protesting the slaughter of cows.

Vince had been furious.

"You dropped the ball."

"But . . . but . . . it wasn't . . . my fault."

"If he had potential commitments, you should have known about it. That's what separates the stars from the hacks."

Hick. Hick. Hick.

"But . . . but . . ."

"And you should have had a write-around prepared."

"Vince, I was assured. Cyndi Bowman is a complete liar—"

Vince's temples pulsated. "I've worked with Cyndi and have always found her nothing but professional." He shook his head. "I don't have time for this now. We're scrambling to get the celeb diet cover going. It's a disaster. Ben mixed up The Zone with Atkins. We'll discuss this with Bernie later."

HOW COULD SOMEONE live in a place for a year and make no friends? No guys to commiserate with about the asshole boss, the shit job, the lack of a love life. Maybe a few days ago, he could have called Lem. He would have understood. Just the other day, Lem had called him "son." How could he have betrayed the only person who'd been nice to him?

There was one place Mike wanted to go. He had her address.

He turned left on Barham. He was almost there, but was it a good idea? Probably not. She hadn't returned his phone call. But what did he have to lose? Nothing. If she hated him already, it didn't matter.

He couldn't handle the rejection. No. He wouldn't go. He'd turn around and head home. A long, sleepless night awaited him. A night of infomercials, of Six-Week Body Makeovers and Seven-Second Abs, of Butt Busters and Fat Blasters.

Maybe if he begged, the hick could get his job back in Rochester. It was just a matter of time before they fired him here. Rochester was the place where he belonged. A place where he didn't have to pretend.

Welcome back, Mike. The big city was too much for you, huh? Happens all the time. Now head over to Pittsford, there's a cow-tipper on the loose.

He continued on Barham. Turned left on Woodrow Wilson.

"MIKE? YOU LOOK horrible."

She opened the door and let him in. He was so grateful that he hugged her and didn't let go. A Dalmation and a small ball of fur jumped on his back. He nearly tumbled to the floor. He squeezed her tighter.

"Mike, what is it?"

He shut his eyes and breathed her in.

"Mike, it's okay. It's going to be okay."

What was it about Catherine that made him tell her everything? Joey Green. The Rolodex. Lem Brac. The stories he'd concocted. It all just poured out of him, almost beyond his control. He felt exhausted but strangely refreshed—the way he did when he went to confession as a kid. A blank slate. Cleansed from sin. His penance would be her rejection, so he knew it didn't matter what he said.

"I'm just completely inadequate," he said. "My first girlfriend didn't even realize it when she lost her virginity."

"Just some weird defense mechanism on her part," she said,

smiling. "Maybe no girl's excited you enough. Maybe you play it safe too often. You need someone completely different. You need to take risks."

He studied her for an explanation. He had a bad feeling she wasn't talking about herself.

"You sound like my mother," he said, laughing. "Well, I guess I've blown it with you."

She looked up at him and smiled. "Mike, it's not that. There's just too much you don't know about me—too much you don't want to know."

"You're perfect."

"I'm so far from perfect it's not funny." Catherine sighed and closed her eyes. "I started drinking when I was thirteen."

"So what? I had my first beer when I was twelve. There's not much to do in Rochester but drink."

Catherine smiled weakly. "By the time I was eighteen, I was doing anything I could get my hands on. Coke. Crack. Heroin. My mom couldn't handle me at all. My father kicked me out of the house. He and my mom divorced because of me."

"Catherine, I don't—"

She put her hand out to silence him.

"I heard him tell my mom that one night. 'She's not my daughter.' He screamed it. Then he left her because of me. He couldn't stand the sight of his own daughter. Can you imagine living with that? I still see the way he looked at me when I go to sleep at night. I don't think I'll ever get over that."

She rubbed tears out of her eyes, and Mike hugged her.

"Shit. I'm sorry, Catherine."

Catherine pushed him lightly. She looked hard at him. "Mike, I did anything to get a high . . . Do you have any idea what that means?"

"Ah . . . I mean, I guess."

"No, you don't. You have no clue."

Mike looked away from her glare.

"It means I did a lot of horrible things. *A lot.* I don't even remember most of it, but every now and then, I'll go somewhere, like a Hollywood party or something, and I'll see a group of guys staring or laughing or pointing at me. And I know I'll never escape my past. I don't know why I stay here. Maybe it's for moments like those to remind me, because the truth is, I have no idea who I was."

Mike nodded his head.

"Look at you. You're not good at lying, despite what you think. Lottie was right. I can see it in those eyes of yours. She calls them newly hatched chicken eyes."

"Lottie," Mike snarled. "Why do you care so much about her?"

"I'm trying to help myself by helping Lottie. Maybe if I can save one person, I'll be able to forgive myself. I'll stop seeing that look of disgust in my own father's eyes."

"You have no idea what kind of person she is."

The Dalmatian barked. Catherine whistled and it climbed into her lap. "Hey there, boy," she said, nuzzling and kissing it. "A family decided to get rid of him because their son grew out of his *101 Dalmatians* phase. The kid likes *Finding Nemo* now so they got him an aquarium instead. Maybe you should adopt him."

Mike laughed. "I can barely take care of myself."

"Maybe that's the problem. You need to take care of someone else to forget about yourself. That's what I do. This dog is so needy, he'll consume you."

The other dog, a runty poodle, yipped and tugged at Mike's jeans.

"That's Arthur," Catherine said. "The shelter found him whimpering on the corner of Hollywood and Gower yesterday."

Mike eyed the poodle suspiciously. It yipped again.

"It couldn't be."

"What?"

Mike leaned over and looked underneath the dog. He nodded his head. "Plastic balls."

"What?"

He laughed. "I don't believe it! I know this dog. It's Root Canal. It's my neighbor's."

"Your neighbor's?"

"I don't fucking believe it. She loved that dog. She was obsessed with that dog. That dog has these little hand-knit outfits and everything. It had its own little doggie bed. I can't believe she'd just abandon it. It doesn't make sense."

He petted the dog. "Root Canal?" The poodle jumped on Mike and licked his cheek. "It's him, all right."

"Root Canal? What a horrible name. I was calling him Arthur, after my first boyfriend. He was this really sweet guy, who's trying to be an actor now, although he has the most horrible lisp. When I saw this little guy, I thought if he could speak, he'd have a lisp."

They stroked Root Canal/Arthur. Mike smiled at Catherine. He realized she reminded him of Liz, another custodian of strays. Maybe Catherine was right. Maybe he needed to go against his type. Maybe he was drawn to women like Catherine and Liz because he considered himself a mangy little mutt with nowhere to go.

"Mike, can I set you up with someone who I think would be good for you?"

"You're trying to set me up with a friend?" He tried to sound casual, but the rejection caught in his throat. "I'm horrible on blind dates."

"It wouldn't be a blind date."

"How could it not be a . . ." Then it dawned on him. "You're talking about her again, aren't you?"

"She likes you, Mike."

"She hates me. You even said that. Besides, you have no idea what she did to me."

"Was it before or after you stole her Rolodex?" Catherine asked, grinning. "I said she thinks she hates you, but she doesn't. She wants to hate you because she knows you're right for her. I know it sounds crazy and illogical. She thinks her type is some vapid actor who doesn't give a shit about her. But you guys would be great together. I can feel it."

"You and Lem."

"The guy you told me about?"

"Yeah. You sound a lot like him. But I can tell you it would never work. We are not at all alike."

Catherine smiled. "Stranger things have happened, Mike Posner."

"Is this how you reject all your men? You introduce them to your friends?"

Friend. A jolt ran through him. Suddenly the rejection didn't sting so badly. He finally had a friend in Los Angeles. And could it really be true that Lottie Love had a crush on him? How could she after she'd humiliated him in front of the entire staff?

Nah. It was too crazy. There was no way. Girls like Lottie Love never even glanced at him. Girls like Lottie Love could never accept his flaws.

Root Canal slathered him with kisses.

A PERSONAL ASSISTANT WITH ENORMOUS BREASTS OPENED THE door.

"Hello, it's Lemuel Brac. I'm here for Ms. Blanchard."

"Um, yes. She'll be right with you."

The assistant ushered him into the living room. Lem sat on the couch. A fire blazed as the air-conditioning thrummed. When the assistant left, Lem pulled the vodka from his pocket and swilled. A few drops landed on the white couch. The poker rooted around at his heart again. Lem wondered if he was having a heart attack.

He always believed Patricia had been a gift from Thom to assuage some kind of guilt that he could never really pinpoint. With a look you were under her spell.

Dear Franny,

Your press junket is set up for September 14, noon, at the Four Seasons. Eat a hamburger for lunch. Everyone hates salad eaters. Eat the fries, too. All of them. And if you gain any weight, I'll kiss the extra pounds.

Yours always,
Thom

Lem closed his eyes. Despite the booze and the pain in his chest, everything was suddenly clear. Thom Bowman had never been his friend.

When he opened his eyes, he saw the photograph. The same one he had in his office. It was from the cover story he had written. He recognized the look now. It was one of deceit. Thom and Franny had pulled one over on him. He walked toward it.

Lisa the Love Witch Reveals All.

Or at least she gives the illusion.

The pain seared through him. He wondered if he was dying, right here, underneath Lisa the Love Witch's gaze. With a spell you were at her command.

AMBER OPENED THE FRONT DOOR TO FRANNY'S HOUSE AND STARED at Lottie. They exchanged estrogen salutes—Lottie could feel Amber's eyes grazing over her black spikey Jimmy Choos, her pencil skirt, and her white cotton button-down with the extra-long cuffs and the third button opened right at her cleavage. Amber paused there.

"Dr. Gene?" Amber asked.

"Don't think so. These are all mammary glands, thank you very much."

She thrust her breasts out as she glided past Amber toward the living room.

"Excuse me, does Franny know you're coming?"

"She's *my* client."

As she walked through the foyer, something caught her eye. A hot pink Rolodex. *Maybe it's a bizarre coincidence,* she thought for an instant. She narrowed her eyes and recognized her penmanship. The *i*'s dotted with fat little hearts. She grabbed it.

"Hey!" Amber rushed up and pulled at it.

"That couldn't be more mine," Lottie said, tugging at it. "How did you—"

"Give it back to me."

Lottie cackled. "Oh my Ga-aad, you are so doing Mike Posner."

"I am not!"

"I couldn't need to know more. Is he like completely horrible in bed? Or is he one of those guys who looks like he'd be a disaster but couldn't be more amazing?"

"Sounds like you wanna know a little too bad," Amber said. "Actually, he's ammma-zing. Enormous. Immense."

Lottie contemplated this. "Really? I so don't believe you . . . Really?"

"OH MY GOD," Franny screamed from another room.

Lottie shut her eyes and shook her head. Was her dad here again?

"PUT THAT DOWN RIGHT NOW!"

Amber and Lottie turned toward each other. Put what down? A gun? A knife?

"HELP! HELP!"

The voice was frantic and scared.

Lottie and Amber raced into the living room.

LEM BRAC LOOKED almost calm as he held the enormous framed photograph above his head. He teetered forward. He teetered backward.

"Oh God, it's the original," Franny gasped. "It was a gift from the photographer. He destroyed the negative so no one else could have it."

Lem struggled to balance it.

Lottie had never seen Lem like this. At work, he'd been reserved. Quietly observing as everyone around him kissed ass, lied, pretended to be something they weren't. She remembered when she started and he took her out to lunch. He told her about celebrity. It was all a lie. An illusion. She hadn't believed him. She'd thought he was a dried-up old raisin of a man with nothing left to offer. And now this? He looked like Atlas holding the world on his shoulders.

"They're not your friends."

No one but Lottie could have understood him. The words were mashed and slurred together. It sounded like "Tearnuffends. Tearnuffends."

"STOP IT! STOP IT!" Franny screeched.

Lem wobbled backward. For an instant, he steadied himself.

He stood perfectly still with the frame resting above him. Then his knees buckled. The frame pitched forward and he tottered with it. As Lem tried desperately to balance himself, the gigantic picture crashed to the tiled floor. Lem fell on top of it.

Franny covered her mouth and shrieked. Then Amber covered her mouth and shrieked.

"Do something," Franny screamed at her assistant. Amber raced toward the frame as if she could somehow fix everything. She stared down at it.

"DO SOMETHING!"

Lem lay on top of the broken mess, his arms stretched out above his head. He was so still that Lottie wondered if he was dead. That frame looked like it weighed a few hundred pounds. How had someone like Lem managed to hoist it up in the first place?

Amber stared down at Lem and the frame.

"DO SOMETHING!"

Lottie walked toward them. She knelt over Lem and gently shook him.

"Lem? Lem?"

Lem opened his eyes and looked at her as if trying to place who she was, and where he was. Then he slowly stood up. He dusted shards of glass off his clothes, his arms. He clutched his heart with a hand. She noticed there was blood on his shirt. One of his palms was bleeding. Lottie pulled a piece of glass out of his hand.

Franny barreled toward Lem and Lottie, pushing them aside. Then she and Amber lifted the frame, raising it surprisingly quickly. Baffled, Lottie grabbed a corner. The frame was hollow. Millions of shards of glass covered the floor. Franny moaned like an animal bleeding out.

Maybe she was: a shard of glass had sliced through Lisa the Love Witch's forehead.

Lottie covered her face to squelch a laugh. Lisa the Love Witch

Reveals All—with a hole in her forehead. Franny continued to howl. When Lottie looked up, Lem was walking out the front door just as her father burst through. She was so surprised to see him, she didn't notice when the Rolodex slipped out of her hand and fell with a bang to the floor. She was oblivious to her hard-earned business cards fluttering about the terra-cotta.

"Hank," Franny sighed. "Oh, Hank." Her father walked over to Franny. He held her for a moment, then looked down at the frame, and tugged at the shard in Lisa's forehead. Franny yelped as if she'd felt the pain. He pulled out the glass and hugged her again.

"Franny. It's okay. It's okay." He stroked her hair.

Lottie had never seen her father so tender, and a wave of envy coursed through her. She mouthed the word "Dad." She didn't say it aloud because she knew her father most likely never mentioned he had a daughter. He probably wanted Franny to think he was too young to have a daughter as old as Lottie. So why blow it for him? Hank Love wasn't a bad person, just someone who lived his life enveloped in shit and piss and service entrances. If it weren't for Lottie, he might have been an actor.

Besides, she needed to help someone who'd been more like a dad to her for an hour than Hank Love had been her whole life.

We'll Make Your Pipes Sing! When Lottie walked outside, her father's gigantic face stared down at her. A twinkle in his eyes. His bleached white shirt. His crooked nose reconfigured to perfection, just like Lottie's.

"SHE'S TOO YOUNG," Dr. Bernstein had said when her mother took her in for a rhinoplasty consultation. "Her cartilage isn't completely developed. Wait a few more years and then make a decision."

"WHY?" her mother had shrieked. "I know exactly where that nose is headed. And nothing good can come of it. Let's nip it in the bud."

"But it's so early."

"If you don't want my business, say so. There are plenty of other doctors who'll do it."

The doctor studied Lottie. He touched her nose. She felt like a puppy being petted for the first time. She wanted to hug him.

Then he said, "Okay, Mrs. Love. I'll take care of it for you."

HER VW WAS boxed in by her dad's van. He never thought of anything but his own libido. It was probably why her mother had despised Lottie's nose so much. It reminded her of all Hank Love's failings—in his career, his marriage, fatherhood. Lottie saw the keys on the front seat. She got behind the wheel, turned the key in the ignition, and peeled down the street toward Lem.

She moved a leash and a dog collar from the passenger seat. Since when did her dad have a dog? She read the name on the tag.

Root Canal.

LOTTIE STOOD AT THE PODIUM. HER HEART POUNDED. HER HANDS shook. Everyone loved her stories. She knew what they were thinking: Would she tell the one about the time she smashed her car into Mann's Chinese Theater just as Sean Connery strode down the red carpet? Or when she threw up in Cher's piña colada at Spago? They smiled at her, clasping their hands together. They wiggled toward the edge of their seats.

Lottie Love cleared her throat. She exhaled. She squeezed her eyes shut.

"Hey, everyone."

"Hey, Lottie!"

"As you guys know, my name's Lottie Love." She smiled too hard and gulped air. "What you guys don't know is that . . . is that . . ." Her heart caught in her throat. "Is that . . . well, I'mnotanalcoholic."

She opened her eyes and stared at her audience. She exhaled for what seemed like the first time in hours—a whole day's worth of oxygen. There was silence. A horrible, interminable silence.

Then they grinned. Lottie relaxed. There were some giggles. The room burst into applause.

The applause died down. Lottie wondered if she should walk back to her seat. They wiggled toward the edge of their seats again. They rested their chins in their hands. They smiled. Lottie's heart beat furiously. She realized they were waiting for more. They were expecting a punch line.

"I'm sorry, but it's true. I couldn't be less of an alcoholic."

"Exactly," someone said. "That means you are one."

"Huh?"

"I thought your name was Lottie—not Cleopatra, the queen of da Nile," someone yelled from the back.

"Listen," she pleaded. "I barely even like liquor. Okay, every now and then there's nothing better than a daiquiri blended with fresh strawberries or a piña colada with little shavings of coconut and a little too much rum. And sometimes, there's nothing better than a buzz, especially when you wanna flirt with the cute guy at the other end of the bar. I so couldn't imagine how you guys can live life without that."

There was more laughter. Then applause followed by silence.

LOTTIE LOVE REVEALS ALL! TONIGHT!

"I'm serious. You wanna know the truth? Okay? I'll tell you." She took another deep, deep breath. Again, a smattering of giggles. She shut her eyes tight.

"The truth is, I did this for work." She clawed the sides of the podium.

Silence. Lottie struggled to swallow.

"I'm a, I'm a . . ." She huffed and squeezed her eyes shut. "I was a . . . reporterfor*Personality*magazine." She paused. Her heart's thumping filled her ears. "I didn't know anything. I spent my whole life in Tarzana. My father is Hank Love, We'll Make Your Pipes Sing. And then I got the greatest, most perfect job in the world. But I needed tons of contacts. I knew nothing. And then . . . and then I came here one night because . . . well, because I heard Chris Mercer came here. And I saw him and all of you guys. And I thought, why not? What's the harm? I can get to know them. I can become friends with them. It's not like I was hurting anyone. And soon I realized I liked coming here. You guys had become my friends. I need this as much as any of you do."

Lottie had never heard such silence in her life. It actually buzzed, flew across the room, hit walls, and landed with a thud in her ears. Her eyes skittered around the audience. She watched the smiles collapse, the faces scrunch in anger. Heads shook angrily. Then someone booed. Another boo. And finally the room was filled with a thunderous, appalling, all-encompassing boo.

"I'm sorry. I'm so sorry," she whispered.

"BOOOOOOOOOOOOOOOOOOOOOOOOOO!!!!!!!!!!!!!!!"

She was pelted with Styrofoam coffee cups, wooden stirrers, packets of Equal and Sugar in the Raw.

THE OTHER DAY when she drove Lem home in her father's van, she realized she had to do this.

Lem sat in the passenger seat. He stared out the window without speaking. After a few minutes, he fell asleep, his head resting on the window. She didn't know where he lived, so she just drove to Malibu. She parked in front of the ocean and watched the waves tumble and carbonate. She watched butterflies dart in and out of yellow and purple wildflowers. She also watched Lem. She envied his sleep. It seemed deep and peaceful. Occasionally she checked his breath.

While he slept, a school of seals—or was it sea lions? She could never tell the difference—swam by. She was so excited, she felt like a kid. She wanted to wake him and tell him, but she let him sleep. He needed to sleep. Finally, after nearly two hours, he started to stir. She drove to the Starbucks at Trancas. He woke up then.

"I'll be back. I'll get us coffees," Lottie said. "How do you like yours?"

Lem rubbed his eyes and shook his head. "Actually, I'll have a grande decaf caramel macchiato with extra whip," he said. Then he smiled and mumbled to himself. "Seven."

Lottie squinted in disbelief. "Huh?"

When she returned, they drank in silence. Lem studied the blood caked on his palm.

"I thought I could do this on my own, but I can't. I can't," he said. “I need help. This booze thing, it’s too much. I’ve lost control of everything. Everything.”

She told him about her AA meetings. “They’re the nicest people ever. Everyone’s really supportive. Please go. They’ll help you.”

Lem looked hard at her. “I’ll go, Lottie. But on one condition.”

“What’s that?”

He swallowed more coffee. He stared out the window. She thought he’d forgotten her question. After a few moments, he said, “That you stop.”

“Stop? Stop what?”

“Going.”

“Going? Going where?”

“To AA.”

“What?”

“That you tell the truth.”

“I can’t do that. I could never do that.”

“How do you feel, Lottie?”

“Oh my God, you couldn’t sound more like Lipless.”

“Lipless?”

“Never mind. What do you mean, how do I feel?”

Lem studied her. He touched her cheek. She felt like a puppy being petted for the first time.

“You don’t feel very well, do you? You haven’t felt well in a long time. You wake up sad. You go to sleep sad. You cry a lot, don’t you?”

Lottie winced. “That’s not . . . that’s not true.”

She couldn’t stop the tears from rushing out.

“It’s okay. It’s okay. If you only have truth in your life, if there are no lies, you’ll be happy, I promise. You won’t have to worry about being caught, even if it’s only by yourself.”

Lottie wiped tears with the back of her hand. She sniffled. “What happened in there?”

Lem shook his head. “Maybe it was the carousel ride.”

“What?”

“I suppose all along I had known the truth. Some part of me

had always known that I'd been used by both of them, but I wouldn't admit it to myself. I didn't want to get caught in my own lie." He sipped his drink. "I thought if I built it up, I could justify all the mistakes I made because of it. I thought maybe part of it had been real. I was silently begging for it from the moment she walked into the room. Then Franny told me she never forgot our carousel ride. How often she thought about it. I knew it was a lie. She was acting. She had no recollection of it."

Lem took a long breath. He turned to Lottie. "In your innocence, you tried to refresh her memory, right? You told her the story I told you."

"I so didn't mean anything by it. I just couldn't believe she could forget something that was so important to you. It made me wonder about myself and my memories. Maybe the ones I thought were so significant meant nothing to, well, whoever it was I was with."

"I know. But she represented everything that was wrong in my life. I was married to a woman who loved me more than she should have. I let her get away for nothing. We had a good life." He shook his head. "We could have had a great life. And I looked at that photograph and I couldn't help myself."

They sat in silence watching the children climb monkey bars in the playground next to Starbucks.

"Always remember, they're not your friends," he said.

"How could they be friends? They're not even human. They're all so fake."

Lem nodded as he studied the playground. A little girl fell off the swings and ran into the arms of her mom. Or was it her nanny? Her personal assistant?

"You know what else is fake?" Lottie asked. She looked down at her chest. "These. I tell everyone they're real. But they're not. I was young. I was completely flat. Now I feel cliché. Another Valley chick with a fake nose and fake boobs. So I lie about it. You're the only person I've ever told that to, and I have no idea why."

"Well, I'm flattered, I guess," Lem said. He coughed into his hand. "You know, I was writing a book. I thought maybe you could finish it. You know, figure out an ending for me."

"Me? I couldn't finish your book."

"You're the only one, and I'm well—"

Then someone banged on the side of the truck.

"Help. My toilet's overflowing!"

"BOOOOOOOOOOOOOOO!!!!!!!!!"

There were more and more boos. Stomping of feet. Banging of hands on desks, on books, whatever. These people were irate. They glared at her. Someone threw another Styrofoam cup.

"I'm so sorry. I couldn't be more sorry."

Lottie's legs quivered as she raced through a row of chairs. She tripped on someone's knapsack but managed to stumble on toward the exit.

"Everyone calm down, please. Leave Lottie alone. Please leave Lottie alone. It was very brave of her to admit her lie."

The room was silent. Lottie could hear tears in Catherine's voice.

"What led Lottie to do what she did shows us that she's battling her own demons. Demons as ugly to her as booze and drugs are to us."

Catherine was unbelievable. She should be leading the charge against her. Instead her words calmed the crowd. Some even applauded. What had Lottie done to deserve Catherine? She wished that by some miracle Catherine could remain in her life. She wished she hadn't been so mean to her.

At the exit, a woman stopped Lottie and handed her a business card.

"I hate what you did," the woman said, "but I've never seen such raw emotion before. You were fabulous up there. You have Drew Barrymore's vulnerability mixed with an Angelina Jolie–like edgy toughness. I'm a casting director. Call me as soon as you, well, lose ten pounds."

Joe smoked a cigarette by the exit. "Remember, you can do anything," he said to her. "I'm living proof." He laughed hysterically, almost demonically. Lottie gave him a hug as she slipped all the money from her wallet into his coat pocket.

She saw Chris Mercer. The worst was far from over. He was waiting for her outside. Just yesterday, he had professed his love for her to Cyndi Bowman. Now he probably hated her.

CHRIS SAID TO meet him at Chateau Marmont. Ask for Pierre Ventura. The desk clerk escorted her to the garden where he sat, his face obscured by overgrown bougainvilleas.

A waiter quickly arrived. She ordered a Diet Coke.

"I don't mind if you have a drink. Really," Chris said.

"Are you sure? 'Cause after tonight I could really use one—I so don't mean that in the alcoholic sense, but just in the I-had-a-hell-night sense."

"That's fine. Order a drink."

She asked for a vodka tonic. Chris looked at Lottie and smiled. He turned toward the waiter. "The usual, Nick."

They sat in silence. Chris smirked at her.

"What's so funny?" she asked.

The waiter reappeared with her drink and his "usual"—a shot of Patron and a Sierra Nevada chaser.

Lottie stared at Chris.

"I thought . . . I thought . . . You shouldn't be doing this. Please don't do this."

He cocked his head back and downed the shot. Then he clinked glasses with her, chugged his beer, and aahed.

"What a tangled web we weave," Chris said.

"This is crazy. What are you doing?"

"Lottie, we're more alike than you know."

"Huh?"

"When I came to this town, I couldn't even get an agent if my life depended on it. So my buddy told me I should check out the

West Hollywood AA. At first I did it as a goof. It was like acting. It was like honing my craft. Before I knew it, I had an agent, who loved the way I emoted. I didn't plan to keep going, but now I have no choice."

"This is a joke, right?"

"Yes . . . and no. Yes, it's a joke that this is how I live my life, but no, it's the truth. I am not an alcoholic." Chris bent in to kiss her. "You won't tell anyone, right?"

"Of course I won't."

"That's why I had to agree to that interview with that reporter. He caught me very drunk and extremely disorderly. No one but good friends and people paid to keep quiet ever see me drinking. Somehow he found out my alias. I have no idea how the fuck he did that. Anyway, Cyndi said he'd blow my cover. I was afraid that she'd force me to go to Promises with her. That woman won't leave me alone for a second."

He leaned in toward her. "But then when you had your 'relapse' the other night, I knew I needed to be there for you. It was more important to me than a month at Promises with Cyndi."

"I'm sorry I lied."

He put a finger on her lips. "That's when I knew I was falling for you. I didn't understand it then. I mean, really, I barely know you. But I understand it now."

"You do?" Lottie guzzled her vodka tonic.

"You see, Lottie, we're the same," Chris said. "Anyway, I know I should be furious with you, but this is all such a relief. I figured if I had a relationship with you, I'd have to pretend to be sober. That would have sucked to have to act all the time."

He kissed her. "You know, why don't we go to my room and . . . talk some more."

She stared at him.

He cleared his throat. "You know . . . you're number one." He smiled.

"I can't."

"What? After the other night, I thought you weren't into the hard-to-get thing . . ." He grabbed a breast.

"I'm so sorry, Chris," Lottie said, shifting away from him. "I just can't."

"What the . . . ?"

She didn't answer, because she didn't know how to explain. He was sexy, beautiful, famous, loaded, the most desirable man in the universe. But she felt nothing. *How fucked up is that?* she thought. It was like the spell had been broken.

The last thing she wanted was a celebrity.

"IT'S BEEN THE CRAZIEST NIGHT WE'VE EVER HAD," THE YOUNG girl at the podium said as he stumbled in. "I think we'll wrap it up and break for coffee—unless someone has something they need to say."

He stood at the back and leaned against the wall. His body shook. He wanted to run out and head for the nearest bar. Instead, he ahemmed and tentatively raised his hand. The young girl pointed to him.

"Yes. Come on up."

A wobbly Lem Brac took center stage. He never liked being the focus of attention, but he had made a promise. He couldn't do this alone. Today he'd sat at his desk and tried to write, but it didn't happen. So he drank and drank and drank. If he sobered up for good, maybe he could salvage something. Maybe he could get to know Cathy.

"Hello, my name is Lem Brac."

"Hello, Lem."

"I didn't want to do this," he said, shaking his head. "I didn't think I needed to do this, but I know I can't do it myself. And then I had this friend . . . this very good friend."

He squinted out at the audience searching for her. She said she'd be there. She had promised.

"Lottie?" He called. "Lottie, are you here? Is Lottie Love here?"

A strange murmur ran through the crowd.

"My friend Lottie Love said you people could help me, and I need some help. Lottie? Lottie?"

He waited a few seconds. "I guess not." He cleared his throat. "I'm a reporter for *Personality* magazine and . . ."

The murmur grew.

"I let my . . ."

The murmur became louder and louder until it was like a tsunami of noise whirring around the room.

"Get out of here!" someone yelled.

Someone else stood up, slid a folding chair across the room, and clomped out. "I've had enough of this," he said.

"I . . . I . . ."

"We know . . . You're an alcoholic."

There was no air left in the room. Lem wheezed. The poker lunged at his heart. He panted and struggled to breathe.

"I . . . I . . ."

"Go tell it to Lottie Love," someone sneered.

Lem had heard about the tough-love approach, but this was ridiculous. He looked out at the faces. Where was the love Lottie had promised? These people were furious. Maybe he'd stumbled upon the wrong meeting. Maybe this was a convention of people who despised lushes.

"I need help. I need help. I need . . ."

He couldn't catch his breath. The room whirled around him. The faces were distorted. Mouths were where eyes should be. Bodies had four arms. Shouts were muffled. Lem closed his eyes. He spun around in the pitch black. His heart arrhythmically lub-dubbed. And then there was darkness and a beautiful silence.

HE DREAMED HE was in a hospital. There were needles and suctions and a tangle of lines hooked to him. There was a heart monitor that didn't *beep beep.*

He had to be dead.

He looked up at the beautiful girl staring down at him. *An angel,* he thought. So after all his cynicism, there is an afterlife. But what had he done to deserve an angel? He looked into her blue eyes. She seemed so familiar. It was the girl from the podium. He squinted to get a better look. He smiled with complete joy. He reached his arms out to her. He struggled to speak. He gasped and choked. Finally the words came out of him, taking all his oxygen, all his energy.

"My daughter."

EVERYTHING FROM HIS CALIFORNIA HEGIRA FIT INTO FIVE BOXES, so he was able to pack up his apartment in a few hours. He figured if he left this afternoon, he could be there Friday morning.

Earlier, Liz had called. It had been more than a year since they'd spoken.

"Hey."

"Hey."

Mike could tell she'd been crying. He imagined she and the guy with the goatee had broken up. She wanted Mike back. He felt warm relief rush through his body. Perfect timing. In an instant, he planned his future: he'd head to New York and find a job with a newspaper that needed to bulk up its entertainment reporting. He'd even work for some rag in the suburbs and commute from their apartment. Suddenly life seemed stable again.

"Is everything okay?" he asked.

Liz panted and sniffled.

"What's wrong?"

"I just wanted you to know that . . . that . . ."

"Yes?" He smiled into the phone.

"Mr. Cat died."

Even though he had assumed Mr. Cat was not long for this world, Mike found himself struggling to catch his breath. Sometimes it seemed as though it was only yesterday that he dropped off Mr. Cat at Liz's and headed straight across the country until he hit palm trees and ocean.

"Mike?"

"Yeah?"

"I knew you'd want to know." She sniffled some more. "I loved that little guy."

"Yeah, remember when you found him? He was too weak to eat so you fed him with a doll's bottle."

Liz laughed. "You said I was crazy, but it worked."

"I know. I thought he'd be dead by the end of the weekend, but you worked a miracle on him."

"You think so? I felt so sorry for him. I always have a soft spot in my heart for strays."

"Yeah, I know."

There was silence. Liz sniffed. "So, are you seeing anybody?"

"Right now, no . . . How about you? Are you and that guy still . . ."

"No. We broke up a while ago . . . I'm not seeing anybody."

"Oh."

"So . . . are you ever coming back to New York? I'm thinking of moving back to Rochester. The city's so crazy. I feel like there's nothing here for me."

He heard Catherine's voice. Liz was safe. But safe wasn't so bad, was it? It may not be an electric current charging through his body, but it was a warm rush of relief.

"I don't know."

HE HUNG UP and continued packing. He called Phil Rossman, the editor in chief in Rochester. After the bullshit small talk, he asked if there were any openings.

"The big city's too much for you, eh, Mike? Of course, we'd love you back here. Love it. We always thought you'd be back. The staff will be thrilled. I can't wait to tell them. All the positions are filled, but we'll invent one for you. Actually, there's a great story coming up that has Mike Posner all over it. The residents of Pittsford are opposing plans for . . ."

Zoning ordinances. Highway interchanges. Retirement communities. Parking garages. Cow tipping. Stoplights. Drainage ditches.

Composting facilities. Disorderly conducts. Mike was bored out of his skull just by the conversation.

He needed a miracle.

"SOME OF YOUR sources have been feeding you misinformation," Vince Reggio said yesterday as Bernie stood behind him, her arms folded, her lips pursed.

"All we need is a Jayson Blair at *Personality*," she said.

He wanted to say that sometimes he felt everyone at *Personality* had a little bit of Jayson Blair in them.

They hadn't fired him—yet. But he knew it was coming. They were going through every story he'd written since he'd been there. To top it off, James Davenworth from the *Daily News* had been hired to run the New York bureau. And he had plenty to say about Mike Poseur.

Hick. Hick. Hick.

SOMEONE KNOCKED ON the door. Mike opened it hesitantly. Amber stood there holding out a disheveled-looking pink Rolodex. One of the rings had cracked and business cards were awkwardly splayed out.

"You left this in my apartment the other night."

Mike opened the door wider. "The other night? That was weeks ago."

"Okay, okay, you caught me. I needed time to Xerox the whole thing. Your friend is connected, big-time. I mean, Ray Young's home phone number."

"I know."

"Anyway, I'm really not a klepto. I swear."

"Well, thanks for bringing it back."

"I need to focus on my acting now more than ever. I was just fired from my job."

"I think that makes two of us. So what happened to you?"

Amber giggled. "This is pretty bad."

"Worse than stealing a Rolodex?"

"Yeah," Amber said, stifling another laugh. "I worked as a personal assistant for Franny Blanchard—you know, Lisa the Love Witch. She caught me putting protein powder in her drink."

"So?"

"She was obsessed with her weight. So I started putting the powder in her drink to fatten her up. She couldn't figure out why her butt was getting enormous. Pretty evil, huh? But she was a nasty-ass bitch. Root Canal is missing. I'm convinced she had her boyfriend steal poor Rootie. She despised him." Amber surveyed the apartment. "OhmyGod, you're moving."

"You could say things aren't really working out."

Amber smirked. "This is Los Angeles; things never work out." She thought about this. "Well, things work out really fantastically for a handful of people and you have to hear about it every fucking day. Like I need to know how fucking great the fucking Olson twins' life is? God, I hate them and they're only like, what, eighteen? But you know what?"

"What?"

"Once you leave, you'll never be happy anywhere else. Trust me, I've tried it. Suddenly, you'll be living in a place where there's no chance of running into the fucking Olson twins at Coffee Bean and Tea Leaf and you'll suddenly wish you could. This place is addicting."

Mike was instantly reminded of what Lem had told him more than a year ago. He said the place eventually seeps into your blood and you can never get it out. He said it just happens, like an overnight transfusion, and you wake up one day knowing you can't imagine anything else. You may have thought it silly or shallow, but now it's part of you. You see that $10 million sprawling manse and you want it. It is so close; just a fence, a few hedges, and a security system away, and sometimes you forget it can never be yours.

Then you attend their parties and mingle with them—even perambulating along the red carpet to your next event—and again, you forget that you are there as a reporter with a publicist watching and pointing to her watch because you have a time limit; you can speak with the stars for only a few minutes. The publicist tells you that your time is up, you must leave the party and stand with the starstruck herds on the other side of the velvet rope.

Then you walk outside and the strobes flash before the photographers realize that you're nobody. And though the cameras snap by mistake, you can't help but feel momentarily important, momentarily blinded by the dazzling lights dancing like savages behind the lids of your closed eyes. So you sneak back in until you are caught. It's easy to spot you, because when it comes down to it, you don't fit in. Your pupils have not adjusted to the flashbulbs. You look dazed; you look a little too much in love.

"You're probably right, Amber," he said.

She checked him for sarcasm. "You think so?"

"Yeah." He took the Rolodex from her. "I have something for you."

"Wait," she said, pulling a shopping bag from behind her back. "I have something else for you."

Mike took the bag, surprised by the weight of it. He peered in. It was filled with little bottles. He pulled one out.

Franny Blanchard's The Cure. Horny Goat Milk.

"What's this?"

"Well, it's just . . . I, um, thought this, um, would help you. I swear the woman has some kinda magical powers, just like Lisa the Love Witch. Anyway, she devised this concoction and it really works. She and her disgusting boyfriend are like nonstop. Since she fired me, I figured I'd help myself. My apartment is like a pharmacy."

Mike felt his face turn red. He coughed nervously.

"You seem a little, well, insecure about some things." Amber looked down at the floor. "I don't know why. Maybe this will help you."

"Help me?"

"Trust me. Take this. It will change everything and then maybe we can get together sometime, okay? You seem like a great guy."

"I'm a greater guy than you can imagine." Mike smiled. He jotted something on a piece of paper and handed it to her. "Here."

"Whose number is this?"

"Root Canal's."

"What?"

When she left, after hugging and kissing him a thousand times, Mike knew where he had to go and what he had to do.

"IS LOTTIE HERE?" He spoke through a slit in the door to a Goth chick with piercings in her eyebrows, nose, and lips and what looked like a doorknob dangling from her chin.

She grunted at Mike and turned.

Mike wondered how those two ever became roommates. She was hardly Lottie's type. Had to be some kind of online roommate service. He shook his head sadly. Lottie Love, who'd lived in L.A. all her life, had to rely on a service to find someone to live with.

He stood there peering into the slit, wondering if the grunt had been a yes or a no when suddenly Lottie appeared. Mike was surprised to see her wearing pajamas dotted with smiling, fluffy white sheep. He chuckled silently. He thought her bedroom attire would be strictly black lace.

He handed her the Rolodex.

"Sorry," he said. "I'm an asshole. But I swear I wasn't always an asshole. This place turned me into one. I can't believe what an asshole I've been."

She smiled. "I know." Her eyes studied her red polished toes. "Sorry about Chris Mercer. I'm an even bigger asshole."

"I don't think I've ever been so pissed at someone in my life. And what you said about me in that meeting. Jeez . . ."

"I'm just happy to inspire such raw emotion."

She smiled, waiting for him to say something, but he couldn't. Her scent wafted through the air. It was the smell of ocean and coconut oil, citrus and night jasmine. California flowed out of her pores like perfume. And he knew Amber was right. He'd never leave. Mike shut his eyes and was swept away by waves tumbling, thundering, and sizzling along a hot sandy shore.

And then it happened.

It was a miracle. Maybe not precisely the miracle he had asked for, but nevertheless a miracle: an aching, throbbing, pulsating erection. The biggest boner of his life. It strained at his pants and begged for air.

Franny Blanchard's Horny Goat Milk had taken effect.

He grinned goofily. He couldn't help but look down at it. Lottie followed his gaze and laughed.

"I guess you're not that angry," Lottie said. "You know, I could never tell if you liked me or hated me."

Mike laughed to himself. He could almost hear Lem.

You didn't listen to me, but I knew, didn't I? This is what you always wanted.

"It was a little of both. Well, probably a lot of both."

Then Mike did something he'd never done in his whole life. He ran straight into the Bouncing Betty. He grabbed Lottie's face with both hands and kissed her on the lips while the world seemed to spin and collapse around him. Mike wasn't sure how Lottie would react. But he didn't really care. All she'd have to do was pull away and he'd leave. No big deal. But when she didn't, he kissed her harder. It was like an electric current stampeding through his veins. The Rolodex fell to the floor.

"Get a fucking room," the Goth chick said.

They stopped kissing and looked at each other. He knew they were probably thinking the same thing: this is crazy. They were completely wrong for each other. He thought about the day at the beach in Santa Barbara, after Thom Bowman's funeral. He thought about her rippled back with its little heart tattoo. Her defined calves and ankles, her knees with little bumps of muscle. His heart galloped.

He'd tell Bernie and Vince that he'd taken the key—not Lem, not Lottie. He didn't care anymore. Then he'd find a rusted Dumpster, grab the handful of newspapers that crammed his passenger seat, and hurl them into the trash. He'd do it again and again until the seat was empty and waiting to be occupied. A passenger seat crammed with newspaper marks a lonely life, Lem had said to him several times. Don't let the flowers die. Mike was finally going to heed Lem's advice. He couldn't wait to tell Lem. He grinned so hard his mouth hurt.

"What are you thinking?" Lottie asked, smiling.

"About how you smell like California," he sighed.

She scowled flirtatiously. "Oh, great. Like smog and exhaust fumes?"

"No. Like orange blossoms and lemon trees and promise."

"This couldn't be the biggest mistake ever," Lottie said.

"You know, I could never decipher your speech. But I think that means it's only a little mistake. And a little mistake is much better than the horrible mistakes I've been making."

"You and me both."

She grabbed his hand and pulled him toward the bedroom.

THE DECK WAS A RIOT OF COLORS. PURPLE, YELLOW, WHITE, RED, pink, lavender, and orange flowers competed like Hollywood stars for attention. Nearly every day Catherine and Lottie pruned and watered and planted some more. Afterward, Lottie always stood back to see if they had arrived yet.

Catherine and Lottie would sprawl on the deck, pulling out gnarled branches that looked like ghosts in midspook, digging out the cement-hard dirt from rotting planters. They tossed away the unsalvageable pots and painted the rest. Then they filled them with Queen Anne's lace, telstars, cosmos, zinnias, sage, and goldenrod.

"Aren't some of those weeds?" Catherine had asked.

"You couldn't need to trust me more," Lottie had replied.

Lottie had spent hours researching and meticulously combing through the aisles at Green Thumb in a quest to find plants and flowers that attracted butterflies and hummingbirds. When she was a child, she had chased after butterflies with a yellow net. She'd forgotten that. She began to wonder if perhaps her childhood wasn't as bad as she had imagined. Maybe Lem had been right. Maybe it wasn't so horrible being Charlotte Love from Tarzana.

Lottie believed the butterflies would eventually discover Lem's deck and settle there, laying eggs that would become caterpillars, pupae, and butterflies. The cycle of life—ad infinitum. She wanted it to be her gift to Lem.

⋆★⋆

CATHERINE HAD BEEN at the hospital with Lem. She held his hand and he smiled at her. He called her "daughter." And Catherine felt an overwhelming sense of peace. Then his hand lost its grip on hers.

For Catherine, this was a moment she'd never forget. The moment when a stranger who seemed so familiar had called her "daughter" and she'd finally felt forgiven. When she learned the truth from her mother, she wasn't even angry. She felt relieved. Lottie wished Lem could have known this. He had been a father at last.

Lem had scrawled out a will on a piece of paper. The apartment legally became Catherine's. She could have sold it and made some money; after all, it was in Beverly Hills. Instead, Catherine asked Lottie to move in with her. Lottie was out of work and couldn't pay the rent at the place she shared with the doorknob dyke. So here was Catherine, coming to her rescue again. At first she said no. But Catherine insisted. "Lem would have wanted it."

Lottie moved in. They had spent the last few days working on it—the deck and the interior. They ripped away Lem's heavy curtains and filled the place with sunlight and air.

Lem had been right. Once Lottie stopped lying, she felt better. She didn't cry herself to sleep anymore. She didn't need actors. Best of all, she didn't need Lipless.

Lipless told her it was a big mistake. "Let's ease out of this slowly. How about once a week?"

"I don't think so."

"Okay, okay. Once a month."

"I couldn't have made my decision more."

"Fine." Lipless squeezed out a smile. "But call me anytime. I'd love to keep in touch with you. And if you ever need an emergency session, don't hesitate."

LOTTIE LOVE REVEALS ALL: THE REUNION SPECIAL

"Emergency session? For the first time in a long time, I feel fine."

"I don't think you really do, Charlotte."

"Lottie."

Lottie knew Lipless was desperate. But she couldn't believe how much so until weeks later when she read an article in the *L.A. Times.* Lipless was under investigation for selling client information to the *Star.* Turns out she had allegedly made hundreds of thousands divulging secrets during the last few years—including a big score for the Ray Young is gay story. Despite Lottie's refusal to divulge, Lipless had figured it out. Apparently she wasn't clueless after all.

Lottie wouldn't need emergency sessions. She felt it. For the first time, she had a roommate she liked. When she stood out on the deck, she breathed in the jasmine-scented air and felt calm. And maybe the butterflies would come.

LOTTIE LOVE LTD: SHE'LL MAKE YOUR CAREER SING

After she quit, Lottie started her own publicity firm. Lottie Love Ltd. Maybe she could accomplish something without thrusting out her boobs. But it hadn't been easy. Cyndi found out about her AA stunt and spread the word to every celebrity, studio, and publicist in her Rolodex. Lottie had a small list of clients, including Earl Montjoy (yes, fat Earl, who had recently signed a two-year contract with *General Hospital*), Amber Pepridge (who was cast as Ray Young's assistant pool cleaner on *Bel Air Belles*), Marlon Lang (who had been making most of his money as a cabdriver lately), and a few unknowns. So far, only some had paid the monthly retainer, but it was a start.

Besides, one day some of them would be the Now Big Things. And if there was one thing Lottie Love knew, it was that.

She also knew that if she used her old tricks or if she threatened to talk about the past, she could get a lot more clients. Chris Mercer, Tristan Keith, and Ray Young wouldn't have a choice. But she didn't want to do that anymore. It was almost like learning to walk again. Hard work, but she thought she could do it.

Franny Blanchard wanted to be Lottie's client. She had called Lottie in a frenzy. The Cure had received a slew of negative press. Franny had been sued by several people claiming the herbal concoction caused heart attacks and other ailments. Marjorie Bowman initiated the suit, saying that although Alzheimer's had ravaged her husband's brain, his heart had been strong and healthy at his last doctor's appointment a month earlier. Lottie made Mike throw away his stash.

"Sorry. I couldn't want to represent you less," Lottie had said.

"What does that even mean?"

"It means no."

"But your father told me you were the best in the business."

"What?" Lottie had felt a mixture of love and sadness. So he *had* told Franny about her. He *was* proud of her!

Hank eventually dumped Franny. He sued her because Horny Goat had caused a strange tingling in his lower extremities. Franny Blanchard: she made his pipes tingle, a KTLA reporter had said smugly.

For a few months, her father had become a joke, but all the negative press had been good for Franny. She was back in the spotlight. She even landed a role as a madame on *Sin Gals,* the new hit comedy from Gregory Perry. But Lottie had heard from a source that they were planning to have her killed off. Karmic comeuppance via gamma rays.

Her dad asked Lottie for help. So she wrote press releases for his business. She knew he was just doing it to make sure she didn't starve, but she pretended to take it seriously. She advised him to paint over his face on the truck in favor of a subtler approach to plumbing. Nothing doing, he said. Oh well, it was worth the try.

The other day when her father helped her move furniture, Lottie told him, "Dad, I know I don't say it, but I appreciate everything you've done for me."

"Thanks, Char—I mean, Lottie—but I wasn't there for you enough."

"But you gave up your dreams for me and became a plumber."

"Are you kidding? I love being a plumber. It's your mother who always made my acting sound more serious than it was. I think she was embarrassed by my career choice. She thought it was beneath her, so she created this romantic version of it. She made plumbing my last resort. In her mind, I was about to be a star, but I sacrificed it all for my family."

"Really?" Even her family history had been a lie.

"Really." He laughed. "Plumbing completes me."

Lottie smiled. Maybe it wasn't so bad being Hank Love from Tarzana. Maybe all the spotlights don't shine on Hollywood.

But Mike Posner was in the spotlight, at least for today. When she clicked on the television, there he was, on *Entertainment Tonight,* talking about Chris Mercer, whom he eventually interviewed for a *Personality* cover.

"He told me that he thinks about drinking every day. He says he sees a bottle of vodka and he can feel the sensation of the booze going down his throat and sometimes he starts to feel buzzed."

She laughed.

CHRIS MERCER REVEALS ALL!
EXCLUSIVELY TO MIKE POSNER!

And with that one story, Bernie suddenly forgot all about the source problems. Chris talked about his battle with alcoholism, his recovery. It was wonderful, the editors said. It was the first truth Mike had thought he'd written. Lottie didn't dare tell him that Chris was lying the whole time.

She realized while watching him on TV that the newly hatched chicken look had disappeared. She didn't know if it had been gone for a while and she was just noticing it. Or had it vanished some time that day?

Vince eventually found out that Mike had stolen the key. He sent Bernie the video, believing she'd fire him. Instead, she said, "I'm impressed. That boy shows initiative. Anything for a story." Mike was on his way to Vince's job.

Was it love? Lottie couldn't say. The word "love" was so much a part of her lexicon that it had lost meaning. But it was all crazy. Here was a guy she couldn't stand a few weeks ago. Catherine said she sought out larger-than-life celebrities because it made her feel better, made her feel like she was worth something. Reality couldn't compete. She had hated Mike because she hated herself.

MIKE STOPPED BY with the Dalmatian he had adopted from Catherine.

He smiled as he scanned Lottie. "Cute overalls."

"I just saw you on TV," she told him.

"How was I?"

"You need to smile more," she said, petting the dog. "Have you figured out a name?"

"Rolo."

"Rolo?" Lottie shook her head. "Ugh."

"After Rolodex," he said, his ears turning red. "If it weren't for that thing, I would have never had the balls to, well . . . get to know you."

"Or Chris Mercer," Lottie couldn't help but add. But she was touched. She gently slapped the dog.

While Mike helped Catherine plant some oleanders around the side of the deck, Lottie unpacked her bedroom. She opened the box full of posters from her office at *Personality*—Brad and Chris and Tom and Marlon and Ray. She decided it was time to throw them away.

She flipped the box over and tossed its contents into the trash. A pile of yellow legal pages fluttered to the floor. She picked them up and didn't recognize the handwriting at first. Then she realized it was Lem Brac's. He must have left the notes in the box by accident.

The pages were numbered, so she organized them. There was a title page.

THEY'RE NOT YOUR FRIENDS

She found a note and realized that this was no accident. He must have shoved it in the box that night at the office.

Dear Lottie,

You may discover this manuscript a week from now or in twenty years. I might never know. But I do know that you've rummaged through this box and decided you no longer need the posters. I tried to purge myself of celebrity once and it got me into a lot of trouble. I know you'll have better luck.

Please read this book and finish it for me. I never will, but you can. An agent told me it was very good. It still needs an ending. Then you can publish it. You're the only one I trust.

Never let the flowers die.

Lemuel

She sat on a chaise lounge on the deck and read. The story started with Lem as a young man arriving in the United States. It was filled with anecdotes from every celebrity he'd ever met. It told the story of Franny Blanchard.

She thought about what she should do. About everything—her career, Mike, this book. Why would Lem think she was capable of an ending? She was barely making a start. Maybe nothing would come to her. Maybe Lem thought she was better than she really was. Maybe Mike and Catherine did, too. Maybe she had always been an actress fooling everybody. She closed her eyes and struggled for an ending.

FROM WHAT SEEMED like miles away, she heard Rolo bark excitedly. She opened her eyes. He was pawing at a butterfly. That's when she noticed them. A swarm of monarchs flitted in and out of the goldenrod.

She slowly moved toward the butterflies. Their gold-and-black wings were like stained glass shimmering in the sunlight. Just like when she was a little girl, she stealthily leaned in and plucked one right off the sage. She lightly pinched it between her thumb and forefinger.

"They found us," she said, knowing at that moment that Lem was right. She could do anything.

ACKNOWLEDGMENTS

Thanks to Shana Drehs, my editor, for her enthusiasm and wisdom, and the entire Crown team responsible for assembling this book, especially Mary Ann Smith, Karen Minster, and Sibylle Kazeroid. Also, wholehearted thanks to Stephanie Kip Rostan, my agent, for her unwavering belief in this book; to my mom and dad, who will promote this book harder than anyone, except for perhaps my sister, Jeannine Schwing, and her husband, Dave; to Renée Lipp, who always provides good juju; and especially to Larry—for encouraging me to write this book, forcing me to finish it, and then reading it at least a hundred times—and for being, along with my daughters, my inspiration.

ABOUT THE AUTHOR

Irene Zutell spent five years as a correspondent in the Los Angeles bureau of *People* magazine. Her work has appeared in many publications, including *Us Weekly*, the *New York Times*, the *New York Daily News*, *Newsday*, and *Crain's New York Business*. Irene cocreated and was co–executive producer of a reality show for CBS, and is a coauthor of *I'll Never Have Sex with You Again! Tales from the Delivery Room*. She lives in Los Angeles with her husband and daughters.